GREAT STORIES BY NOBEL PRIZE WINNERS

Great Stories

EDITED BY LEO HAMALIAN AND EDMOND L. VOLPE

THE NOONDAY PRESS   NEW YORK

by Nobel Prize Winners

ACKNOWLEDGMENTS

The editors wish to express their thanks to the persons and publishers listed below for their kind cooperation in granting permission to reprint copyrighted material.

The Father, by Björnsterne Björnsen. Translated by R. B. Anderson and used with permission of The American-Scandinavian Foundation.

Flagman Thiel, by Gerhart Hauptmann. Translated by Adele S. Seltzer and reprinted from *Great German Short Novels and Stories*, edited by Victor Lang, by permission of Random House, Inc. Copyright, 1933, by The Modern Library, Inc.

Saved, by Sir Rabindranath Tagore. Published by The Macmillan Company and reprinted by permission of the Publisher.

A Fisher Nest, by Henrik Pontoppidan. Translated by Juliane Sarauw and used with permission of The American-Scandinavian Foundation.

The Call of Life, by Knut Hamsun. Translated by Anders Orbeck and used with permission of The American-Scandinavian Foundation.

The Crucifixion of the Outcast, by William Butler Yeats. Published by The Macmillan Company and reprinted with permission of the Publisher.

Death, by Wladyslaw Reymont. Translated by Else Benecke and Marie Bush. Published by Oxford University Press and reprinted with permission of the Publisher.

The Miraculous Revenge, by George Bernard Shaw. Reprinted by permission of the Public Trustee and The Society of Authors, London, England.

The Sardinian Fox, by Grazia Deladda. Translated by William Fense Weaver and reprinted from *Modern Italian Short Stories*, edited by Marc Slonim, and published by Simon and Schuster, Inc. Copyright 1954 by Marc Slonim. Used with permission of the Publisher.

Little Lizzie, by Thomas Mann. Copyright 1936 by Alfred A. Knopf, Inc. Translated from the German by H. T. Lowe-Porter. Reprinted from *Stories of Three Decades* by Thomas Mann by permission of Alfred A. Knopf, Inc.

What That Kind of Mush Gets You, by Sinclair Lewis. From *Cass Timberlane* by Sinclair Lewis, copyright 1945 by Sinclair Lewis. Reprinted by permission of Random House, Inc.

Sunstroke, by Ivan Bunin. Translated by Teka Matheson and reprinted with the permission of William Aspenwall Bradley.

War, by Luigi Pirandello. Translated by Michael Pettinati. From *The Medals and Other Stories*, by Luigi Pirandello. Copyright, 1939, by E. P. Dutton & Co., Inc. Reprinted by permission of the Publisher.

The Operation, by Roger Martin du Gard. Translated by Stuart Gilbert and taken from *The Thibaults*, by Roger Martin du Gard. Copyright 1939 by The Viking Press, Inc. Reprinted by permission of The Viking Press, Inc.

Lost Forests, by Johannes v. Jensen. Translated by Henry Commager and used with permission of The American-Scandinavian Foundation.

Within and Without, by Herman Hesse. Translation by T. K. Brown reprinted from *The World's Best* edited by Whit Burnett. The Dial Press, Inc., New York, 1950.

That Evening Sun, by William Faulkner. Reprinted from *Collected Stories of William Faulkner*, © Copyright, 1931, renewed, 1958, by William Faulkner. Reprinted by permission of Random House, Inc.

The Lift That Went Down Into Hell, by Par Lagerkvist. Translated by Alan Blair. From *The Eternal Smile* by Par Lagerkvist © Copyright, 1954, by Random House, Inc. Reprinted by permission of Random House, Inc.

Lily, by Haldor Laxness. Reprinted from *Icelandic Poems and Stories* by permission of the Publisher, Princeton University Press.

The Guest, by Albert Camus. Copyright 1957, 1958 by Alfred A. Knopf, Inc. Translated from the French by Justin O'Brien. Reprinted from *Exile and the Kingdom* by Albert Camus by permission of Alfred A. Knopf, Inc.

Il Tratto de Apelle, by Boris Pasternak. Translated by Robert Payne and reprinted with the permission of the Translator.

To Kay and Rose

Contents

Preface

TO THE READER

The stories in this volume, though varied in locale, subject, style and inspiration, share a unique distinction: all were written by recipients of the most coveted award in the world of letters, the Nobel Prize for Literature.

The Nobel Prize is highly esteemed for several reasons. It is the only literary award of true international prestige. And by bringing the writer to the attention of a world-wide audience it elevates the solitary figure of the artist to his rightful distinction as international hero. Furthermore, in an age in which the cheap and the shoddy is hailed by so many as art, the award invites that audience to join in the celebration of the true artist's devotion to his craft. Finally, there is the attractive cash prize (worth about $30,000) that accompanies the medallion bearing the likeness of Nobel on one side and a symbolic representation of literature on the reverse side.

Some writers (rarely those who win it) openly sneer at the Nobel Prize, asserting that such awards are irrelevant, even antagonistic, to the life of art. Gore Vidal, for instance, has compared the award to the Roman custom of opening the veins in the bath. Part of this prejudice against the prize probably stems from the strong feeling that still surrounds the name of its founder, Alfred Bernhard Nobel. He is remembered as the first man to make and explode dynamite, as the Swedish industrialist who amassed a vast fortune through the manufacture of explosives, as the conscience-stricken magnate who turned philanthropist before his death in San Remo, Italy, in 1896. As far as it goes, the picture is not inaccurate, but it omits those elements which yield the image of the whole man.

In reality, Nobel was also a quiet, peaceful, and studious man who devoted most of his life to research in chemistry, engineering, agriculture; he studied in the United States with the inventor of the ironclad, the *Monitor*, and helped to develop synthetic rubber. He was deeply interested in the cause of peace and the arts and sciences that helped to perpetuate peace. In his will, he left a nine million dollar trust fund, the interest from which was to be distributed annually (on December 10th) "in the form of prizes to those who have, within the respective twelve months successively elapsed, rendered the greatest service to mankind" in chemistry, medicine, physics, and peace. He also specified that the Swedish Academy of Stockholm was to award an equal portion to the "person who shall have produced in the field of literature the most distinguished work of an idealistic tendency."

The Academy clarified the somewhat turgid phrases of Nobel's will. Literature was interpreted to mean not only belles-lettres, but also other works, provided that they possessed literary merit. It also indicated that while the prize was to be awarded for the author's latest work, older achievements would be taken into account if their importance had become apparent within the specified period. Hence, while the Academy over the years has preferred the poet, playwright, or novelist, historians such as Winston Churchill and Theodor Mommsen and philosophers such as Bertrand Russell and Henri Bergson are among the recipients; and while the Academy has often cited a particular work as the basis of the award, such writers as Ernest Hemingway, T. S. Eliot, Andre Gide, and Ivan Bunin—to mention a few—were honored for their entire output.

The Academy also determined that a prize could be divided or allotted jointly to two or more candidates, and that it could be retained for the following year if no worthwhile work appeared in the year under consideration. As a result, the prize was divided between two authors in 1904 (Frederic Mistral and Don Jose Echergaray) and 1917 (Karl Gjellerup and Henrik Pontoppidan), and was withheld seven other years, all, except 1935, years in which the world was at war.

However it has seen fit to interpret Nobel's intentions, the Academy has scrupulously observed his injunction that "no consideration whatever is to be given to the nationality of the candidate"—except during the war years, when writers of neutral countries were apparently given preference (hence the preponderance of Scandinavian names during these periods). The fifty-four winners represent eighteen nations. Most of the recipients have been continental Europeans, but Great Britain, Iceland, India, Chile, and the Irish Free State have been honored; and the United States, though a late starter, has been represented by five winners since Sinclair Lewis received the prize in 1930. French writers have been chosen nine times, English writers six times, and German writers five times. Until Boris Pasternak was named in 1958, no writer living in Russia had ever (Bunin lived abroad) been chosen for the distinction.

The first award was made in 1901 to the Frenchman Rene F. A. Sully-Prudhomme and for the first twenty-five years, at least, the prize went to writers who had matured and written during the previous century. Because great writers invariably reflect the thoughts and tastes of their times and because they usually account for the artistic advances of their craft, this collection of stories is more than an anthology of world-renowned writers. It is a historical survey of the changing literary styles and tastes over the past hundred years, and perhaps of more interest to an age primarily interested in fiction, it is a survey of the developing form of fiction during that period in literary history when that form was becoming an art.

Like the novel, the short story, which was first proclaimed as a distinct art form by Edgar Allen Poe, has undergone drastic changes in the past century. Its development has in many ways coincided with the development of the art of fiction. Among the many advances that took place in fiction during the years covered by this anthology, two are most obvious in these stories: subtlety of presentation and a shift from external physical action to internal mental or spiritual action. The nineteenth-century short story, like the novel of that period, seldom required more of the reader than an ability to read. The writer took infinite pains to clarify his intention and his meaning, spelling out in what seems to us today an obvious, often discursive manner the significance of each character and event. The modern author, on the other hand, is likely to expect a creative participation from his reader. The reader must immerse himself in the story; he must be sensitive to the subtle touches through which the atmosphere and setting are developed, to the skillfully-handled symbols through which character and significance of action are revealed. Earlier fiction writers were content to present their characters from the outside; today the writer probes, through symbol and suggestion beyond the external facade of his characters and enters the complex emotional and psychological inner terrain of the human being.

Therefore, we have tried to include in this collection stories which not only appeal to modern tastes but which also represent their authors and their period. Unfortunately, as a record of the advances made in fiction, the book has some evident gaps. Some of the greatest writers of our age could not be included. Though their influence is apparent in the work of a number of writers represented here, Leo Tolstoy, Henry James, Marcel Proust, Joseph Conrad, James Joyce, and D. H. Lawrence are missing from the list of prize-winners.

Two other writers whom we should have liked to include—Andre Gide and Ernest Hemingway—are among the missing. Their publishers refused to give us permission to reprint any of their work. Such omissions, though painful to the specialist in fiction, need not bother the general reader, whose enjoyment depends upon the quality of the story he reads, not upon the reputation of the writer. Our major aim has been to assemble a collection of quality fiction, and this aim we believe we have succeeded in achieving. These stories, like all great literature, reveal to us the individual artist coming to grips with life in terms of the creative and thinking human being. Several of them are notable for the way they bring focus upon man as a creature of feeling and vision searching for a dimly-remembered dream, crying out the anguish of a soul crushed by its own will, looking into the heart of light or darkness when the veil is twitched away for a moment, reflecting the life of the mind and the promptings of the spirit.

Leo Hamalian and Edmond L. Volpe

City College of New York

GREAT STORIES BY NOBEL PRIZE WINNERS

Björnsterne Björnsen

BJÖRNSTERNE BJÖRNSEN *is regarded, with Hendrik Ibsen, as one of the fathers of modern Norwegian literature. Born in 1832 in the northern mountains, he attended the University of Christiana and soon afterwards embarked upon a distinguished career as a dramatist, critic, poet, novelist, and moral and political leader. In 1903, he was the third recipient of the Nobel Prize. Like two other award winners, Wladyslaw Reymont and Grazia Deledda, he sought to transmit to his reader the life of the peasant, whom he considered the true representative of his nation. Simple and direct, his short stories convey the reality of nature in the austere life he depicts, and this compressed little masterpiece, "The Father," published in 1881, reveals his ability to convey emotional intensity in a few words. When he died in Paris in 1910, his body was returned to Norway in state.*

The man whose story is here to be told was the wealthiest and most influential person in his parish; his name was Thord Overass. He appeared in the priest's study one day, tall and earnest.

"I have gotten a son," said he, "and I wish to present him for baptism."

"What shall his name be?"

"Finn—after my father."

"And the sponsors?"

They were mentioned, and proved to be the best men and women of Thord's relations in the parish.

"Is there anything else?" inquired the priest, and looked up. The peasant hesitated a little.

"I should like very much to have him baptized by himself," he said, finally.

"That is to say on a week-day?"

"Next Saturday, at twelve o'clock noon."

"Is there anything else?" inquired the priest.

"There is nothing else," and the peasant twirled his cap, as though he were about to go.

Then the priest rose. "There is yet this, however," said he, and walking toward Thord, he took him by the hand and looked gravely into his eyes. "God grant that the child may become a blessing to you!"

One day sixteen years later, Thord stood once more in the priest's study.

"Really, you carry your age astonishingly well, Thord," said the priest; for he saw no change whatever in the man.

"That is because I have no troubles," replied Thord.

To this the priest said nothing, but after a while he asked: "What is your pleasure this evening?"

"I have come this evening about that son of mine who is to be confirmed tomorrow."

"He is a bright boy."

"I did not wish to pay the priest until I heard what number the boy would have when he takes his place in church tomorrow."

"He will stand number one."

"So I have heard; and here are ten dollars for the priest."

"Is there anything else I can do for you?" inquired the priest, fixing his eyes on Thord.

"There is nothing else."

Thord went out.

Eight years more rolled by, and then one day a noise was heard outside of the priest's study, for many men were approaching, and at their head was Thord, who entered first.

The priest looked up and recognized him.

"You come well attended this evening, Thord," said he.

"I am here to request that the banns may be published for my son; he is about to marry Karen Storliden, daughter of Gudmund, who stands here beside me."

"Why, that is the richest girl in the parish."

"So they say," replied the peasant, stroking back his hair with one hand.

The priest sat a while as if in deep thought, then entered the names in his book, without making any comments, and the men wrote their signatures underneath. Thord laid three dollars on the table.

"One is all I am to have," said the priest.

"I know that very well; but he is my only child, and I want to do it handsomely."

The priest took the money.

"This is now the third time, Thord, that you have come here on your son's account."

"But now I am through with him," said Thord, and folding up his pocketbook he said farewell and walked away.

The men slowly followed him.

A fortnight later, the father and son were rowing across the lake, one calm still day, to Storliden's to make arrangements for the wedding.

"This thwart is not secure," said the son, and stood up to straighten the seat on which he was sitting.

At the same moment the board he was standing on slipped from under him; he threw up his arms, uttered a shriek, and fell overboard.

"Take hold of the oar!" shouted the father, springing to his feet and holding out the oar.

But when the son had made a couple of efforts, he grew stiff.

"Wait a moment!" cried the father, and began to row toward his son. Then the son rolled over on his back, gave his father one long look, and sank.

Thord could scarcely believe it; he held the boat still, and stared at the spot where his son had gone down, as though he must surely come to the surface again. There rose some bubbles, then some more, and finally one large one that burst; and the lake lay there as smooth and bright as a mirror again.

For three days and three nights people saw the father rowing round and round the spot, without taking either food or sleep; he was dragging the lake for the body of his son. And toward morning of the third day he found it, and carried it in his arms up over the hills to his gard.

It might have been about a year from that day, when the priest, late one autumn evening, heard someone in the passage outside of the door, carefully trying to find the latch. The priest opened the door, and in walked a tall, thin man, with bowed form and white hair. The priest looked long at him before he recognized him. It was Thord.

"Are you out walking so late?" said the priest, and stood still in front of him.

"Ah, yes? it is late," said Thord, and took a seat.

The priest sat down also, as though waiting. A long, long silence followed. At last Thord said:

"I have something with me that I should like to give to the poor; I want it to be invested as a legacy in my son's name."

He rose, laid some money on the table, and sat down again. The priest counted it.

"It is a great deal of money," said he.

"It is half the price of my gard. I sold it today."

The priest sat long in silence. At last he asked, but gently: "What do you propose to do now, Thord?"

"Something better."

They sat there for a while, Thord with downcast eyes, the priest with his eyes fixed on Thord. Presently the priest said, slowly and softly:

"I think your son has at last brought you a true blessing."

"Yes, I think so myself," said Thord, looking up, while two big tears coursed slowly down his cheeks.

[Translated by R. B. Anderson]

Rudyard Kipling

THE MAN WHO WAS

RUDYARD KIPLING *was born in 1865 in Bombay, India, and educated in England. Working for Anglo-Indian newspapers provided him with the raw materials for the "soldier tales, Indian tales, and tales of the opposite sex" he later wrote for an Allahbad journal. English editors eagerly competed for his work when he returned to London in 1889, and soon he was producing his finest poems and stories, among them "The Man Who Was," a masterpiece of compression, suspense, and prophecy. During the next years in Brattleboro, Vermont (his American wife's home) and in Sussex, he continued the brilliant performances that led to the Nobel Prize in 1907. His subsequent work consolidated an international reputation in some eyes, left him a second-rate Tory hack in others'. Since his death in 1935, he has been increasingly recognized as a matchless master of the short-story technique.*

> *The Earth gave up her dead that tide,*
> *Into our camp he came,*
> *And said his say, and went his way,*
> *And left our hearts aflame.*
>
> *Keep tally—on the gun-butt score*
> *The vengeance we must take,*
> *When God shall bring full reckoning,*
> *For our dead comrade's sake.*
>
> Ballad

Let it be clearly understood that the Russian is a delightful person till he tucks in his shirt. As an Oriental he is charming. It is only when he insists upon being treated as the most easterly of western peoples instead of the most westerly of easterns that he becomes a racial anomaly extremely difficult to handle. The host never knows which side of his nature is going to turn up next.

Dirkovitch was a Russian—a Russian of the Russians—who appeared to get his bread by serving the Czar as an officer in a Cossack regiment, and corresponding for a Russian newspaper with a name that was never twice alike. He was a handsome young Oriental, fond of wandering through unexplored portions of the earth, and he arrived in India from nowhere in particular. At least no living man could ascertain whether it was by way of Balkh, Badakshan, Chitral, Beluchistan, or Nepal, or anywhere else. The Indian Government, being in an unusually affable mood, gave orders that he was to be civilly treated and shown everything that was to be seen. So he drifted, talking bad English and worse French, from one city to another, till he foregathered with Her Majesty's White Hussars in the city of Peshawur, which stands at the mouth of that narrow swordcut in the hills that men call the Khyber Pass. He was undoubtedly an officer, and he was decorated after the manner of the Russians with little enameled crosses, and he could talk, and (though this has nothing to do with his merits) he had been given up as a hopeless task, or cask, by the Black Tyrone, who individually and collectively, with hot whisky and honey, mulled brandy, and mixed spirits of every kind, had striven in all hospitality to make him drunk. And when the Black Tyrone, who are exclusively Irish, fail to disturb the peace of head of a foreigner—that foreigner is certain to be a superior man.

The White Hussars were as conscientious in choosing their wine as in charging the enemy. All that they possessed, including some wondrous brandy, was placed at the absolute disposition of Dirkovitch, and he enjoyed himself hugely—even more than among the Black Tyrones.

But he remained distressingly European through it all. The White Hussars were "My dear true friends," "Fellow-soldiers glorious," and "Brothers inseparable." He would unburden himself by the hour on the glorious future that awaited the combined arms of England and Russia when their hearts and their territories should run side by side and the great mission of civilizing Asia should begin. That was unsatisfactory, because Asia is not going to be civilized after the methods of the West. There is too much Asia and she is too old. You cannot reform a lady of many lovers, and Asia has been insatiable in her flirtations aforetime. She will never attend Sunday-school or learn to vote save with swords for tickets.

Dirkovitch knew this as well as any one else, but it suited him to talk special-correspondently and to make himself as genial as he could. Now and then he volunteered a little, a very little, information about his own sotnia of Cossacks, left apparently to look after themselves somewhere at the back of beyond. He had done rough work in Central Asia, and had seen rather more help-yourself fighting than most men of his years. But he was careful never to betray his superiority, and more than careful to praise on all occasions the appearance, drill, uniform, and organization of Her Majesty's White Hussars. And indeed they were a regiment to be admired. When Lady Durgan, widow of the late Sir John Durgan, arrived in their station, and after a short time had been proposed to by every single man at mess, she put the public sentiment very neatly when she explained that they were all so nice that unless she could marry them all, including the colonel and some majors already married, she was not going to content herself with one hussar. Wherefore she wedded a little man in a rifle regiment, being by nature contradictious; and the White Hussars were going to wear crape on their arms, but compromised by attending the wedding in full force, and lining the aisle with unutterable reproach. She had jilted them all—from Basset-Holmer the senior captain to little Mildred the junior subaltern, who could have given her four thousand a year and a title.

The only persons who did not share the general regard for the

White Hussars were a few thousand gentlemen of Jewish extraction who lived across the border, and answered to the name of Pathan. They had once met the regiment officially and for something less than twenty minutes, but the interview, which was complicated with many casualties, had filled them with prejudice. They even called the White Hussars children of the devil and sons of persons whom it would be perfectly impossible to meet in decent society. Yet they were not above making their aversion fill their money-belts. The regiment possessed carbines—beautiful Martini-Henri carbines that would lob a bullet into an enemy's camp at one thousand yards, and were even handier than the long rifle. Therefore they were coveted all along the border, and since demand inevitably breeds supply, they were supplied at the risk of life and limb for exactly their weight in coined silver— seven and one-half pounds weight of rupees, or sixteen pounds sterling reckoning the rupee at par. They were stolen at night by snaky-haired thieves who crawled on their stomachs under the nose of the sentries; they disappeared mysteriously from locked arm-racks, and in the hot weather, when all the barrack doors and windows were open, they vanished like puffs of their own smoke. The border people desired them for family vendettas and contingencies. But in the long cold nights of the northern Indian winter they were stolen most extensively. The traffic of murder was liveliest among the hills at that season, and prices ruled high. The regimental guards were first doubled and then trebled. A trooper does not much care if he loses a weapon—Government must make it good—but he deeply resents the loss of his sleep. The regiment grew very angry, and one rifle-thief bears the visible marks of their anger upon him to this hour. That incident stopped the burglaries for a time, and the guards were reduced accordingly, and the regiment devoted itself to polo with unexpected result; for it beat by two goals to one that very terrible polo corps the Lushkar Light Horse, though the latter had four ponies apiece for a short hour's fight, as well as a native officer who played like a lambent flame across the ground.

They gave a dinner to celebrate the event. The Lushkar team

came, and Dirkovitch came, in the fullest full uniform of a Cossack officer, which is as full as a dressing-gown, and was introduced to the Lushkars, and opened his eyes as he regarded. They were lighter men than the Hussars, and they carried themselves with the swing that is the peculiar right of the Punjab Frontier Force and all Irregular Horse. Like everything else in the Service it has to be learnt, but, unlike many things, it is never forgotten, and remains on the body till death.

The great beam-roofed mess-room of the White Hussars was a sight to be remembered. All the mess plate was out on the long table—the same table that had served up the bodies of five officers after a forgotten fight long and long ago—the dingy, battered standards faced the door of entrance, clumps of winter-roses lay between the silver candlesticks, and the portraits of eminent officers deceased looked down on their successors from between the heads of sambhur, nilghai, markhor, and, pride of all the mess, two grinning snow-leopards that had cost Basset-Holmer four months' leave that he might have spent in England, instead of on the road to Thibet and the daily risk of his life by ledge, snow-slide, and grassy slope.

The servants in spotless white muslin and the crest of their regiments on the brow of their turbans waited behind their masters, who were clad in the scarlet and gold of the White Hussars, and the cream and silver of the Lushkar Light Horse. Dirkovitch's dull green uniform was the only dark spot at the board, but his big onyx eyes made up for it. He was fraternizing effusively with the captain of the Lushkar team, who was wondering how many of Dirkovitch's Cossacks his own dark wiry down-countrymen could account for in a fair charge. But one does not speak of these things openly.

The talk rose higher and higher, and the regimental band played between the courses, as is the immemorial custom, till all tongues ceased for a moment with the removal of the dinner-slips and the first toast of obligation, when an officer rising said, "Mr. Vice, the Queen," and little Mildred from the bottom of the table answered, "The Queen, God bless her," and the big spurs clanked as the big men heaved themselves up and drank the Queen upon whose pay they were falsely supposed to settle their mess-bills. That Sacrament of the Mess never grows old, and never ceases to bring a lump into the throat of the listener wherever he be by sea or by land. Dirkovitch rose with his "brothers glorious," but he could not understand. No one but an officer can tell what the toast means; and the bulk have more sentiment than comprehension. Immediately after the little silence that follows on the ceremony there entered the native officer who had played for the Lushkar team. He could not, of course, eat with the mess, but he came in at dessert, all six feet of him, with the blue and silver turban atop, and the big black boots below. The mess rose joyously as he thrust forward the hilt of his saber in token of fealty for the colonel of the White Hussars to touch, and dropped into a vacant chair amid shouts of: "*Rung ho*, Hira Singh!" (which being translated means "Go in and win"). "Did I whack you over the knee, old man?" "Ressaidar Sahib, what the devil made you play that kicking pig of a pony in the last ten minutes?" "*Shabash*, Ressaidar Sahib!" Then the voice of the colonel, "The health of Ressaidar Hira Singh!"

After the shouting had died away Hira Singh rose to reply, for he was the cadet of a royal house, the son of a king's son, and knew what was due on these occasions. Thus he spoke in the vernacular:—"Colonel Sahib and officers of this regiment. Much honor have you done me. This will I remember. We came down from afar to play you. But we were beaten." ("No fault of yours, Ressaidar Sahib. Played on our own ground y'know. Your ponies were cramped from the railway. Don't apologize!") "Therefore perhaps we will come again if it be so ordained." ("Hear! Hear! Hear, indeed! Bravo! Hsh!") "Then we will play you afresh" ("Happy to meet you.") "till there are left no feet upon our ponies. Thus far for sport." He dropped one hand on his sword-hilt and his eye wandered to Dirkovitch lolling back in his chair. "But if by the will of God there arises any other game which is not the polo game, then be assured, Colonel Sahib and officers, that we will play it out side by side, though *they*," again his eye sought Dirkovitch, "though *they* I say have fifty ponies to our one horse." And with a deep-mouthed *Rung ho!* that sounded like a musket-butt on flagstones he sat down amid leaping glasses.

Dirkovitch, who had devoted himself steadily to the brandy—the terrible brandy aforementioned—did not understand, nor did the expurgated translations offered to him at all convey the point. Decidedly Hira Singh's was the speech of the evening, and the clamor might have continued to the dawn had it not been broken by the noise of a shot without that sent every man feeling at his defenseless left side. Then there was a scuffle and a yell of pain.

"Carbine-stealing again!" said the adjutant, calmly sinking back in his chair. "This comes of reducing the guards. I hope the sentries have killed him."

The feet of armed men pounded on the veranda flags, and it was as though something was being dragged.

"Why don't they put him in the cells till the morning?" said the colonel testily. "See if they've damaged him, sergeant."

The mess sergeant fled out into the darkness and returned with two troopers and a corporal, all very much perplexed.

"Caught a man stealin' carbines, sir," said the corporal. "Least-ways 'e was crawlin' towards the barricks, sir, past the main road sentries, an' the sentry 'e sez, sir——"

The limp heap of rags upheld by the three men groaned. Never was seen so destitute and demoralized an Afghan. He was turbanless, shoeless, caked with dirt, and all but dead with rough handling. Hira Singh started slightly at the sound of the man's pain. Dirkovitch took another glass of brandy.

"*What* does the sentry say?" said the colonel.

"*Sez* 'e speaks English, sir," said the corporal.

"So you brought him into mess instead of handing him over to the sergeant! If he spoke all the Tongues of the Pentecost you've no business——"

Again the bundle groaned and muttered. Little Mildred had risen from his place to inspect. He jumped back as though he had been shot.

"Perhaps it would be better, sir, to send the men away," said he to the colonel, for he was a much privileged subaltern. He put his arms round the ragbound horror as he spoke, and dropped him into a chair. It may not have been explained that the littleness of Mildred lay in his being six feet four and big in proportion. The corporal seeing that an officer was disposed to look after the capture, and that the colonel's eye was beginning to blaze, promptly removed himself and his men. The mess was left alone with the carbine-thief, who laid his head on the table and wept bitterly, hopelessly, and inconsolably, as little children weep.

Hira Singh leapt to his feet. "Colonel Sahib," said he, "that man is no Afghan, for they weep *Ai! Ai!* Nor is he of Hindustan, for they weep *Oh! Ho!* He weeps after the fashion of the white men, who say *Ow! Ow!*"

"Now where the dickens did you get that knowledge, Hira Singh?" said the captain of the Lushkar team.

"Hear him!" said Hira Singh simply, pointing at the crumpled figure that wept as though it would never cease.

"He said, 'My God!' " said little Mildred. "I heard him say it."

The colonel and the mess-room looked at the man in silence. It is a horrible thing to hear a man cry. A woman can sob from the top of her palate, or her lips, or anywhere else, but a man must cry from his diaphragm, and it rends him to pieces.

"Poor devil!" said the colonel, coughing tremendously. "We ought to send him to the hospital. He's been manhandled."

Now the adjutant loved his carbines. They were to him as his grandchildren, the men standing in the first place. He grunted rebelliously: "I can understand an Afghan stealing, because he's built that way. But I can't understand his crying. That makes it worse."

The brandy must have affected Dirkovitch, for he lay back in his chair and stared at the ceiling. There was nothing special in the ceiling beyond a shadow as of a huge black coffin. Owing to some peculiarity in the construction of the mess-room this shadow was always thrown when the candles were lighted. It never disturbed the digestion of the White Hussars. They were in fact rather proud of it.

"Is he going to cry all night?" said the colonel, "or are we supposed to sit up with little Mildred's guest until he feels better?"

The man in the chair threw up his head and stared at the mess. "Oh, my God!" he said, and every soul in the mess rose to his feet. Then the Lushkar captain did a deed for which he ought to have been given the Victoria Cross—distinguished gallantry in a fight against overwhelming curiosity. He picked up his team with his eyes as the hostess picks up the ladies at the opportune moment, and pausing only by the colonel's chair to say, "This isn't *our* affair, you know, sir," led them into the veranda and the gardens. Hira Singh was the last to go, and he looked at Dirkovitch. But Dirkovitch had departed into a brandy-paradise of his own. His lips moved without sound and he was studying the coffin on the ceiling.

"White—white all over," said Basset-Holmer, the adjutant. "What a pernicious renegade he must be! I wonder where he came from?"

The colonel shook the man gently by the arm, and "Who are you?" said he.

There was no answer. The man stared round the mess-room and smiled in the colonel's face. Little Mildred, who was always more of a woman than a man till "Boot and saddle" was sounded, repeated the question in a voice that would have drawn confidences from a geyser. The man only smiled. Dirkovitch at the far end of the table slid gently from his chair to the floor. No son of Adam in this present imperfect world can mix the Hussars' champagne with the Hussars' brandy by five and eight glasses of each without remembering the pit whence he was digged and descending thither. The band began to play the tune with which the White Hussars from the date of their formation have concluded all their functions. They would sooner be disbanded than abandon that tune; it is a part of their system. The man straightened himself in his chair and drummed on the table with his fingers.

"I don't see why we should entertain lunatics," said the colonel.

"Call a guard and send him off to the cells. We'll look into the business in the morning. Give him a glass of wine first though."

Little Mildred filled a sherry-glass with the brandy and thrust it over to the man. He drank, and the tune rose louder, and he straightened himself yet more. Then he put out his long-taloned hands to a piece of plate opposite and fingered it lovingly. There was a mystery connected with that piece of plate, in the shape of a spring which converted what was a seven-branched candlestick, three springs on each side and one in the middle, into a sort of wheel-spoke candelabrum. He found the spring, pressed it, and laughed weakly. He rose from his chair and inspected a picture on the wall, then moved on to another picture, the mess watching him without a word. When he came to the mantelpiece he shook his head and seemed distressed. A piece of plate representing a mounted hussar in full uniform caught his eye. He pointed to it, and then to the mantelpiece with inquiry in his eyes.

"What is it—Oh what is it?" said little Mildred. Then as a mother might speak to a child, "That is a horse. Yes, a horse."

Very slowly came the answer in a thick, passionless guttural —"Yes, I—have seen. But—where is *the* horse?"

You could have heard the hearts of the mess beating as the men drew back to give the stranger full room in his wanderings. There was no question of calling the guard.

Again he spoke—very slowly, "Where is *our* horse?"

There is but one horse in the White Hussars, and his portrait hangs outside the door of the mess-room. He is the piebald drum-horse, the king of the regimental band, that served the regiment for seven-and-thirty years, and in the end was shot for old age. Half the mess tore the thing down from its place and thrust it into the man's hands. He placed it above the mantelpiece, it clattered on the ledge as his poor hands dropped it, and he staggered towards the bottom of the table, falling into Mildred's chair. Then all the men spoke to one another something after this fashion, "The drum-horse hasn't hung over the mantelpiece since '67." "How does he know?" "Mildred, go and speak to him again." "Colonel, what are you going to do?" "Oh, dry up, and give the poor devil a chance to pull himself together." "It isn't possible anyhow. The man's a lunatic."

Little Mildred stood at the colonel's side talking in his ear. "Will you be good enough to take your seats please, gentlemen!" he said, and the mess dropped into the chairs. Only Dirkovitch's seat, next to little Mildred's, was blank, and little Mildred himself had found Hira Singh's place. The wide-eyed mess-sergeant filled the glasses in deep silence. Once more the colonel rose, but his hand shook and the port spilled on the table as he looked straight at the man in little Mildred's chair and said hoarsely, "Mr. Vice, the Queen." There was a little pause, but the man sprung to his feet and answered without hesitation, "The Queen, God bless her!" and as he emptied the thin glass he snapped the shank between his fingers.

Long and long ago, when the Empress of India was a young woman and there were no unclean ideals in the land, it was the custom of a few messes to drink the Queen's toast in broken glass, to the vast delight of the mess-contractors. The custom is now dead, because there is nothing to break anything for, except now and again the word of a Government, and that has been broken already.

"That settles it," said the colonel, with a gasp. "He's not a sergeant. What in the world is he?"

The entire mess echoed the word, and the volley of questions would have scared any man. It was no wonder that the ragged, filthy invader could only smile and shake his head.

From under the table, calm and smiling, rose Dirkovitch, who had been roused from healthful slumber by feet upon his body. By the side of the man he rose, and the man shrieked and groveled. It was a horrible sight coming so swiftly upon the pride and glory of the toast that had brought the strayed wits together.

Dirkovitch made no offer to raise him, but little Mildred heaved him up in an instant. It is not good that a gentleman who can answer to the Queen's toast should lie at the feet of a subaltern of Cossacks.

The hasty action tore the wretch's upper clothing nearly to the waist, and his body was seamed with dry black scars. There is only one weapon in the world that cuts in parallel lines, and it is neither the cane or the cat. Dirkovitch saw the marks, and the pupils of his eyes dilated. Also his face changed. He said something that sounded like *Shto ve takete*, and the man fawning answered, *Chetyre*.

"What's that?" said everybody together.

"His number. That is number four, you know." Dirkovitch spoke very thickly.

"What has a Queen's officer to do with a qualified number?" said the colonel, and an unpleasant growl ran round the table.

"How can I tell?" said the affable Oriental with a sweet smile. "He is a—how you have it?—escape—run-a-way, from over there." He nodded toward the darkness of the night.

"Speak to him if he'll answer you, and speak to him gently," said little Mildred, settling the man in a chair. It seemed most improper to all present that Dirkovitch should sip brandy as he talked in purring, spitting Russian to the creature who answered so feebly and with such evident dread. But since Dirkovitch appeared to understand no one said a word. All breathed heavily, leaning forward, in the long gaps of the conversation. The next time that they have no engagements on hand the White Hussars intend to go to St. Petersburg in a body to learn Russian.

"He does not know how many years ago," said Dirkovitch, facing the mess, "but he says it was very long ago in a war. I think that there was an accident. He says he was of this glorious and distinguished regiment in the war."

"The rolls! The rolls! Holmer, get the rolls!" said little Mildred, and the adjutant dashed off bare-headed to the orderly-room, where the muster-rolls of the regiment were kept. He returned just in time to hear Dirkovitch conclude, "Therefore, my dear friends, I am most sorry to say there was an accident which would have been reparable if he had apologized to that our colonel, which he had insulted."

Then followed another growl which the colonel tried to beat

down. The mess was in no mood just then to weigh insults to Russian colonels.

"He does not remember, but I think that there was an accident, and so he was not exchanged among the prisoners, but he was sent to another place—how do you say?—the country. So, he says, he came here. He does not know how he came. Eh? He was at Chepany"—the man caught the word, nodded, and shivered—"at Zhigansk and Irkutsk. I cannot understand how he escaped. He says, too, that he was in the forests for many years, but how many years he has forgotten—that with many things. It was an accident; done because he did not apologize to that our colonel. Ah!"

Instead of echoing Dirkovitch's sigh of regret, it is sad to record that the White Hussars livelily exhibited un-Christian delight and other emotions, hardly restrained by their sense of hospitality. Holmer flung the frayed and yellow regimental rolls on the table, and the men flung themselves at these.

"Steady! Fifty-six—fifty-five—fifty-four," said Holmer. "Here we are. 'Lieutenant Austin Limmason. *Missing.*' That was before Sebastopol. What an infernal shame. Insulted one of their colonels, and was quietly shipped off. Thirty years of his life wiped out."

"But he never apologized. Said he'd see him damned first," chorused the mess.

"Poor chap! I suppose he never had the chance afterwards. How did he come here?" said the colonel.

The dingy heap in the chair could give no answer.

"Do you know who you are?"

It laughed weakly.

"Do you know that you are Limmason—Lieutenant Limmason of the White Hussars?"

Swiftly as a shot came the answer, in a slightly surprised tone, "Yes, I'm Limmason, of course." The light died out in his eyes, and the man collapsed, watching every motion of Dirkovitch with terror. A flight from Siberia may fix a few elementary facts in the mind, but it does not seem to lead to continuity of thought. The man could not explain how, like a homing pigeon, he had found his way to his own old mess again. Of what he had suffered or seen he knew nothing. He cringed before Dirkovitch as instinctively as he had pressed the spring of the candlestick, sought the picture of the drum-horse, and answered to the toast of the Queen. The rest was a blank that the dreaded Russian tongue could only in part remove. His head bowed on his breast, and he giggled and cowered alternately.

The devil that lived in the brandy prompted Dirkovitch at this extremely inopportune moment to make a speech. He rose, swaying slightly, gripped the table-edge, while his eyes glowed like opals, and began:

"Fellow-soldiers glorious—true friends and hospitables. It was an accident, and deplorable—most deplorable." Here he smiled sweetly all round the mess. "But you will think of this little, little thing. So little, is it not? The Czar! Posh! I slap my fingers—I snap my fingers at him. Do I believe in him? No! But in us Slav who has done nothing, *him* I believe. Seventy—how much—millions peoples that have done nothing—not one thing. Posh! Napoleon was an episode." He banged a hand on the table. "Hear you, old peoples, we have done nothing in the world—out here. All our work is to do; and it shall be done, old peoples. Get a-way!" He waved his hand imperiously, and pointed to the man. "You see him. He is not good to see. He was just one little—oh, so little—accident, that no one remembered. Now he is *That!* So will you be, brother-soldiers so brave—so will you be. But you will never come back. You will all go where he is gone, or"—he pointed to the great coffin-shadow on the ceiling, and muttering, "Seventy millions—get a-way, you old peoples," fell asleep.

"Sweet, and to the point," said little Mildred. "What's the use of getting wroth? Let's make this poor devil comfortable."

But that was a matter suddenly and swiftly taken from the loving hands of the White Hussars. The lieutenant had returned only to go away again three days later, when the wail of the

Dead March, and the tramp of the squadrons, told the wondering Station, who saw no gap in the mess-table, that an officer of the regiment had resigned his new-found commission.

And Dirkovitch, bland, supple, and always genial, went away too by a night train. Little Mildred and another man saw him off, for he was the guest of the mess, and even had he smitten the colonel with the open hand, the law of that mess allowed no relaxation of hospitality.

"Good-bye, Dirkovitch, and a pleasant journey," said little Mildred.

"*Au revoir*," said the Russian.

"Indeed! But we thought you were going home?"

"Yes, but I will come again. My dear friends, is that road shut?" He pointed to where the North Star burned over the Khyber Pass.

"By Jove! I forgot. Of course. Happy to meet you, old man, any time you like. Got everything you want? Cheroots, ice, bedding? That's all right. Well, *au revoir*, Dirkovitch."

"Um," said the other man, as the tail-lights of the train grew small. "Of—all—the—unmitigated——!"

Little Mildred answered nothing, but watched the North Star and hummed a selection from a recent Simla burlesque that had much delighted the White Hussars. It ran—

> *I'm sorry for Mister Bluebeard,*
> *I'm sorry to cause him pain;*
> *But a terrible spree there's sure to be*
> *When he comes back again.*

Selma Lagerlof

SELMA LAGERLOF, *the first authoress to win the Nobel Prize* (1909), *was born in 1858 in Varmland, Sweden. She gave up a teaching career to write when her first book,* Gosta Berling, *an original and imaginative saga based upon stories and folk tales of her native province, proved an immediate success. Her talent shows itself most maturely in the novel* Jerusalem, *about a group of Swedish farmers who emigrate to the Holy Land, and in two collections of tales,* Invisible Links, *from which "The Outlaws" is taken, and* The Queen of Kunghalla. *Generations of children throughout the world (and recently television viewers) have been delighted by her fantasy,* The Wonderful Adventures of Nils. *Her deeply religious spirit and profound knowledge of the forces that move men, observable also in her poetry, autobiography, essays, and other fiction, make the following story one of the most memorable in Scandinavian literature. She died in 1940 at her estate of Marbacka, the subject of one of her books.*

A peasant had killed a monk and fled to the woods. He became an outlaw, upon whose head a price was set. In the forest he met another fugitive, a young fisherman from one of the outermost islands, who had been accused of the theft of a herring net. The two became companions, cut themselves a home in a cave, laid their nets together, cooked their food, made their arrows, and held watch one for the other. The peasant could never leave the forest. But the fisherman, whose crime was less serious, would now and then take upon his back the game they had killed, and would creep down to the more isolated houses on the outskirts of the village. In return for milk, butter, arrow-heads, and clothing he would sell his game, the black mountain cock, the moor hen, with her shining feathers, the toothsome doe, and the long-eared hare.

The cave which was their home cut down deep into a mountain-side. The entrance was guarded by wide slabs of stone and ragged thornbushes. High up on the hillside there stood a giant pine, and the chimney of the fireplace nestled among its coiled roots. Thus the smoke could draw up through the heavy hanging branches and fade unseen into the air. To reach their cave the men had to wade through the stream that sprang out from the hill slope. No pursuer thought of seeking their trail in this merry brooklet. At first they were hunted as wild animals are. The peasants of the district gathered to pursue them as if for a baiting wolf or bear. The bowmen surrounded the wood while the spear carriers entered and left no thicket or ravine unsearched. The two outlaws cowered in their gloomy cave, panting in terror and listening breathlessly as the hunt passed on with noise and shouting over the mountain ranges.

For one long day the young fisherman lay motionless, but the murderer could stand it no longer, and went out into the open where he could see his enemy. They discovered him and set after him, but this was far more to his liking than lying quiet in impotent terror. He fled before his pursuers, leaped the streams, slid down the precipices, climbed up perpendicular walls of rock. All his remarkable strength and skill awoke to energy under the spur of danger. His body became as elastic as a steel spring, his foot held firm, his hand grasped sure, his eye and ear were doubly sharp. He knew the meaning of every murmur in the foliage; he could understand the warning in an upturned stone.

When he had clambered up the side of a precipice he would stop to look down on his pursuers, greeting them with loud songs of scorn. When their spears sang above him in the air, he would catch them and hurl them back. As he crashed his way through tangled underbrush something within him seemed to sing a wild song of rejoicing. A gaunt, bare hilltop stretched itself through the forest, and all alone upon its crest there stood a towering pine. The red brown trunk was bare, in the thick grown boughs at the top a hawk's nest rocked in the breeze. So daring had the fugitive grown that on another day he climbed to the nest while his pursuers sought him in the woody slopes below. He sat there and twisted the necks of the young hawks as the hunt raged far beneath him. The old birds flew screaming about him in anger. They swooped past his face, they struck at his eyes with their beaks, beat at him with their powerful wings, and clawed great scratches in his weather-hardened skin. He battled with them laughing. He stood up in the rocking nest as he lunged at the birds with his knife, and he lost all thought of danger and pursuit in the joy of battle. When recollection came again and he turned to look for his enemies, the hunt had gone off in another direction. Not one of the pursuers had thought of raising his eyes to the clouds to see the prey hanging there, doing schoolboy deeds of recklessness while his life hung in the balance. But the man trembled from head to foot when he saw that he was safe. He caught for a support with his shaking hands; he looked down giddily from the height to which he had climbed. Groaning in fear of a fall, afraid of the birds, afraid of the possibility of being seen, weakened through terror of everything and anything, he slid back down the tree trunk. He laid himself flat upon the earth and crawled over the loose stones until he reached the underbrush. There he hid among the tangled branches of the young pines, sinking down, weak and helpless, upon the soft moss. A single man might have captured him.

Tord was the name of the fisherman. He was but sixteen years old, but was strong and brave. He had now lived for a whole year in the wood.

The peasant's name was Berg, and they had called him "The Giant." He was handsome and well-built, the tallest and strongest man in the entire county. He was broad-shouldered and yet slender. His hands were delicate in shape, as if they had never known hard work, his hair was brown, his face soft-coloured. When he had lived for some time in the forest his look of strength was awe-inspiring. His eyes grew piercing under bushy brows wrinkled by great muscles over the forehead. His lips were more firmly set than before, his face more haggard, with deepened hollows at the temples, and his strongly marked cheek-bones stood out plainly. All the softer curves of his body disappeared, but the muscles grew strong as steel. His hair turned grey rapidly.

Tord had never seen any one so magnificent and so mighty before. In his imagination, his companion towered high as the forest, strong as the raging surf. He served him humbly, as he would have served a master, he revered him as he would have revered a god. It seemed quite natural that Tord should carry the hunting spear, that he should drag the game home, draw the water, and build the fire. Berg, the Giant, accepted all these services, but scarce threw the boy a friendly word. He looked upon him with contempt, as a common thief.

The outlaws did not live by pillage, but supported themselves by hunting and fishing. Had not Berg killed a holy man, the peasants would soon have tired of the pursuit and left them to themselves in the mountains. But they feared disaster for the villages if he who had laid hands upon a servant of God should go unpunished. When Tord took his game down into the valley they would offer him money and a pardon for himself if he would lead them to the cave of the Giant, that they might catch the latter in his sleep. But the boy refused, and if they followed him he would lead them astray until they gave up the pursuit.

Once Berg asked him whether the peasants had ever tried to persuade him to betrayal. When he learned what reward they had promised he said scornfully that Tord was a fool not to accept such offers. Tord looked at him with something in his eyes that Berg, the Giant, had never seen before. No beautiful woman whom he had loved in the days of his youth had ever looked at him like that; not even in the eyes of his own children, or of his wife, had he seen such affection. "You are my God, the ruler I have chosen of my own free will." This was what the eyes said.

"You may scorn me, or beat me, if you will, but I shall still remain faithful."

After this, Berg gave more heed to the boy and saw that he was brave in action but shy in speech. Death seemed to have no terrors for him. He would deliberately choose for his path the fresh formed ice on the mountain pools, the treacherous surface of the morass in springtime. He seemed to delight in danger. It gave him some compensation for the wild ocean storms he could no longer go out to meet. He would tremble in the night darkness of the wood, however, and even by day the gloom of a thicket or a deeper shadow could frighten him. When Berg asked him about this he was silent in embarrassment.

Tord did not sleep in the bed by the hearth at the back of the cave, but every night, when Berg was asleep the boy would creep to the entrance and lie there on one of the broad stones. Berg discovered this, and although he guessed the reason he asked the boy about it. Tord would not answer. To avoid further questions he slept in the bed for two nights, then returned to his post at the door.

One night, when a snow-storm raged in the treetops, piling up drifts even in the heart of the thickets, the flakes swirled into the cave of the outlaws. Tord, lying by the entrance, awoke in the morning to find himself wrapped in a blanket of melting snow. A day or two later he fell ill. Sharp pains pierced his lungs when he tried to draw breath. He endured the pain as long as his strength would stand it, but one evening, when he stooped to blow up the fire, he fell down and could not rise again. Berg came to his side and told him to lie in the warm bed. Tord groaned in agony, but could not move. Berg put his arm under the boy's body and carried him to the bed. He had a feeling while doing it as if he were touching a clammy snake; he had a taste in his mouth as if he had eaten unclean horseflesh, so repulsive was it to him to touch the person of this common thief. Berg covered the sick boy with his own warm bear-skin rug and gave him water. This was all he could do, but the illness was not dangerous, and Tord recovered quickly.

But now that Berg had had to do his companion's work for a few days, and had had to care for him, they seemed to have come nearer to one another. Tord dared to speak to Berg sometimes, as they sat together by the fire cutting their arrows.

"You come of good people, Berg," Tord said one evening. "Your relatives are the richest peasants in the valley. The men of your name have served kings and fought in their castles."

"They have more often fought with the rebels and done damage to the king's property," answered Berg.

"Your forefathers held great banquets at Christmas time. And you held banquets too, when you were at home in your house. Hundreds of men and women could find place on the benches in your great hall, the hall that was built in the days before St. Olaf came here to Viken for christening. Great silver urns were there, and mighty horns, filled with mead, went the rounds of your table."

Berg looked at the boy again. He sat on the edge of the bed with his head in his hands, pushing back the heavy tangled hair that hung over his eyes. His face had become pale and refined through his illness. His eyes still sparkled in fever. He smiled to himself at the pictures called up by his fancy—pictures of the great hall and of the silver urns, of the richly clad guests, and of Berg, the Giant, lording it in the place of honor. The peasant knew that even in the days of his glory no one had ever looked at him with eyes so shining in admiration, so glowing in reverence, as this boy did now, as he sat by the fire in his worn leather jacket. He was touched, and yet displeased. This common thief had no right to admire him.

"Were there no banquets in your home?" he asked.

Tord laughed: "Out there on the rocks where father and mother live? Father plunders the wrecks and mother is a witch. When the weather is stormy she rides out to meet the ships on a seal's back, and those who are washed overboard from the wrecks belong to her."

"What does she do with them?" asked Berg.

"Oh, a witch always needs corpses. She makes salves of them, or perhaps she eats them. On moonlit nights she sits out in the wildest surf and looks for the eyes and fingers of drowned children."

"That is horrible!" said Berg.

The boy answered with calm confidence: "It would be for others, but not for a witch. She can't help it."

This was an altogether new manner of looking at life for Berg.

"Then thieves have to steal, as witches have to make magic?" he questioned sharply.

"Why, yes," answered the boy. "Every one has to do the thing he was born for." But a smile of shy cunning curled his lips, as he added: "There are thieves who have never stolen."

"What do you mean by that?" spoke Berg.

The boy still smiled his mysterious smile and seemed happy to have given his companion a riddle. "There are birds that do not fly; and there are thieves who have not stolen," he said.

Berg feigned stupidity, in order to trick the other's meaning: "How can any one be called a thief who has never stolen?" he said.

The boy's lips closed tight as if to hold back the words. "But if one has a father who steals—" he threw out after a short pause.

"A man may inherit house and money, but the name thief is given only to him who earns it."

Tord laughed gently. "But when one has a mother—and that mother comes and cries, and begs one to take upon one's self the father's crime—and then one can laugh at the hangman and run away into the woods. A man may be outlawed for the sake of a fish net he has never seen."

Berg beat his fist upon the stone table, in great anger. Here this strong, beautiful boy had thrown away his whole life for another. Neither love, nor riches, nor the respect of his fellow men could ever be his again. The sordid care for food and clothing was all that remained to him in life. And this fool had let him, Berg, despise an innocent man. He scolded sternly, but Tord was not frightened any more than a sick child is frightened at the scolding of his anxious mother.

High up on one of the broad wooded hills there lay a black swampy lake. It was square in shape, and its banks were as straight, and their corners as sharp as if it had been the work of human hands. On three sides steep walls of rock rose up, with hardy mountain pines clinging to the stones, their roots as thick as a man's arm. At the surface of the lake, where the few strips of grass had been washed away, these naked roots twisted and coiled, rising out of the water like myriad snakes that had tried to escape from the waves, but had been turned to stone in their struggle. Or was it more like a mass of blackened skeletons of long-drowned giants which the lake was trying to throw off? The arms and legs were twisted in wild contortions, the long fingers grasped deep into the rocks, the mighty ribs formed arches that upheld ancient trees. But now and again these iron-hard arms, these steel fingers with which the climbing pines supported themselves, would loosen their hold, and then the strong north wind would hurl the tree from the ridge far out into the swamp. There it would lie, its crown burrowing deep in the muddy water. The fishes found good hiding places amid its twigs, while the roots rose up over the water like the arms of some hideous monster, giving the little lake a repulsive appearance.

The mountains sloped down on the fourth side of the little lake. A tiny rivulet foamed out here; but before the stream could find its path it twisted and turned among boulders and mounds of earth, forming a whole colony of islands, some of which scarce offered foothold, while others carried as many as twenty trees on their back.

Here, where the rocks were not high enough to shut out the sun, the lighter foliaged trees could grow. Here were the timid, grey-green alders, and the willows with their smooth leaves. Birches were here, as they always are wherever there is a chance to shut out the evergreens, and there were mountain ash and elder bushes, giving charm and fragrance to the place.

At the entrance to the lake there was a forest of rushes as high as a man's head, through which the sunlight fell as green upon the water as it falls on the moss in the true forest. There were little clearings among the reeds, little round ponds where the water lilies slumbered. The tall rushes looked down with gentle gravity upon these sensitive beauties, who closed their white leaves and their yellow hearts so quickly in their leather outer dress as soon as the sun withdrew his rays.

One sunny day the outlaws came to one of these little ponds to fish. They waded through the reeds to two high stones, and sat there throwing out their bait for the big green, gleaming pike that slumbered just below the surface of the water. These men, whose life was now passed entirely among the mountains and the woods, had come to be as completely under the control of the powers of nature as were the plants or the animals. When the sun shone they were open-hearted and merry, at evening they became silent, and the night, which seemed to them so all-powerful, robbed them of their strength. And now the green light that fell through the reeds and drew out from the water stripes of gold, brown, and black-green, smoothed them into a sort of magic mood. They were completely shut out from the outer world. The reeds swayed gently in the soft wind, the rushes murmured, and the long, ribbon-like leaves struck them lightly in the face. They sat on the grey stones in their grey leather garments, and the shaded tones of the leather melted into the shade of the stones. Each saw his comrade sitting opposite him as quietly as a stone statue. And among the reeds they saw giant fish swimming, gleaming and glittering in all colours of the rainbow. When the men threw out their lines and watched the rings on the water widen amid the reeds, it seemed to them that the motion grew and grew until they saw it was not they themselves alone that had occasioned it. A Nixie, half human, half fish, lay sleeping deep down in the water. She lay on her back, and the waves clung so closely to her body that the men had not seen her before. It was her breath that stirred the surface. But it did not seem to the watchers that there was anything strange in the fact that she lay there. And when she had disappeared in the next moment they did not know whether her appearance had been an illusion or not.

The green light pierced through their eyes into their brains like a mild intoxication. They saw visions among the reeds, visions which they would not tell even to each other. There was not much fishing done. The day was given up to dreams and visions.

A sound of oars came from among the reeds, and they started up out of their dreaming. In a few moments a heavy boat, hewn out of a tree trunk, came into sight, set in motion by oars not much broader than walking sticks. The oars were in the hands of a young girl who had been gathering water-lilies. She had long, dark brown braids of hair, and great dark eyes, but she was strangely pale, a pallor that was not grey, but softly pink tinted. Her cheeks were no deeper in colour than the rest of her face; her lips were scarce redder. She wore a bodice of white linen and a leather belt with a golden clasp. Her skirt was of blue with a broad red hem. She rowed past close by the outlaws without seeing them. They sat absolutely quiet, less from fear of discovery than from the desire to look at her undisturbed. When she had gone, the stone statues became men again and smiled:

"She was as white as the water-lilies," said one. "And her eyes were as dark as the water back there under the roots of the pines."

They were both so merry that they felt like laughing, like really laughing as they had never laughed in this swamp before, a laugh that would echo back from the wall of rock and loosen the roots of the pines.

"Did you think her beautiful?" asked the Giant.

"I do not know, she passed so quickly. Perhaps she was beautiful."

"You probably did not dare to look at her. Did you think she was the Nixie?"

And again they felt a strange desire to laugh.

While a child, Tord had once seen a drowned man. He had found the corpse on the beach in broad daylight, and it had not frightened him, but at night his dreams were terrifying. He had seemed to be looking out over an ocean, every wave of which threw a dead body at his feet. He saw all the rocks and islands covered with corpses of the drowned, the drowned that were dead and belonged to the sea, but that could move, and speak, and threaten him with their white stiffened fingers.

And so it was again. The girl whom he had seen in the reeds appeared to him in his dreams. He met her again down at the bottom of the swamp lake, where the light was greener even than in the reeds, and there he had time enough to see that she was beautiful. He dreamed that he sat on one of the great pine roots in the midst of the lake while the tree rocked up and down, now under, now over the surface of the water. Then he saw her on one of the smallest islands. She stood under the red mountain ash and laughed at him. In his very last dream it had gone so far that she had kissed him. But then it was morning, and he heard Berg rising, but he kept his eyes stubbornly closed that he might continue to dream. When he did awake he was dazed and giddy from what he had seen during the night. He thought much more about the girl than he had done the day before. Toward evening it occurred to him to ask Berg if he knew her name.

Berg looked at him sharply. "It is better for you to know it at once," he said. "It was Unn. We are related to each other."

And then Tord knew that it was this pale maiden who was the cause of Berg's wild hunted life in forest and mountain. He tried to search his memory for what he had heard about her.

Unn was the daughter of a free peasant. Her mother was dead, and she ruled in her father's household. This was to her taste, for she was independent by nature, and had no inclination to give herself to any husband. Unn and Berg were cousins, and the rumor had long gone about that Berg liked better to sit with Unn and her maids than to work at home in his own house. One Christmas, when the great banquet was to be given in Berg's hall, his wife had invited a monk from Draksmark, who, she hoped, would show Berg how wrong it was that he should neglect her for another. Berg and others besides him hated this monk because of his appearance. He was very stout and absolutely white. The ring of hair around his bald head, the brows above his moist eyes, the color of his skin, of his hands, and of his garments, were all white. Many found him very repulsive to look at.

But the monk was fearless, and as he believed that his words would have greater weight if many heard them, he rose at the table before all the guests, and said: "Men call the cuckoo the vilest of birds because he brings up his young in the nest of others. But here sits a man who takes no care for his house and his children, and who seeks his pleasure with a strange woman. Him I will call the vilest of men." Unn rose in her place. "Berg, this is said to you and to me," she cried. "Never have I been so shamed, but my father is not here to protect me." She turned to go, but Berg hurried after her. "Stay where you are," she said. "I do not wish to see you again." He stopped her in the corridor, and asked her what he should do that she might stay with him. Her eyes glowed as she answered that he himself should know best what he must do. Then Berg went into the hall again and slew the monk.

Berg and Tord thought on awhile with the same thoughts, then Berg said: "You should have seen her when the white monk fell. My wife drew the children about her and cursed Unn. She turned the faces of the children toward her, that they might always remember the woman for whose sake their father had become a murderer But Unn stood there so quiet and so beautiful that the men who saw her trembled. She thanked me for the deed, and prayed me to flee to the woods at once. She told me never to become a robber, and to use my knife only in some cause equally just."

"Your deed had ennobled her," said Tord.

And again Berg found himself astonished at the same thing that had before now surprised him in the boy. Tord was a heathen, or worse than a heathen; he never condemned that which was wrong. He seemed to know no sense of responsibility. What had to come, came. He knew of God, of Christ, and the Saints, but he knew them only by name, as one knows the names of the gods of other nations. The ghosts of the Scheeren Islands were his gods. His mother, learned in magic, had taught him to believe in

the spirits of the dead. And then it was that Berg undertook a task
which was as foolish as if he had woven a rope for his own neck.
He opened the eyes of this ignorant boy to the power of God, the
Lord of all justice, the avenger of wrong who condemned sinners
to the pangs of hell everlasting. And he taught him to love Christ
and His Mother, and all the saintly men and women who sit before the throne of God praying that His anger may be turned
away from sinners. He taught him all that mankind has learned
to do to soften the wrath of God. He told him of the long trains
of pilgrims journeying to the holy places; he told him of those who
scourged themselves in their remorse; and he told him of the pious
monks who flee the joys of this world.

The longer he spoke the paler grew the boy and the keener his
attention as his eyes widened at the visions. Berg would have
stopped, but the torrent of his own thoughts carried him away.
Night sank down upon them, the black forest night, where the
scream of the owl shrills ghostly through the stillness. God came
so near to them that the brightness of His throne dimmed the
stars, and the angels of vengeance descended upon the mountain
heights. And below them the flames of the underworld fluttered
up to the outer curve of the earth and licked greedily at this last
refuge of a race crushed by sin and woe.

Autumn came, and with it came storm. Tord went out alone
into the woods to tend the traps and snares, while Berg remained
at home to mend his clothes. The boy's path led him up a wooded
height along which the falling leaves danced in circles in the gust.
Again and again the feeling came to him that some one was walking behind him. He turned several times, then went on again
when he had seen that it was only the wind and the leaves. He
threatened the rustling circles with his fist, and kept on his way.
But he had not silenced the sounds of his vision. At first it was the
little dancing feet of elfin children; then it was the hissing of a
great snake moving up behind him. Beside the snake there came a
wolf, a tall, grey creature, waiting for the moment when the adder
should strike at his feet to spring upon his back. Tord hastened
his steps, but the visions hastened with him. When they seemed

but two steps behind him, ready for the spring, he turned. There was nothing there, as he had known all the time. He sat down upon a stone to rest. The dried leaves played about his feet. The leaves of all the forest trees were there: the little yellow birch leaves, the red-tinged mountain ash leaves, the dried, black-brown foliage of the elm, the bright red aspen leaves, and the yellow-green fringes of the willows. Faded and crumpled, broken and scarred, they were but little like the soft, tender shoots of green that had unrolled from the buds a few months ago.

"Ye are sinners," said the boy. "All of us are sinners. Nothing is pure in the eyes of God. Ye have already been shrivelled up in the flame of His wrath."

Then he went on again, while the forest beneath him waved like a sea in storm, although it was still and calm on the path around him. But he heard something he had never heard before. The wood was full of voices. Now it was like a whispering, now a gentle plaint, now a loud threat, or a roaring curse. It laughed, and it moaned. It was as the voice of hundreds. This unknown something that threatened and excited, that whistled and hissed, a something that seemed to be, and yet was not, almost drove him mad. He shivered in deadly terror, as he had shivered before, the day that he lay on the floor of his cave, and heard his pursuers rage over him through the forest. He seemed to hear again the crashing of the branches, the heavy footsteps of the men, the clanking of their arms, and their wild, bloodthirsty shouts.

It was not alone the storm that roared about him. There was something else in it, something yet more terrible; there were voices he could not understand, sounds as of a strange speech. He had heard many a mightier storm than this roar through the rigging. But he had never heard the wind playing on a harp of so many strings. Every tree seemed to have its own voice, every ravine had another song, the loud echo from the rocky wall shouted back in its own voice. He knew all these tones, but there were other stranger noises with them. And it was these that awoke a storm of voices within his own brain.

He had always been afraid when alone in the darkness of the

wood. He loved the open sea and the naked cliffs. Ghosts and spirits lurked here in the shadows of the trees.

Then suddenly he knew who was speaking to him in the storm. It was God, the Great Avenger, the Lord of all Justice. God pursued him because of his comrade. God demanded that he should give up the murderer of the monk to vengeance.

Tord began to speak aloud amid the storm. He told God what he wanted to do, but that he could not do it. He had wanted to speak to the Giant and to beg him make his peace with God. But he could not find the words; embarrassment tied his tongue. "When I learned that the world is ruled by a God of Justice," he cried, "I knew that he was a lost man. I have wept through the night for my friend. I know that God will find him no matter where he may hide. But I could not speak to him; I could not find the words because of my love for him. Do not ask that I shall speak to him. Do not ask that the ocean shall rise to the height of the mountains."

He was silent again, and the deep voice of the storm, which he knew for God's voice, was silent also. There was a sudden pause in the wind, a burst of sunshine, a sound as of oars, and the gentle rustling of stiff reeds. These soft tones brought up the memory of Unn.

Then the storm began again, and he heard steps behind him, and a breathless panting. He did not dare to turn this time, for he knew that it was the white monk. He came from the banquet in Berg's great hall, covered with blood, and with an open axe cut in his forehead. And he whispered: "Betray him. Give him up, that you may save his soul."

Tord began to run. All this terror grew and grew in him, and he tried to flee from it. But as he ran he heard behind him the deep, mighty voice, which he knew was the voice of God. It was God Himself pursuing him, demanding that he should give up the murderer. Berg's crime seemed more horrible to him than ever it had seemed before. A weaponless man had been murdered, a servant of God cut down by the steel. And the murderer still dared to live. He dared to enjoy the light of the sun and the fruits of the earth. Tord halted, clinched his fists, and shrieked a threat. Then, like a madman, he ran from the forest, the realm of terror, down into the valley.

When Tord entered the cave the outlaw sat upon the bench of stone, sewing. The fire gave but a pale light, and the work did not seem to progress satisfactorily. The boy's heart swelled in pity. This superb Giant seemed all at once so poor and so unhappy.

"What is the matter?" asked Berg. "Are you ill? Have you been afraid?"

Then for the first time Tord spoke of his fear. "It was so strange in the forest. I heard the voices of spirits and I saw ghosts. I saw white monks."

"Boy!"

"They sang to me all the way up the slope to the hilltop. I ran from them, but they ran after me, singing. Can I not lay the spirits? What have I to do with them? There are others to whom their appearance is more necessary."

"Are you crazy to-night, Tord?"

Tord spoke without knowing what words he was using. His shyness had left him all at once, speech seemed to flow from his lips. "They were white monks, as pale as corpses. And their clothes are spotted with blood. They draw their hoods down over their foreheads, but I can see the wound shining there. The great, yawning, red wound from the axe."

"Tord," said the Giant, pale and deeply grave, "the Saints alone know why you see wounds of axe thrusts. I slew the monk with a knife."

Tord stood before Berg trembling and wringing his hands. "They demand you of me. They would compel me to betray you."

"Who? The monks?"

"Yes, yes, the monks. They show me visions. They show me Unn. They show me the open, sunny ocean. They show me the camps of the fishermen, where there is dancing and merriment. I close my eyes, and yet I can see it all. 'Leave me,' I say to them. 'My friend has committed a murder, but he is not bad. Leave me alone, and I will talk to him, that he may repent and atone. He will see the wrong he has done, and he will make a pilgrimage to the Holy Grave.' "

"And what do the monks answer?" asked Berg. "They do not want to pardon me. They want to torture me and to burn me at the stake."

" 'Shall I betray my best friend?' I ask them. He is all that I have in the world. He saved me from the bear when its claws were already at my throat. We have suffered hunger and cold together. He covered me with his own garments while I was ill. I have brought him wood and water, I have watched over his sleep, and led his enemies off the trail. Why should they think me a man who betrays his friend? My friend will go to the priest himself, and will confess to him, and then together we will seek absolution?"

Berg listened gravely, his keen eyes searching in Tord's face. "Go to the priest yourself, and tell him the truth. You must go back again among mankind."

"What does it help if I go alone? The spirits of the dead follow me because of your sin. Do you not see how I tremble before you? You have lifted your hand against God himself. What crime is like unto yours? Why did you tell me about the just God? It is you yourself who compel me to betray you. Spare me this sin. Go to the priest yourself." He sank down on his knees before Berg.

The murderer laid his hand on his head and looked at him. He measured his sin by the terror of his comrade, and it grew and grew to a monstrous size. He saw himself in conflict with the Will that rules the world. Remorse entered his heart.

"Woe unto me that I did what I did," he said. "And is not this miserable life, this life we lead here in terror, and in deprivation, is it not atonement enough? Have I not lost home and fortune? Have I not lost friends, and all the joys that make the life of a man? What more?"

As he heard him speak thus, Tord sprang up in wild terror. "You can repent!" he cried. "My words move your heart? Oh, come with me, come at once. Come, let us go while yet there is time."

Berg the Giant sprang up also. "You—did it—?"

"Yes, yes, yes. I have betrayed you. But come quickly. Come now, now that you can repent. We must escape. We will escape."

The murderer stooped to the ground where the battle-ax of his fathers lay at his feet. "Son of a thief," he hissed. "I trusted you— I loved you."

But when Tord saw him stoop for the axe, he knew that it was his own life that was in peril now. He tore his own axe from his girdle, and thrust at Berg before the latter could rise. The Giant fell headlong to the floor, the blood spurting out over the cave. Between the tangled masses of hair Tord saw the great, yawning, red wound of an axe thrust.

Then the peasants stormed into the cave. They praised his deed and told him that he should receive full pardon.

Tord looked down at his hands, as if he saw there the fetters that had drawn him on to kill the man he loved. Like the chains of the Fenrir wolf, they were woven out of empty air. They were woven out of the green light amid the reeds, out of the play of shadows in the woods, out of the song of the storm, out of the rustling of the leaves, out of the magic vision of dreams. And he said aloud: "God is great."

He crouched beside the body, spoke amid his tears to the dead, and begged him to awake. The villagers made a litter of their spears, on which to carry the body of the free peasant to his home. The dead man aroused awe in their souls, they softened their voices in his presence. When they raised him on to the bier, Tord stood up, shook the hair from his eyes, and spoke in a voice that trembled:

"Tell Unn, for whose sake Berg the Giant became a murderer, that Tord the fisherman, whose father plunders wrecks, and whose mother is a witch—tell her that Tord slew Berg because Berg had taught him that justice is the corner-stone of the world."

[*Translated by Pauline Bancroft Flach*]

Maurice Maeterlinck

MAURICE MAETERLINCK *was born in Ghent, Belgium, in 1862. He gave up an early career in law to follow his literary inclinations, shaped by his acquaintance with the Symbolist poets in Paris. Though his chief contributions to literature are not in fiction, he created several distinctive stories, among which is "The Massacre of the Innocents," his first published work (1886). The story lacks conventional plot, but like his masterpieces that were to come, it finds strength in its simplicity of expression, its bare and poignant imagery, and its Breughel-like attention to detail and background. Unlike most of his other work, it makes no attempt to explore the shadowy regions beyond the visible world. Maeterlinck was awarded the Nobel Prize in 1911 for his artistic achievements, notably his outstanding accomplishments in the theater,* The Blue Bird *and* Pelleas and Melisande *and his delicately-beautiful essays in* The Life of the Bees. *He made an unsuccessful lecture tour of the United States in 1920 and returned as a refugee from the war in 1940. He died at his home in Nice in 1949.*

On Friday the 26th of December about supper time, a little shepherd came into Nazareth crying terribly.

Some peasants who were drinking ale at the Blue Lion threw open the shutters to look into the village orchard, and saw the lad running across the snow. They recognized him as Korneliz' son, and shouted at him from the window: "What's the matter? Go to bed, you!"

But the boy answered in a voice of terror, telling them that the

Spaniards had come, having already set fire to the farm, hanged his mother from a chestnut bough, and bound his nine little sisters to the trunk of a large tree. The peasants quickly came forth from the inn, surrounded the boy and plied him with questions. He went on to tell them that the soldiers were clad in steel armor and mounted on horseback, that they had seized the cattle of his uncle, Petrus Krayer, and would soon enter the wood with the sheep and cattle.

They all ran to the Golden Sun, where Korneliz and his brother-in-law were drinking ale, while the innkeeper hastened out into the village to spread the news of the approach of the Spaniards.

There was great excitement in Nazareth. Women threw open windows and peasants ran forth from their houses carrying lights which they extinguished as soon as they came to the orchard, where it was bright as midday, because of the snow and the full moon. They gathered round Korneliz and Krayer in the public square before the inn. Many had brought pitchforks and rakes. They took counsel, speaking in tones of terror, out under the trees.

As they were uncertain what to do, one of them ran to fetch the curé, who owned the farm that was worked by Korneliz. He came forth from his house with the keys of the church, in company with the sacristan, while all the others followed him to the churchyard, where he proclaimed from the top of the tower that he could see nothing, either across the fields or in the wood, but that there were red clouds in the direction of his farm. Over all the rest of the horizon the sky was blue and filled with stars.

After deliberating a long while in the churchyard, they decided to hide in the wood which the Spaniards were to come through, attack them if they were not too numerous, and recover Petrus Krayer's cattle and any booty they might have taken at the farm.

The men armed themselves with forks and spades while the women remained with the curé by the church. Looking for a favorable place for an ambuscade, the men reached a hilly spot near a mill at the edge of the wood, where they could see the fire glowing against the stars of night. They took up their position under some enormous oaks by the side of an ice-covered pond.

A shepherd, who was called the Red Dwarf, mounted to the top of the hill in order to warn the miller, who had already stopped his mill when he saw flames on the horizon. But he allowed the peasant to enter, and the two went to a window to look out over the countryside.

The moon shone down brightly upon the conflagration, and the men could see a long procession of people wending their way across the snow. After they had done watching, the Dwarf went down again to the others waiting in the wood. They could soon distinguish in the distance four riders behind a herd of cattle browsing over the fields. As they stood, clad in their blue breeches and red mantles, looking about by the pond's edge under trees made luminous by the heavy snowfall, the sacristan showed them a box-hedge, and behind this they crouched.

The Spaniards, driving before them flocks and cattle, made their way over the ice, and when the sheep came to the hedge and began nibbling at the greenery, Korneliz broke through, the others following him into the moonlight, armed with their forks. There was then a great massacre in the presence of the huddled sheep and cows, that looked on frightened at the terrible slaughter under the light of the moon.

When they had killed the men and their horses, Korneliz went out into the fields toward the blazing farm, while the others stripped the dead. Then they all returned to the village with the flocks and cattle. The women, who were looking out toward the dense wood from behind the churchyard walls, saw them coming out from among the trees and in company with the curé ran to meet them. They all returned dancing amid laughing children and barking dogs. As they made merry under the pear-trees, where the Dwarf had hung lanterns as for a kermesse, they asked the curé what ought to be done next. They decided to send a cart for the body of the woman who had been hanged and her nine little girls, and bring them all back to the village. The sisters of the dead woman and various other relatives got into the cart, and the curé as well, for he was old and very fat and could walk only with the greatest difficulty. They drove off into the wood, and in silence reached the wide open fields, where they saw the dead soldiers, stripped naked, and the horses lying on their backs on the shining ice among the trees. They went on toward the farm, which was still burning in the midst of the open fields.

When they reached the orchard of the burning house, they stopped short before the garden gate and looked upon the terrible tragedy. Korneliz' wife hung, naked, from the branches of a huge chestnut. He himself climbed up a ladder into the branches of the tree, below which his nine little girls awaited their mother on the lawn. Korneliz made his way through the arching boughs overhead when all at once, outlined against the bright snow, he caught sight of the crowd beneath, looking up at him. Weeping, he signed to them to come to his help, and they came into the garden, and the sacristan, the Red Dwarf, the innkeepers of the Blue Lion and the Golden Sun, the curé carrying a lantern, and several other peasants, climbed into the snow-covered chestnut to cut down the body of the hanged woman. The women took the body into their arms at the foot of the tree, as those other women once received Our Lord Jesus Christ.

She was buried on the following day, and for the next week nothing unusual occurred in Nazareth, but the next Sunday famished wolves ran through the village after High Mass, and the snow fell until noon. Then the sun came out and shone bright in the sky, and the peasants went home to dinner as usual, and dressed for Benediction.

At this time there was no one out on the square, for it was bitter cold. Only dogs and chickens wandered here and there among the trees, and sheep nibbled at the triangular spot of grass, and the curé's maid swept the snow in the garden.

Then a troop of armed men crossed the stone bridge at the far end of the village, and pulled up at the orchard. A few peasants came out of their houses, but hurried back terror-stricken when they saw that the horsemen were Spaniards, and went to their windows to watch what was going to happen. There were thirty horsemen, in armor. They gathered round an old man with a white beard. Each horseman carried with him a foot-soldier dressed in yellow or red. These dismounted and ran about over the snow to warm themselves, while a number of armored soldiers also dismounted.

They made their way toward the Golden Sun and knocked at the door. It was opened with some hesitancy, and the Spaniards entered, warmed themselves before the fire, and demanded ale. They then left the inn, taking with them pots, pitchers, and bread for their companions, and the old man with the white beard who stood waiting among his soldiers. As the street was still deserted, the commanding officer sent off some horsemen behind the houses to guard the village on the side facing the open country, and ordered the footmen to bring to him all children two years old or under, as he intended to massacre them, in accordance with what is written in the Gospel of St. Matthew.

The men went first to the small inn of the Green Cabbage and the barber's hut, which stood close to each other in the central part of the street. One of them opened the pigsty and a whole litter of pigs escaped and roamed about through the village. The innkeeper and the barber came out of their houses and humbly inquired of the soldiers what was wanted, but the Spaniards understood no Flemish, and entered the houses in search of the children. The innkeeper had one who, dressed in its little shirt, was sitting on the dinner table, crying. One of the soldiers took it in his arms and carried it off out under the apple trees, while its parents followed weeping. The foot-soldiers next threw open the stables of the barrel-maker, the blacksmith, and the cobbler, and cows, calves, asses, pigs, goats and sheep wandered here and there over the square. When they broke the windows of the carpenter's house, a number of the wealthiest and oldest peasants of the parish gathered in the street and advanced toward the Spaniards. They respectfully took off their caps and hats to the velvet-clad chief, asking him what he intended to do, but he too did not understand their language, and one of them ran off to get the curé. He was about to go to Benediction, and was putting on his

golden chasuble in the sacristy. The peasants cried, "The Spaniards are in the orchard!" Terror-stricken, he ran to the church
door, followed by the choir-boys carrying their censers and candles. From the door he could see the cattle and other animals set
loose from their stables wandering over the grass and snow, the
Spanish horsemen, the foot-soldiers before the doors of the
houses, horses tied to trees all along the street, and men and
women supplicating the soldier who carried the child still clad in
its shirt. He hastened into the churchyard, the peasants turning
anxiously toward him, their priest, who arrived like a god covered
with gold, out there among the pear-trees. They pressed close
about him as he stood facing the white-bearded man. He spoke
both in Flemish and Latin, but the officer slowly shrugged his
shoulders to show that he failed to understand.

The parishioners inquired of him in undertones, "What does he
say? What is he going to do?" Others, seeing the curé in the orchard, emerged cautiously from their huts, and women hastily
came near and whispered in small groups among themselves, while
the soldiers who had been besieging the inn, came out again when
they saw the crowd assembling in the square.

Then he who held the innkeeper's child by one leg, cut off its
head with a stroke of the sword. The peasants saw the head fall,
and the body bleeding on the ground. The mother gathered it to
her arms, forgetting the head, and ran toward her house. On the
way she stumbled against a tree, fell flat on the snow and lay in a
faint, while the father struggled with two soldiers.

Some of the younger peasants threw stones and wood at the
Spaniards, but the horsemen rallied and lowered their lances, the
women scattered in all directions, while the curé with his other
parishioners, shrieked with horror to the accompaniment of the
noises made by the sheep, geese, and dogs.

As the soldiers went off once more down the street, they were
quiet again, waiting to see what would happen. A group went
into the shop of the sacristan's sisters, but came out again without
touching the seven women, who were on their knees praying
within. Then they entered the inn of the Hunchback of St. Nich-

olas. There too the door was instantly opened in the hope of placating them, but when they appeared again in the midst of a great tumult, they carried three children in their arms, and were surrounded by the Hunchback, his wife and daughters, who were begging for mercy with clasped hands. When the soldiers came to their leader they laid the children down at the foot of an elm, all dressed in their Sunday clothes. One of them, who wore a yellow dress, got up and ran with unsteady feet toward the sheep. A soldier ran after it with his naked sword. The child died with its face on the earth. The others were killed near the tree. The peasants and the innkeeper's daughters took flight, screaming, and went back to their houses. Alone in the orchard, the curé fell to his knees and begged the Spaniards, in a piteous voice, with arms crossed over his breast, going from one to the other on his knees, while the father and mother of the murdered children, seated on the snow, wept bitterly as they bent over the lacerated bodies.

As the foot-soldiers went along the street they noticed a large blue farmhouse. They tried to break in the door, but this was of oak and studded with huge nails. They therefore took tubs which were frozen in a pond near the entrance, and used them to enter the house from the second story windows.

There had been a kermesse in this house: relatives had come to feast on waffles, hams, and custards. At the sound of the smashing of windows they crouched together behind the table, still laden with jugs and dishes. The soldiers went to the kitchen and after a savage fight in which many were wounded, they seized all the small boys and girls, and a little servant who had bitten the thumb of one soldier, left the house and closed the door behind them to prevent their being followed.

Those who had no children cautiously came forth from their houses and followed the soldiers at a distance. They could see them throw down their victims on the ground before the old man, and cold-bloodedly massacre them with lances or swords. Meanwhile men and women crowded the windows of the blue farmhouse and the barn, cursing and raising their arms to heaven as they contemplated the pink, red, and white clothes of their motionless children on the ground among the trees. Then the soldiers hanged the servant from the Half Moon Inn on the other side of the street. There was a long silence in the village.

It had now become a general massacre. Mothers escaped from their houses, trying to flee through vegetable and flower gardens out into the open country, but mounted soldiers pursued them and drove them back into the street. Peasants, with caps held tight between their hands, fell to their knees before the soldiers who dragged off their little ones, and dogs barked joyously amid the disorder. The curé, his hands raised heavenward, rushed back and forth from house to house and out among the trees, praying in desperation like a martyr. The soldiers, trembling from the cold, whistled in their fingers as they moved about, or stood idly with their hands in their pockets, their swords under their arms, in front of houses that were being entered. Small groups in all directions, seeing the fear of the peasants, were entering the farmhouses, and in every street similar scenes were enacted. The market-gardener's wife, who lived in an old hut with pink tiles near the church, pursued with a chair two soldiers who were carrying off her children in a wheelbarrow. She was terribly sick when she saw her children die, and made to sit on a chair against a tree.

Other soldiers climbed into the lime trees in front of a farmhouse painted the color of lilacs, and made their way in by taking off the tiles. When they reappeared on the roof, the parents with extended arms followed them until the soldiers forced them back, finding it necessary finally to strike them over the head with their swords before they could shake themselves free and return again to the street below.

One family, who had concealed themselves in the cellar of a large house, stood at the gratings and wildly lamented, while the father desperately brandished his pitchfork through the grating. Outside, an old bald-headed fellow sat on a manure-heap, sobbing to himself. In the square a woman dressed in yellow had fainted away, her weeping husband holding her up by the arms against a pear-tree. Another woman, in red, clutched her little girl, whose hands had been cut off, and lifted the child's arms to see whether she could move. Still another woman was escaping toward the open country, the soldiers running after her among the haystacks, which stood out in sharp relief against the snow-covered fields.

Before the Four Sons of Aymon confusion reigned. The peasants had made a barricade while the soldiers encircled the inn, unable to effect an entrance. They were trying to climb up to the sign-board by means of the vines, when they caught sight of a ladder behind the garden gate. Setting this against the wall, they scaled it, one after another. But the landlord and his family threw down at them tables and chairs, crockery and cradles from the window, upsetting ladder and soldiers together.

In a wooden cottage at the outskirts of the village another group of soldiers came upon an old woman washing her children in a tub before the open fire. She was old and deaf, and did not hear them when they entered. Two soldiers carried off the tub with the children in it, while the bewildered old woman set off in pursuit, carrying the clothes which she had been about to put on the infants. Out in the village she saw traces of blood, swords in the orchard, smashed cradles in the open streets, women praying and wringing their hands over their dead children, and began to scream and strike the soldiers who had to set down the tub in order to defend themselves. The curé hurried over to her, his hands still folded over his chasuble, and entreated the Spaniards for mercy, in the presence of the naked children screaming in the tub. Other soldiers came up, bound the distracted mother to a tree, and went off with the children.

The butcher, having hidden his baby girl, leaned against the front of his shop with apparent unconcern. A foot-soldier and one of the armed horsemen entered his home and found the child in a copper pot. The butcher desperately seized a knife and rushed off in pursuit, but the soldiers disarmed him and suspended him by the hands from some hooks in the wall, where he kicked and wriggled among his dead animals until evening.

Round the churchyard a multitude gathered in front of a long low green farmhouse. The proprietor wept bitterly as he stood in his doorway. He was a fat, jolly-looking man, and happened to arouse the compassion of a few soldiers who sat near the wall in the sunlight, patting a dog. The soldier who was taking off his child made gestures as if to convey the meaning, "What can I do? I'm not to blame!"

One peasant who was being pursued leaped into a boat near the stone bridge, and, with his wife and children, rowed quickly across that part of the pond that was not frozen. The Spaniards, who dared not follow, walked angrily among the reeds by the shore. They climbed into the willows along the bankside, trying to reach the boat with their lances. Unable to do so, they continued to threaten the fugitives, who drifted out over the dark water.

The orchard was still thronged with people: it was there, in the presence of the white-bearded commanding officer, that most of the children were being murdered. The children who were over two and could just walk, stood together eating bread and jam, staring in wide-eyed wonder at the massacre of their helpless play-mates, or gathered round the village fool, who was playing his flute.

All at once there was a concerted movement in the village, and the peasants made off in the direction of the castle that stood on rising ground at the far end of the street. They had caught sight of their lord on the battlements, watching the massacre. Men and women, young and old, extended their hands toward him in supplication as he stood there in his velvet cloak and golden cap like a king in Heaven. But he only raised his hands and shrugged his shoulders to show that he was powerless, while the people supplicated him in growing despair, kneeling with heads bared in the snow, and crying piteously. He turned slowly back into his tower. Their last hope had vanished.

When all the children had been killed, the weary soldiers wiped their swords on the grass and ate their supper among the pear-trees, then mounting in pairs, they rode out of Nazareth across the bridge over which they had come.

The setting sun turned the wood into a flaming mass, dyeing the village a blood red. Utterly exhausted, the curé threw himself down in the snow before the church, his servant standing at his side. They both looked out into the street and the orchard, which were filled with peasants dressed in their Sunday clothes. Before the entrances of many houses were parents holding the bodies of children on their knees, still full of blank amazement, lamenting over their grievous tragedy. Others wept over their little ones where they had perished, by the side of a cask, under a wheelbarrow, or by the pond. Others again carried off their dead in silence. Some set to washing benches, chairs, tables, bloody underclothes, or picking up the cradles that had been hurled into the street. Many mothers sat bewailing their children under the trees, having recognized them by their woolen dresses. Those who had had no children wandered through the square, stopping by grief-stricken mothers, who sobbed and moaned. The men, who had stopped crying, doggedly pursued their strayed beasts to the accompaniment of the barking of dogs; others silently set to work mending their broken windows and damaged roofs.

As the moon quietly rose through the tranquil sky, a sleepy silence fell upon the village, where at last the shadow of no living thing stirred.

[*Translated by Barrett H. Clark*]

Gerhart Hauptmann

FLAGMAN THIEL

GERHART HAUPTMANN, *who won the Nobel Prize in 1912, was born in 1862 in Silesia, Germany, the son of an inn keeper. Although his family wanted him to take up farming, Hauptmann was determined to become an artist, and tried his hand at sculpture, music, poetry, and fiction before he discovered his true calling, the drama. His first play,* Before Dawn *(1889) produced a literary controversy and catapulted him to fame. Under the influence of naturalism, he wrote a series of dramas about the working and the poor middle classes, such as his masterpiece* The Weavers, The Red Cock, *and* The Rats. *His transition to poetic mysticism is first noticeable in* Hannele, *the dream vision of an abused dying girl. Three years later he achieved his greatest popular success with his most obviously neo-Romantic play,* The Sunken Bell *(1886). Of particular interest to Americans is the novel* Atlantis *(1912), based upon his trip to the United States and describing in amazing detail the disaster of the* Titanic *two years before it actually happened. He was the only important man of letters to remain in Germany after Hitler had proclaimed the lack of pity as the official policy of that country. Before his death in 1946, he accepted a Soviet invitation to visit Berlin.* "Flagman Thiel" *reveals his interest in the oppressed character whose greatest difficulty is his own weakness; as a ballet, it won great popularity in Berlin during the thirties.*

I

Every Sunday Thiel, the flagman, was to be seen sitting in a pew in the church at Neu Zittau. If he was absent, you might be sure he was on Sunday duty or else—as happened twice in the course of ten years—at home ill in bed. Once a great lump of coal from the tender of a passing locomotive had struck his leg and sent him rolling into the ditch at the bottom of the embankment. The second time the trouble was a wine bottle that had come flying from an express and had hit him in the middle of his chest. Nothing but these two mishaps had ever succeeded in keeping Thiel from church the instant he was off duty.

The first five years he had had to come alone to Neu Zittau from Schön-Schornstein, a small collection of homes on the Spree. Then, one fine day, he appeared in the company of a delicate, sickly looking woman. The people thought she ill suited his herculean build. And on a later Sunday afternoon, at the altar of the church, he solemnly gave her his hand and pledged his troth.

So, for two years, the delicate young creature sat beside him in the pew. For two years her fine, hollow-cheeked face bent over the ancient hymnal beside his weather-tanned face.

And suddenly the flagman was to be seen sitting alone, as of old.

On one of the preceding weekdays the bell had tolled for the dead. That was all.

Scarcely any change, so the people declared, was to be observed in the flagman. The brass buttons of his clean Sunday uniform were as brightly polished as before, his red hair as sleekly pomaded and as neatly parted, military fashion. Only he held his broad, hairy neck a little bent, and sang more eagerly, and listened to the sermon more devoutly. The general opinion was that his wife's death had not hit him very hard. A view that was strengthened when in the course of the year he married again. The second wife was a strong, stout milkmaid from Altegrund.

Even the pastor felt free to express his doubts when Thiel came to announce his engagement.

"So soon again? You really want to marry so soon again?"

"I can't keep my house running, sir, with the wife who's gone."

"To be sure. But I mean—aren't you in a bit of a hurry?"

"It's on account of the boy."

Thiel's wife had died in childbirth. The boy had lived and been named Tobias.

"Yes, yes, to be sure, the boy," said the pastor, with a gesture clearly revealing that he had not thought of the infant until that moment. "That throws a different light on the matter. What have you been doing with him until now while you are at work?"

Thiel explained that he left Tobias in the care of an old woman. Once she had nearly let him get burned, and another time had let him roll from her lap to the floor. Fortunately the child had not been badly hurt—only a big surface bruise. Such a state of things could not continue, the flagman said, especially as the child, being delicate, required particular attention. For that reason and also because he had sworn to his wife on her deathbed that he would always take exceedingly good care of the child, he had decided to marry again.

The people found absolutely nothing to cavil with in the new couple that now visited the church regularly on Sundays. The milkmaid seemed to have been made for the flagman. She was but a few inches shorter than he and exceeded him in girth, while her features were just as coarsely molded as his, though, in contrast, they lacked soul.

If Thiel had cherished the desire for an inveterate worker and paragon of a housewife in his second wife, then his hopes were surprisingly fulfilled. However, without knowing it, he had purchased three other qualities, too, a hard, domineering disposition, quarrelsomeness, and brutal passion.

Within half a year the whole place knew who was lord and master in the flagman's little house. Thiel became the object of general pity. It was a piece of good luck for the "creature," the exercised husbands said, that she had got such a gentle lamb as Thiel for a husband. With other men she wouldn't come off so easy, she'd receive some hard knocks. An animal like that had to be managed—with blows, if need be—a good sound thrashing to make her behave herself.

But Thiel, despite his sinewy arms, was not the man to thrash his wife. What got the people so annoyed seemed to cause him no perturbation. As a rule, he let his wife's endless sermonizings pass without a word, and when he did occasionally make a response, the slow drag of his speech and the quiet coolness of his tone contrasted oddly with her high-pitched bawling.

The outside world seemed scarcely to touch him. It was as though he carried something within him that heavily overbalanced all of the evil it brought by good.

Nevertheless, for all his phlegm, there were occasions on which he would not allow things to pass—when little Toby was concerned. Then his childlike goodness, his yieldingness took on a dash of determination that even so untamed a temperament as Lena's did not dare to oppose.

The moments, however, in which he revealed this side of his character became rarer and rarer, and finally ceased completely. During the first year of his marriage he had shown a certain suffering resistance to Lena's tyranny. In the second year this also ceased completely. After a quarrel he no longer left for his work with his earlier indifference in case he had not previously placated her. Often he even stooped to beg her to be kind again. His solitary post in the heart of the Brandenburg pine forest was no longer, as it had been, the place where he would rather be than anywhere else on earth. The quiet devout thoughts of his dead wife were crossed by thoughts of the living wife. It was not with repugnance, as in the first months of his marriage, that he trod the homeward way, but often with passionate haste, after having counted the hours and minutes till the time of his release.

He who had been united to his first wife by a more spiritual love fell into his second wife's grip through the power of crude impulses. He became almost wholly dependent upon her.

At times he experienced pangs of conscience at this turn, and resorted to a number of unusual devices to bring about a change. For one thing, he declared his hut and his beat to be holy ground, dedicated exclusively to the shades of the dead. And he actually succeeded by all sorts of pretexts in preventing Lena from accompanying him there. He hoped he should always be able to keep her off. The very number of his hut and the direction in which it lay were still unknown to her.

Thus, by conscientiously dividing the time at his disposal between the living and the dead, Thiel actually succeeded in soothing his conscience.

Often, to be sure, especially in moments of solitary devotion, when he felt the tie between him and his dead wife deeply and warmly, he beheld his present condition in the light of truth, and he experienced disgust.

If he was doing day duty, his spiritual intercourse with her was limited to dear recollections of their life together. But in the dark, when a snowstorm raged among the pines and along the embankment, his hut at midnight, by the light of his lantern, became a chapel.

With a faded photograph of the departed before him on the table, and the hymnal and the Bible turned open, he alternately read and sang the whole night long, interrupted only at intervals by the trains rushing past. He would attain a state of ecstasy in which he had visions of his wife standing there in person.

In its remoteness this post, which Thiel had held for ten years, contributed to the intensification of his mystic inclinations. To the north, east, south and west, it was separated by a walk of at least three quarters of an hour from the nearest habitation. It lay in the very heart of the forest. But there was a grade crossing there, and Thiel's duty was to lower and raise the gates.

In the summer days passed, in the winter weeks without a single person except other railroad workers setting foot on Thiel's beat. Almost the only changes in the solitude came from the weather and the periodic mutations of the seasons. It was not difficult to recall the events—besides the two mishaps to his body—that had broken into the regular course of the hours of service.

Four years previous the imperial special bearing the Kaiser to Breslau had gone dashing by. Once on a winter's night an express had run over a stag. And once on a hot summer's day, as Thiel was making an inspection of his beat, he had found a corked bottle of wine. It was scorching hot to the touch, and Thiel had esteemed its contents because when he uncorked it a geyser spouted out, showing that the stuff was well fermented. Thiel had laid the bottle on the edge of a pond in the woods to cool off. Somehow it had disappeared from the spot, and even after the passage of years Thiel never thought of that bottle without a pang of regret.

A bit of diversion was provided by a spring behind the hut. From time to time men at work on the road bed or on the telegraph lines came for a drink, and stayed, of course, to talk a while. Sometimes the forest ranger would also come when he was thirsty.

Tobias developed slowly. It was not until he was two years old that he learned to walk and talk. For his father he displayed unusual affection, and as he grew more understanding Thiel's old love for his child was re-awakened. Accordingly Lena's love for the child decreased, turning into unmistakable dislike when the next year a baby boy was born to her, too.

After that bad times began for Tobias. In his father's absence he was particularly made to suffer. He had to dedicate his feeble powers unrewarded to the service of the little cry-baby. He became more and more exhausted. His head grew too large round, and his fiery red hair, with the chalky face beneath, on top of his wretched little body, made an unlovely and pitiful impression. When the backward mite was seen dragging himself down to the Spree with his baby brother bursting with health in his arms, curses were muttered behind the windows of the cottages. But no one ever ventured to utter the curses in the open.

Thiel, who was most of all concerned, seemed to have no eyes for what was going on, and refused to understand the hints of well-meaning neighbors.

II

Once Thiel returned from night duty at seven o'clock of a June morning. Directly Lena had greeted him, she burst into her usual complaining.

A few weeks before notice had been given that they could no

longer cultivate the piece of land which they rented for planting potatoes for their own use, and no other land had been found to replace it. Though everything pertaining to the land was part of Lena's duty, Thiel none the less had to listen to a hundred iterations that he would be to blame if they had to buy ten sacks of potatoes for dear money. Thiel merely muttered a word or two. Paying slight attention to Lena's tirade, he went straight over to Tobias's bed, which he shared with the boy on nights when he was off duty.

He sat down and watched the sleeping child with an anxious expression on his good face. For a while he contented himself with chasing away the persistent flies, then he woke him up. A touching joy lighted up the boy's blue, deep-set eyes. He snatched for his father's hand, and a pitiful smile drew the corners of his mouth. Thiel helped him put on his few bits of clothing. Suddenly a shadow chased across his face. He noticed that his son's right cheek was slightly swollen and bore finger marks designed white on red.

At breakfast Lena brought up the same subject again, pursuing it with even more vigor. Thiel cut her off by telling her that the railroad inspector had given him for nothing the use of a stretch of land alongside the tracks not far from his hut, probably because it was too distant for the inspector to use for himself.

Lena was incredulous, then gradually her doubts melted away and she became noticeably good-humored. How big was the lot? How good was the soil? She plied him with questions. And when she learned that there were actually two dwarf fruit trees on the land, she fairly lost her head. At length the questions were all asked, and as the shopkeeper's bell, which could be heard in every house in the place, kept ringing incessantly, Lena ran forth to ferret out the latest news.

While she remained in the dark shop crowded with wares, Thiel occupied himself at home with Tobias, who sat on his knee playing with pine cones that his father had brought from the woods.

"What do you want to be when you grow up?" asked Thiel. The stereotyped question was invariably answered by the equally stereotyped reply, "Railroad inspector." It was not asked in fun. The flagman's dreams actually soared so high. It was in all seriousness that he cherished the hope that with God's help Tobias would become something extraordinary. The instant "railroad inspector" left the child's bloodless lips, Thiel's face brightened, fairly radiated bliss.

"Go play now, Tobias," he said soon afterward, lighting his pipe with a shaving kindled at the hearth fire. The boy showing shy pleasure went out.

Thiel undressed and got into bed. For a long while he lay staring up at the low, cracked ceiling. Finally he fell asleep and woke up shortly before twelve o'clock. While Lena in her noisy fashion prepared the midday meal, he dressed and went out on the street to fetch Tobias, whom he found scratching plaster out of a hole in the wall and stuffing it into his mouth. Thiel led him by the hand past the eight houses that constituted the hamlet down to the Spree. The stream lay dark and glassy between sparsely foliaged poplars. Thiel sat down on a block of granite close to the water's edge.

Every fair day the villagers were accustomed to see him on this spot. The children were devoted to him. They called him Father Thiel. He taught them games that he remembered from his own childhood, reserving, however, the best of his memories for Tobias. He whittled him arrows that flew farther than those of the other boys, he carved him willow pipes, and even deigned to sing ditties in his rusty bass, and tap the beat with the horn handle of his knife against the bark of a tree.

The people thought him silly. They blamed him. They could not understand how he could go to so much trouble for the little brats. Though they should have been richly content, seeing that the children were well taken care of when in his charge. Besides, Thiel did more than play with them. He took up serious things, too. He heard the older ones recite their lessons, helped them study their Bible and hymn verses, and spelled out c-a-t and d-o-g with the younger ones.

After the midday meal Thiel rested again a while, drank a cup of coffee, and began to prepare for work. It took him a lot of time, as for everything he did. Each move had been regulated for years. The objects carefully spread out on the walnut dresser went into his various pockets always in the same order—knife, notebook, comb, a horse's tooth, an old watch in a case, and a small book wrapped in red paper. The last was handled with especial care. During the night it lay under Thiel's pillow, and by day was carried in his breast pocket. On a label pasted on the cover was written in Thiel's awkward yet flourished hand, "Savings Account of Tobias Thiel."

The clock on the wall with the long pendulum and sickly yellow face indicated a quarter to five when Thiel left. A small boat, his own property, ferried him across the Spree. Arrived at the further side, he stood still a moment and listened back in the direction he had come from. Then he turned into a broad path through the woods and within a few moments reached the depths of the deep-booming pine forest, its mass of needles like a dark green undulating sea.

The moist layers of needles and moss made a carpet as inaudible to the tread as felt. Thiel made his way without looking up, now past the rusty brown columns of the older trees, now between the thickly enmeshed younger growth, and farther on across broad stretches of nursery, over-shadowed by a few tall slim pines for the protection of the young saplings. A transparent bluish haze rising from the earth laden with mingled fragrances blurred the forms of the trees. A heavy, drab sky hung low over the tops. Flocks of cawing crows seemed to bathe in the gray of the atmosphere. Black puddles filled the depressions in the path and cast a still drearier reflection of a dreary nature.

"Fearful weather," thought Thiel when he roused out of deep reflection and looked up.

Suddenly his thoughts were deflected. A dim feeling came to him that he must have forgotten something. And surely enough, when he searched his pockets, he discovered that he had not brought along the sandwich that he required on account of the long hours on duty. For a while he stood undecided. Then turned and hurried back.

In a short while he reached the Spree, rowed himself across in a few powerful strokes, and without delay, perspiring from every pore, ascended the gradual slope of the village street. The shopkeeper's old, mangy poodle lay in the middle of the road. On the tarred board fence around a cottager's yard perched a hooded crow. It spread its feathers, shook itself, nodded, uttered an ear-splitting caw, caw, and with a slapping sound of its wings rose in the air and let the wind drive it in the direction of the forest.

Nothing was to be seen of the villagers—about twenty fishermen and lumbermen with their families.

The stillness was broken—by a high-pitched voice. The flagman involuntarily stopped. A volley of violent, jangling tones assailed his ears. It seemed to come from the open dormer window of a low house that he knew only too well.

Treading as silently as possible, he glided nearer. Now he quite clearly recognized his wife's voice. Only a few steps more, and he could understand almost everything she said.

"You horrid little beast, you! Is the poor baby to scream its belly inside out from hunger? What? Just you wait—just you wait. I'll teach you to mind. You'll never forget."

For a few moments there was silence. Then a sound could be heard like the beating out of clothes. And the next instant another hailstorm of abuse was let loose.

"You miserable little puppy, you! Do you think I'll let my own child die of hunger because of a mean little thing like you?—Shut your mouth!" A slight whimper had been audible. "If you don't shut your mouth, I'll give you something that'll keep you going a whole week."

The whimpering did not subside.

The flagman felt his heart pounding in irregular beats. He began to tremble slightly. His glance fastened on the ground as though his mind were wandering, and again and again his coarse, hard hand went up to his freckled forehead to brush back a dank strand of hair. For a second he was about to give way. He stood shaken by a convulsion that swelled his muscles and drew his fingers into a clenched ball. The convulsion subsided. He was left in a state of dull exhaustion.

With unsteady steps he entered the narrow, brick-paved vestibule and slowly, wearily mounted the creaking wooden stairs.

"Pugh, pugh, pugh!" You could hear how with every sign of scorn and fury someone spat out three times in succession. "You horrid, mean, sneaking, cowardly, low-down good-for-nothing!" The epithets followed one another in crescendo, the voice that uttered them breaking several times from strain. "You want to hit my boy, do you? You ugly little brat you, don't you dare to hit the poor helpless child on its mouth. What's that? Huh? If I wanted to soil my hands on you, I'd—"

At that moment the door to the living room was opened, and the rest of the sentence remained unspoken on the frightened woman's tongue. She was livid with passion, her lips twitched evilly. Her right hand raised in the air sank and grasped the saucepan with milk in it. She tried to pour some into the baby's bottle, but desisted as the larger part of the milk flowed down the outside of the bottle on to the table. She clutched at various objects without being able to hold them any length of time. Finally she recovered herself sufficiently to address her husband with violence. What did he mean by coming home at this unusual hour? Was he thinking of spying on her? That would be too much. This last was directly followed by the asseveration that she had a clear conscience and need not lower her eyes before any one.

Thiel scarcely heard what she said. He gave a hasty look at Toby, who was crying aloud, and for a few moments he had to restrain forcibly a something dreadful rising within him. Then the old phlegm spread over his taut features, and at the same time a furtive, lustful light came into his eyes. His glance played over his wife's heavy limbs while she, with averted face, bustled about still making an effort to be composed. Her full, half-bared breasts swelled with excitement and threatened to burst her corset. Her drawn-up skirts accentuated the width of her broad hips. A force seemed to emanate from the woman, indomitable, inescapable. Thiel felt himself powerless to cope with it. Tightly, like a cobweb, yet firmly as a mesh of steel, it laid itself around him, chaining him down, robbing him of his strength. In this condition he was incapable of saying a word to her, much less a harsh word.

Thus it was that Tobias, bathed in tears, cowering in a corner, saw his father go over to the oven bench without looking round at him, pick up the forgotten sandwich, hold it out to Lena by way of the only explanation, give a short, distraught nod of his head in good-by, and disappear.

III

Thiel made all possible haste back to his solitary post in the woods. Even so he was a quarter of an hour late. The assistant who relieved him, a consumptive, the victim of the unavoidably rapid changes in temperature to which the work subjected one, was waiting prepared to leave on the sanded little platform of the hut, on which the number, black on white, gleamed from a distance between the tree trunks.

The two men shook hands, exchanged a few brief reports, and parted, the one disappearing within the hut, the other taking the continuation of the road by which Thiel had come. His convulsive cough sounded further and further away among the trees, until finally the one human sound in the solitude fell silent.

Thiel as always, after his fashion, set about preparing the small square room for the night. He worked mechanically, his mind occupied with the impression of the past hour.

First he laid his supper on the narrow, brown-painted table beside one of the windows like slits through which the stretch of track could be conveniently viewed. Next he kindled a fire in the small, rusty stove and placed a pot of cold water on top. After that he straightened out his utensils, a shovel, a spade, a wrench and a few other things, and then cleaned his lantern and filled it with fresh oil.

Scarcely were his arrangements completed when the signal rang shrilly, three times, and three times again, to announce that a train from the direction of Breslau was pulling out of the near station. Thiel showed no hurry, allowing a few minutes to pass before emerging from the hut with flag and cartridge case in his hand. And it was with a lazy, dragging shuffle that he walked along the narrow strip of sand to the crossing, about sixty feet away. Though there was scarcely any traffic along the road at that point, still he conscientiously let down and raised the gates before and after the passage of each train.

This operation now concluded, he leaned idly on one of the black-and-white barred anchor-posts.

The tracks cut in a straight line right and left into the green forest stretching beyond the reach of the eye. On each side the mass of needles stood apart to leave, as it were, an avenue free for the reddish-brown graveled embankment. The black tracks running parallel looked like the strands of a huge iron net drawn together to a point on the horizon in the extreme south and north.

The wind had risen, it drove light waves of mist along the edge of the forest into the distance. A humming came from the telegraph poles alongside the tracks. On the wires that stretched from pole to pole like the sustaining cords spun by a huge spider perched swarms of chirping birds. A woodpecker flew with a laugh over Thiel's head. The man did not so much as look up.

The sun hanging from under the edge of vast masses of clouds and about to sink into the dark-green sea of treetops poured streams of purple over the forest. The pillared arcades of the pine trunks on the yon side of the embankment took fire as from within and glowed like metal. The tracks, too, began to glow, turning into the semblance of fiery snakes. They were the first to pale. The glow, leaving the ground, slowly ascended upward, resigning first the bodies of the trees, then the lower tops to the cold light of dissolution. For a while a reddish sheen lingered on the extreme crowns.

Silently and solemnly was the exalted drama enacted.

The flagman still stood at the gates motionless. At length he made a step forward. A dark point on the horizon where the tracks joined, became more than a point. Increasing from second to second it yet seemed to stand still. Then of a sudden it acquired movement, and drew nearer. A vibrating and humming went through the tracks, a rhythmic clang, a muted thunder. It grew louder and louder until at length it sounded not unlike the hoof beats of a storming cavalry regiment. From a distance the air pulsated intermittently with a panting and a blustering. Then suddenly the serenity of the forest snapped. A mad uproar filled the welkin, the tracks curved, the earth shook—a blast of air, a cloud of dust and steam and smoke—and the snorting monster had gone by.

The noises waned as they had waxed. The exhalations thinned away. Shrunken to a point again the train vanished in the distance, and the old solemn hush again settled upon this corner of the forest.

"Minna," whispered the flagman, as if coming out of a dream.

He returned to the hut, where he brewed himself some weak coffee, then sat down, sipping from time to time and all the while staring at a dirty piece of newspaper that he had picked up on his round.

Gradually a curious unrest came upon him. Attributing it to the heat from the stove, he tore off his coat and waistcoat. That proving to be of no help, he got up, took a spade from a corner, and went out to the lot that the inspector had presented to him.

It was a narrow strip of soil, overgrown with weeds. The blossoms on the two fruit trees were like snowy white foam. Thiel calmed down, a quiet content possessed him.

To work now.

The spade cut into the earth with a crunch. The wet clods flew and crumbled as they fell.

For a long while he dug uninterruptedly. Then he paused and said to himself audibly, shaking his head gravely:

"No, no, it won't do. No, it won't do."

The thought had suddenly struck him that Lena would be

coming there often to look after the lot, and his accustomed life would be seriously disturbed. At one blow pleasure in the possession of the bit of ground turned into distaste. Hastily, as if he had been about to do wrong, he ripped the spade out of the earth and carried it back to the hut.

Again he sank into gloomy reflections. Almost without knowing why, he could not endure the prospect of Lena's presence for whole days at a stretch while he was on duty. Much as he might try he could not reconcile himself to the idea. It seemed to him he had something valuable to defend, against someone who was attempting to violate his holiest sanctuary. Involuntarily his muscles tautened in a slight cramp, and a short, defiant laugh escaped him.

The sound of his own laughter was alarming. He looked about and lost the thread of his thoughts. Finding it again he went back to the same dismal broodings.

Then suddenly a heavy black curtain was torn apart, his eyes so long befogged had now a clear view. He had the sensation of awakening from a deathlike sleep that had lasted two years. With an incredulous shake of the head he contemplated all the awful things he must have been guilty of in that condition. The long-suffering of his child, which the impressions of the earlier afternoon should only have confirmed, now were clearly revealed to his soul. Pity and penitence overcame him, and also great shame, that all this long while he had lived in disgraceful resignation, never taking the dear, helpless child's part, not even finding the strength to admit how much the child suffered.

From the self-tormenting contemplation of his sins of omission a great tiredness came over him. He fell asleep, bent over the table with his forehead resting on his hand.

For a long while he lay like that, and several times uttered the name Minna in a choked voice.

A rushing and roaring filled his ears, as of great masses of water. He tore his eyes open and looked about. Darkness enveloped him. His limbs gave way, the sweat of terror oozed from every pore, his pulse beat irregularly, his face was wet with tears.

He wanted to look toward the door, but in the inky darkness did not know which way to turn. He rose reeling. And still terror possessed him. The woods outside boomed like the ocean, the wind drove rain and sleet against the panes. Thiel groped about helplessly. For a moment he felt himself to be drowning. Then suddenly there was a dazzling bluish flare, as of drops of super-natural light falling down into the earth's atmosphere to be instantly extinguished by it.

The moment sufficed to restore the flagman to reason. He fumbled for his lantern and found it. At the same instant the thunder awoke on the farthest edge of the heavens over Brandenburg. At first a dull, restrained rumble, it rolled nearer in surging metallic waves, until overhead it discharged itself in great peals, menacing roars that shook the earth to its foundations.

The window panes clattered. Thiel lighted the lantern, and his first glance after he regained self-control was at the clock. In a bare five minutes the express was due. Thinking he had failed to hear the signal, he made for the crossing as quickly as the dark and the storm permitted. Just as he was letting down the gates the signal rang—the sound was scattered by the wind in all directions.

The pine-trees bent over, their branches scraped against each other with uncanny creakings and squeakings. For a few moments the moon was visible, a pale yellow chalice amid the torn clouds. By its light could be seen the wind's mauling of the black tree-tops. The foliage of the birches along the embankment waved and fluttered like ghostly horses' tails. Beneath them lay the rails gleaming wet, absorbing the pale moonlight in spots here and there.

Thiel tore the cap from his head. The rain soothed him. It ran down his face mingled with tears.

His brain was in a ferment with confused recollections of his dream. Tobias seemed to be undergoing maltreatment, and such horrible maltreatment that the mere thought of it stopped his heart. Another vision was clearer, of his dead wife. She had come from somewhere along the railroad tracks. She had looked very ill and was wearing rags for clothes. Without looking round she passed the hut, and then—here his memory became vague—she had great difficulty somehow in proceeding, she even collapsed several times.

Thiel pondered. And then he knew that she was in flight. No doubt of it. Else why those anxious backward glances as she dragged herself forward with her legs giving way under her? Oh, those awful looks of hers!

But there was something that she was carrying, wrapped in cloths, something limp, bloody, pale. And the way she looked down on it reminded him of a past scene.

A dying woman who kept her gaze fixed on her new-born babe with an expression of the deepest pain, intolerable torture. It was an expression he could no more forget than that he had a father and a mother.

Where had she gone? He did not know. But one thing was clear in his soul: she had withdrawn from him, disregarded him, dragged herself further and further away into the dark, stormy night. "Minna, Minna," he had cried, and the sound of his own cry awakened him.

Two round red lights like the staring eyes of a huge monster penetrated the dark. A bloody sheen glided in advance, transforming the drops of rain in its course into drops of blood. A veritable rain of blood seemed to descend from heaven.

Horror fell upon Thiel, mounting and mounting as the train drew nearer. Dream and reality fused into one. He still saw the woman wandering down the tracks. His hand wavered toward the cartridge case, as if to stop the speeding train. Fortunately it was too late. Lights flared before his eyes, the train had rushed past.

The remainder of the night there was little peace for Thiel. He felt a great urgency to be at home, a great longing to see little Toby, from whom, it seemed to him, he had been separated for years. Several times, in his growing anxiety over the child's condition he was tempted to quit duty.

To shorten the hours until his release he determined as soon as day dawned to walk his beat. So, with a cane in one hand and a large iron wrench in the other, he went out into the dirty-gray twilight and stepped along on the spine of a rail, halting every now and then to tighten a bolt with the wrench or to hammer at one of the fish-plates that held the rails together.

The wind and rain had stopped, fragments of a pale blue sky became visible between rifts in the banked clouds. The monotonous tap-tap of his soles on the hard metal and the sleepy drip-drop from the wet trees gradually calmed Thiel.

At six o'clock he was relieved. Without delay he started home.

It was a glorious Sunday morning. The clouds had broken and drifted beyond the horizon. The sun, gleaming like a great blood-red gem, poured veritable masses of light upon the forest. Through the network of the branches the beams shot in sharp straight lines casting a glow upon islets of lacy ferns and here and there turning silvery grey patches on the ground into bits of coral. The tops of the trees, the trunks, the grass shed fire like dew. The world seemed to lie under a deluge of light. And the freshness of the air penetrated to the very core of one's being.

Even in Thiel's brain the fantasies of the night could not but grow pale. And when he entered the room where little Toby was lying in bed with the sun shining on him and more color in his cheeks than usual, they disappeared completely.

To be sure, in the course of the day Lena thought she noticed something odd about him. At church instead of looking in the book he observed her sidewise, and in the middle of the day, when Toby was supposed as usual to carry the baby out on the street, he took it from the boy's arms and laid it in her lap. Otherwise there was nothing conspicuously different about him.

Having no chance to take a nap and as he was to do day duty that week, he went to bed early, at nine o'clock. Exactly as he was about to fall asleep, his wife told him that she intended to accompany him the next morning to dig the lot and plant potatoes.

Thiel winced. He awoke completely, but kept his eyes shut.

Lena went on. If the potatoes were to amount to anything, she said, it was high time to do the planting. And she would have to take the children along because it would probably occupy her the entire day.

Thiel muttered a few unintelligible words, to which she paid no attention. She had turned her back and by the light of a tallow candle was occupied with unfastening her corset and letting down her skirts. Suddenly, without herself knowing why, she turned round and beheld her husband's ashen face distorted by a play of passions. He had raised himself partly, supporting himself by his hands on the edge of the bed, his burning eyes fastened upon her.

"Thiel!" cried the woman, half in anger, half in fear.

Like a somnambulist who hears his name called, Thiel came out of his daze. He stammered something, threw his head back on the pillow, and pulled the quilt over his ears.

Lena was the first to get up the next morning. She went about noiselessly, making the necessary preparations for the excursion. The baby was put into the perambulator, then Tobias was awakened and dressed. He smiled when he was told where he was going.

When everything was ready and even the coffee was made and set on the table, Thiel awoke. His first sensation on seeing the arrangements was of displeasure. He wanted to protest, but the proper opening refused to frame itself. Besides, what arguments could he advance that would weigh with Lena? And there was his child's little face beaming with joy, growing happier and happier each instant, until Thiel, from the sight of his delight in the approaching excursion, could not think of opposing it.

Nevertheless, on the way through the woods, as he pushed the baby-carriage with difficulty through the deep soil, Thiel was not free from anxiety.

Tobias gathered flowers and laid them in the carriage. He was happier than almost any time his father had seen him. In his little brown plush cap he hopped about among the ferns and tried, helplessly to be sure, to catch the glassy-winged dragon flies that darted above them.

As soon as they reached the spot, Lena made a survey. She

threw the sack of seed potatoes on the grassy edge of a small grove of birches, kneeled down, and let the darkish soil run between her fingers.

Thiel watched her eagerly.

"Well," he said, "how is it?"

"Every bit as good as the corner on the Spree."

A burden fell from the flagman. He contentedly scratched the stubble on his face. He had feared she would be dissatisfied.

After hastily devouring a thick slice of bread the woman tossed aside head cloth and jacket, and began to spade up the earth with the speed and endurance of a machine. At regular intervals she straightened up and took several deep breaths. But the pauses were never for long, except when she had to suckle the baby, which she did quickly, with panting, perspiring breasts.

After a while the flagman called to her from the platform in front of the hut:

"I must inspect the beat. I'm taking Tobias with me."

"What!" she screamed back. "Nonsense! Who'll stay with the baby? You'll come here," she shouted still louder.

But the flagman as if not hearing walked off with Toby. For a moment she considered whether she should not run after the two, then desisted because of the loss of time.

Thiel walked down the tracks with his son. The boy was quite excited, everything was so new and strange. Those narrow black rails warmed by the sun—he could not comprehend what they could be meant for. And he kept up an incessant stream of funny questions. What struck him as strangest of all was the resonance of the telegraph poles.

Thiel knew the sound of each pole on his beat so well that with closed eyes he could tell at exactly what spot he stood. And now he stopped several times, holding Tobias by the hand, to listen to the wonderful tones that came from the wood like sonorous chorals from inside a church. The pole at the extreme south end made a particularly full, beautiful sound. It was a mingling of tones that seemed to come without pausing for breath.

Tobias ran round the weathered post to see if he could not through some hole discover the originators of the lovely music. His father listening sank into a devout mood, as in church. He distinguished a voice that reminded him of his dead wife, and fancied it was a choir of blessed spirits, her voice mingling with the others. A deep emotion, a great yearning brought the tears to his eyes.

Tobias asked to be allowed to gather the flowers in the field alongside the tracks. Thiel as always let the child have his way.

Fragments of the blue sky seemed to have dropped on to the meadow, so thickly was it strewn with small, blue blossoms. Like colored pennants the butterflies fluttered and floated among the shining white trunks of the birches. The delicate green foliage gave forth a soft rustle.

Tobias plucked flowers. His father watched him meditatively. Occasionally the flagman raised his eyes and searched between the leaves for a glimpse of the sky, which held the golden sunlight like a huge, spotless bowl.

"Father," said the child, pointing to a brown squirrel which with small scratching sounds was darting up a solitary pine-tree, "Father, is that the good Lord?"

"Silly boy," was all that Thiel could find to reply as bits of loosened bark fell from the trunk of the tree to his feet.

Lena was still digging when Thiel and Tobias returned. She had already spaded up half the plot!

The trains passed at intervals. Each time they rushed by Tobias watched with mouth agape. Even his stepmother was amused by the funny faces he made.

The midday meal, consisting of potatoes and a remnant of roast pork, was consumed inside the hut. Lena was in good spirits. Even Thiel seemed ready to resign himself to the inevitable with good grace. While they ate, he entertained his wife by telling her various things connected with his work. Could she, for instance, imagine that there were forty-six screws in one rail, and more like that.

By mealtime the spading had been done, and in the afternoon Lena was going to sow the potatoes. This time, insisting that Tobias must look after the baby, she took him along.

"Watch out!" Thiel called after her, suddenly gripped by concern. "Watch out that he doesn't go too close to the tracks."

A shrug of Lena's shoulders was her only answer.

The signal rang for the Silesian express. Scarcely had Thiel taken his place in readiness at the gates when the approaching rumble became audible. Within a fraction of a minute he could see the train. On it came, the black funnel spitting steam in countless puffs, one chasing upward after the other. There! One—two—three milk-white geysers gushing up straight as candles—the engine whistling. Three times in succession, short, shrill, alarming.

"They're putting on the brakes," Thiel said to himself. "I wonder why."

He stepped out beyond the gates to look down the tracks, mechanically pulling the red flag from its case and holding it straight in front of him.

Good heavens! Had he been blind? God, O God, what was that? There—between the rails.

"Stop!" he screamed with every atom of breath in his lungs.

Too late. A dark mass had gone down under the train and was being tossed between the wheels like a rubber ball.

Only a few seconds more and with a grating and squeaking of the brakes, the train came to a standstill.

Instantly the lonely stretch became a scene of animation. The conductor and brakeman ran along the gravel path beside the tracks back to the rear end. From every window curious faces peered. And then the crowd that had gathered in the rear formed into a cluster, and moved forward.

Thiel panted. He had to hold on to something not to sink to the ground like a slaughtered steer.

How's that? Were they actually waving to him?

"No!"

A scream came from the spot where the accident had occurred, followed by a howling as from an animal. Who was that? Lena? It was not her voice, yet—

A man came hurrying down the tracks.

"Flagman!"

"What's the matter?"

"An accident."

The messenger shrank before the strange expression in the flagman's eyes. His cap hung on the side of his head, his red hair stood straight up.

"He's still alive. Maybe something can be done."

A rattle in the flagman's throat was the only answer.

"Come quickly—quickly."

With a tremendous effort Thiel pulled himself together. His slack muscles tautened, he drew himself to his full height, his face was empty and dead.

He followed the man at a run, oblivious of the pale, frightened faces at the windows. A young woman looked out, a traveling salesman with a fez on his head, a young couple apparently on their honeymoon. What were they to him? The contents of those rattling, thumping boxes on wheels had never concerned him. His ears were filled with Lena's lamentations.

Yellow dots swam before his eyes, countless yellow dots like fireflies. He shrank back, he stood still. From out of the dance of fireflies it came toward him, pale, limp, bloody—a forehead beaten black and blue, blue lips with dark blood trickling from them. Tobias!

Thiel said nothing. His face went a dirty white. He grinned as if out of his senses. At length he bent over, he felt the limp, dead limbs heavy in his arms. The red flag went round them.

He started to leave.

Where?

"To the railroad doctor, to the railroad doctor, came from all sides."

"We'll take him," called the baggage-master, and turned to prepare a couch of coats and books in his car. "Well?"

Thiel made no move to let go of the boy. They urged him. In vain. The baggage-master had a stretcher handed out from the car and ordered a man to remain with the father. Time was precious. The conductor's whistle shrilled. Coins rained from the windows.

Lena raved like a madwoman. "The poor woman," they said in the coaches, "the poor, poor mother."

The conductor whistled several times, the engine blew a signal, sent white clouds hissing up from its cylinders, and stretched its sinews of iron. In a few seconds, the mail express, with floating flags of smoke, was dashing with redoubled speed through the forest.

The flagman, whose mood had altered, laid the half-dead child on the stretcher.

There he lay with his racked tiny body. Every now and then a long wheeze raised the bony chest, which was visible under the tattered shirt. The little arms and legs, broken not only at the joints, assumed the most unnatural positions. The heel of one small foot was twisted to the front, the arms hung over the sides of the stretcher.

Lena kept up a continuous whimper. Every trace of her former insolence had disappeared. Over and over again she repeated a story to exonerate herself.

Thiel seemed not to notice her. With an expression of awful anxiety he kept his eyes riveted on the child.

A hush had fallen, a deadly hush. The tracks rested hot and black on the glaring gravel. The noon had stifled the wind, and the forest stood motionless, as if carved in stone.

In muffled voices the two men took counsel. The quickest way to reach Friedrichshagen would be to go back to the neighboring station in the direction of Breslau, because the next train, a fast commutation, did not stop at the station that was nearer to Friedrichshagen.

Thiel seemed to consider if he should go along. At the time there was no one there who understood the duties of the position, so with a mute motion of his head he indicated to his wife that she should take hold of the stretcher. She did not dare to refuse though she was concerned about having to leave the baby behind.

Thiel accompanied the cortège of two to the end of his beat, then stood still and looked after them long. Suddenly he clapped his hand to his forehead with a blow that resounded afar. It might wake him up, he thought. Because this was a dream like the one he had had yesterday. No use. Reeling rather than walking he reached his hut. There he fell face downward on the floor. His cap flew into a corner, his carefully kept watch fell from his pocket, the case sprang open, the glass broke. An iron fist seemed to be clamped on his neck, so tight that he could not move no matter how he moaned and groaned and tried to free himself. His forehead was cold, his throat parched.

The ringing of the signal roused him. Under the influence of those three repeated sounds the attack abated. Thiel could rise and do his duty. To be sure, his feet were heavy as lead, and the stretch of rails circled about him like the spokes of an enormous wheel with his head for its axis. But at least he could stand up a while.

The commutation train approached. Tobias must be in it. The nearer it drew the more the pictures before Thiel's eyes blurred. Finally all he saw was the mutilated boy with the bloody mouth. Then darkness fell.

After a while he awoke from the swoon. He found himself lying in the hot sun close to the gates. He rose, shook the sand from his clothes and spat it from his mouth. His head cleared a bit, he could think more quietly.

In the hut he immediately picked his watch up from the floor and laid it on the table. It was still going. For two hours he counted the seconds, then the minutes, while representing to himself what was happening to Tobias. Now Lena was arriving with him, now she stood in front of the doctor. The doctor observed the boy and felt him all over, and shook his head.

"Bad, very bad—but perhaps—who can tell?"

He made a more thorough examination.

"No," he then said, "no, it's all over."

"All over, all over," groaned the flagman. But then he drew himself up, raised his unconsciously clenched fist, rolled his eyes to the ceiling, and shouted as if the narrow little room must burst with the sound of his voice. "He must live, he must. I tell you, he must live."

He flung open the door of the hut—the red glow of evening fell through—and ran rather than walked to the gates. Here he stood still seemingly bewildered. Then suddenly spreading his arms he went to the middle of the road-bed, as if to stop something that was coming from the same direction as the commutation. His wide-open eyes made the impression of blindness. While stepping backward to make way for something, a stream of half-intelligible words came from between his gritted teeth.

"Listen. Don't go. Listen, listen. Don't go. Stay here. Give him back to me. He's beaten black and blue. Yes, yes. All right. I'll beat her black and blue, too. Do you hear? Stay. Give him back to me."

Something seemed to move past him, because he turned and made as if to follow.

"Minna, Minna,"—his voice was weepy like a small child's— "Minna, listen. Give him back to me. I will—" He groped in the air as if to catch and hold someone fast. "My little wife—yes, yes —and I'll—and I'll beat her—so she's black and blue, too—I'll beat her, too—with the hatchet—you see?—with the kitchen hatchet— I'll beat her with the kitchen hatchet. And that'll be the end of her. And then—yes, yes—with the hatchet—yes, with the kitchen hatchet—black blood."

Foam gathered on his lips, his glassy eyeballs rolled incessantly.

A gentle breath of the evening blew steadily over the forest, a rosy cloud mass hung in the western sky.

He had followed the invisible something about a hundred paces when he stood still, apparently having lost courage. With fearful dread in his eyes, he stretched out his arms, pleading, adjuring. He strained his eyes, shaded them with his hand, as if to discern the inessential being in the far distance. Finally his head sank, and the tense expression of his face changed into apathy. He turned and dragged himself the way he had come.

The sunlight laid its final glow over the forest, then was extinguished. The trunks of the pines rose among the tops like pale, decayed bones, and the tops weighed upon them like greyish black layers of mold. The hammering of a woodpecker penetrated the silence. Up above one last dilatory pink cloud traversed the steely blue of the sky. The breath of the wind turned dankly cold as if blowing from a cellar.

The flagman shivered. Everything was new and strange. He did not know what he was walking on, or what was about him. A squirrel hopped along the road-bed. Thiel pondered. He had to think of the Lord. But why? "The Lord is hopping along the tracks, the Lord is hopping along the tracks." He said it several times as if to get at something associated with it. He interrupted himself. A ray of illumination fell upon his brain. "Good heavens! That's madness." He forgot everything else and turned upon this new enemy. He tried to order his thoughts. In vain. They'd come and go and ramble away and shoot off at a tangent. He caught himself in the absurdest fancies, and shuddered at the consciousness of his impotence.

The sound of a child crying came from the birch grove near by. It was the signal for madness. Almost against his will he had to hurry to the spot where the baby, whom everybody had neglected, was crying and kicking on the unblanketed floor of its carriage.

What did he mean to do? What had driven him there? The questions were submerged in a whirling eddy of thoughts and emotions.

"The Lord is hopping along the tracks." Now he knew. Tobias —she had murdered him—Lena—the child had been entrusted to her care. "Stepmother! Beast of a mother!" he hissed between clenched teeth. "And her brat lives."

A red mist enveloped his senses. Two baby eyes penetrated through it. He felt something soft, fleshy between his fingers. He heard gurgling, whistling sounds, mingled with hoarse cries that came from he did not know whom.

Then something fell upon his brain like hot drops of sealing wax, and his spirit was cleared as from a cataleptic trance. Aroused to consciousness, he caught the quiver in the air that was the final reverberation of the signal, and in a trice he realized what he had been about to do. His hand relaxed its grip on the throat, under which the infant had writhed and squirmed. It gasped for breath, then began to cough and bawl.

"It's alive. Thank the Lord, it's alive."

He let it lie and hastened to the crossing. Dark clouds of smoke rolled in the distance, the wind drove them to the ground. He distinguished the panting of an engine that sounded like the intermittent, tortured breathing of a giant.

The stretch was shrouded in a cold twilight. But after a while the clouds of smoke parted, and Thiel recognized the train as being the freight that was returning with open empty cars and bringing home the men who had been working on the road-bed during the day. It had ample running time to stop at each station to drop or pick up the men.

Quite a distance from Thiel's hut the brakes began to be put on, and a loud clanking and clanging and rattling and screeching tore the silence before the train came to a standstill with a single shrill, long-drawn whistle.

About fifty men and women were in the different cars. Nearly all of them stood, some of the men with bared heads. There was a mystifying air of solemnity about them. When they caught sight of the flagman, a whispering began among them, and the old men drew their pipes from between their yellow teeth and held them respectfully in their hands. Here and there a woman would turn to blow her nose.

The conductor descended and advanced toward Thiel. The workmen saw him solemnly shake the flagman's hand, and then saw Thiel with slow steps almost military in their stiffness go back to the rear. None of them dared to address him, though they all knew him.

From the rear wagon they were lifting little Toby.

He was dead.

Lena followed. Her face was a bluish white, brown rings under-
lined her eyes.

Thiel did not so much as cast a glance at her. She, however,
was shocked at sight of her husband. His cheeks were hollow, his
eyelashes and beard were plastered, his hair, it seemed to her, was
gone grayer. Traces of dried tears all over his face. And an unsteady light in his eyes that made her shudder.

The stretcher had been brought back for transporting the body
home.

For a while there was gruesome silence. Thiel lost himself in
black depths of awful thoughts. Darkness deepened. A herd of
deer started to cross the embankment. The stag stood still between the rails and turned his agile neck curiously. The engine
whistled. He and the rest of the herd disappeared in a flash.

At the moment that the train was about to start Thiel collapsed. The train stood still, and counsel was held as to what had
now best be done. Since every effort they made to bring the flagman back to his senses, proved futile, they decided to let the
child's body lie in the hut temporarily, and use the stretcher for
conveying the flagman instead. Two men carried the stretcher,
Lena followed, pushing the baby carriage, sobbing the whole way,
the tears running down her cheeks.

The great purplish ball of the moon shone low between the
trunks of the pine-trees. As it rose it paled and diminished in size
until finally it hung high in the heavens like a swinging lamp, and
cast a pale sheen over the forest, through every chink and cranny
of the foliage, painting the faces of the processionists a livid white.

Cautiously but sturdily they made their way through the close
second growth, then past broad nurseries with the larger trees
scattered among the younger ones. Here the pale light seemed to
have collected itself in great dark bowls.

Occasionally a rattle came from the unconscious man's throat,
and occasionally he raved. Several times he clenched his fists and
tried to raise himself, his eyes all the time remaining closed. Getting him across the Spree was difficult, and a return trip had to be
made to fetch Lena and the baby.

As they ascended the slight eminence on which the hamlet was situated, they met a few of the inhabitants, who forthwith spread the news of the misfortune. The whole colony came running.

Among her gossips Lena broke into fresh lamentations.

Thiel was with difficulty carried up the narrow stairway of his home and put to bed. And the men returned immediately to bring little Toby's body back.

Some of the old, experienced people advised cold compresses. Lena carried out their prescription eagerly, properly, dropping cloths into icy cold spring water and renewing them as soon as the unconscious man's burning forehead had heated them. Anxiously she observed his breathing. It seemed to come more regularly and to continue to improve each minute.

However, the day's excitement had told upon her, and she decided to try to get a little sleep. No use! Whether she held her eyes open or shut, she kept seeing the events of the past hours. The baby slept. Contrary to her wont, she had not paid much attention to it. Altogether she had turned into a different person. Not a trace of her former arrogance. The sick man with the colorless face shining with sweat dominated her even in sleep.

A cloud passed, obscuring the moon and throwing the room into complete darkness. Lena heard nothing but her husband's heavy though regular breathing. She felt creepy in the dark and considered whether she should not rise and kindle a light. But as she attempted to get up, a leaden weight on her limbs pulled her back, her lids drooped, she fell asleep.

Some time later the men returning with the boy's body found the front door wide open. Surprised at this, they mounted and found the upstairs door also open. They called the woman by her name. No answer. They struck a match. The flare of it revealed awful havoc.

"Murder, murder!"

Lena lay in her blood, her face unrecognizable, her skull broken open.

"He murdered his wife, he murdered his wife!"

They ran about witless. Neighbors came. One bumped against the cradle.

"Good heavens!" He shrank back, ashen pale, his eyes fixed in a horrified stare. The baby lay with its throat cut.

The flagman had disappeared. The search made for him that night proved fruitless. The next morning, however, the man who replaced him found him on the tracks at the spot where little Toby had been run over, holding the shaggy brown cap in his arm and caressing it as if it were a living thing.

The block signaler, apprised of his discovery, telegraphed for help. Several men tried with kindly inducements to lure Thiel from the tracks. He was not to be budged. The express then due had to be stopped, and it was only by the united efforts of the entire crew and the use of force that the man, who had begun to rave fearfully, could be removed from the railroad. They had to bind his hands and feet, and the policeman summoned to the spot guarded his transportation the whole way to Berlin, where he was examined in the jail and the next day was sent to a free psychopathic ward. He never let go of the shaggy brown cap. He watched over it with jealous tenderness.

[*Translated by Adele S. Seltzer*]

Sir Rabindranath Tagore

SIR RABINDRANATH TAGORE, *author of about fifty dramas, a hundred books of verses, forty books of fiction, and books of essays and philosophy, was born in 1861 in Calcutta, the eldest son of a wealthy Brahmin. In 1878, he went to London to study law, but soon gave up his studies to return to India and to participate in the nationalist movement by writing poems and songs of inspiration. In 1885 he went to Shilaida, on the banks of the Ganges, to oversee his father's estates, and there became familiar with the native life he depicted in his fiction. Tagore's writing soon made him a national figure in India and in the West. When he was awarded the Nobel Prize in 1913, he was on a lecture tour of the United States. Knighted in 1915, Tagore surrendered his title to protest the British suppression of the Punjab riots. At the age of sixty-eight, already an accomplished musician, he took up painting and was exhibited throughout the world. Known as the "Bengal Shelley," Tagore, even in his short stories, displays the imagination of the poet. A new edition of his translated works makes him easily available to Americans.*

Gouri was the beautiful, delicately nurtured child of an old and wealthy family. Her husband, Paresh, had recently by his own efforts improved his straitened circumstances. So long as he was poor, Gouri's parents had kept their daughter at home, unwilling to surrender her to privation; so she was no longer young when at last she went to her husband's house. And Paresh never felt quite that she belonged to him. He was an advocate in a small western town, and had no close kinsman with him. All his thought was about his wife, so much so that sometimes he would come home before the rising of the Court. At first Gouri was at a loss to understand why he came back suddenly. Sometimes, too, he would dismiss one of the servants without reason; none of them ever suited him long. Especially if Gouri desired to keep any particular servant because he was useful, that man was sure to be got rid of forthwith. The high-spirited Gouri greatly resented this, but her resentment only made her husband's behavior still stranger.

At last when Paresh, unable to contain himself any longer, began in secret to cross-question the maid about her, the whole thing reached his wife's ears. She was a woman of few words; but her pride raged within like a wounded lioness at these insults, and this mad suspicion swept like a destroyer's sword between them. Paresh, as soon as he saw that his wife understood his motive, felt no more delicacy about taxing Gouri to her face; and the more his wife treated it with silent contempt, the more did the fire of his jealousy consume him.

Deprived of wedded happiness, the childless Gouri betook herself to the consolations of religion. She sent for Paramananda Swami, the young preacher of the Prayer-House hard by, and, formally acknowledging him as her spiritual preceptor, asked him to expound the *Gita* to her. All the wasted love and affection of her woman's heart was poured out in reverence at the feet of her Guru.

No one had any doubts about the purity of Paramananda's character. All worshiped him. And because Paresh did not dare to hint at any suspicion against him, his jealousy ate its way into his heart like a hidden cancer.

One day some trifling circumstance made the poison overflow. Paresh reviled Paramananda to his wife as a hypocrite, and said: "Can you swear that you are not in love with this crane that plays the ascetic?"

Gouri sprang up like a snake that has been trodden on, and, maddened by his suspicion, said with bitter irony: "And what if I am?" At this Paresh forthwith went off to the Court-house, and locked the door on her.

In a white heat of passion at this last outrage, Gouri got the door open somehow, and left the house.

Paramananda was poring over the scriptures in his lonely room in the silence of noon. All at once, like a flash of lightning out of a cloudless sky, Gouri broke in upon his reading.

"You here?" questioned her Guru in surprise.

"Rescue me, O my lord Guru," said she, "from the insults of my home life, and allow me to dedicate myself to the service of your feet."

With a stern rebuke, Paramananda sent Gouri back home. But I wonder whether he ever again took up the snapped thread of his reading.

Paresh, finding the door open, on his return home, asked: "Who has been here?"

"No one!" his wife replied. "I have been to the house of my Guru."

"Why?" asked Paresh, pale and red by turns.

"Because I wanted to."

From that day Paresh had a guard kept over the house, and behaved so absurdly that the tale of his jealousy was told all over the town.

The news of the shameful insults that were daily heaped on his disciple disturbed the religious meditations of Paramananda. He felt he ought to leave the place at once; at the same time he could not make up his mind to forsake the tortured woman. Who can say how the poor ascetic got through those terrible days and nights?

At last one day the imprisoned Gouri got a letter.

"My child," it ran, "it is true that many holy women have left the world to devote themselves to God. Should it happen that the trials of this world are driving your thoughts away from God, I will with God's help rescue his handmaid for the holy service of his feet. If you desire, you may meet me by the tank in your garden at two o'clock tomorrow afternoon."

Gouri hid the letter in the loops of her hair. At noon next day when she was undoing her hair before her bath she found that the letter was not there. Could it have fallen onto the bed and got into her husband's hands, she wondered. At first, she felt a kind of fierce pleasure in thinking that it would enrage him; and then she could not bear to think that this letter, worn as a halo of deliverance on her head, might be defiled by the touch of insolent hands.

With swift steps she hurried to her husband's room. He lay groaning on the floor, with eyes rolled back and foaming mouth. She detached the letter from his clenched fist, and sent quickly for a doctor.

The doctor said it was a case of apoplexy. The patient had died before his arrival.

That very day, as it happened, Paresh had an important appointment away from home. Paramananda had found this out, and accordingly had made his appointment with Gouri. To such a depth had he fallen!

When the widowed Gouri caught sight from the window of her Guru stealing like a thief to the side of the pool, she lowered her eyes as at a lightning flash. And in that flash she saw clearly what a fall his had been.

The Guru called: "Gouri."

"I am coming," she replied.

When Paresh's friends heard of his death, and came to assist in the last rites, they found the dead body of Gouri lying beside that of her husband. She had poisoned herself. All were lost in admiration of the wifely loyalty she had shown in her *sati*, a loyalty rare indeed in these degenerate days.

Henrik Pontoppidan

A FISHER NEST

HENRIK PONTOPPIDAN, *the great realist of Danish literature, was born in Fredericia in 1857, the son of a clergyman. Prior to his becoming a writer, he taught geography and surveying in a rural high school headed by his brother. After marrying the daughter of a local proprietor, he produced two volumes of short tales whose titles*—Village Pictures *and* From the Cottages—*reflect their contents. These realistic stories are remarkable for their minute, unflinching pictures of the drab, unromantic, confined life the peasant was forced to lead. Pontoppidan's reputation was made, however, by three novel-cycles;* The Promised Land, Lucky-Per, *and* The Kingdom of the Dead. *For these marathon performances, he shared with Karl Gjellerup, a fellow Dane residing in Germany, the Nobel Prize for 1917, and gained a measure of fame outside of Denmark. He died in 1943 at Charlottenlund.*

Far out by the open sea there was a poor little fisher-hamlet—ten small, black, wooden huts. Half buried in the sand, the string of low houses crept like a caterpillar behind the high, naked sand-down over which the breakers scattered their foam.

On calm summer days, while the sun was melting the tar out of the timber walls and heating the sand till it glowed and burned under the feet, the little hamlet would sometimes expand in its solitude with a beauty as ephemeral as that of a butterfly bursting its chrysalis and hovering on bright wings above the desolation of its usual dreary existence. On the downs wet fishing nets sagged from row upon row of high poles. On the beach below, crowds of half naked, noisy children played, and here and there sun-burned women in scarlet skirts squatted around a fire in the sand, boiling pitch.

But at the first equinoctial storm, when the clouds came low down over the desolate, sand-swept hills, when the big white sea-gulls huddled together in the rolling surf, and the wind-chafed dunes foamed like driven snow, then the little hamlet would again hide behind the down. Loopholes and hatches were closed, and the doors barred; even the smoke would not rise from the openings in the black-burned buildings, but hung timidly over the roofs. Day after day the little fisher-colony seemed plunged in a heavy sleep, while great flakes of white foam were carried past it on the wind.

But sometimes on dark nights it happened that, through the roar of the sea breaking against the shore, another sound could be heard—a door was opened against the wind, but instantly forced back and closed by the storm. A man crawled up the slope of the down, and holding one hand behind his ear, lay flat on the ground to listen. After a while another man came and lay down beside him. A few drowsy words, punctured by hours of silence, passed between them.

Then, suddenly, they both rose and, running quickly toward the houses, knocked at a door in one place, at a shutter in another, and everywhere they called out the same word.

In a moment, square-shouldered men with bearded faces emerged from the darkness. Clad in heavy, stiff cloaks, they moved about without speaking, busying themselves with ropes, ladders, and boat-hooks. At last they gathered around a little horn lantern and marched in a troop toward the east, behind the downs.

Here and there in an open door appeared the head and bust of a half naked woman with her hair hanging in disorder around her shoulders; but as soon as the men disappeared, the doors were closed—and again nothing was heard but the never ceasing, hollow roar of the sea.

A moment later a flame rose against the black sky, high up in the sand-hills to the east. It was a lighted pitch torch from which dark, red sparks were flying over the country.

An hour or two passed.

Suddenly a shriek of many voices is heard from the sea. In the same moment the torch is extinguished. All is darkness.

But out there in the breakers it is as if the gale had gathered all its force and risen in its wildest strength. It sounds like the flapping wings of a giant bird in distress. Near the shore a ship's cables are broken, there is a commotion on deck, and the sound of a loud, commanding voice is drowned in a confused shouting from many men mingled with the piercing, agonized cry of a woman.

Under the dune by the sea the stocky little men are sitting in a circle, gathered around the lantern which throws a ruddy glow over the sand and the bearded faces. They sit in quiet expectation, folding their hands around their raised knees or resting their heads on their hands, as if asleep.

No one speaks. Now and then, when the woman's cry of anguish and the monotonous howling of the sailors fighting in the rigging becomes heart-rending, they look stealthily at each other and try to smile. An old fellow, the last in the line, steals away and mutters something over a rosary which he has managed to pull out of his jacket.

Then there comes a moment when the sea seems to rise and, trembling, gathers all its strength. A series of rolling, thundering sounds like reports of distant cannon is heard on land. Then all is silent. Not a cry.

But soon the seething waters between the dunes and the sea are filled with broken wreckage tossed about and whirled around as in a boiling caldron. Something is washed ashore; other things are carried away again by the waves or crushed on the spot. A big piece of the mast with a rope attached to it is thrown on land, and a cry is heard from a shipwrecked man who is clinging to it.

He is saved.

But in the same moment he is stabbed with a knife in his side, and falls backward. The men surround him, and the lantern is put close to his face, as he sinks feebly on the sand with a last startled gaze.

"It's wine!" mutters the man who holds the lantern, after looking at the dark hair and olive skin of the dying sailor.

The others nod approvingly. A bandy-legged little fellow bends down and fumbles at the clothes of the stranger and examines the glittering ear-rings in his ears. To make sure that he will not revive, he stabs him again, and leaving him with the deep, oozing wound in his side, he waddles toward the sea.

Here his comrades are busy saving wreckage out of the surf with hooks and ropes. When the morning slowly dawns over the sea in a cold, gray mist, barrels of wine and broken planks are pulled ashore. As fast as the waves carry them toward the beach, the dead bodies are hauled on land and plundered. Boxes and cases with colored silk goods are broken open and examined.

While this is going on, the women from the fisher-huts bring hot beer in big, wooden pitchers which they circulate among the men. Trembling in the morning cold, they crowd together on the edge of the down, and with a greedy flash in their eyes, they glance at the wealth heaped together there.

Toward noon, when there is nothing more to save, and when the naked corpses have been buried carefully under the sand, the barrels are rolled into the huts with great merriment, and the big, wooden pitchers are placed on the table. The men and women, the latter clad in silk dresses, sit down on benches around them, and day after day the little fisher-hamlet abandons itself to a wild intoxication, singing and rioting through the long, dark nights, while sand and white foam-flakes are whirling past.

But all this belongs to a very remote age, far, far back in time. The saga of the fisher-hamlet is almost forgotten to-day, up there in the desolate solitude, where year after year sea and sand have effaced and leveled, smoothed and buried everything.

It may happen, however, on fine summer evenings when the sun is setting in blood-red clouds, throwing a fiery glow over the sea, that a respectable head of a family, who is taking a pleasure trip through this beautiful part of the country, will stop before a

wreck on the beach half washed away by the sea, and lost in admiration at the sight, will repeat the tales of the bloody scenes
and nightly terrors of that remote age while his children listen
attentively.

As he explains this, he shows them the solidly built life-boat
station on the dune, or he points to the east, toward the narrow,
flat peninsula, where the high lighthouse proudly rises toward the
sky as a last stronghold of the land.

In time the downs, too, have been influenced by civilization,
and long, straight lines of lymegrass and sea reed have been
planted as a protection against the flying sand. Stretchers of light
brown heather and peaceful moors are now seen among the
dunes, where the fox abides on silent summer nights.

The fisher-hamlet itself, which has kept its strange, caterpillar
shape, is now a thriving village, with a church and a clergyman,
with merchants and an inn, with many small houses, whose tile-
covered roofs appear more intensely red among the greenish white
sand-hills.

On quiet summer days, when the sun melts the tar in the few
remaining old wooden huts, and heats the sand till it burns under
the feet, the village again unfolds itself in its solitude, as it did in
bygone days. It spreads over the dunes, with black poles and nets
and drying fish, with noisy crowds of bare-legged children on the
beach, and sunburned women in scarlet skirts who crouch in the
sand around a steaming kettle, peeling potatoes.

Along the shore painters are sitting—one behind the other—
under large yellow umbrellas like frogs under mushrooms. Poets
with long hair and notebooks are seen everywhere, while in the
village crowds of tourists eagerly observe this unfamiliar scene and
the interesting primitive life of its inhabitants.

Toward noon the heat grows oppressive. There is no air stirring.
From the stifling heat a white haze rises and hangs over the village.

Outside the houses, ducks, pigs, and children are asleep on the
glaring sand. Heavy and sleepy looking women with bare legs and
half-fastened dresses are passing in and out, glancing sullenly

toward a small door in one of the tiny houses where a young tourist with a mosquito veil around his hat is joking with a group of lively fisher girls. The laughter of these young girls is soon the only sound heard in the village.

Even the bare-legged little maids who have been running around the whole morning, their skirts tucked up, splashing in the surf, are tired out and sit down in the shade, under some boats that have been hauled on land. Here they rest with hands folded in their laps and let their eyes follow the little chattering sea-birds that skim over the surface of the water and dive down to catch fish.

An elderly gentleman with a high, gray hat pushed to the back of his head, a gray dust-coat, and an immense spy-glass hanging down on his stomach, comes out on the hotel steps and with a satisfied grimace breathes the polluted air, heavy with the odor of dung and of fish rotting on the strand.

High up on the downs the fishermen are sitting, with small pipes in their mouths, mending their nets. A few among them have fallen asleep, chin on chest, but most of them are chattering, now and then looking toward the sea with a dull glance—this large, empty, milky-blue sea, lying there, quiet and shining, so hopelessly desolate that all life would have seemed extinct save for the heaving and sinking of the waves down below the beach.

Suddenly one day, a big steamer hove in sight in the northeast. It was the Two Brothers, an English freighter headed toward the Kattegat, bound evidently for one of the Baltic ports. Behind it trailed for miles a streak of dense, woolly smoke, as the boat pressed on with full steam ahead.

On deck all was quiet. Soundings had just been taken with no report of shoals.

The sailors were lying in the shade on the lower deck—a mixed crew of Germans, Swedes, and Irishmen, in red-checked woolen shirts. They were sleeping face downward on the deck. The captain himself was keeping watch. He sat in his cosy little cabin on the bridge, whence he might comfortably observe the course of the ship and examine the sunny coast they were passing.

He was a little, short-necked Englishman, stuffed with beef and porter, with a face red and shining like a copper kettle. The motionless, milky eyes expressed deadly dullness. Not a line in his face moved while he was sitting there, quietly smoking a sweet-smelling shag after lunch.

But he was not alone. Sitting close to him, almost on his lap, was a young, slender woman, twisting his coarse beard with her white, quick fingers. Neither spoke. Sometimes, when the strong smoke which he was blowing unceremoniously down over her made her cough, she would mischievously pull his shaggy beard. But at the slightest impatient grumbling from this lump of flesh she would let the beard go and nestle close to him with a droll expression like a frightened kitten.

This was Little Mary. That is what she called herself. Captain Charles—if ever he deigned to speak to her at all—called her simply Mary.

The crew—who rarely saw her—the cook, and the steward, addressed her as "Miss." And when she went for her daily walk in the afternoon, up and down the deck, quiet, erect, with English correctness, her hands in the pockets of her tightly buttoned jacket, the first mate and the sailors politely made way for her, and nothing in their manner showed that they knew all about her.

She had come on board more than two months ago at Liverpool, and Captain Charles had several times brought his fist down on the table before her, swearing that he would put her on shore in the first English port they entered and send her back to the den of misery where she belonged. But the mild summer winds and several lucky trips had made him soft. There was always an imploring glance in her eyes which he could not resist, and she had put her little hand around his neck so gently that he regularly withdrew his order, and he even felt something like a heart move beneath the fat under his vest. Mary was only seventeen.

He now rested, satiated and motionless after his lunch, and abandoned himself to daydreams. Strange fancies had come. Why should he not keep her for the rest of the summer—and perhaps for the winter, too? He might even marry the girl. He had got into the habit of having her about, and he did not like to think of being without her. Of course he would be the laughing-stock of his comrades if he really married her. And there would be a great commotion home in Grangemouth. But why not let them laugh? As long as he was at sea he would not know. And then— Mary was only seventeen. As for her past, there was an excuse in the home she had come from. Her father was a worthless fellow who had more than once in a fit of drunkenness ill-treated and half killed her, and her mother, a dissolute old woman, had herself taught the girl her profession. Besides, Mary was only a child and hardly knew what sort of life she had been drawn into. While he was lost in this revery, and Mary amused herself by letting her head rest on his chest, rocked up and down by his breathing, they suddenly felt a few light shocks through the ship, and a moment later, it stopped, while the stamping of the machinery increased to a furious speed.

Captain Charles's heavy body was alert in a moment. Throwing Mary off, he rushed out of the door with an oath, made the machine stop, and bent over the railing of the bridge. Yes— to be sure! The ship had stopped. Through the clear, glassy green water pebbles and shells were shining down on the sandy shoal which they had struck quite softly.

His face, which for a moment had been colorless, turned purple, but after having looked along the ship's side, and after having, as he thought, made sure that no harm was done, he turned to the crew, who had come running from all parts of the ship, looked over the railing, and reassured them with a calm "All right."

"Half speed!—back—half speed!" he called out to the engineers.

And when the machine again began to work he walked up and down the bridge several times, puffing violently at his shag-pipe, to get over his fright.

But the ship did not move. Not even at his command "Full speed back!" did it move. However much the machine puffed and heaved, however black and angry the smoke gushed out of the smoke-stack, the heavy ship did not stir. It only groaned a little at the exertion with a clattering noise of iron.

Meanwhile the catastrophe had been noticed on shore by a painter and some fishermen who posed for him, standing in the shallow water dressed in heavy sea-boots and pulling their nets. A hurried message was sent to the slumbering city to wake the people from their siesta.

And now there was a stir. At first one by one, then crowds, the men came sauntering across the dunes with laughter gurgling in their stomachs, while the women and children invaded the highest part of the down behind the village and from this vantage point, shading their eyes with their hands, looked steadily toward the north. Everywhere people were hurrying over the sand, shouting and beckoning to each other from a distance. The stranding commissioner and the police officer were passing in an open carriage, and all the tourists had left the lunch table of the inn in haste to rush toward the stranding place. The man in the high, gray hat was ahead of the others, using his long legs like stilts. A napkin, which in the confusion he had pushed into his pocket, was hanging out behind.

The whole town stirred with feverish commotion. People paused before the front doors to ask questions or explain. But it was not till it became known as an incontestable fact that the ship was stuck, solidly stuck, in the sand, that the anxiety gave way to a stormy mirth, which extended even to the children and made them run up and down the streets, shouting "Hurrah." The merchant jumped up on the office chair, and with a smile he ordered the big cask of whisky to be brought up from the cellar. Neighbors and friends called on each other, and everywhere there was a smell of coffee. Even old folks and cripples who could scarcely walk hobbled on till they reached the top of the nearest dune, where they revelled in the sight of the big, smoking sea-monster lying out there, groaning and struggling to free itself.

In front of the place where the steamer had run ashore, the beach was black with people, and around the steamer—it was stuck several hundred yards from land, on the third reef—there was a gathering of boats from the salvage corporation, shouting to the captain whenever he showed himself on the bridge.

Captain Charles, however, pretended not to see or hear anything of this. Through the first mate he had forbidden all strangers to board his ship and obstinately refused all offers of help. He ordered his own big boat to be lowered and had some men row two anchors away from the ship, tugging with strong chains at the rear bar. The engineers had been given orders to increase the steam, and even to go as far as the red line; for off they must.

While this was going on, he walked up and down the bridge, his hands in the pockets of his jacket, or he sat in the cabin on the bridge, drinking straight whisky out of a big beer glass. Mary's round cat's eyes followed his every movement and watched anxiously the expression of his red face. A few times she had ventured to approach him, but with a snarl he had pushed her away violently.

At last the two anchors were cast. Again the machine began to work, the steam whirled, and the chains tightened, but the ship did not move an inch; it only sank deeper into the sand after each vain attempt.

The group on the shore grew larger, and the number of boats on the water kept increasing. Fishermen from the remotest part of the peninsula and from a neighboring village toward the south were dragging their boats along the shore. At last a whole fleet of small vessels gathered around the stranded steamer, pushing each other, and paddling along with shouts and laughter. They were especially interested in guessing at the kind of cargo the ship might carry. Cotton or iron would make the biggest salvage money, and that was what they hoped for. It could hardly be coal, as no apparatus for unloading could be seen.

At some distance from the others lay a six-oar boat carrying the stranding commissioner. He was a portly, thick-set man, who tried to look at the whole scene with an air of sublime indifference. In reality no one could be more interested in the value of cargo and ship than he, as he had—through his mere presence—a legal claim to one half percent of the salvage sum.

The customs officer, a fat man with gold-rimmed glasses, approached in another boat and saluted him.

"What do you think of this, consul?" he said, and laughed in his fiery red beard which seemed to be ablaze in the sun. "To run ashore in the middle of the day and in this kind of weather. If that is not a present!" The stranding commissioner shrugged his shoulders, a movement that might be interpreted in any way.

"I suppose it is iron," the officer continued. "Anyhow, that is what people say."

"Heaven knows!" the other answered with an almost priestly solemnity, and looked into the air. "She looks like a coal steamer —English, of course."

The customs officer laughed again.

"English, yes. And as tough and tenacious as English beef. Can you understand, consul, how it is possible that he still hopes to get off?"

"Well now—he may still succeed," the commissioner answered with a delusive expression of Christian sympathy. Only in the corners of his mouth the play of muscles betrayed the anxiety of his soul.

"Pardon me, gentlemen, is it true, what they say that the salvage-steamer has been telegraphed for?" It was the man with the gray silk hat. He had hired a boat with four seasoned old fishermen and, trembling with excitement, he was sitting in the stern with the spyglass in his hand. "Can it really be so?" he continued, as no one answered. "I was told that, according to a reliable report, the boat was expected here."

"Yes, she may be here in a moment," said the consul, looking toward the east.

And there, coming from the south, around the peninsula, appeared a small steamer. The consul gave a signal to his sailors, and the oars dipped into the water. A few minutes later the boat was at the side of the stranded ship.

He made himself known to the first mate and asked if help was wanted. Captain Charles, who from his cabin on the bridge had seen the little steamer stop and anchor at some distance, answered, "No." "No," he repeated with clenched teeth, bringing his fist down on the table. The mate hesitated before taking this answer.

A whisky bottle was standing before the captain, and he had emptied the third glass.

The consul left and rowed away at once toward land.

Some hours passed. The crowd kept increasing, as the women came and brought food for their husbands. They camped on the sand. The whisky bottles were circulating. All were hilarious, as if celebrating a national festival.

Toward sunset the surface of the sea suddenly ruffled, and the boats still lying around the ship began to rock. As yet there were no clouds to be seen, but there was a strange, dim look about the sun, and the sea seemed to rise out there against the horizon.

A quarter of an hour passed, and the sea grew so rough that the boats had to seek land. The men pushed them on shore by stemming their shoulders against the sides, and the women began to seek shelter under the large prows.

Now the sky was hidden by clouds, and the winds increased in strength, so that the position of the ship became critical. It was lying in the breakers with its broad-side turned toward the sea, which already began to pound against it. From the shore one could see how one white-crested wave after the other splashed over the gunwale.

Those of the spectators on the seashore who were provided with telescopes suddenly noticed that there was a great activity on board. The sailors were running to and fro on deck. A boat was lowered, and the clattering of an anchor chair was heard. It was clear that a last decisive attempt would be made. Huge masses of smoke with showers of sparks rolled out against the dark sky, and then the crew began to work.

It looked quite ghastly seen from the shore. Some of the women began to wail. But for this, it was very quiet on land now. Toward the northwest a blood-red sun was setting behind large masses of dark clouds.

Then the machine suddenly stopped again. After a long delay, they saw through the growing darkness how the flag of distress was slowly hoisted. At the same time, a feeble, long-winded and hoarse signal was heard from the steam whistle.

"She's crying now," they said, and they laughed.

The eight-oar boat of the district had been brought and was pushed into the sea, with the stranding commissioner and the attorney who had to accredit the salvage conditions with the seal of the law. There was still a third person seated in the boat, a thin little man in a gray cloak, holding his hat with his black-gloved left hand. It was the agent of the salvage company, who had been landed by the small steamer, directly after its arrival, and who, since then, had been on the shore.

The gale had almost blown up a storm, yet the skilled crew led the boat through the waves, with steady strokes of the oars, and twenty minutes later the three officials were put on board. The first mate received them and led them below deck into the officers' mess. Here Captain Charles was sitting, much intoxicated, behind a table over which a lamp was hanging. The light, thrown back from the inside of a white painted tin shade, was falling on the mahogany table-top, the rest of the room was left in a greenish twilight.

He received the strangers without any greeting and asked shortly how much it would cost.

The agent of the salvage company asked permission to look over the shipping-papers. When they were brought and he had learned the value of the cargo, the age of the ship, the amount of the insurance, etc., he answered: "Six thousand pounds."

A convulsive shock passed through the frame of Captain Charles. It was as if his intoxication suddenly left him, and he became sober again. Then a strange, proud smile of despair played around his bluish-white lips.

"I see," he said half to himself.

There was silence for a few minutes. The sea was knocking against the side of the ship, right at the Captain's back, and in there in the narrow room, the chafing of the waves had a strange, hollow, and ghostly sound. The young attorney, who was not yet accustomed to these scenes, grew paler and paler and looked toward the door. Over their heads on deck heavy boots were tramping.

"Four thousand pounds," the captain said at last.

The agent shrugged his shoulders regretfully. "Impossible."

The stranding commissioner, whose duty it was to assist the captain and to look after the interests of the ship, then made an effort to mediate. But as he knew that the salvage company made it a rule never to change an estimate, and it was to his own interest to keep the salvage sum as high as possible, he quickly turned against the captain with many sympathetic words, and in passable English tried to make him understand that on account of the increasing danger of the position in which the ship was placed, there was no other way; he would have to accept.

The agent, who quite agreed with this statement, added that, if his conditions were not accepted before an hour had elapsed, the salvage-steamer would have to return, as he, under the present circumstances, did not dare to let it remain here during the night. Besides he begged to say that only for ten minutes longer would he feel bound to the very favorable offer he had made.

Captain Charles still remained silent. He put his short, fat arms on the table and was looking from one to the other of the men with slow, understanding nods. After the last words of the agent his pale lips quivered for a moment. Then he turned to the first mate, who had been present during the negotiations as his witness, and asked him for writing materials.

A few hours later the Two Brothers was tugged loose and found seaworthy. In the dark stormy night, when the lights were shining from every hut in the small village in the downs, when the people had already begun to feast on the third part of the salvage-money, when the tables of the inn and the bars of the tavern were crowded with people, the foreign steamer passed on toward the east, around the neck of land, continuing its solitary trip out across the sea.

The first mate kept the watch. Captain Charles had shut himself up in his quarters with a bottle of whisky, but without Mary. The poor child was sitting in the corner of her narrow berth in her own small cabin, looking into the darkness with her round cat's eyes. She had read her fate in the furious glance of her master when he had pushed her away in the afternoon. Her hour of freedom had passed. In the first port the ship entered he would carry out his order and send her back to the old den of misery, hunger, and dirt, to the blows of her father and the curses of her mother.

Or?

The sea is deep. The sea is merciful . . .

The next morning, when the Two Brothers sailed into the Sound, Mary was no longer on board.

[Translated by Juliane Sarauw]

Knut Hamsun

KNUT HAMSUN *was born in Lom, Norway, in 1859 and spent his childhood in the North, the scene of many of his grimly-realistic novels and tales. He worked at miscellaneous jobs—clerk, peddler, shoemaker, dockhand, sheriff, teacher, and wanderer (twice, for two year periods, to the United States)—before he attracted attention as a writer.* Hunger *caused a sensation in Scandinavian letters by its lyric glorification of the irrational processes in a starving man's mind. Exchanging vagabondage for bucolic comfort, Hamsun produced* The Growth of the Soil, *an epic which brought him the Nobel Prize in 1920. His growing aversion to the industrial-democratic society aligned him with the Nazi invaders of his country, and after the liberation he was tried for treason. Though he escaped prison because of his age, he was stripped of his fortune and forced to submit to psychiatric examination in an Oslo sanitarium. After his release, he returned to his estate near Grimstad, where he died in 1952.*

Down near the inner harbor in Copenhagen, there is a street called Vestervold, a relatively new, yet desolate boulevard. There are few houses to be seen on it, few gas lamps, and almost no people whatever. Even now, in summer, it is rare that one sees people promenading there.

Well, last evening I had something of a surprise in that street.

I had taken a few turns up and down the sidewalk when a lady came towards me from the opposite direction. There were no other people in sight. The gas lamps were lighted, but it was nevertheless dark—so dark that I could not distinguish the lady's face. One of the usual creatures of the night, I thought to myself, and passed her by.

At the end of the boulevard, I turned about and walked back. The lady had also turned about, and I met her again. She is waiting for someone, I thought, and I was curious to see whom she could be waiting for. And again I passed her by.

When I met her the third time I tipped my hat and spoke to her.

"Good evening! Are you waiting for someone?"

She was startled. No—that is, yes—she was waiting for someone.

Did she object to my keeping her company till the person she was expecting arrived?

No—she did not object in the least, and she thanked me. For that matter, she explained, she was not expecting anyone. She was merely taking the air—it was so still here.

We strolled about side by side. We began talking about various things of no great consequence. I offered my arm.

"Thank you, no," she said, and shook her head.

There was no great fun promenading in this way; I could not see her in the dark. I struck a match to see what time it was. I held the match up and looked at her too.

"Nine-thirty," I said.

She shivered as if she were freezing. I seized the opportunity.

"You are freezing?" I asked. "Shan't we drop in some place and get something to drink? At Tivoli? At the National?"

"But, don't you see, I can't go anywhere now," she answered.

And I noticed then for the first time that she wore a very long black veil. I begged her pardon, and blamed the darkness for my mistake. And the way in which she took my apology at once convinced me that she was not one of the usual night wanderers.

"Won't you take my arm?" I suggested again. "It may warm you a bit."

She took my arm.

We paced up and down a few turns. She asked me to look at the time again.

"It is ten," I said. "Where do you live?"

"On Gamle Kongevei."

I stopped her.

"And may I see you to your door?" I asked.

"Not very well," she answered. "No, I can't let you . . . You live on Bredgade, don't you?"

"How do you know that?" I asked in surprise.

"Oh, I know who you are," she answered.

A pause. We walked arm in arm down the lighted streets. She walked rapidly, her long veil streaming behind.

"We had better hurry," she said.

At her door in Gamle Kongevei she turned toward me as if to thank me for my kindness in escorting her. I opened the door for her, and she entered slowly. I thrust my shoulder gently against the door and followed her in. Once inside she seized my hand. Neither of us said anything.

We mounted two flights of stairs and stopped on the third floor. She herself unlocked the door to her apartment, then opened a second door, and took me by the hand and led me in. It was presumably a drawing room; I could hear a clock ticking on the wall. Once inside the door the lady paused a moment, threw her arms about me suddenly, and kissed me tremblingly, passionately on the mouth. Right on the mouth.

"Won't you be seated?" she suggested. "Here is a sofa. Meanwhile I'll get a light."

And she lit a lamp.

I looked about me, amazed, yet curious. I found myself in a spacious and extremely well-furnished drawing room with other, half-open doors leading into several rooms on the side. I could not for the life of me make out what sort of person it was I had come across.

"What a beautiful room!" I exclaimed. "Do you live here?"

"Yes, this is my home," she answered.

"Is this your home? You live with your parents then?"

"Oh, no," she laughed. "I am an old woman, as you'll see!"

And she removed her veil and her wraps.

"There—see! What did I tell you!" she said, and threw her arms about me once again, abruptly, driven by some uncontrollable urge.

She might have been twenty-two or three, wore a ring on her right hand, and might for that matter really have been a married woman. Beautiful? No, she was freckled, and had scarcely any eyebrows. But there was an effervescent life about her, and her mouth was strangely beautiful.

I wanted to ask her who she was, where her husband was, if she had any, and whose house this was I was in, but she threw herself about me every time I opened my mouth and forbade me to be inquisitive.

"My name is Ellen," she explained. "Would you care for something to drink? It really won't disturb anyone if I ring. Perhaps you'd step in here, in the bedroom, meanwhile."

I went into the bedroom. The light from the drawing room illuminated it partially. I saw two beds. Ellen rang and ordered wine, and I heard a maid bring in the wine and go out again. A little later Ellen came into the bedroom after me, but she stopped short in the door. I took a step toward her. She uttered a little cry and at the same time came toward me.

This was last evening.

What further happened? Ah, patience! There is much more!

It was beginning to grow light this morning when I awoke. The daylight crept into the room on either side of the curtain. Ellen was also awake and smiled toward me. Her arms were white and velvety, her breast unusually high. I whispered something to her, and she closed my mouth with hers, mute with tenderness. The day grew lighter and lighter.

Two hours later I was on my feet. Ellen was also up, busy dressing herself—she had got her shoes on. Then it was I experienced something which even now strikes me as a gruesome dream. I was at the wash stand. Ellen had some errand or other in the adjoining room, and as she opened the door I turned around and glanced in. A cold draft from the open window in the room rushed in upon me, and in the center of the room I could just make out a corpse stretched out on a table. A corpse, in a coffin, dressed in white, with a gray beard, the corpse of a man. His bony knees protruded like madly clenched fists underneath the sheet and his face was sallow and ghastly in the extreme. I could see everything in full daylight. I turned away and said not a word.

When Ellen returned I was dressed and ready to go out. I could scarcely bring myself to respond to her embraces. She put on some additional clothes; she wanted to accompany me down as far as the street door, and I let her come, still saying nothing. At the door she pressed close to the wall so as not to be seen.

"Well, good-bye," she whispered.

"Till tomorrow?" I asked, in part to test her.

"No, not tomorrow."

"Why not tomorrow?"

"Not so many questions, dear. I am going to a funeral tomorrow, a relation of mine is dead. Now there—you know it."

"But the day after tomorrow?"

"Yes, the day after tomorrow, at the door here. I'll meet you. Goodbye."

I went.

Who was she? And the corpse? With its fists clenched and the corners of its mouth drooping—how ghastly comic! The day after tomorrow she would be expecting. Ought I see her again?

I went straight down to the Bernina Café and asked for a directory. I looked up the number so and so Gamle Kongevei and—there—there was the name. I waited some little time till the morning papers were out. Then I turned quickly to the announcements of deaths. And—sure enough—there I found hers too, the very first in the list, in bold type: "My husband, fifty-three years old, died today after a long illness." The announcement was dated the day before.

I sat for a long time and pondered.

A man marries. His wife is thirty years younger than he. He contracts a lingering illness. One fair day he dies.

And the young widow breathes a sigh of relief.

[*Translated by Anders Orbeck*]

Anatole France

ANATOLE FRANCE, *baptized Jacques Anatole Francois Thibault in 1844, was the son of a Parisian bookseller and bibliophile. His literary career began slowly and late, for he was thirty-five years old when his first volume of stories was published. In 1921, he was awarded the Nobel Prize. During the greater part of his life, he assumed an air of detachment and irresponsibility (apparent rather than real, for he helped Zola defend Dreyfus, and attacked willful ignorance, superstition, and immorality wherever he found them, advocating reforms such as mass education, labor organization, and minority rights). He never ceased to remain skeptical of contemporary judgment, whether of the present or the past, a skepticism he dramatized in "The Procurator of Judea." Though his present-day reputation has receded, it is reported that his funeral procession in 1924 was attended by crowds as large as those attending the 1919 Victory Parade.*

Lælius Lamia, born in Italy of illustrious parents, had not yet discarded the *toga prætexta* when he set out for the schools of Athens to study philosophy. Subsequently he took up his residence at Rome, and in his house on the Esquiline, amid a circle of youthful wastrels, abandoned himself to licentious courses. But being accused of engaging in criminal relations with Lepida, the wife of Sulpicius Quirinus, a man of consular rank, and being found guilty, he was exiled by Tiberius Cæsar. At that time he was just entering his twenty-fourth year. During the eighteen years that his exile lasted he traversed Syria, Palestine, Cappadocia, and Armenia, and made prolonged visits to Antioch, Cæsarea, and Jerusalem. When, after the death of Tiberius, Caius was raised to the purple, Lamia obtained permission to return to Rome. He even regained a portion of his possessions. Adversity had taught him wisdom.

He avoided all intercourse with the wives and daughters of Roman citizens, made no efforts towards obtaining office, held aloof from public honors, and lived a secluded life in his house on the Esquiline. Occupying himself with the task of recording all the remarkable things he had seen during his distant travels, he turned, as he said, the vicissitudes of his years of expiation into a diversion for his hours of rest. In the midst of these calm employments, alternating with assiduous study of the works of Epicurus, he recognized with a mixture of surprise and vexation that age was stealing upon him. In his sixty-second year, being afflicted with an illness which proved in no slight degree troublesome, he decided to have recourse to the waters at Baiæ. The coast at that point, once frequented by the halcyon, was at this date the resort of the wealthy Roman, greedy of pleasure. For a week Lamia lived alone, without a friend in the brilliant crowd. Then one day, after dinner, an inclination to which he yielded urged him to ascend the incline, which, covered with vines that resembled bacchantes, looked out upon the waves.

Having reached the summit he seated himself by the side of a path beneath a terebinth, and let his glances wander over the lovely landscape. To his left, livid and bare, the Phlegræn plain stretched out towards the ruins of Cumæ. On his right, Cape Misenum plunged its abrupt spur beneath the Tyrrhenian sea. Beneath his feet luxurious Baiæ, following the graceful outline of the coast, displayed its gardens, its villas thronged with statues, its porticos, its marble terraces along the shores of the blue ocean where the dolphins sported. Before him, on the other side of the bay, on the Campanion coast, gilded by the already sinking sun, gleamed the temples which far away rose above the laurels of

Posilippo, whilst on the extreme horizon Vesuvius looked forth smiling.

Lamia drew from a fold of his toga a scroll containing the *Treatise upon Nature,* extended himself upon the ground, and began to read. But the warning cries of a slave necessitated his rising to allow of the passage of a litter which was being carried along the narrow pathway through the vineyards. The litter being uncurtained, permitted Lamia to see stretched upon the cushions as it was borne nearer to him the figure of an elderly man of immense bulk, who, supporting his head on his hand, gazed out with a gloomy and disdainful expression. His nose, which was aquiline, and his chin, which was prominent, seemed desirous of meeting across his lips, and his jaws were powerful.

From the first moment Lamia was convinced that the face was familiar to him. He hesitated a moment before the name came to him. Then suddenly hastening towards the litter with a display of surprise and delight—

"Pontius Pilate!" he cried. "The gods be praised who have permitted me to see you once again!"

The old man gave a signal to the slaves to stop, and cast a keen glance upon the stranger who had addressed him.

"Pontius, my dear host," resumed the latter, "have twenty years so far whitened my hair and hollowed my cheeks that you no longer recognize your friend Ælius Lamia?"

At this name Pontius Pilate dismounted from the litter as actively as the weight of his years and the heaviness of his gait permitted him, and embraced Ælius Lamia again and again.

"Gods! what a treat it is to me to see you once more! But, alas, you call up memories of those long-vanished days when I was Procurator of Judæa in the province of Syria. Why, it must be thirty years ago that I first met you. It was at Cæsarea, whither you came to drag out your weary term of exile. I was fortunate enough to alleviate it a little, and out of friendship, Lamia, you followed me to that depressing place Jerusalem, where the Jews filled me with bitterness and disgust. You remained for more than ten years my guest and my companion, and in converse about Rome and things Roman we both of us managed to find consolation—you for your misfortunes, and I for my burdens of State."

Lamia embraced him afresh.

"You forget two things, Pontius; you are overlooking the facts that you used your influence on my behalf with Herod Antipas, and that your purse was freely open to me."

"Let us not talk of that," replied Pontius, "since after your return to Rome you sent me by one of your freedmen a sum of money which repaid me with usury."

"Pontius, I could never consider myself out of your debt by the mere payment of money. But tell me, have the gods fulfilled your desires? Are you in the enjoyment of all the happiness you deserve? Tell me about your family, your fortunes, your health."

"I have withdrawn to Sicily, where I possess estates, and where I cultivate wheat for the market. My eldest daughter, my best-beloved Pontia, who has been left a widow, lives with me, and directs the household. The gods be praised, I have preserved my mental vigor; my memory is not in the least degree enfeebled. But old age always brings in its train a long procession of griefs and infirmities. I am cruelly tormented with gout. And at this very moment you find me on my way to the Phlegræan plain in search of a remedy for my sufferings. From the burning soil, whence at night flames burst forth, proceed acrid exhalations of sulphur, which, so they say, ease the pains and restore suppleness to the joints. At least, the physicians assure me that it is so."

"May you find it so in your case, Pontius! But, despite the gout and its burning torments, you scarcely look as old as myself, although in reality you must be my senior by ten years. Unmistakably you have retained a greater degree of vigor than I ever possessed, and I am overjoyed to find you looking so hale. Why, dear friend, did you retire from the public service before the customary age? Why, on resigning your governorship in Judæa, did you withdraw to a voluntary exile on your Sicilian estates? Give me an account of your doings from the moment that I ceased to be a witness of them. You were preparing to suppress a Samaritan rising when I set out for Cappadocia, where I hoped to draw some profit from the breeding of horses and mules. I have not seen you since then. How did that expedition succeed? Pray tell me. Everything interests me that concerns you in any way."

Pontius Pilate sadly shook his head.

"My natural disposition," he said, "as well as a sense of duty, impelled me to fulfill my public responsibilities, not merely with diligence, but even with ardor. But I was pursued by unrelenting hatred. Intrigues and calumnies cut short my career in its prime, and the fruit it should have looked to bear has withered away. You ask me about the Samaritan insurrection. Let us sit down on this hillock. I shall be able to give you an answer in a few words. Those occurrences are as vividly present to me as if they had happened yesterday.

"A man of the people, of persuasive speech—there are many such to be met with in Syria—induced the Samaritans to gather together in arms on Mount Gerizim (which in that country is looked upon as a holy place) under the promise that he would disclose to their sight the sacred vessels which in the ancient days of Evander and our father, Æneas, had been hidden away by an eponymous hero, or rather a tribal deity, named Moses. Upon this assurance the Samaritans rose in rebellion; but having been warned in time to forestall them, I dispatched detachments of infantry to occupy the mountain, and stationed cavalry to keep the approaches to it under observation.

"These measures of prudence were urgent. The rebels were already laying siege to the town of Tyrathaba, situated at the foot of Mount Gerizim. I easily dispersed them, and stifled the as yet scarcely organized revolt. Then, in order to give a forcible example with as few victims as possible, I handed over to execution the leaders of the rebellion. But you are aware, Lamia, in what strait dependence I was kept by the proconsul Vitellius, who governed Syria not in, but against the interests of Rome, and looked upon the provinces of the empire as territories which could be farmed out to tetrarchs. The head-men among the Samaritans, in their resentment against me, came and fell at his feet lamenting. To listen to them, nothing had been further from their thoughts than to

disobey Cæsar. It was I who had provoked the rising, and it was
purely in order to withstand my violence that they had gathered
together round Tyrathaba. Vitellius listened to their complaints,
and handling over the affairs of Judæa to his friend Marcellus,
commanded me to go and justify my proceedings before the Emperor himself. With a heart overflowing with grief and resentment
I took ship. Just as I approached the shores of Italy, Tiberius, worn
out with age and the cares of empire, died suddenly on the self-
same Cape Misenum, whose peak we see from this very spot magni-
fied in the mists of evening. I demanded justice of Caius, his suc-
cessor, whose perception was naturally acute, and who was acquainted with Syrian affairs. But marvel with me, Lamia, at the
maliciousness of fortune, resolved on my discomfiture. Caius then
had in his suite at Rome the Jew Agrippa, his companion, the
friend of his childhood, whom he cherished as his own eyes. Now
Agrippa favored Vitellius, inasmuch as Vitellius was the enemy
of Antipas, whom Agrippa pursued with his hatred. The Emperor
adopted the prejudices of his beloved Asiatic, and refused even to
listen to me. There was nothing for me to do but bow beneath
the stroke of unmerited misfortune. With tears for my meat and
gall for my portion, I withdrew to my estates in Sicily, where I
should have died of grief if my sweet Pontia had not come to console her father. I have cultivated wheat, and succeeded in producing the fullest ears in the whole province. But now my life is
ended; the future will judge between Vitellius and me."

"Pontius," replied Lamia, "I am persuaded that you acted towards the Samaritans according to the rectitude of your character,
and solely in the interests of Rome. But were you not perchance
on that occasion a trifle too much influenced by that impetuous
courage which has always swayed you? You will remember that in
Judæa it often happened that I who, younger than you, should
naturally have been more impetuous than you, was obliged to urge
you to clemency and suavity."

"Suavity towards the Jews!" cried Pontius Pilate. "Although
you have lived amongst them, it seems clear that you ill understand those enemies of the human race. Haughty and at the same

time base, combining an invincible obstinacy with a despicably mean spirit, they weary alike your love and your hatred. My character, Lamia, was formed upon the maxims of the divine Augustus. When I was appointed Procurator of Judæa, the world was already penetrated with the majestic ideal of the *pax romana*. No longer, as in the days of our internecine strife, were we witnesses to the sack of a province for the aggrandisement of a proconsul. I knew where my duty lay. I was careful that my actions should be governed by prudence and moderation. The gods are my witnesses that I was resolved upon mildness, and upon mildness only. Yet what did my benevolent intentions avail me? You were at my side, Lamia, when, at the outset of my career as ruler, the first rebellion came to a head. Is there any need for me to recall the details for you? The garrison had been transferred from Cæsarea to take up its winter quarters at Jerusalem. Upon the ensigns of the legionaries appeared the presentment of Cæsar. The inhabitants of Jerusalem, who did not recognize the indwelling divinity of the Emperor, were scandalized at this, as though, when obedience is compulsory, it were not less abject to obey a god than a man. The priests of their nation appeared before my tribunal imploring me with supercilious humility to have the ensigns removed from within the holy city. Out of reverence for the divine nature of Cæsar and the majesty of the empire, I refused to comply. Then the rabble made common cause with the priests, and all around the pretorium portentous cries of supplication arose. I ordered the soldiers to stack their spears in front of the tower of Antonia, and to proceed, armed only with sticks like lictors, to disperse the insolent crowd. But, heedless of blows, the Jews continued their entreaties, and the more obstinate amongst them threw themselves on the ground and, exposing their throats to the rods, deliberately courted death. You were a witness of my humiliation on that occasion, Lamia. By the order of Vitellius I was forced to send the insignia back to Cæsarea. That disgrace I had certainly not merited. Before the immortal gods I swear that never once during my term of office did I flout justice and the laws. But I am grown old. My enemies and detractors are dead. I shall die unavenged. Who will now retrieve my character?"

He moaned and lapsed into silence. Lamia replied—

"That man is prudent who neither hopes nor fears anything from the uncertain events of the future. Does it matter in the least what estimate men may form of us hereafter? We ourselves are after all our own witnesses, and our own judges. You must rely, Pontius Pilate, on the testimony you yourself bear to your own rectitude. Be content with your own personal respect and that of your friends. For the rest, we know that mildness by itself will not suffice for the work of government. There is but little room in the actions of public men for that indulgence of human frailty which the philosophers recommend."

"We'll say no more at present," said Pontius. "The sulphureous fumes which rise from the Phlegræan plain are more powerful when the ground which exhales them is still warm beneath the sun's rays. I must hasten on. Adieu! But now that I have rediscovered a friend, I should wish to take advantage of my good fortune. Do me the favor, Ælius Lamia, to give me your company at supper at my house tomorrow. My house stands on the seashore, at the extreme end of the town in the direction of Misenum. You will easily recognize it by the porch which bears a painting representing Orpheus surrounded by tigers and lions, whom he is charming with the strains from his lyre.

"Till tomorrow, Lamia," he repeated, as he climbed once more into his litter. "Tomorrow we will talk about Judæa."

The following day at the supper hour Lamia presented himself at the house of Pontius Pilate. Two couches only were in readiness for occupants. Creditably but simply equipped, the table held a silver service in which were set out beccaficos in honey, thrushes, oysters from the Lucrine lake, and lampreys from Sicily. As they proceeded with their repast, Pontius and Lamia interchanged inquiries with one another about their ailments, the symptoms of which they described at considerable length, mutually emulous of communicating the various remedies which had been recommended to them. Then, congratulating themselves on being thrown together once more at Baiæ, they vied with one another in praise of the beauty of that enchanting coast and the mildness of the climate they enjoyed. Lamia was enthusiastic about the charms of the courtesans who frequented the seashore laden with golden ornaments and trailing draperies of barbaric broidery. But the aged Procurator deplored the ostentation with which by means of trumpery jewels and filmy garments foreigners and even enemies of the empire beguiled the Romans of their gold. After a time they turned to the subject of the great engineering feats that had been accomplished in the country; the prodigious bridge constructed by Caius between Puteoli and Baiæ, and the canals which Augustus excavated to convey the waters of the ocean to Lake Avernus and the Lucrine lake.

"I also," said Pontius, with a sigh, "I also wished to set afoot public works of great utility. When, for my sins, I was appointed Governor of Judæa, I conceived the idea of furnishing Jerusalem with an abundant supply of pure water by means of an aqueduct. The elevation of the levels, the proportionate capacity of the various parts, the gradient for the brazen reservoirs to which the distribution pipes were to be fixed—I had gone into every detail, and decided everything for myself with the assistance of mechanical experts. I had drawn up regulations for the superintendents so as to prevent individuals from making unauthorized depredations. The architects and the workmen had their instructions. I gave orders for the commencement of operations. But far from viewing with satisfaction the construction of that conduit, which was intended to carry to their town upon its massive arches not only water but health, the inhabitants of Jerusalem gave vent to lamentable outcries. They gathered tumultuously together, exclaiming against the sacrilege and impiousness, and, hurling themselves upon the workmen, scattered the foundation stones. Can you picture to yourself, Lamia, a filthier set of barbarians? Nevertheless, Vitellius decided in their favor, and I received orders to put a stop to the work."

"It is a knotty point," said Lamia, "how far one is justified in devising things for the commonweal against the will of the populace."

Pontius Pilate continued as though he had not heard this interruption.

"Refuse an aqueduct! What madness! But whatever is of Roman origin is distasteful to the Jews. In their eyes we are an unclean race, and our very presence appears a profanation to them. You will remember that they would never venture to enter the pretorium for fear of defiling themselves, and that I was consequently obliged to discharge my magisterial functions in an open-air tribunal on that marble pavement your feet so often trod.

"They fear us and they despise us. Yet is not Rome the mother and warden of all those peoples who nestle smiling upon her venerable bosom? With her eagles in the van, peace and liberty have been carried to the very confines of the universe. Those whom we have subdued we look on as our friends, and we leave those conquered races, nay, we secure to them the permanence of their customs and their laws. Did Syria, aforetime rent asunder by its rabble of petty kings, ever even begin to taste of peace and prosperity until it submitted to the armies of Pompey? And when Rome might have reaped a golden harvest as the price of her goodwill, did she lay hands on the hoards that swell the treasuries of barbaric temples? Did she despoil the shrine of Cybele at Pessinus, or the Morimene and Cilician sanctuaries of Jupiter, or the temple of the Jewish god of Jerusalem? Antioch, Palmyra, and Apamea, secure despite their wealth, and no longer in dread of the wandering Arab of the desert, have erected temples to the genius of Rome and the divine Cæsar. The Jews alone hate and withstand us. They withhold their tribute till it is wrested from them, and obstinately rebel against military service."

"The Jews," replied Lamia, "are profoundly attached to their ancient customs. They suspected you, unreasonably I admit, of a desire to abolish their laws and change their usages. Do not resent it, Pontius, if I say that you did not always act in such a way as to disperse their unfortunate illusion. It gratified you, despite your habitual self-restraint, to play upon their fears, and more than once have I seen you betray in their presence the contempt with which their beliefs and religious ceremonies inspired you. You irritated them particularly by giving instructions for the sacerdotal garments and ornaments of their high priest to be kept in ward by your legionaries in the Antonine tower. One must admit that though they have never risen like us to an appreciation of things divine, the Jews celebrate rites which their very antiquity renders venerable."

Pontius Pilate shrugged his shoulders.

"They have very little exact knowledge of the nature of the gods," he said. "They worship Jupiter, yet they abstain from naming him or erecting a statue of him. They do not even adore him under the semblance of a rude stone, as certain of the Asiatic peoples are wont to do. They know nothing of Apollo, of Neptune, of Mars, nor of Pluto, nor of any goddess. At the same time, I am convinced that in days gone by they worshipped Venus. For even to this day their women bring doves to the altar as victims; and you know as well as I that the dealers who trade beneath the arcades of their temple supply those birds in couples for sacrifice. I have even been told that on one occasion some madman proceeded to overturn the stalls bearing these offerings, and their owners with them. The priests raised an outcry about it, and looked on it as a case of sacrilege. I am of opinion that their custom of sacrificing turtle-doves was instituted in honor of Venus. Why are you laughing, Lamia?"

"I was laughing," said Lamia, "at an amusing idea which, I hardly know how, just occurred to me. I was thinking that perchance some day the Jupiter of the Jews might come to Rome and vent his fury upon you. Why should he not? Asia and Africa have already enriched us with a considerable number of gods. We have seen temples in honor of Isis and the dog-faced Anubis erected in Rome. In the public squares, and even on the race-courses, you may run across the Bona Dea of the Syrians mounted on an ass. And did you never hear how, in the reign of Tiberius, a young patrician passed himself off as the horned Jupiter of the Egyptians,

Jupiter Ammon, and in this disguise procured the favors of an illustrious lady who was too virtuous to deny anything to a god?
Beware, Pontius, lest the invisible Jupiter of the Jews disembark
some day on the quay at Ostia!"

At the idea of a god coming out of Judæa, a fleeting smile
played over the severe countenance of the Procurator. Then he
replied gravely—

"How would the Jews manage to impose their sacred law on
outside peoples when they are in a perpetual state of tumult
amongst themselves as to the interpretation of that law? You have
seen them yourselves, Lamia, in the public squares, split up into
twenty rival parties, with staves in their hands, abusing each other
and clutching one another by the beard. You have seen them on
the steps of the temple, tearing their filthy garments as a symbol
of lamentation, with some wretched creature in a frenzy of pro-
phetic exaltation in their midst. They have never realized that it
is possible to discuss peacefully and with an even mind those matters concerning the divine which yet are hidden from the profane
and wrapped in uncertainty. For the nature of the immortal gods
remains hidden from us, and we cannot arrive at a knowledge of it.
Though I am of the opinion, none the less, that it is a prudent
thing to believe in the providence of the gods. But the Jews are devoid of philosophy, and cannot tolerate any diversity of opinions.
On the contrary, they judge worthy of the extreme penalty all those
who on divine subjects profess opinions opposed to their law. And
as, since the genius of Rome has towered over them, capital sentences pronounced by their own tribunals can only be carried out
with the sanction of the proconsul or the procurator, they harry
the Roman magistrate at any hour to procure his signature to their
baleful decrees, they besiege the pretorium with their cries of
'Death!' A hundred times, at least, have I known them, mustered,
rich and poor together, all united under their priests, make a furious onslaught on my ivory chair, seizing me by the skirts of my
robe, by the thongs of my sandals, and all to demand of me—nay,
to exact from me—the death sentence on some unfortunate whose
guilt I failed to perceive, and as to whom I could only pronounce

that he was as mad as his accusers. A hundred times, do I say! Not a hundred, but every day and all day. Yet it was my duty to execute their law as if it were ours, since I was appointed by Rome not for the destruction, but for the upholding of their customs, and over them I had the power of the rod and the axe. At the outset of my term of office I endeavored to persuade them to hear reason; I attempted to snatch their miserable victims from death. But this show of mildness only irritated them the more; they demanded their prey, fighting around me like a horde of vultures with wing and beak. Their priests reported to Cæsar that I was violating their law, and their appeals, supported by Vitellius, drew down upon me a severe reprimand. How many times did I long, as the Greeks used to say, to dispatch accusers and accused in one convoy to the crows!

"Do not imagine, Lamia, that I nourish the rancor of the discomfited, the wrath of the superannuated, against a people which in my person has prevailed against both Rome and tranquillity. But I foresee the extremity to which sooner or later they will reduce us. Since we cannot govern them, we shall be driven to destroy them. Never doubt it. Always in a state of insubordination, brewing rebellion in their inflammatory minds, they will one day burst forth upon us with a fury beside which the wrath of the Numidians and the mutterings of the Parthians are mere child's play. They are secretly nourishing preposterous hopes, and madly premeditating our ruin. How can it be otherwise, when, on the strength of an oracle, they are living in expectation of the coming of a prince of their own blood whose kingdom shall extend over the whole earth? There are no half measures with such a people. They must be exterminated. Jerusalem must be laid waste to the very foundation. Perchance, old as I am, it may be granted me to behold the day when her walls shall fall and the flames shall envelop her houses, when her inhabitants shall pass under the edge of the sword, when salt shall be strown on the place where once the temple stood. And in that day I shall at length be justified."

Lamia exerted himself to lead the conversation back to a less acriminious note.

"Pontius," he said, "it is not difficult for me to understand both your long-standing resentment and your sinister forebodings. Truly, what you have experienced of the character of the Jews is nothing to their advantage. But I lived in Jerusalem as an interested onlooker, and mingled freely with the people, and I succeeded in detecting certain obscure virtues in these rude folk which were altogether hidden from you. I have met Jews who were all mildness, whose simple manners and faithfulness of heart recalled to me what our poets have related concerning the Spartan lawgiver. And you yourself, Pontius, have seen perish beneath the cudgels of your legionaries simple-minded men who have died for a cause they believed to be just without revealing their names. Such men do not deserve our contempt. I am saying this because it is desirable in all things to preserve moderation and an even mind. But I own that I never experienced any lively sympathy for the Jews. The Jewesses, on the contrary, I found extremely pleasing. I was young then, and the Syrian women stirred all my senses to response. Their ruddy lips, their liquid eyes that shone in the shade, their sleepy gaze pierced me to the very marrow. Painted and stained, smelling of nard and myrrh, steeped in odors, their physical attractions are both rare and delightful."

Pontius listened impatiently to these praises.

"I was not the kind of man to fall into the snares of the Jewish women," he said; "and since you have opened the subject yourself, Lamia, I was never able to approve of your laxity. If I did not express with sufficient emphasis formerly how culpable I held you for having intrigued at Rome with the wife of a man of consular rank, it was because you were then enduring heavy penance for your misdoings. Marriage from the patrician point of view is a sacred tie; it is one of the institutions which are the support of Rome. As to foreign women and slaves, such relations as one may enter into with them would be of little account were it not that they habituate the body to a humiliating effeminacy. Let me tell you that you have been too liberal in your offerings to the Venus of the Market-place; and what, above all, I blame in you is that you have not married in compliance with the law and given children to the Republic, as every good citizen is bound to do."

But the man who had suffered exile under Tiberius was no longer listening to the venerable magistrate. Having tossed off his cup of Falernian, he was smiling at some image visible to his eye alone.

After a moment's silence he resumed in a very deep voice, which rose in pitch by little and little—

"With what languorous grace they dance, those Syrian women! I knew a Jewess at Jerusalem who used to dance in a poky little room, on a threadbare carpet, by the light of one smoky little lamp, waving her arms as she clanged her cymbals. Her loins arched, her head thrown back, and, as it were, dragged down by the weight of her heavy red hair, her eyes swimming with voluptuousness, eager, languishing, compliant, she would have made Cleopatra herself grow pale with envy. I was in love with her barbaric dances, her voice—a little raucous and yet so sweet—her atmosphere of incense, the semi-somnolescent state in which she seemed to live. I followed her everywhere. I mixed with the vile rabble of soldiers, conjurers, and extortioners with which she was surrounded. One day, however, she disappeared, and I saw her no more. Long did I seek her in disreputable alleys and taverns. It was more difficult to learn to do without her than to lose the taste for Greek wine. Some months after I lost sight of her, I learned by chance that she had attached herself to a small company of men and women who were followers of a young Galilean thaumaturgist. His name was Jesus; he came from Nazareth, and he was crucified for some crime, I don't quite know what. Pontius, do you remember anything about the man?"

Pontius Pilate contracted his brows, and his hand rose to his forehead in the attitude of one who probes the deeps of memory. Then after a silence of some seconds—

"Jesus?" he murmured, "Jesus—of Nazareth? I cannot call him to mind."

[Translated by Frederick Chapman]

William Butler Yeats

WILLIAM BUTLER YEATS, *Ireland's greatest poet, was born near Dublin in 1865, the son of a well-known landscape painter. A sensitive, lonely boy at school in England, he enjoyed his sojourns with his mother's people (including an astrologer and a race-horse owner) in County Sligo. Here he came to know the Irish peasants and their past, on which he was to draw later for his books. As a young writer in London, he published prose and poetry of great promise ("The Outcast" is from this period), but his truly creative span did not begin until his return to Dublin. He broadened his interest in occult philosophy, helped nurture the Irish theater and literary revival, and became involved with the Irish Revolution. These experiences in and out of this world transmuted the decorative embroideries of his early lyrics* (The Wanderings of Oisin *and* The Wind Among the Reeds) *into the austere but magnificent style of* The Green Helmet, The Wild Swans at Coole, The Tower, *and* Four Plays for Dancers, *and also resulted in* Essays *and* Autobiography. *He was elected a senator of the Irish Free State in 1922 and awarded the Nobel Prize in 1923—the news of which he celebrated by frying sausages at midnight. Before his death on the French Riviera in 1939, he was already acknowledged as one of the most important poets of our language. The following story, the product of his left-hand, Oscar Wilde regarded as the best thing to come from the pen of young Yeats.*

A man, with thin brown hair and a pale face, half ran, half walked, along the road that wound from the south to the town of Sligo. Many called him Cumhal, the son of Cormac, and many called him the Swift, Wild Horse; and he was a gleeman, and he wore a short parti-colored doublet, and had pointed shoes, and a bulging wallet. Also he was of the blood of the Ernaans, and his birth-place was the Field of Gold; but his eating and sleeping places were the four provinces of Eri, and his abiding place was not upon the ridge of the earth. His eyes strayed from the Abbey tower of the White Friars and the town battlements to a row of crosses which stood out against the sky upon a hill a little to the eastward of the town, and he clenched his fist, and shook it at the crosses. He knew they were not empty, for the birds were fluttering about them; and he thought how, as like as not, just such another vagabond as himself was hanged on one of them; and he muttered: "If it were hanging or bowstringing, or stoning or beheading, it would be bad enough. But to have the birds pecking your eyes and the wolves eating your feet! I would that the red wind of the Druids had withered in his cradle the soldier of Dathi, who brought the tree of death out of barbarous lands, or that the lightning, when it smote Dathi at the foot of the mountain, had smitten him also, or that his grave had been dug by the green-haired and green-toothed merrows deep at the roots of the deep sea."

While he spoke, he shivered from head to foot, and the sweat came out upon his face, and he knew not why, for he had looked upon many crosses. He passed over two hills and under the battlemented gate, and then round by a left-hand way to the door of the Abbey. It was studded with great nails, and when he knocked at it, he roused the lay brother who was the porter, and of him he asked a place in the guest-house. Then the lay brother took a glowing turf on a shovel, and led the way to a big and naked outhouse strewn with very dirty rushes; and lighted a rush-candle fixed between two of the stones of the wall, and set the glowing turf upon the hearth and gave him two unlighted sods and a wisp of straw, and showed him a blanket hanging from a nail, and a shelf with a loaf of bread and a jug of water, and a tub in a far corner. Then the lay brother left him and went back to his place by the door. And Cumhal the son of Cormac began to blow upon the glowing turf that he might light the two sods and the wisp of straw; but the sods and the straw would not light, for they were damp. So he took off his pointed shoes, and drew the tub out of the corner with the thought of washing the dust of the highway from his feet; but the water was so dirty that he could not see the bottom. He was very hungry, for he had not eaten all that day; so he did not waste much anger upon the tub, but took up the black loaf, and bit into it, and then spat out the bite, for the bread was hard and mouldy. Still he did not give way to his anger, for he had not drunken these many hours; having a hope of heath beer or wine at his day's end, he had left the brooks untasted, to make his supper more delightful. Now he put the jug to his lips, but he flung it from him straightway, for the water was bitter and ill-smelling. Then he gave the jug a kick, so that it broke against the opposite wall, and he took down the blanket to wrap it about him for the night. But no sooner did he touch it than it was alive with skipping fleas. At this, beside himself with anger, he rushed to the door of the guest-house, but the lay brother, being well accustomed to such outcries, had locked it on the outside; so he emptied the tub and began to beat the door with it, till the lay brother came to the door and asked what ailed him, and why he woke him out of sleep. "What ails me!" shouted Cumhal, "are not the sods as wet as the sands of the Three Rosses? and are not the fleas in the blanket as many as the waves of the sea and as lively? and is not the bread as hard as the heart of a lay brother who has forgotten God? and is not the water in the jug as bitter and as ill-smelling as his soul? and is not the foot-water the color that shall be upon him when he has been charred in the Undying Fires?" The lay brother saw that the lock was fast, and went back to his niche, for he was too sleepy to talk with comfort. And Cumhal went on beating at the door, and presently he heard the lay brother's foot once more, and cried out at him, "O cowardly and tyrannous race of friars, persecutors of the bard and the gleeman, haters of life and joy! O race that does not draw the sword and tell the truth! O race that melts the bones of the people with cowardice and with deceit!"

"Gleeman," said the lay brother, "I also make rhymes; I make many while I sit in my niche by the door, and I sorrow to hear the bards railing upon the friars. Brother, I would sleep, and therefore I make known to you that it is the head of the monastery, our gracious abbot, who orders all things concerning the lodging of travelers."

"You may sleep," said Cumhal, "I will sing a bard's curse on the abbot." And he set the tub upside down under the window, and stood upon it, and began to sing in a very loud voice. The singing awoke the abbot, so that he sat up in bed and blew a silver whistle until the lay brother came to him. "I cannot get a wink of sleep with that noise," said the abbot. "What is happening?"

"It is a gleeman," said the lay brother, "who complains of the sods, of the bread, of the water in the jug, of the foot-water, and of the blanket. And now he is singing a bard's curse upon you, O brother abbot, and upon your father and your mother, and your grandfather and your grandmother, and upon all your relations."

"Is he cursing in rhyme?"

"He is cursing in rhyme, and with two assonances in every line of his curse."

The abbot pulled his night-cap off and crumpled it in his hands, and the circular brown patch of hair in the middle of his bald head looked like an island in the midst of a pond, for in Connaught they had not yet abandoned the ancient tonsure for the style then coming into use. "If we do not somewhat," he said, "he will teach his curses to the children in the street, and the girls spinning at the doors, and to the robbers upon Ben Bulben."

"Shall I go, then," said the other, "and give him dry sods, a fresh loaf, clean water in a jug, clean foot-water, and a new blanket, and make him swear by the blessed Saint Benignus, and by the sun and moon, that no bond be lacking, not to tell his rhymes to the children in the street, and the girls spinning at the doors, and the robbers upon Ben Bulben?"

"Neither our blessed Patron nor the sun and moon would avail at all," said the abbot; "for tomorrow or the next day the mood to curse would come upon him, or a pride in those rhymes would move him, and he would teach his lines to the children, and the girls, and the robbers. Or else he would tell another of his craft how he fared in the guest-house and he in his turn would begin to curse, and my name would wither. For learn there is no stead-fastness of purpose upon the roads, but only under roofs, and be-tween four walls. Therefore I bid you go and awaken Brother Kevin, Brother Dove, Brother Little Wolf, Brother Bald Patrick, Brother Bald Brandon, Brother James and Brother Peter. And they shall take the man, and bind him with ropes, and dip him into the river that he may cease to sing. And in the morning, lest this but make him curse the louder, we will crucify him."

"The crosses are all full," said the lay brother.

"Then we must make another cross. If we do not make an end of him another will, for who can eat and sleep in peace while men like him are going about the world? Ill should we stand before blessed Saint Benignus, and sour would be his face when he comes to judge us at the Last Day, were we to spare an enemy of his when we had him under our thumb! Brother, the bards and the gleemen are an evil race, ever cursing and ever stirring up the peo-ple, and immoral and immoderate in all things, and heathen in their hearts, always longing after the Son of Lir, and Aengus, and Bridget, and the Dagda, and Dana the Mother, and all the false gods of the old days; always making poems in praise of those kings and queens of the demons, Finvaragh, whose home is under Cru-achmaa, and Red Aodh of Cnoc-na-Sidhe, and Cleena of the Wave, and Aoibhell of the Grey Rock, and him they call Donn of the Vats of the Sea; and railing against God and Christ and the blessed Saints." While he was speaking he crossed himself, and when he had finished he drew the nightcap over his ears, to shut out the noise, and closed his eyes, and composed himself to sleep.

The lay brother found Brother Kevin, Brother Dove, Brother Little Wolf, Brother Bald Patrick, Brother Bald Brandon, Brother James and Brother Peter sitting up in bed, and he made them get up. Then they bound Cumhal, and they dragged him to the river, and they dipped him in it at the place which was afterwards called Buckley's Ford.

"Gleeman," said the lay brother, as they led him back to the guesthouse, "why do you ever use the wit which God has given you to make blasphemous and immoral tales and verses? For such is the way of your craft. I have, indeed, many such tales and verses well nigh by rote, and so I know that I speak true! And why do you praise with rhyme those demons, Finvaragh, Red Aodh, Cleena, Aoibhell and Donn? I, too, am a man of great wit and learning, but I ever glorify our gracious abbot, and Benignus our Patron, and the princes of the province. My soul is decent and orderly, but yours is like the wind among the salley gardens. I said what I could for you, being also a man of many thoughts, but who could help such a one as you?"

"Friend," answered the gleeman, "my soul is indeed like the wind, and it blows me to and fro, and up and down, and puts many things into my mind and out of my mind, and therefore am I called the Swift, Wild Horse." And he spoke no more that night, for his teeth were chattering with the cold.

The abbot and the friars came to him in the morning, and bade him get ready to be crucified, and led him out of the guest-house. And while he still stood upon the step a flock of great grass-barnacles passed high above him with clanking cries. He lifted his arms to them and said, "O great grass-barnacles, tarry a little, and mayhap my soul will travel with you to the waste places of the shore and to the ungovernable sea!" At the gate a crowd of beggars gathered about them, being come there to beg from any traveler or pilgrim who might have spent the night in the guest-house. The abbot and the friars led the gleeman to a place in the woods at some distance, where many straight young trees were growing, and they made him cut one down and fashion it to the right length, while the beggars stood round them in a ring, talking and gesticulating. The abbot then bade him cut off another and shorter piece of wood, and nail it upon the first. So there was his cross for him; and they put it upon his shoulder, for his crucifixion was to be on the top of the hill where the others were. A half-mile on the way he asked them to stop and see him juggle for them; for he knew, he said, all the tricks of Aengus the Subtle-hearted. The old friars were for pressing on, but the young friars would see him: so he did many wonders for them, even to the drawing of live frogs out of his ears. But after a while they turned on him, and said his tricks were dull and a shade unholy, and set the cross on his shoulders again. Another half-mile on the way, and he asked them to stop and hear him jest for them, for he knew, he said, all the jests of Conan the Bald, upon whose back a sheep's wool grew. And the young friars, when they had heard his merry tales, again bade him take up his cross, for it ill became them to listen to such follies. Another half-mile on the way, he asked them to stop and hear him sing the story of White-breasted Deirdre, and how she endured many sorrows, and how the sons of Usna died to serve her. And the young friars were mad to hear him, but when he had ended they grew angry, and beat him for waking forgotten longings in their hearts. So they set the cross upon his back, and hurried him to the hill.

When he was come to the top, they took the cross from him, and began to dig a hole to stand it in, while the beggars gathered round, and talked among themselves. "I ask a favor before I die," says Cumhal.

"We will grant you no more delays," says the abbot.

"I ask no more delays, for I have drawn the sword, and told the truth, and lived my vision, and am content."

"Would you, then, confess?"

"By sun and moon, not I; I ask but to be let eat the food I carry in my wallet. I carry food in my wallet whenever I go upon a journey, but I do not taste of it unless I am well-nigh starved. I have not eaten now these two days."

"You may eat, then," says the abbot, and he turned to help the friars dig the hole.

The gleeman took a loaf and some strips of cold fried bacon out of his wallet and laid them upon the ground. "I will give a tithe to the poor," says he, and he cut a tenth part from the loaf and the bacon. "Who among you is the poorest?" And thereupon was a great clamor, for the beggars began the history of their sorrows and their poverty, and their yellow faces swayed like Gara Lough when the floods have filled it with water from the bogs.

He listened for a little, and, says he, "I am myself the poorest, for I have traveled the bare road, and by the edges of the sea; and the tattered doublet of particolored cloth upon my back and the torn pointed shoes upon my feet have ever irked me, because of the towered city full of noble raiment which was in my heart. And I have been the more alone upon the roads and by the sea because I heard in my heart the rustling of the rose-bordered dress of her who is more subtle than Aengus, the Subtle-hearted, and more full of the beauty of laughter than Conan the Bald, and more full of the wisdom of tears than White-breasted Deirdre, and more lovely than a bursting dawn to them that are lost in the darkness. Therefore, I award the tithe to myself; but yet, because I am done with all things, I give it unto you."

So he flung the bread and the strips of bacon among the beggars, and they fought with many cries until the last scrap was eaten. But meanwhile the friars nailed the gleeman to his cross, and set it upright in the hole, and shovelled the earth in at the foot, and trampled it level and hard. So then they went away, but the beggars stared on, sitting round the cross. But when the sun was sinking, they also got up to go, for the air was getting chilly. And as soon as they had gone a little way, the wolves, who had been showing themselves on the edge of a neighboring coppice, came nearer, and the birds wheeled closer and closer. "Stay, outcasts, yet a little while," the crucified one called in a weak voice to the beggars, "and keep the beasts and the birds from me." But the beggars were angry because he had called them outcasts, so they threw stones and mud at him, and went their way. Then the wolves gathered at the foot of the cross, and the birds flew lower and lower. And presently the birds lighted all at once upon his head and arms and shoulders, and began to peck at him, and the wolves began to eat his feet. "Outcasts," he moaned, "have you also turned against the outcast?"

Wladyslaw Reymont

WLADYSLAW REYMONT *was born in* 1868 *near Radom, Poland.
Before becoming a professional writer, he spent a restless youth in various occupations and wrote his first novel while in charge of a railway
section. There followed a series of novels and a number of short stories,
all displaying Reymont's keen sense of observation and his deep compassion for the peasant class about which he usually wrote. The ruth-
less realism of the terrifying drama he was sometimes able to attain is
well represented in "Death," one of the most powerful stories in Polish
fiction. His epic tetraology of native life,* The Peasants, *shows his special gifts at their height and earned him world-wide fame. He received
the Nobel Prize in* 1924 *and died in Warsaw the following year.*

"Father, eh, father, get up, do you hear?—Eh, get a
move on!"

"Ohm God, or Blessed Virgin! Aoh!" groaned the old man,
who was being violently shaken. His face peeped out from under
his sheepskin, a sunken, battered, and deeply-lined face, of the
same color as the earth he had tilled for so many years; with a
shock of hair, gray as the furrows of the ploughed fields in autumn. His eyes were closed; breathing heavily he dropped his
tongue from his half-open bluish mouth with cracked lips.

"Get up! Hi!" shouted his daughter.

"Grandad!" whimpered a little girl who stood in her chemise

and a cotton apron tied across her chest, and raised herself on tip-toe to look at the old man's face.

"Grandad!" There were tears in her blue eyes and sorrow in her grimy little face. "Grandad!" she called out once more, and plucked at the pillow.

"Shut up!" screamed her mother, took her by the nape of the neck and thrust her against the stove.

"Out with you, damned dog!" she roared, when she stumbled over the old half-blind bitch who was sniffing the bed. "Out you go! will you. . . . you carrion!" and she kicked the animal so violently with her clog that it tumbled over, and, whining, crept toward the closed door. The little girl stood sobbing near the stove, and rubbed her nose and eyes with her small fists.

"Father, get up while I am still in a good humor!"

The sick man was silent, his head had fallen on one side, his breathing became more and more labored. He had not much longer to live.

"Get up. What's the idea? Do you think you are going to do your dying here? Not if I know it! Go to Julina, you old dog! You've given the property to Julina, let her look after you . . . come now . . . while I'm yet asking you!"

"Oh blessed Child Jesus! oh Mary. . . ."

A sudden spasm contracted his face, wet with anxiety and sweat. With a jerk his daughter tore away the feather-bed, and, taking the old man round the middle, she pulled him furiously half out of bed, so that only his head and shoulders were resting on it; he lay motionless like a piece of wood, and like a piece of wood, stiff and dried up.

"Priest . . . His Reverence . . ." he murmured under his heavy breathing.

"I'll give you your priest! You shall kick the bucket in the pigsty, you sinner . . . like a dog!" She seized him under the armpits, but dropped him again directly, and covered him entirely with the feather-bed, for she had noticed a shadow flitting past the window. Someone was coming up to the house.

She scarcely had time to push the old man's feet back into the bed. Blue in the face, she furiously banged the feather-bed and pushed the bedding about.

The wife of the peasant Dyziak came into the room.

"Christ be praised!"

"In Eternity . . ." growled the other, and glanced suspiciously at her out of the corners of her eyes.

"How do you do? Are you well?"

"Thank God . . . so so . . ."

"How's the old man? Well?"

She was stamping the snow off her clogs near the door.

"Eh . . . how should he be well? He can hardly fetch breath any more."

"Neighbor . . . you don't say say . . . neighbor . . ." She was bending down over the old man.

"Priest," he sighed.

"Dear me . . . just fancy . . . dear me, he doesn't know me! The poor man wants the priest. He's dying, that's certain; he's all but dead already . . . dear me! Well, and did you send for his Reverence?"

"Have I got any one to send?"

"But you don't mean to let a Christian soul die without the sacrament?"

"I can't run off and leave him alone, and perhaps . . . he may recover."

"Don't you believe it . . . hoho . . . just listen to his breathing. That means that his inside is withering up. It's just as it was with my Walek last year when he was so ill."

"Well, dear, you'd better go for the priest, make haste . . . look!"

"All right, all right. Poor thing! He looks as if he couldn't last much longer. I must make haste . . . I'm off . . ." and she tied her apron more firmly over her head.

"Good-bye, Antkowa."

"Go with God."

Dyziakowa went out, while the other woman began to put the room in order; she scraped the dirt off the floor, swept it up, strewed wood-ashes, scrubbed her pots and pans and put them in a row. From time to time she turned a look of hatred on to the bed, spat, clenched her fists, and held her head in helpless despair.

"Fifteen acres of land, the pigs, three cows, furniture, clothes—half of it, I'm sure, would come to six thousand . . . good God!"

And as though the thought of so large a sum was giving her fresh vigor, she scrubbed her saucepans with a fury that made the walls ring, and banged them down on the board.

"May you . . . may you!" She continued to count up: "Fowls, geese, calves, all the farm implements. And all left to that trull! May misery eat you up . . . may the worms devour you in the ditch for the wrong you have done me, and for leaving me no better off than an orphan!"

She sprang toward the bed in a towering rage and shouted:

"Get up!" And when the old man did not move, she threatened him with her fists and screamed into his face:

"That's what you've come here for, to do your dying here, and I am to pay for your funeral and buy you a hooded cloak. . . . that's what you think! I don't think so! You won't live to see me do it! If your Julina is so sweet, you'd better make haste and go to her. Was it I who was supposed to look after you in your dotage? She is the pet, and if you think . . ."

She did not finish, for she heard the tinkling of the bell, and the priest entered with the sacrament.

Antkowa bowed down to his feet, wiping tears of rage from her eyes, and after she had poured the holy water into a chipped basin and put the asperges-brush beside it, she went out into the passage, where a few people who had come with the priest were waiting already.

"Christ be praised."

"In Eternity."

"What is it?"

"Oh, nothing! Only that he's come here to give up . . . with us, whom he has wronged. And now he won't give up. Oh, dear me . . . poor me!"

She began to cry.

"That's true! He will have to rot, and you will have to live," they all answered in unison and nodded their heads.

"One's own father," she began again . . . "Have we, Antek and I, not taken care of him, worked for him, sweated for him, just as much as they? Not a single egg would I sell, not half a pound of butter, but put it all down his throat; the little drop of milk I have taken away from the baby and given it to him, because he was an old man and my father . . . and now he goes and gives it all to Tomek. Fifteen acres of land, the cottage, the cows, the pigs, the calf, and the farm carts and all the furniture . . . is that nothing? Oh, pity me! There's no justice in this world, none . . . Oh, oh!"

She leant against the wall, sobbing loudly.

"Don't cry, neighbor, don't cry. God is full of mercy, but not always toward the poor. He will reward you some day."

"Idiot, what's the good of talking like that?" interrupted the speaker's husband. "What's wrong is wrong. The old man will go, and poverty will stay."

"It's hard to make an ox move when he won't lift up his feet," another man said thoughtfully.

"Eh . . . You can get used to everything in time, even to hell," murmured a third, and spat from between his teeth.

The little group relapsed into silence. The wind rattled the door and blew snow through the crevices on to the floor. The peasants stood thoughtfully, with bared heads, and stamped their feet to get warm. The women, with their hands under the cotton aprons, and huddled together, looked with patient resigned faces toward the door of the living room.

At last, the bell summoned them into the room; they entered one by one, pushing each other aside. The dying man was lying on his back, his head deeply buried in the pillows; his yellow chest, covered with white hair, showed under the open shirt. The priest bent over him and laid the wafer upon his outstretched tongue. All knelt down, and, with their eyes raised to the ceiling, violently smote their chests, while they sighed and sniffled audibly. The women bent down to the ground and babbled: "Lamb of God that takest away the sins of the world."

The dog, worried by the frequent tinkling of the bell, growled ill-temperedly in the corner.

The priest had finished the last unction, and beckoned to the dying man's daughter.

"Where's yours, Antokowa?"

"Where should he be, your Reverence, if not at his daily job?"

For a moment the priest stood, hesitating, looked at the assembly, pulled his expensive fur tighter round his shoulders; but he could not think of anything suitable to say; so he only nodded to them and went out, giving them his white, aristocratic hand to kiss, while they bent toward his knees.

When he had gone they immediately dispersed. The short December day was drawing to its close. The wind had gone down, but the snow was now falling in large, thick flakes. The evening twilight crept into the room. Antokowa was sitting in front of the fire; she broke off twig after twig of the dry firewood, and carelessly threw them upon the fire.

She seemed to be purposing something, for she glanced again and again at the window, and then at the bed. The sick man had been lying quite still for a considerable time. She got very impatient, jumped up from her stool and stood still, eagerly listening and looking about; then she sat down again.

Night was falling fast. It was almost quite dark in the room. The little girl was dozing, curled up near the stove. The fire was flickering feebly with a reddish light which lighted up the woman's knees and a bit of the floor.

The dog started whining and scratched at the door. The chickens on the ladder cackled low and long.

Now a deep silence reigned in the room. A damp chill rose from the wet floor.

Antkowa suddenly got up to peer through the window at the village street; it was empty. The snow was falling thickly, blotting out everything at a few steps' distance. Undecided, she paused in front of the bed, but only for a moment; then she suddenly pulled away the feather-bed roughly and determinedly, and threw it on to the other bedstead. She took the dying man under the armpits and lifted him high up.

"Magda! Open the door!"

Magda jumped up, frightened, and opened the door.

"Come here . . . take hold of his feet."

Magda clutched at her grandfather's feet with her small hands and looked up in expectation.

"Well, get on . . . help me to carry him! Don't stare about . . . carry him, that's what you've got to do!" she commanded again, severely.

The old man was heavy, perfectly helpless, and apparently unconscious; he did not seem to realize what was being done to him. She held him tight and carried, or rather dragged him along, for the little girl had stumbled over the threshhold and had dropped his feet, which were drawing two deep furrows in the snow.

The penetrating cold had restored the dying man to consciousness, for in the yard he began to moan and utter broken words:

"Julisha . . . oh God . . . Ju . . ."

"That's right, you scream . . . scream as much as you like, nobody will hear you, even if you shout your mouth off."

She dragged him across the yard, opened the door of the pigsty with her foot, pulled him in, and propped him close to the wall.

The sow came forward, grunting, followed by her piglets.

"Malusha! malu, malu, malu!"

The pigs came out of the sty and she banged the door, but returned almost immediately, tore the shirt open on the old man's chest, tore off his chaplet, and took it with her.

"Now die, you leper!"

She kicked his naked leg, which was lying across the opening, with her clog, and went out.

The pigs were running about in the yard; she looked back at them from the passage.

"Malusha! malu, malu, malu!"

The pigs came running up to her, squeaking; she brought out a bowlful of potatoes and emptied it. The mother-pig began to eat greedily, and the piglets poked their pink noses into her and pulled at her until nothing but their loud smacking could be heard.

Antkowa lighted a small lamp above the fireplace and tore open the chaplet, with her back turned toward the window. A sudden gleam came into her eyes, when a number of banknotes and two silver roubles fell out.

"It wasn't just talk then, his saying that he'd put by the money for the funeral." She wrapped the money up in a rag and put it into the chest.

"You Judas! May eternal blindness strike you!" she said.

She put the pots and pans straight and tried to cheer the fire which was going out.

"Damn it! That plague of a boy has left me without a drop of water."

She stepped outside and called, "Ignatz! Hi! Ignatz!"

A good half-hour passed, then the snow creaked under stealthy footsteps and a shadow stole past the window. Antkowa seized a piece of wood and stood by the door which was flung wide open; a small boy of about nine entered the room.

"You stinking idler! Running about the village, are you? And not a drop of water in the house!"

Clutching him with one hand she beat the screaming child with the other.

"Mommy! I won't do it again . . . Mommy, leave off . . . Mom. . . ."

She beat him long and hard, giving vent to all her pent-up rage.

"Mother! Ow! Oh, you Saints! She's killing me!"

"You dog! You're loafing about, and not a drop of water do you fetch me, and there's no wood . . . am I to feed you for nothing, and you worrying me into the bargain?" She hit harder.

At last he tore himself away, jumped out by the window, and shouted at her with a tear-choked voice:

"May your paws rot off to the elbows, you dog of a mother! May you be stricken down, you sow! . . . . You may wait till you're manure before I fetch you any water!"

And he ran back to the village.

The room suddenly seemed strangely empty. The lamp above the fireplace trembled feebly. The little girl was sobbing to herself.

"What are you snivelling about?"

"Mommy . . . oh . . . oh . . . grandad . . ."

She leant, weeping, against her mother's knee.

"Leave off, idiot!"

She took the child on her lap, and pressing her close, she began to clean her head. The little thing babbled incoherently; she looked feverish; she rubbed her eyes with her small fists and presently went to sleep, still sobbing convulsively from time to time.

Soon afterwards the husband returned home. He was a huge fellow in a sheepskin, and wore a muffler round his cap. His face was blue with cold; his moustache, covered with hoar frost, looked like a brush. He knocked the snow off his boots, took muffler and cap off together, dusted the snow off his fur, clapped his stiff hands against his arms, pushed the bench toward the fire, and sat down heavily.

Antkowa took a saucepan full of cabbage off the fire and put it in front of her husband, cut a piece of bread and gave it to him, together with the spoon. The peasant ate in silence, but when he had finished he undid his fur, stretched his legs, and said: "Is there any more?"

She gave him the remains of their midday porridge; he spooned it up after he had cut himself another piece of bread; then he took out his pouch, rolled a cigarette and lighted it, threw some sticks on the fire and drew closer to it. A good while later he looked round the room. "Where the old man?"

"Where should he be? In the pigsty."

He looked questioningly at her.

"I should think so! What should he loll in bed for, and dirty the bedclothes? If he's got to give up, he will give up all the quicker in there. . . . Has he given me a single thing? What should he come to me for? Am I to pay for his funeral and give him his food? If he doesn't give up now—and I tell you, he is a tough one—then he'll eat us out of house and home. If Julina is to have everything let her look after him—that's nothing to do with me."

"Isn't my father . . . and cheated us, he has. I don't care . . . The old speculator!"

Antek swallowed the smoke of his cigarette and spat into the middle of the room.

"If he hadn't cheated us we should now have . . . wait a minute . . . we've got five . . . and seven and a half . . . makes . . . five and . . . seven. . . ."

"Twelve and a half. I had counted that up long ago; we could have kept a horse and three cows . . . bah! . . . the carrion!"

Again he spat furiously.

The woman got up, laid the child down on the bed, took the little rag bundle from the chest and put it into her husband's hand.

"What is that?"

"Look at it."

He opened the linen rag. An expression of greed came into his face; he bent forward toward the fire with his whole frame, so as to hide the money, and counted it over twice.

"How much is it?"

She did not know the money values.

"Fifty-four roubles."

"Lord! So much?"

Her eyes shone; she stretched out her hand and fondled the money.

"How did you come by it?"

"Ah, bah! . . . how? Don't you remember the old man telling us last year that he had put by enough to pay for his funeral?"

"That's right, he did say that."

"He had stitched it into his chaplet and I took it from him; holy things shouldn't knock about in a pigsty; that would be sinful; then I felt the silver through the linen, so I tore that off and took the money. That is ours; hasn't he wronged us enough?"

"That's God's truth. It's ours; that little bit at least is coming back to us. Put it with the other money; we can just do with it. Only yesterday Smoletz told me he wanted to borrow a thousand roubles from me; he will give his five acres of ploughed fields near the forest as security."

"Have you got enough?"

"I think I have."

"And will you begin to sow the fields yourself in the spring?"

"Rather . . . if I shouldn't have quite enough now, I will sell the sow; even if I should have to sell the little ones as well I must lend him the money. He won't be able to redeem it," he added. "I know what I know. We shall go to the lawyer and make a proper contract that the ground will be mine unless he repays the money within five years."

"Can you do that?"

Of course I can. How did Dumin get hold of Dyziak's fields? . . . Put it away; you may keep the silver; buy what you like with it. Where's Ignatz?"

"He's run off somewhere. Ha! no water, it's all gone . . ."

The peasant got up without a word, looked after the cattle, went in and out, fetched water and wood.

The supper was boiling in the saucepan. Ignatz cautiously crept into the room; no one spoke to him. They were all silent and strangely ill at ease. The old man was not mentioned; it was as if he had never been.

Antek thought of his five acres; he looked upon them as a certainty. Momentarily the old man came into his mind, and then again the sow he had meant to kill when she had finished with the sucking-pigs. Again and again he spat when his eyes fell on the empty bedstead, as if he wanted to get rid of an unpleasant thought. He was worried, did not finish his supper, and went to bed immediately after. He turned over from side to side; the potatoes and cabbage, groats and bread gave him indigestion, but he got over it and went to sleep.

When all was silent, Antkowa gently opened the door into the next room where the bundles of flax lay. From underneath these she fetched a packet of banknotes wrapped up in a linen rag, and added the money. She smoothed the notes many times over, opened them out, folded them up again, until she had gazed her fill; then she put out the light and went to bed beside her husband.

Meanwhile the old man had died. The pigsty, a miserable lean-to run up of planks and thatched with branches, gave no protection against wind and weather. No one heard the helpless old man entreating for mercy in a voice trembling with despair. No one saw him creep to the closed door and raise himself with a superhuman effort to try and open it. He felt death gaining upon him; from his heels it crept upwards to his chest, holding it as in a vise, and shaking him in terrible spasms; his jaws closed upon each other, tighter and tighter, until he was no longer able to open them and scream. His veins were hardening until they felt like wires. He reared up feebly, till at last he broke down on the threshold, with foam on his lips, and a look of horror at being left to die of cold, in his broken eyes; his face was distorted by an expression of anguish which was like a frozen cry. There he lay.

The next morning before dawn Antek and his wife got up. His first thought was to see what had happened to the old man.

He went to look, but could not get the door of the pigsty to open, for the corpse was barring it from the inside like a beam. At last, after a great effort, he was able to open it far enough to slip in, but he came out again at once, terror-stricken. He could hardly get across the yard and into the house fast enough; he was almost senseless with fear. He could not understand what was happening to him; his whole frame shook as in a fever, and he stood by the door panting and unable to utter a word.

Antkowa was at that moment teaching little Magda her prayer. She turned her head toward her husband with questioning eyes.

"Thy will be done . . ." she babbled thoughtlessly.

"Thy will. . . ."

". . . be done . . ."

". . . be done . . ." the kneeling child repeated like an echo.

"Well, is he dead?" she jerked out, ". . . on earth . . ."

". . . on earth . . ."

"To be sure, he's lying across the door," he answered under his breath.

". . . as it is in Heaven . . ."

". . . is in Heaven . . ."

"But we can't leave him there; people might say we took him there to get rid of him—we can't have that. . . ."

"What do you want me to do with him?"

"How do I know? You must do something."

"Perhaps we can get him across here?" suggested Antek.

"Look at that now . . . let him rot! Bring him in here? Not if . . ."

"Idiot, he will have to be buried."

"Are we to pay for his funeral? . . . but deliver us from evil . . . what are you blinking your silly eyes for? . . . go on praying."

". . . deliver . . . us . . . from . . . evil . . ."

"I shouldn't think of paying for that, that's Tomek's business by law and right."

". . . Amen . . ."

"Amen."

She made the sign of the cross over the child, wiped its nose with her fingers and went up to her husband.

He whispered: "We must get him across."

"Into the house . . . here?"

"Where else?"

"Into the cowshed; we can lead the calf out and lay him down on the bench, let him lie in state there, if he likes . . . such a one as he has been!"

"Monika!"

"Eh?"

"We ought to get him out there."

"Well, fetch him out then."

"All right . . . but . . ."

"You're afraid, what?"

"Idiot . . . damned . . ."

"What else?"

"It's dark."

"If you wait till it's day, people will see you."

"Let's go together."

"You go if you are so keen."

"Are you coming, you carrion, or are you not?" he shouted at her; "he's your father, not mine." And flung out of the room in a rage.

The woman followed him without a word.

When they entered the pigsty, a breath of horror struck them, like the exhalation from a corpse. The old man was lying there, cold as ice; one half of his body had frozen to the floor; they had to tear him off forcibly before they could drag him across the threshold and into the yard.

Antkowa began to tremble violently at the sight of him; he looked terrifying in the light of the grey dawn, on the white coverlet of snow, with his anguished face, wide-open eyes, and drooping tongue, on which the teeth had closed firmly. There were blue patches on his skin, and he was covered with filth from head to foot.

"Take hold," whispered the man, bending over him. "How horribly cold he is!"

The icy wind which rises just before the sun, blew into their faces, and shook the snow off the swinging twigs with a dry cackle.

Here and there a star was still visible against the leaden background of the sky. From the village came the creaking noise of the hauling of water, and the cocks crew as if the weather were going to change.

Antkowa shut her eyes and covered her hands with her apron, before she took hold of the old man's feet; they could hardly lift him, he was so heavy. They had barely put him down on a bench when she fled back into the house, throwing out a linen-rag to her husband to cover the corpse.

The children were busy scraping potatoes; she waited impatiently at the door.

"Have done . . . come in! . . . Lord, how long you are!"

"We must get someone to come and wash him," she said, laying the breakfast, when he had come in.

"I will fetch the deaf-mute."

"Don't go to work today."

"Go . . . no, not I . . ."

They did not speak again, and ate their breakfast without appetite, although as a rule they finished their four quarts of soup between them.

When they went out into the yard they walked quickly, and did not turn their heads toward the other side. They were worried, but did not know why; they felt no remorse; it was perhaps more a vague fear of the corpse, or fear of death, that shook them and made them silent.

When it was broad day, Antek fetched the village deaf-mute, who washed and dressed the old man, laid him out, and put a consecrated candle at his head.

Antek then went to give notice to the priest and to the Soltys of his father-in-law's death and of his own inability to pay for the funeral.

"Let Tomek bury him; he has got all the money."

The news of the old man's death spread rapidly throughout the village. People soon began to assemble in little groups to look at the corpse. They murmured a prayer, shook their heads, and went off to talk it over.

On the third day, shortly before the burial was to take place, Tomek's wife made her appearance at Antek's cottage.

In the passage she almost came nose to nose with her sister, who was just taking a pail of dishwater out to the cowshed.

"Blessed be Jesus Christ," she murmured, and kept her hand on the doorhandle.

"Now: look at that . . . soul of a Judas!" Antkowa put the pail down hard. "She's come to spy about here. Got rid of the old one somehow, didn't you? Hasn't he given everything to you . . . and you dare show yourself here, you trull! Have you come for the rest of the rags he left here, what?"

"I bought him a new sukmana at Whitsuntide; he can keep that on, of course, but I must have the sheepskin back, because it has been bought with money I have earned by the sweat of my brow," Tomekowa replied calmly.

"Have it back, you mangy dog, have it back?" screamed Antkowa. "I'll give it to you . . . you'll see what you will have . . ." and she looked round for an object that would serve her purpose. "Take it away? You dare! You have crawled to him and lickspittled till he became the idiot he was and made everything over to you and wronged me, and then . . ."

"Everybody knows that we bought the land from him; there are witnesses . . ."

"Bought it? Look at her! You mean to say you're not afraid to lie like that under God's living eyes? Bought it! Cheats, that's what you are, thieves, dogs! You stole the money from him first, and then . . . Didn't you make him eat out of the pig pail? Adam is a witness that he had to pick the potatoes out of the pig pail, ha! You've let him sleep in the cowshed, because, you said, he stank so that you couldn't eat. Fifteen acres of land and a dower-life like that . . . for so much property! And you've beaten him too, you swine, you monkey!"

"Hold your snout, or I'll shut it for you and make you remember, you sow, you trull!"

"Come on then, come on, you destitute creature!"

"I . . . destitute?"

"Yes, you! You would have rotted in a ditch, the vermin would have eaten you up, if Tomek hadn't married you."

"I, destitute? Oh, you carrion!"

They sprang at each other, clutching at each other's hair; they fought in the narrow passage, screaming themselves hoarse all the time.

"You street-walker, you loafer . . . there! that's one for you! There's one for my fifteen acres, and for all the wrong you have done me, you dirty dog!"

"For the love of God, you women, leave off, leave off! It's a sin and a shame!" cried the neighbors.

"Let me go, you leper, will you let me go?"

"I'll beat you to death, I will tear you to pieces, you filth!"

They fell down, hitting each other indiscriminately, knocked over the pail and rolled about in the pigwash. At last, speechless with rage and only breathing hard, they still banged away at each other. The men were hardly able to separate them. Purple in the face, scratched all over, and covered with filth, they looked like witches. Their fury was boundless; they sprang at each other again, and had to be separated a second time.

At last Antkowa began to sob hysterically with rage and exhaustion, tore her own hair and wailed: "Oh Jesus! Oh little child Jesus! Oh Mary! Look at this pestiferous woman . . . curse those heathen . . . oh! oh! . . ." she was only able to roar, leaning against the wall.

Tomekowa, meanwhile, was cursing and shouting outside the house, and banging her heels against the door.

The spectators stood in little groups, taking counsel with each other, and stamping their feet in the snow. The women looked like red spots dabbed onto the wall; they pressed their knees together, for the wind was penetratingly cold. They murmured remarks to each other from time to time, while they watched the road leading to the church, the spires of which stood out clearly behind the branches of the bare trees. Every minute some one or other wanted to have another look at the corpse; it was a perpetual coming and going. The small yellow flames of the candles could be seen through the half-open door, flaring in the draught, and momentarily revealing a glimpse of the dead man's sharp profile as he lay in the coffin. The smell of burning juniper floated through the air, together with the murmurings of prayers and the grunts of the deaf-mute.

At last the priest arrived with the organist. The white pine coffin was carried out and put into the cart. The women began to sing the usual lamentations, while the procession started down the long village street towards the cemetery.

The priest intoned the first words of the Service for the Dead, walking at the head of the procession with his black biretta on his head; he had thrown a thick fur cloak over his surplice; the wind made the ends of the stole flutter; the words of the Latin hymn fell from his lips at intervals, dully, as though they had been frozen; he looked bored and impatient, and let his eyes wander into the distance. The wind tugged at the black banner, and the pictures of heaven and hell on it wobbled and fluttered to and fro, as though anxious to display themselves to the rows of cottages on either side, where women with shawls over their heads and bare-headed men were standing huddled together.

They bowed reverently, made the sign of the cross, and beat their breasts.

The dogs were barking furiously from behind the hedges; some jumped on to the stone walls and broke into long-drawn howls.

Eager little children peeped out from behind closed windows, beside toothless used-up old people's faces, furrowed as fields in autumn.

A small crowd of boys in linen trousers and blue jackets with brass buttons, their bare feet stuck into wooden sandals, ran behind the priest, staring at the pictures of heaven and hell, and intoning the intervals of the chant with thin, quivering voices: a! o! . . . They kept it up as long as the organist did not change the chant.

Ignatz proudly walked in front, holding the banner with one hand and singing the loudest of all. He was flushed with exertion and cold, but he never relaxed, as though eager to show that he alone had a right to sing, because it was his grandfather who was being carried to the grave.

They left the village behind. The wind threw itself upon Antek, whose huge form towered above all the others, and ruffled his hair; but he did not notice the wind; he was entirely taken up with the horses and with steadying the coffin, which was tilting dangerously at every hole in the road.

The two sisters were walking close behind the coffin, murmuring prayers and eyeing each other with furious glances.

"Tsutsu! Go home! . . . Go home at once, you carrion!" One of the mourners pretended to pick up a stone. The dog, who had been following the cart, whined, put her tail between her legs, and fled behind a heap of stones by the roadside; when the procession had moved on a good bit, she ran after it in a semi-circle, and anxiously kept close to the horses, lest she should be prevented from following.

The Latin chant had come to an end. The women, with shrill voices, began to sing the old hymn: "He who dwelleth under the protection of the Lord."

It sounded thin. The blizzard, which was getting up, did not allow the singing to come to much. Twilight was falling.

The wind drove clouds of snow across from the endless, steppe-like plains, dotted here and there with skeleton trees, and lashed the little crowd of human beings as with a whip.

". . . and loves and keeps with faithful heart His word . . ." they intoned through the whistling of the tempest and the frequent shouts of Antek, who was getting breathless with cold: "Whoa! Whoa, my lads!"

Snowdrifts were beginning to form across the road like huge wedges, starting from behind trees and heaps of stones.

Again and again the singing was interrupted when the people looked round anxiously into the white void: it seemed to be moving when the wind struck it with dull thuds; now it towered in huge walls, now it dissolved like breakers, turned over, and furiously darted sprays of a thousand sharp needles into the faces of the mourners. Many of them returned half-way, fearing an increase of the blizzard; the others hurried on to the cemetery in the greatest haste, almost at a run. They got through the ceremony as fast as they could; the grave was ready; they quickly sang a little more, the priest sprinkled holy water on the coffin; frozen clods of earth and snow rolled down, and the people fled home.

Tomek invited everybody to his house, because "the reverend Father had said to him, that otherwise the ceremony would doubtless end in an ungodly way at the public-house."

Antek's answer to the invitation was a curse. The four of them, including Ignatz and the peasant Smoletz, turned into the inn.

They drank four quarts of spirits mixed with fat, ate three pounds of sausages, and talked about the money transaction.

The heat of the room and the spirits soon made Antek very drunk. He stumbled so on the way home that his wife took him firmly under the arm.

Smoletz remained at the inn to drink an extra glass in prospect of the loan, but Ignatz ran home ahead as fast as he could, for he was horribly cold.

"Look here, mother . . ." said Antek, "the five acres are mine! aha! mine, do you hear? In the autumn I shall sow wheat and barley, and in the spring we will plant potatoes . . . mine they are mine! . . . God is my comfort, sayest thou . . ." he suddenly began to sing.

The storm was raging and howling.

"Shut up! You'll fall down, and that will be the end of it."

". . . His angel keepeth watch . . ." he stopped abruptly. The darkness was impenetrable; nothing could be seen at a distance of two feet. The blizzard had reached its highest fury; whistling and howling on a gigantic scale filled the air, and mountains of snow hurled themselves upon the couple.

From Tomek's cottage came the sound of funeral chants and loud talking when they passed by.

"These heathen! These thieves! You wait—I'll show you my five acres! Then I shall have ten. You won't lord it over me! Dogs'-breed . . . aha! I'll work, I'll slave, but I shall get it, eh, mother? we will get it, what?" he hammered his chest with his fist, and rolled his drunken eyes.

He went on like this for a while, but as soon as they reached their home, the woman dragged him into bed, where he fell down like a dead man. But he did not go to sleep yet, for after a time he shouted: "Ignatz!"

The boy approached, but with caution, for fear of contact with the paternal foot.

"Ignatz, you dead dog! Ignatz, you shall be a first-class peasant, not a beggarly professional man," he bawled, and brought his fist down on the bedstead.

"The five acres are mine, mine! Foxy Germans,* you. . . . da. . . ." He went to sleep.

* The term "German" is used for foreigner generally, whom the Polish peasant despises.

[*Translated by Else Benecke and Marie Bush*]

George Bernard Shaw

GEORGE BERNARD SHAW *was born in 1856 to a family of Dublin "downstarts." After an unsuccessful start as a novelist—in nine years the pen that was to make his fortune earned him no more than twelve pounds—he became an unorthodox newspaper critic of the arts. Meanwhile he had joined the Fabian League and was propagating its brand of socialism in brilliant lectures and pamphlets. In 1892 he struck out in a new direction as a playwright* (Mrs. Warren's Profession, Arms and the Man, Caesar and Cleopatra, Man and Superman), *but not until King Edward VII attended a performance of* John Bull's Other Island *in 1905 did he overcome British prejudice against his witty, outrageous attacks upon marriage, religion, morality, and especially the politics and diplomacy of Great Britain. A red-bearded vegetarian who hated vivisection and who loved his wife Charlotte, he extended his reputation as an eccentric and rebel by pronouncements deliberately shocking to the public (he once addressed a New York audience as "boobs" without diminishing his vast American popularity). He received the Nobel Prize in 1925 and died in 1950 in his Victorian house at Ayot St. Lawrence. His plays (and the musicals based upon them) are continually produced throughout the civilized world, but few people know his lively short stories, of which the following selection is a sample.*

I arrived in Dublin on the evening of the 5th of August, and drove to the residence of my uncle, the Cardinal Archbishop. He is, like most of my family, deficient in feeling, and consequently cold to me personally. He lives in a dingy house, with a side-long view of the portico of his cathedral from the front windows, and of a monster national school from the back. My uncle maintains no retinue. The people believe that he is waited upon by angels. When I knocked at the door, an old woman, his only servant, opened it, and informed me that her master was then officiating in the cathedral, and that he had directed her to prepare dinner for me in his absence. An unpleasant smell of salt fish made me ask her what the dinner consisted of. She assured me that she had cooked all that could be permitted in His Holiness's house on a Friday. On my asking her further why on a Friday, she replied that Friday was a fast day. I bade her tell His Holiness that I had hoped to have the pleasure of calling on him shortly, and drove to a hotel in Sackville Street, where I engaged apartments and dined.

After dinner I resumed my eternal search—I know not for what: it drives me to and fro like another Cain. I sought in the streets without success. I went to the theater. The music was execrable, the scenery poor. I had seen the play a month before in London, with the same beautiful artist in the chief part. Two years had passed since, seeing her for the first time, I had hoped that she, perhaps, might be the long sought mystery. It had proved otherwise. On this night I looked at her and listened to her for the sake of that bygone hope, and applauded her generously when the curtain fell. But I went out lonely still. When I had supped at a restaurant, I returned to my hotel, and tried to read. In vain. The sound of feet in the corridors as the other occupants of the hotel went to bed distracted my attention from my book. Suddenly it occurred to me that I had never quite understood my uncle's character. He, father to a great flock of poor and ignorant Irish; an austere and saintly man, to whom livers of hopeless lives daily appealed for help heavenward; who was reputed never to have sent away a troubled peasant without relieving him of his burden by sharing it; whose knees were worn less by the altar steps than by the tears and embraces of the guilty and wretched: *he* had refused to humor my light extravagances, or to find time to talk with me of books, flowers, and music. Had I not been mad to expect it? Now that I needed sympathy myself, I did him justice. I desired to be with a true-hearted man, and to mingle my tears with his.

I looked at my watch. It was nearly an hour past midnight. In the corridor the lights were out, except one jet at the end. I threw a cloak upon my shoulders, put on a Spanish hat, and left my apartment, listening to the echoes of my measured steps retreating through the deserted passages. A strange sight arrested me on the landing of the grand staircase. Through an open door I saw the moonlight shining through the windows of a saloon in which some entertainment had recently taken place. I looked at my watch again: it was but one o'clock; and yet the guests had departed. I entered the room, my boots ringing loudly on the waxed boards. On a chair lay a child's cloak and a broken toy. The entertainment had been a children's party. I stood for a time looking at the shadow of my cloaked figure upon the floor, and at the disordered decorations, ghostly in the white light. Then I saw that there was a grand piano, still open, in the middle of the room. My fingers throbbed as I sat down before it; and expressed all that I felt in a grand hymn which seemed to thrill the cold stillness of the shadows into a deep hum of approbation, and to people the radiance of the moon with angels. Soon there was a stir without too, as if the rapture were spreading abroad. I took up the chant triumphantly with my voice, and the empty saloon resounded as though to the thunder of an orchestra.

"Hallo, sir!" "Confound you, sir—" "Do you suppose that this—" "What the deuce—?"

I turned; and silence followed. Six men, partially dressed, and with dishevelled hair, stood regarding me angrily. They all carried candles. One of them had a bootjack, which he held like a truncheon. Another, the foremost, had a pistol. The night porter was behind trembling.

"Sir," said the man with the revolver, coarsely, "may I ask whether you are mad, that you disturb people at this hour with such an unearthly noise?"

"Is it possible that you dislike it?" I replied, courteously.

"Dislike it!" said he, stamping with rage. "Why—damn everything—do you suppose we were enjoying it?"

"Take care: he's mad," whispered the man with the bootjack. I began to laugh. Evidently they did think me mad. Unaccustomed to my habits, and ignorant of music as they probably were, the mistake, however absurd, was not unnatural. I rose. They came closer to one another; and the night porter ran away.

"Gentlemen," I said, "I am sorry for you. Had you lain still and listened, we should all have been the better and happier. But what you have done, you cannot undo. Kindly inform the night porter that I am gone to visit my uncle, the Cardinal Archbishop. Adieu!"

I strode past them, and left them whispering among themselves. Some minutes later I knocked at the door of the Cardinal's house. Presently a window on the first floor was opened; and the moonbeams fell on a gray head, with a black cap that seemed ashy pale against the unfathomable gloom of the shadow beneath the stone sill.

"Who are you?"

"I am Zeno Legge."

"What do you want at this hour?"

The question wounded me. "My dear uncle," I exclaimed, "I know you do not intend it, but you make me feel unwelcome. Come down and let me in, I beg."

"Go to your hotel," he said sternly. "I will see you in the morning. Goodnight." He disappeared and closed the window.

I felt that if I let this rebuff pass, I should not feel kindly toward my uncle in the morning, nor, indeed, at any future time. I therefore plied the knocker with my right hand, and kept the bell ringing with my left until I heard the door-chain rattle within. The Cardinal's expression was grave nearly to moroseness as he confronted me on the threshold.

"Uncle," I cried, grasping his hand, "do not reproach me. Your door is never shut against the wretched. I am wretched. Let us sit up all night and talk."

"You may thank my position and not my charity for your admission, Zeno," he said. "For the sake of the neighbors, I had rather you played the fool in my study than upon my doorstep at this hour. Walk upstairs quietly, if you please. My house-keeper is a hard-working woman: the little sleep she allows herself must not be disturbed."

"You have a noble heart, uncle. I shall creep like a mouse."

"This is my study," he said, as we entered an ill-furnished den on the second floor. "The only refreshment I can offer you, if you desire any, is a bunch of raisins. The doctors have forbidden you to touch stimulants, I believe."

"By heaven—!" He raised his finger. "Pardon me: I was wrong to swear. But I had totally forgotten the doctors. At dinner I had a bottle of *Graves*."

"Humph! You have no business to be travelling alone. Your mother promised me that Bushy should come over here with you."

"Pshaw! Bushy is not a man of feeling. Besides, he is a coward. He refused to come with me because I purchased a revolver."

"He should have taken the revolver from you, and kept to his post."

"Why will you persist in treating me like a child, uncle? I am very impressionable, I grant you; but I have gone around the world alone, and do not need to be dry-nursed through a tour in Ireland."

"What do you intend to do during your stay here?"

I had no plans; and instead of answering I shrugged my shoulders and looked round the apartment. There was a statuette of the Virgin upon my uncle's desk. I looked at its face, as he was wont to look in the midst of his labors. I saw there eternal peace. The air became luminous with an infinite network of the jewelled rings of Paradise descending in roseate clouds upon us.

"Uncle," I said, bursting into the sweetest tears I had ever shed, "my wanderings are over. I will enter the Church, if you will help me. Let us read together the third part of *Faust*; for I understand it at last.

"Hush, man," he said, half rising with an expression of alarm. "Control yourself."

"Do not let my tears mislead you. I am calm and strong. Quick, let us have Goethe:

> *Das Unbeschreibliche,*
> *Hier ist gethan;*
> *Das Ewig-Weibliche,*
> *Zieht uns hinan."*

"Come, come. Dry your eyes and be quiet. I have no library here."

"But I have—in my portmanteau at the hotel," I said, rising. "Let me go for it, I will return in fifteen minutes."

"The devil is in you, I believe. Cannot—"

I interrupted him with a shout of laughter. "Cardinal," I said noisily, "you have become profane; and a profane priest is always the best of good fellows. Let us have some wine; and I will sing a German beer song."

"Heaven fogive me if I do you wrong," he said; "but I believe God has laid the expiation of some sin on your unhappy head. Will you favor me with your attention for a while? I have something to say to you, and I have also to get some sleep before my hour for rising, which is half-past five."

"My usual hour for retiring—when I retire at all. But proceed. My fault is not inattention, but over-susceptibility."

"Well, then, I want you to go to Wicklow. My reasons—"

"No matter what they may be," said I, rising again. "It is enough that you desire me to go. I shall start forthwith."

"Zeno, will you sit down and listen to me?"

I sank upon my chair reluctantly. "Ardor is a crime in your eyes, even when it is shown in your service," I said. "May I turn down the light?"

"Why?"

"To bring on my sombre mood, in which I am able to listen with tireless patience."

"I will turn it down myself. Will that do?"

I thanked him, and composed myself to listen in the shadow. My eyes, I felt, glittered. I was like Poe's raven.

"Now for my reasons for sending you to Wicklow. First, for your own sake. If you stay in town, or in any place where excitement can be obtained by any means, you will be in Swift's Hospital in a week. You must live in the country, under the eye of one upon whom I can depend. And you must have something to do to keep you out of mischief, and away from your music and painting and poetry, which, Sir John Richards writes to me, are dangerous for you in your present morbid state. Second, because I can entrust you with a task which, in the hands of a sensible man, might bring discredit on the Church. In short, I want you to investigate a miracle."

He looked attentively at me. I sat like a statue.

"You understand me?" he said.

"Nevermore," I replied, hoarsely. "Pardon me," I added, amused at the trick my imagination had played me, "I understand you perfectly. Proceed."

"I hope you do. Well, four miles distant from the town of Wicklow is a village called Four Mile Water. The resident priest is Father Hickey. You have heard of the miracles at Knock?"

I winked.

"I did not ask you what you think of them, but whether you have heard of them. I see you have. I need not tell you that even a miracle may do more harm than good to the Church in this country, unless it can be proved so thoroughly that her powerful and jealous enemies are silenced by the testimony of followers of their heresy. Therefore, when I saw in a Wexford newspaper last week a description of a strange manifestation of the Divine Power which was said to have taken place at Four Mile Water, I was troubled in my mind about it. So I wrote to Father Hickey, bidding him give me an account of the matter if it were true, and, if not, to denounce from the altar the author of the report, and to contradict it in the paper at once. This is his reply. He says—well, the first part is about Church matters: I need not trouble you with it. He goes on to say—"

"One moment. Is that his own handwriting? It does not look like a man's."

"He suffers from rheumatism in the fingers of his right hand; and his niece, who is an orphan, and lives with him, acts as his amanuensis. Well—"

"Stay. What is her name?"

"Her name? Kate Hickey."

"How old is she?"

"Tush, man, she is only a little girl. If she were old enough to concern you, I should not send you into her way. Have you any more questions to ask about her?"

"None. I can fancy her in a white veil at the rite of confirmation, a type of faith and innocence. Enough of her. What says the Reverend Hickey of the apparitions?"

"They are not apparitions. I will read you what he says. Ahem! 'In reply to your inquiries concerning the late miraculous event in this parish, I have to inform you that I can vouch for its truth, and that I can be confirmed not only by the inhabitants of the place, who are all Catholics, but by every person acquainted with the former situation of the graveyard referred to, including the Protestant Archdeacon of Baltinglas, who spends six weeks annually in the neighborhood. The newspaper account is incomplete and inaccurate. The following are the facts: About four years ago, a man named Wolfe Tone Fitzgerald settled in this village as a farrier. His antecedents did not transpire; and he had no family. He lived by himself; was very careless of his person; and when in his cups, as he often was, regarded the honor neither of God nor man in his conversation. Indeed if it were not speaking ill of the dead, one might say that he was a dirty, drunken, blasphemous blackguard. Worse again, he was, I fear, an atheist; for he never attended Mass, and gave His Holiness worse language even than he gave the Queen. I should have mentioned that he was a bitter rebel, and boasted that his grandfather had been out in '98, and his father with Smith O'Brien. At last he went by the name of Brimstone Billy, and was held up in the village as the type of all wickedness.

" 'You are aware that our graveyard, situated on the north side of the water, is famous throughout the country as the burial-place of the nuns of St. Ursula, the hermit of Four Mile Water, and many other holy people. No Protestant has ever ventured to enforce his legal right of interment there, though two have died in the parish within my own recollection. Three weeks ago, this Fitzgerald died in a fit brought on by drink; and a great hullabaloo was raised in the village when it became known that he would be buried in the graveyard. The body had to be watched to prevent its being stolen and buried at the cross-roads. My people were greatly disappointed when they were told I could do nothing to stop the burial, particularly as I of course refused to read any service on the occasion. However, I bade them not interfere; and the interment was effected on the 14th of July, late in the evening, and long after the legal hour. There was no disturbance. Next morning, the graveyard was found moved to the south side of the water, with the one newly-filled grave left behind on the north side; and thus they both remain. The departed saints would not lie with the reprobate. I can testify to it on the oath of a Christian priest; and if this will not satisfy those outside the Church, everyone, as I said before, who remembers where the graveyard was two months ago, can confirm me.

" 'I respectfully suggest that a thorough investigation into the truth of this miracle be proposed to a committee of Protestant gentlemen. They shall not be asked to accept a single fact on hearsay from my people. The ordnance maps show where the graveyard was; and anyone can see for himself where it is. I need not tell your Eminence what a rebuke this would be to those enemies of the holy Church that have sought to put a stain on her by discrediting the late wonderful manifestations at Knock Chapel. If they come to Four Mile Water, they need cross-examine no one. They will be asked to believe nothing but their own senses.

" 'Awaiting your Eminence's counsel to guide me further in the matter,

" ' I am, etc.' "

"Well, Zeno," said my uncle: "what do you think of Father Hickey now?"

"Uncle: do not ask me. Beneath this roof I desire to believe everything. The Reverend Hickey has appealed strongly to my love of legend. Let us admire the poetry of his narrative, and ignore the balance of probability between a Christian priest telling a lie on his oath and a graveyard swimming across a river in the middle of the night and forgetting to return."

"Tom Hickey is not telling a lie, sir. You may take my word for that. But he may be mistaken."

"Such a mistake amounts to insanity. It is true that I myself, awaking suddenly in the depth of night, have found myself convinced that the position of my bed had been reversed. But on opening my eyes the illusion ceased. I fear Mr. Hickey is mad. Your best course is this. Send down to Four Mile Water a perfectly sane investigator; an acute observer; one whose perceptive faculties, at once healthy and subtle, are absolutely unclouded by religious prejudice. In a word, send me. I will report to you the true state of affairs in a few days; and you can then make arrangements for transferring Hickey from the altar to the asylum."

"Yes, I had intended to send you. You are wonderfully sharp; and you would make a capital detective if you could only keep your mind to one point. But your chief qualification for this business is that you are too crazy to excite the suspicion of those whom you may have to watch. For the affair may be a trick. If so, I hope and believe that Hickey has no hand in it. Still, it is my duty to take every precaution."

"Cardinal: may I ask whether traces of insanity have ever appeared in our family?"

"Except in you and in my grandmother, no. She was a Pole; and you resemble her personally. Why do you ask?"

"Because it has often occurred to me that you are, perhaps, a little cracked. Excuse my candor; but a man who has devoted his life to the pursuit of a red hat; who accuses everyone else beside himself of being mad; and who is disposed to listen seriously to a tale of a peripatetic graveyard, can hardly be quite sane. Depend upon it, uncle, you want rest and change. The blood of your Polish grandmother is in your veins."

"I hope I may not be committing a sin in sending a ribald on the Church's affairs," he replied, fervently. "However, we must use the instruments put into our hands. Is it agreed that you go?"

"Had you not delayed me with this story, which I might as well have learned on the spot, I should have been there already."

"There is no occasion for impatience, Zeno. I must first send to Hickey to find a place for you. I shall tell him that you are going to recover your health, as, in fact, you are. And, Zeno, in Heaven's name be discreet. Try to act like a man of sense. Do not dispute with Hickey on matters of religion. Since you are my nephew, you had better not disgrace me."

"I shall become an ardent Catholic, and do you infinite credit, uncle."

"I wish you would, although you would hardly be an acquisition to the Church. And now I must turn you out. It is nearly three o'clock; and I need some sleep. Do you know your way back to your hotel?"

"I need not stir. I can sleep in this chair. Go to bed, and never mind me."

"I shall not close my eyes until you are safely out of the house. Come, rouse yourself, and say goodnight."

The following is a copy of my first report to the Cardinal:

FOUR MILE WATER, COUNTY WICKLOW,
"10th August.

MY DEAR UNCLE,

The miracle is genuine. I have affected perfect credulity in order to throw the Hickeys and the countryfolk off their guard with me. I have listened to their method of convincing skeptical strangers. I have examined the ordnance maps, and cross-examined the neighboring Protestant gentlefolk. I have spent a day upon the ground on each side of the water, and have visited it at midnight. I have considered the upheaval theories, subsidence theories, volcanic theories, and tidal wave theories which the provincial *savants* have suggested. They are all untenable. There is only one scoffer in the district, an Orangeman; and he admits the removal of the cemetery, but says it was dug up and transplanted in the night by a body of men under the command of Father Tom. This also is out of the question. The interment of Brimstone Billy was the first which had taken place for four years; and his is the only grave which bears a trace of recent digging. It is alone on the north bank; and the inhabitants shun it after nightfall. As each passer-by during the day throws a stone upon it, it will soon be marked by a large cairn. The graveyard, with a ruined stone chapel still standing in its midst, is on the south side. You may send down a committee to investigate the matter as soon as you please. There can be no doubt as to the miracle having actually taken place, as recorded by Hickey. As for me, I have grown so accustomed to it that if the county Wicklow were to waltz off with me to Middlesex, I should be quite impatient of any expressions of surprise from my friends in London.

Is not the above a businesslike statement? Away, then, with this stale miracle. If you would see for yourself a miracle which can never pall, a vision of youth and health to be crowned with garlands for ever, come down and see Kate Hickey, whom you suppose to be a little girl. Illusion, my lord cardinal, illusion! She is seventeen, with a bloom and a brogue that would lay your asceticism in ashes at a flash. To her I am an object of wonder, a strange man bred in wicked cities. She is courted by six feet of farming material, chopped off a spare length of coarse humanity by the Almighty, and flung into Wicklow to plough the fields. His name is Phil Langan; and he hates me. I have to consort with him for the sake of Father Tom, whom I entertain vastly by stories of your wild oats sown at Salamanca. I exhausted all my authentic anecdotes the first day; and now I invent gallant escapades with Spanish donnas, in which you figure as a youth of unstable morals. This delights Father Tom infinitely. I feel that I have done you a service by thus casting on the cold sacerdotal abstraction which formerly represented you in Kate's imagination a ray of vivifying passion.

What a country this is! A Hesperidean garden: such skies! Adieu, uncle.

Zeno Legge

Behold me, then, at Four Mile Water, in love. I had been in love frequently; but not oftener than once a year had I encountered a woman who affected me as seriously as Kate Hickey. She was so shrewd, and yet so flippant! When I spoke of art she yawned. When I deplored the sordidness of the world she laughed, and called me "poor fellow!" When I told her what a treasure of beauty and freshness she had she ridiculed me. When I reproached her with her brutality she became angry, and sneered at me for being what she called a fine gentleman. One sunny afternoon we were standing at the gate of her uncle's house, she looking down the dusty road for the detestable Langan, I watching the spotless azure sky, when she said:

"How soon are you going back to London?"

"I am not going back to London, Miss Hickey. I am not yet tired of Four Mile Water."

"I'm sure Four Mile Water ought to be proud of your approbation."

"You disapprove of my liking it, then? Or is it that you grudge me the happiness I have found there? I think Irish ladies grudge a man a moment's peace."

"I wonder you have ever prevailed on yourself to associate with Irish ladies, since they are so far beneath you."

"Did I say they were beneath me, Miss Hickey? I feel that I have made a deep impression on you."

"Indeed! Yes, you're quite right. I assure you I can't sleep at night for thinking of you, Mr. Legge. It's the best a Christian can do, seeing you think so mighty little of yourself."

"You are triply wrong, Miss Hickey: wrong to be sarcastic with me, wrong to pretend that there is anything unreasonable in my belief that you think of me sometimes, and wrong to discourage the candor with which I always avow that I think constantly of myself."

"Then you had better not speak to me, since I have no manners."

"Again! Did I say you had no manners? The warmest expressions of regard from my mouth seem to reach your ears transformed into insults. Were I to repeat the Litany of the Blessed Virgin, you would retort as though I had been reproaching you. This is because you hate me. You never misunderstand Langan, whom you love."

"I don't know what London manners are, Mr. Legge; but in Ireland gentlemen are expected to mind their own business. How dare you say I love Mr. Langan?"

"Then you do not love him?"

"It is nothing to you whether I love him or not."

"Nothing to me that you hate me and love another?"

"I didn't say I hated you. You're not so very clever yourself at understanding what people say, though you make such a fuss because they don't understand you." Here, as she glanced down the road again, she suddenly looked glad.

"Aha!" I said.

"What do you mean by 'Aha!'"

"No matter. I will now show you what a man's sympathy is. As you perceived just then, Langan—who is too tall for his age, by the bye—is coming to pay you a visit. Well, instead of staying with you, as a jealous woman would, I will withdraw."

"I don't care whether you go or stay, I'm sure. I wonder what you would give to be as fine a man as Mr. Langan."

"All I possess: I swear it! But solely because you admire tall men more than broad views. Mr. Langan may be defined geometrically as length without breadth; altitude without position; a line on the landscape, not a point in it."

"How very clever you are!"

"You do not understand me, I see. Here comes your lover, stepping over the wall like a camel. And here go I, out through the gate like a Christian. Good afternoon, Mr. Langan. I am going because Miss Hickey has something to say to you about me which she would rather not say in my presence. You will excuse me?"

"Oh, I'll excuse you," said he boorishly. I smiled, and went out. Before I was quite out of hearing, Kate whispered vehemently to him, "I *hate* that fellow."

I smiled again; but I had scarcely done so when my spirits fell. I walked hastily away with a coarse threatening sound in my ears like that of the clarionets whose sustained low notes darken the woodland in "Der Freischütz." I found myself presently at the graveyard. It was a barren place, enclosed by a mud wall with a gate to admit funerals, and numerous gaps to admit the peasantry, who made short cuts across it as they went to and fro between Four Mile Water and the market town. The graves were mounds overgrown with grass: there was no keeper; nor were there flowers, railings or any of the conventionalities that make an English graveyard repulsive. A great thorn bush, near what was called the grave of the holy sisters, was covered with scraps of cloth and flannel, attached by peasant women who had prayed before it. There were three kneeling there as I entered; for the reputation of the place had been revived of late by the miracle; and a ferry had been established close by, to conduct visitors over the route taken by the graveyard. From where I stood I could see on the opposite bank the heap of stones, perceptibly increased since my last visit, marking the deserted grave of Brimstone Billy. I strained my eyes broodingly at it for some minutes, and then descended the river bank and entered the boat.

"Good evenin t'your honor," said the ferryman, and set to work to draw the boat hand over hand by a rope stretched across the water.

"Good evening. Is your business beginning to fall off yet?"

"Faith, it never was as good as it mightabeen. The people that comes from the south side can see Billy's grave—Lord have mercy on him!—across the wather; and they think bad of payin a penny to put a stone over him. It's them that lives towrst Dublin that makes the journey. Your honor is the third I've brought from the south to north this blessed day."

"When do most people come? In the afternoon, I suppose?"

"All hours, sur, except afther dusk. There isn't a sowl in the counthry ud come within sight of that grave wanst the sun goes down."

"And you! do you stay here all night by yourself?"

"The holy heavens forbid! Is it me stay here all night? No, your honor: I tether the boat at siven o'hlyock, and lave Brimstone Billy—God forgimme!—to take care of it t'll mornin."

"It will be stolen some night, I'm afraid."

"Arra, who'd dar come next or near it, let alone stale it? Faith,

I'd think twice before lookin at it meself in the dark. God bless your honor, and gran'che long life."

I had given him sixpence. I went to the reprobate's grave and stood at the foot of it, looking at the sky, gorgeous with the descent of the sun. To my English eyes, accustomed to giant trees, broad lawns, and stately mansions, the landscape was wild and inhospitable. The ferryman was already tugging at the rope on his way back (I had told him I did not intend to return that way), and presently I saw him make the painter fast to the south bank; put on his coat; and trudge homeward. I turned toward the grave at my feet. Those who had interred Brimstone Billy, working hastily at an unlawful hour, and in fear of molestation by the people, had hardly dug a grave. They had scooped out earth enough to hide their burden, and no more. A stray goat had kicked away a corner of the mound and exposed the coffin. It occurred to me, as I took some of the stones from the cairn, and heaped them so as to repair the breach, that had the miracle been the work of a body of men, they would have moved the one grave instead of the many. Even from a supernatural point of view, it seemed strange that the sinner should have banished the elect, when, by their superior numbers, they might so much more easily have banished him.

It was almost dark when I left the spot. After a walk of half a mile, I recrossed the water by a bridge, and returned to the farmhouse in which I lodged. Here, finding that I had had enough of solitude, I only stayed to take a cup of tea. Then I went to Father Hickey's cottage.

Kate was alone when I entered. She looked up quickly as I opened the door, and turned away disappointed when she recognized me.

"Be generous for once," I said. "I have walked about aimlessly for hours in order to avoid spoiling the beautiful afternoon for you by my presence. When the sun was up I withdrew my shadow from your path. Now that darkness has fallen, shed some light on mine. May I stay half an hour?"

"You may stay as long as you like, of course. My uncle will soon be home. He is clever enough to talk to you."

"What! More sarcasms! Come, Miss Hickey, help me to spend a pleasant evening. It will only cost you a smile. I am somewhat cast down. Four Mile Water is a paradise; but without you, it would be a little lonely."

"It must be very lonely for you. I wonder why you came here."

"Because I heard that the women here were all Zerlinas, like you, and the men Masettos, like Mr. Phil—where are you going to?"

"Let me pass, Mr. Legge. I had intended never speaking to you again after the way you went on about Mr. Langan today; and I wouldn't either, only my uncle made me promise not to take any notice of you, because you were—no matter; but I won't listen to you any more on the subject."

"Do not go. I swear never to mention his name again. I beg your pardon for what I said: you shall have no further cause for complaint. Will you forgive me?"

She sat down, evidently disappointed by my submission. I took a chair, and placed myself near her. She tapped the floor impatiently with her foot. I saw that there was not a movement I could make, not a look, not a tone of my voice, which did not irritate her.

"You were remarking," I said, "that your uncle desired you to take no notice of me because—"

She closed her lips, and did not answer.

"I fear I have offended you again by my curiosity. But indeed, I had no idea that he had forbidden you to tell me the reason."

"He did not forbid me. Since you are so determined to find out—"

"No: excuse me. I do not wish to know, I am sorry I asked."

"Indeed! Perhaps you would be sorrier still to be told. I only made a secret of it out of consideration for you."

"Then your uncle has spoken ill of me behind my back. If that be so, there is no such thing as a true man in Ireland. I would not have believed it on the word of any woman alive save yourself."

"I never said my uncle was a backbiter. Just to show you what he thinks of you, I will tell you, whether you want to know it or not, that he bid me not mind you because you were only a poor mad creature, sent down here by your family to be out of harm's way."

"Oh, Miss Hickey!"

"There now! you have got it out of me; and I wish I had bit my tongue out first. I sometimes think—that I maytnt sin!—that you have a bad angel in you."

"I am glad you told me this," I said gently. "Do not reproach yourself for having done so, I beg. Your uncle has been misled by what he has heard of my family, who are all more or less insane. Far from being mad, I am actually the only rational man named Legge in the three kingdoms. I will prove this to you, and at the same time keep your indiscretion in countenance, by telling you something I ought not to tell you. It is this. I am not here as an invalid or a chance tourist. I am here to investigate the miracle. The Cardinal, a shrewd if somewhat erratic man, selected mine from all the long heads at his disposal to come down here, and find out the truth of Father Hickey's story. Would he have entrusted such a task to a madman, think you?"

"The truth of—who dared to doubt my uncle's word? And so you are a spy, a dirty informer."

I started. The adjective she had used, though probably the commonest expression of contempt in Ireland, is revolting to an Englishman.

"Miss Hickey," I said: "there is in me, as you have said, a bad angel. Do not shock my good angel—who is a person of taste—quite away from my heart, lest the other be left undisputed monarch of it. Hark! The chapel bell is ringing the angelus. Can you, with that sound softening the darkness of the village night, cherish a feeling of spite against one who admires you?"

"You come between me and my prayers," she said hysterically, and began to sob. She had scarcely done so, when I heard voices without. Then Langan and the priest entered.

"Oh, Phil," she cried, running to him, "take me away from him: I can't bear—" I turned towards him, and shewed him my dog-tooth in a false smile. He felled me at one stroke, as he might have felled a poplar-tree.

"Murdher!" exclaimed the priest. "What are you doin, Phil?"

"He's an informer," sobbed Kate. "He came down here to spy on you, uncle, and to try and show that the blessed miracle was a make-up. I knew it long before he told me, by his insulting ways. He wanted to make love to me."

I rose with difficulty from beneath the table, where I had lain motionless for a moment.

"Sir," I said, "I am somewhat dazed by the recent action of Mr. Langan, whom I beg, the next time he converts himself into a fulling-mill, to do so at the expense of a man more nearly his equal in strength than I. What your niece has told you is partly true. I am indeed the Cardinal's spy; and I have already reported to him that the miracle is a genuine one. A committee of gentlemen will wait on you tomorrow to verify it, at my suggestion. I have thought that the proof might be regarded by them as more complete if you were taken by surprise. Miss Hickey: that I admire all that is admirable in you is but to say that I have a sense of the beautiful. To say that I love you would be mere profanity. Mr. Langan: I have in my pocket a loaded pistol, which I carry from a silly English prejudice against your countrymen. Had I been the Hercules of the ploughtail, and you in my place, I should have been a dead man now. Do not redden: you are safe as far as I am concerned."

"Let me tell you before you leave my house for good," said Father Hickey, who seemed to have become unreasonably angry, "that you should never have crossed my threshold if I had known you were a spy: no, not if your uncle were his Holiness the Pope himself."

Here a frightful thing happened to me. I felt giddy, and put my hand to my head. Three warm drops trickled over it. Instantly I became murderous. My mouth filled with blood, my eyes were blinded with it; I seemed to drown in it. My hand went involuntarily to the pistol. It is my habit to obey my impulses instantaneously. Fortunately the impulse to kill vanished before a sudden perception of how I might miraculously humble the mad vanity in which these foolish people had turned upon me. The blood receded from my ears; and I again heard and saw distinctly.

"And let *me* tell you," Langan was saying, "that if you think yourself handier with cold lead than you are with your fists, I'll exchange shots with you, and welcome, whenever you please. Father Tom's credit is the same to me as my own; and if you say a word against it, you lie."

"His credit is in my hands," I said. "I am the Cardinal's witness. Do you defy me?"

"There is the door," said the priest, holding it open before me. "Until you can undo the visible work of God's hand your testimony can do no harm to me."

"Father Hickey," I replied, "before the sun rises again upon Four Mile Water, I will undo the visible work of God's hand, and bring the pointing finger of the scoffer upon your altar."

I bowed to Kate, and walked out. It was so dark that I could not at first see the garden-gate. Before I found it, I heard through the window Father Hickey's voice, saying, "I wouldn't for ten pound that this had happened, Phil. He's as mad as a march hare. The Cardinal told me so."

I returned to my lodging, and took a cold bath to cleanse the blood from my neck and shoulder. The effect of the blow I had received was so severe, that even after the bath and a light meal I felt giddy and languid. There was an alarm-clock on the mantelpiece: I wound it; set the alarm for half-past twelve; muffled it so that it should not disturb the people in the adjoining room; and went to bed, where I slept soundly for an hour and a quarter. Then the alarm roused me, and I sprang up before I was thoroughly awake. Had I hesitated, the desire to relapse into perfect sleep would have overpowered me. Although the muscles of my

neck were painfully stiff, and my hands unsteady from the nervous disturbance produced by the interruption of my first slumber,
I dressed myself resolutely, and, after taking a draught of cold
water, stole out of the house. It was exceedingly dark; and I had
some difficulty in finding the cowhouse, whence I borrowed a
spade, and a truck with wheels, ordinarily used for moving sacks
of potatoes. These I carried in my hands until I was beyond earshot of the house, when I put the spade on the truck, and
wheeled it along the road to the cemetery. When I approached
the water, knowing that no one would dare to come thereabout
at such an hour, I made greater haste, no longer concerning myself about the rattling of the wheels. Looking across to the opposite bank, I could see a phosphorescent glow, marking the
lonely grave of Brimstone Billy. This helped me to find the ferry
station, where, after wandering a little and stumbling often, I
found the boat, and embarked with my implements. Guided by
the rope, I crossed the water without difficulty; landed; made fast
the boat; dragged the truck up the bank; and sat down to rest on
the cairn at the grave. For nearly a quarter of an hour I sat
watching the patches of jack-o'-lantern fire, and collecting my
strength for the work before me. Then the distant bell of the
chapel clock tolled one. I rose; took the spade; and in about ten
minutes uncovered the coffin, which smelt horribly. Keeping to
windward of it, and using the spade as a lever, I contrived with
great labor to place it on the truck. I wheeled it without accident
to the landing-place, where, by placing the shafts of the truck
upon the stern of the boat and lifting the foot by main strength,
I succeeded in embarking my load after twenty minutes' toil, during which I got covered with clay and perspiration, and several
times all but upset the boat. At the southern bank I had less
difficulty in getting truck and coffin ashore, and dragging them
up to the graveyard.

It was now past two o'clock, and the dawn had begun; so that
I had no further trouble from want of light. I wheeled the coffin
to a patch of loamy soil which I had noticed in the afternoon
near the grave of the holy sisters. I had warmed to my work; my

neck no longer pained me; and I began to dig vigorously, soon making a shallow trench, deep enough to hide the coffin with the addition of a mound. The chill pearl-colored morning had by this time quite dissipated the darkness. I could see, and was myself visible, for miles around. This alarmed me, and made me impatient to finish my task. Nevertheless, I was forced to rest for a moment before placing the coffin in the trench. I wiped my brow and wrists, and again looked about me. The tomb of the holy women, a massive slab supported on four stone spheres, was grey and wet with dew. Near it was the thornbush covered with rags, the newest of which were growing gaudy in the radiance which was stretching up from the coast on the east. It was time to finish my work. I seized the truck; laid it alongside the grave; and gradually prized the coffin off with the spade until it rolled over into the trench with a hollow sound like a drunken remonstrance from the sleeper within. I shovelled the earth round and over it, working as fast as possible. In less than a quarter of an hour it was buried. Ten minutes more sufficed to make the mound symmetrical, and to clear the traces of my work from the adjacent sward. Then I flung down the spade; threw up my arms; and vented a sigh of relief and triumph. But I recoiled as I saw that I was standing on a barren common, covered with furze. No product of man's handiwork was near me except my truck and spade and the grave of Brimstone Billy, now as lonely as before. I turned towards the water. On the opposite bank was the cemetery, with the tomb of the holy women, the thornbush with its rags stirring in the morning breeze, and the broken mud wall. The ruined chapel was there too, not a stone shaken from its crumbling walls, not a sign to shew that it and its precinct were less rooted in their place than the eternal hills around.

I looked down at the grave with a pang of compassion for the unfortunate Wolfe Tone Fitzgerald, with whom the blessed would not rest. I was even astonished, though I had worked expressly to this end. But the birds were astir, and the cocks crowing. My landlord was an early riser. I put the spade on the truck again, and hastened back to the farm, where I replaced them in the cow-house. Then I stole into the house, and took a clean pair of boots, an overcoat, and a silk hat. These, with a change of linen, were sufficient to make my appearance respectable. I went out again, bathed in the Four Mile Water, took a last look at the cemetery, and walked to Wicklow, whence I travelled by the first train to Dublin.

Some months later, at Cairo, I received a packet of Irish newspapers, and a leading article, cut from The Times, on the subject of the miracle. Father Hickey had suffered the meed of his inhospitable conduct. The committee, arriving at Four Mile Water the day after I left, had found the graveyard exactly where it had formerly stood. Father Hickey, taken by surprise, had attempted to defend himself by a confused statement, which led the committee to declare finally that the miracle was a gross imposture. The Times, commenting on this after adducing a number of examples of priestly craft, remarked, "We are glad to learn that the Rev. Mr. Hickey has been permanently relieved of his duties as the parish priest of Four Mile Water by his ecclesiastical superior. It is less gratifying to have to record that it has been found possible to obtain two hundred signatures to a memorial embodying the absurd defense offered to the committee, and expressing unabated confidence in the integrity of Mr. Hickey."

Grazia Deledda

THE SARDINIAN FOX

GRAZIA DELEDDA was born in Sardinia in 1875. Though her schooling stopped at the primary level, when she was thirteen she started writing her first novel, Sangue Sardo. At scarcely twenty, she won high praise for her volume of Sardinian tales from which "The Sardinian Fox" is drawn. These and other successes, notably Elias Portolu, which brought her fame throughout Europe, encouraged her to continue writing, and by the time of her death in 1936, she could boast of more than thirty novels, numerous short stories, and the Nobel Prize for 1926. A Roman by address after her marriage in 1900, in her books she seldom left the world of the intense, rather simple native folk of the type she knew as neighbors in Sardinia. She understood their psychology perfectly, and her short stories, while lacking intellectual profundity, reveal with emotional penetration and authenticity the passions and persuasions, the manners and morals of the peasant personality.

The long, warm May days had come back, and Ziu* Tomas again sat as he had the year before—ten years before—in the open courtyard in front of his house, which was the last in a bunch of little, black buildings huddled against the gray slope of a mountain. But in vain spring sent its breath of wild voluptuousness up there: the decrepit old man, motionless be-

---

* "Zia" and "Ziu" literally mean "aunt" and "uncle" but are sometimes used as complimentary titles for older people of some standing.

tween his old black dog and his old yellow cat, seemed as stony and insensible as everything around him.

Only, at night, the smell of the grass reminded him of the pastures where he had spent most of his life; and when the moon rose out of the sea, far off, as huge and golden as the sun, and the coastal mountains, black beneath a silver sky, and all the huge valley and the fantastic semicircle of hills before and to the right of the horizon were covered with shimmering veils and areas of light and shadow, then the old man used to think of childish things, of Lusbé, the devil who leads damned souls to the pasture, after they have been changed into wild boars; and if the moon hid behind a cloud, he thought seriously of the seven calving cows which the planet, at that moment going to supper, devoured calmly in its hiding place.

He almost never spoke; but one evening his granddaughter Zana, when she shook him to tell him it was bedtime, found him so stubbornly silent, erect, and rigid on his stool that she thought he was dead. Frightened, she called Zia Lenarda, her neighbor, and both women succeeded in moving the old man, helping him into the house where he stretched out on the mat in front of the hearth.

"Zia Lenarda, we have to call a doctor. Grandfather is as cold as a corpse," the girl said, touching the old man.

"Our doctor's gone away. He went to the mainland for two months to study ear diseases, because he says they're all deaf around here when he asks them to pay the rent on his pastures . . . as if he hadn't bought all that land with the people's money, may justice find him! And now, instead of him, we have that foolish snob of a city doctor, who thinks he's the court physician of the king of Spain. Who knows if he'll come or not?"

"Zia Lenarda, he has to come. He charges twenty lire a visit!" Zana said haughtily.

And the woman went off.

The substitute was living in the regular doctor's house, the only habitable one in the whole village. Surrounded by gardens, with terraces and arbors, with a great courtyard covered with grapevines and wistaria, the house was a comfort even to this substitute, who came from a town that, though small, had all the necessities, vices, murderers, loose women, and gambling houses that the larger cities have.

Zia Lenarda found him reading a yellow-backed book in the dining room, which opened onto the courtyard; no doubt a medical work, she thought, judging by the intensity with which he consumed it, his nearsighted eyes stuck to the page, his white fists supporting his dark, rather soft cheeks, his thick lips parted to show his protruding teeth.

The maid had to call him twice before he noticed the woman's presence. He closed the book sharply and, slack and distracted, followed Zia Lenarda. She didn't dare to speak, and went before him as if to show him the way, leaping, agile and silent, down from rock to rock over the rough lanes, struck by the moon.

Below, in the valley's depth, in front of the woman's darkened window, the doctor looked up and saw the mountains' silver peaks. The pure smell of the valley was mixed with the sheepfold odor that came from the hovels, from the forms of shepherds crouched here and there on the steps before their doors: all was sad and magnificent. But in the courtyard of Ziu Tomas the smell of hay and sage dominated; and in front of the low wall by the embankment, with the huge moon and a star almost scraping her head, the doctor saw a woman's form so slender, especially from the waist down, so shrouded, without outlines, that she gave him the impression of a bust set on a narrow pedestal.

Seeing him, she went back to the kitchen, got a light, and knelt down beside her grandfather's mat, while Zia Lenarda ran into the other room to fetch a painted chair for the doctor.

Then the girl raised her head and looked into his eyes, and he felt a sensation that he would never forget. He thought he had never seen a woman's face more lovely and more enigmatic: a broad forehead covered almost to the eyebrows (one higher than the other) by two bands of black, shiny hair; a narrow, prominent chin; smooth cheekbones that cast a little shadow on her cheeks; and white, straight teeth, which gave a suggestion of cruelty to her proud mouth; while her great black eyes were full of sadness and a deep languor.

Seeing herself examined in this way, Zana lowered her eyes and didn't raise them again; but when her grandfather didn't answer the doctor's questions, she murmured: "He's been deaf for twenty years or more."

"You don't say? Well, at least you might prepare a foot bath for him; his feet are frozen."

"A foot bath? Won't that hurt him?" Zia Lenarda asked, consulting Zana. "He hasn't taken his shoes off for eight months."

"Well, then, are you going to leave him here now?"

"Where else can I put him? He's always slept here."

The doctor got up, and after he had written out a prescription, he gave it to Zana and looked around him.

The place was black as a cave; he could make out a passage at the back, with a wooden ladder; everything indicated the direst poverty. He looked with pity at Zana, so white and thin that she reminded him of an asphodel blooming at the mouth of a cavern.

"The old man is undernourished," he said hesitantly, "and you are, too, I believe. You'd both need a more plentiful diet. If you can . . ."

She understood at once. "We can do anything!"

Her expression was so full of scorn that he went away almost intimidated.

Up, from stone to stone, along the sandstone path he went back to his oasis; the moon silvered the arbor, and the wistaria blooms hung like bunches of fantastic grapes whose very perfume was intoxicating. The old maidservant was spinning in the doorway, and with Zana's strange face still before his eyes, he asked: "Do you know Ziu Tomas Acchittu?"

Who didn't know the Acchittu family?

"They're known even in Nuoro, my prize! More than one learned man wants to marry Zana."

"Yes, she's beautiful. I had never seen her before."

"She never goes out. There's no need of that, to be sure. The rose smells sweet even indoors. Foreigners come from everywhere, even from Nuoro, and pass by just to see her."

"What? Has the town crier gone around to announce her beauty?"

"That's not it, my soul! The old man is so rich he doesn't know how much he has. Land as big as all of Spain, and they say he has more than twenty thousand *scudi** in a hole somewhere. Only Zana knows the place. That's why she doesn't want even Don Juacchinu, who's noble but not so rich."

"And may I ask where these riches come from?"

"Where do the things of this world come from? They say the old man (on my life, I can't say yes or no about it, myself) had a hand in more than one bandit raid in the good old days when the dragoons weren't as quick as the *carabinieri* are nowadays. Then, in those days, more than one shepherd came home with one sack full of cheese and the other of gold coins and silver plate . . ."

The old woman began to relate all this, and it seemed that she drew the stories from her memory like the thread from her distaff; the man listened, in the shadow of the arbor, sprinkled with gold pieces, and now he understood Zana's laugh and her words: "We can do anything!"

The day after the first visit he was back at the house: the old man was sitting on the mat, calmly gumming his barley bread soaked in cold water, the dog on one side of him, the cat on the other. The sun slanted in through the low door, and the May wind bore away the wild, leathery smell of the old man.

"How's it going?"

"Well, as you can see," Zana said, with a hint of scorn in her voice.

"Yes, I can see. How old are you, Ziu Tomas?"

"Yes, I still can," the old man said, showing the few, blackened teeth he had left.

"He thought you said *chew*. Grandfather—" Zana said, bend-

* "Scudo"—a former Italian silver coin equivalent to about 97 U.S. cents.

ing over the old man, showing him her hands with all the fingers sticking out except the right thumb, "—like this, isn't that right?"

"Yes, ninety, may God preserve me."

"Good for you. I hope you live to be a hundred—more than a hundred! And you, Zana, you've stayed here with him, alone?"

She told him how all her relatives were dead, her aunts, uncles, cousins, the old, the children; and she spoke calmly of death as of a simple event without importance; but when the doctor turned to the old man, shouting: "Change your way of living! Cleanliness! Roast meat! Good wine! and make Zana enjoy herself a little, Ziu Tomas."

Then the old man asked: "When's he coming back?"

"Who?"

"Oh," Zana said, "it's just that he's waiting for our regular doctor to come back and cure his ears."

"Wonderful! Our doctor's fame is assured then."

The old man, who went on understanding everything in his own way, touched the sleeve of his torn jacket, which was shiny with grease. "Dirty? It's the custom. People who are well off don't have to make a show of it."

As a matter of fact, the doctor observed that the cleanest people in town were the poor; the rich paid no attention to their clothes, scorning appearances, and also finding it convenient perhaps. Here, one day, was Zia Lenarda, waiting for the doctor in the courtyard, dressed like a servant, though she too was a woman of means, with property and flocks, so rich that in spite of her forty-three years she had married a handsome boy of twenty.

"Good morning, doctor, your honor. I'd like to ask a favor of you. My husband Jacu is off on military service: now it's shearing time and I want him to come home on leave. Your honor doesn't know anyone at the Court?"

"No, unfortunately, my good woman."

"I asked our regular doctor about it. Take care of it, I said, if you pass through Rome. But he always says yes, then he forgets. My Jacu is a handsome boy (I'm not boasting just because I'm his wife) and just as good as honey . . . with a little pushing he could get everything. . . ."

She made a gesture of pushing with her spindle, but the doctor went off, sighing.

"It's not enough to be handsome and good in this world to get what we want, my dear lady."

And he went back to his oasis, thinking of Zana and of many things in his past. He was thinking that in his youth he had been handsome and good and yet he had got nothing, not love, or wealth, or even pleasure. True, he had not hunted for them; perhaps he had been waiting for them to offer themselves spontaneously; and as he had waited and waited, time had passed in futility. But in the past few years he had been seized sometimes by fits of mad rebellion; he sold his property and went off to search urgently for love, wealth, pleasure. But one day he realized that these cannot be bought, and when his wallet was empty, he went back to his few patients, joked with them good-naturedly, took long, absent-minded walks, and read yellow-backed French novels.

Zia Lenarda, on her side, convinced that good looks can obtain everything, seeing that the doctor went to the Acchittu's every day even though the old man was well, turned to Zana.

"You tell him, treasure! Everyone's getting ready for the shearing. What can I do, with everything turned over to the hired hands? The doctor looks at you with eyes as big as doorknobs. . . . How can he help it, dear heart? If you tell him to ask for Jacu's leave, he can't say no."

But Zana didn't promise; and when, after the tedium of those long days when the warm wind, the empty blue sky, the bright sun created an ineffable sadness, the doctor went at evening to the courtyard of Ziu Tomas, where he sat astride the painted chair in front of the hedge, full of fireflies and stars, she joked with him and asked him what causes certain diseases, how poisons are made, and she spoke calmly of many things, but she didn't ask the favor her neighbor wanted.

Sometimes Zia Lenarda herself, seated on the low wall, spun in the dark and joined in the conversation. This annoyed the doctor, who wanted to be alone with Zana after he had convinced the old man to go to bed early because the night air was bad for the deaf. The older woman spoke of nothing but the shearing.

"If you could just see the celebration, your honor! Nothing is more fun, not even the feast of San Michele and San Constantino. I'd invite you if Jacu came, but without him the feast would be like a funeral for me."

"Well, my good woman, do you want to know the truth? They'd give Jacu leave only if you were ill, and you're as healthy as a goat."

Then she began to complain; she had had so many aches since Jacu left, and now that shearing time approached, she really was suffering mortally. To convince the doctor more readily, she took to her bed. He was touched. He wrote out the certificate and ordered some medicine. Zana waited on her neighbor, poured out the dosage, looking at it in the reddish light of the oil lantern, and murmured: "It's not poison, is it?"

Then she went back to the courtyard, where the doctor was sitting on the painted chair. It was an evening in early June, warm already and scented. Night of love and memories! And the memories came, sweet and bitter, from the doctor's dark, tortuous past, as from the dark and tortuous valley came the sweet and bitter odor of the oleander. He drew his chair closer to the low wall were Zana was sitting, and they began their usual conversation. Occasionally a shepherd passed in the lane, without too much surprise at hearing the doctor's voice in the courtyard of Ziu Tomas. By now everybody believed that the doctor was regularly courting Zana, and they were sure that Zana would accept him, otherwise she would have kept him at a distance. But the two of them spoke of matters apparently innocent, of grasses, poisonous plants, medicaments.

"Oleander? No, that isn't poisonous, but hemlock is. Do you know what it looks like?"

"Who doesn't?"

"It's called the sardonic plant. It makes people die laughing
. . . like you!"

"Let go of my wrist, doctor. I don't have the fever like Zia
Lenarda."

"I have the fever, Zana."

"Well, take some quinine. Or is that poison, too?"

"Why do you keep talking about poisons tonight? Are you plan-
ning to kill somebody? If you are, I'll kill him for you at once . . .
but . . ."

"But?"

"But . . ."

He took her wrist again, and she allowed it. It was dark anyway,
and nobody could see from the lane.

"Yes, I do want some poison. For the fox."

"What? She comes this close?"

"She certainly does! Let go of me," she added in a whisper,
twisting threateningly, but he took her other hand and held her
fast, as if she were a thief.

"Give me a kiss, Zana. Just one."

"You can go and kiss a firebrand. Well, all right, if you give me
the poison. That fox even comes and steals our newborn
lambs . . ."

When Jacu's application for leave had been mailed off, along
with the doctor's certificate, Zia Lenarda recovered and went
back to minding her neighbors' business. And without any surprise
she realized that the doctor was aflame like a field of stubble. He
went back and forth in the lane like a boy, and even twice in a
day he visited Ziu Tomas, claiming he would cure the old man's
deafness before his colleague came back from the mainland. Zana
seemed impassive; often she wouldn't make an appearance, but
stayed shut in her room, like a spider in its hole.

On Sundays, the only day she went out—to go to mass—the
doctor waited for her in front of the church.

One after another, the women came up the winding lane, stiff
in their holiday clothes, their hands folded on their embroidered

aprons, or carrying their babies on their arms, in red cloaks marked
with a blue cross. When they reached a certain spot they turned
toward Mount Nuoro, guarded by a statue of the Redeemer, and
blessed themselves. The sun gleamed on the gold of their sashes
and illuminated their fine Greek profiles. But the doctor, as if
bewitched, looked only at Zana, and the old gossips thought:
"The daughter of Tomas Acchittu has given him mandrake to
drink. . . ."

One day, among the few men who took part in the women's
procession, there was Jacu, home on leave. He was really handsome, no two ways about it: tall, ruddy, clean-shaven, with green
eyes so bright that the women lowered theirs when they went by
him, even if he were paying no attention to them. Military life
had given him the air of a conqueror, but of things far more
serious than mere women. As soon as he arrived, he had gone up
to the doctor's to thank him, bringing him a young kid and an
invitation to the famous shearing. The doctor spoke to him in
dialect; he answered in proper Italian. And when the doctor
asked, rather pointedly: "Are you inviting many people?" he
answered: "Yes, because it's a big family, and a man like me—
well, I may have many enemies, but I also have many friends.
Besides, I'm broad-minded, and I'm inviting even the relatives of
Lenarda's first husband. They can kill me, if I'm lying. And if she
had had three husbands, I'd invite the relatives of them all."

"You're a man of the world, I see. Good for you. I suppose
you'll invite your neighbors, too."

Being a man of the world, Jacu pretended to know nothing of
the doctor's madness over Zana.

"Of course, a neighbor is more than a relative."

The day of the shearing came, and Zana, Zia Lenarda, and the
other women took seats in the cart that Jacu drove.

The sheepfold was on the plateau, and the heavy vehicle,
drawn by two black steers, scarcely broken, bounced up along the
rocky path; but the women weren't afraid, and Zana, her hands
clasping her knees, was calmly crouched down as if in front of her

own hearth. She seemed sad, but her eyes gleamed with a kind of hidden lightning, like a far-off blaze, shining on a dark night in the heart of a forest.

"Neighbor," Jacu said, good-humoredly, "hang me, but you have a face like a funeral. He'll come, he'll come. He's coming later, with the priest, as soon as mass is over. . . ."

"Cheer up, Zana," the women said then, joking a little maliciously, "I hear a horse now, trotting like the devil himself."

"What a chair that is! How much would that chain cost? Nine *reali?*"*

Then Zana grew angry. "Evil take you all. Leave me alone. I can't bear him. The crows can pluck out my eyes if I even look at that man's face today. . . ."

The doctor and the priest arrived a little before noon, welcomed with shouts of joy. In the shade of a cork tree Jacu, the servant, and his friends sheared the sheep, laying them out, carefully bound, on a broad stone that looked like a sacrificial altar. The dogs chased one another through the grass, birds chirped in the oak, an old man who looked like the prophet Elijah gathered the wool into a sack, and all around the asphodel and the wild lilies, bent by the scent-laden wind, seemed to lean forward, curious to see what was happening in the midst of that group of men who stooped down, the shears in their hands. Once they were sheared and released, the sheep jumped up from the heap of wool, as from a foaming wave, and bounded off, shrunken, the muzzles rubbing the earth.

For a while the doctor stood watching, his hands clasped behind him, then he turned to the hut, where the women were cooking, assisted by Jacu's old father, who reserved for himself the honor of roasting a whole kid on the spit. Farther on, the priest, stretched out on the grass in the shade of another cork tree, was telling a Boccaccian tale to a select group of youths. The women nudged Zana and pointed to the doctor; and all at once, with a

* One *real*—a former Spanish silver coin—was equal to about 13 U.S. cents.

change of mood, she began to joke with him, asking him to make himself useful at least, by going to get some water at the spring. He went along with her jokes and, taking a cork pail, walked off in the bright sunlight that scorched the grass and the sage and made a perfume that was enough to intoxicate a man.

The group around the priest sent whistles and shouts after the doctor, and the old man roasting the kid caught his thumb in his fingers as a gesture of contempt. A learned man, a grown man, letting himself be made a fool of like this by the women! Then Zana cursed and ran off, holding her kerchief to her head, until she caught up with the doctor and took the pail out of his hand. From a distance, the women saw the man follow her along the path that led to the spring, and Jacu's old father began to spit furiously on the fire, as if he wanted to put it out.

"The granddaughter of Tomas Acchittu—you see her? She wanted to be alone with the man. If she was my daughter, I'd put my foot on her neck."

"Let her be, father-in-law," Zia Lenarda said kindly. Ah, she knew what love was, how it made you mad, like drinking bewitched water.

The doctor, in fact, dazed by the bright sun, followed Zana into the thicket around the spring, and again he tried to take her in his arms. She looked at him with those eyes of hers, like the Queen of Sheba's; but she pushed him away, threatening to pour the pail full of water on his head. Always the same, since the first evening there by the low wall of the courtyard; she led him on and repulsed him, half ingenuous, half treacherous, and asked him always for the same thing: some poison.

"All right, then, Zana, I'll make you happy. Tonight I'll come to your house, and I'll bring one of those little bottles with a skull on it. But be careful you don't end in jail."

"It's for the fox, I tell you. All right, but leave me now. You hear? Someone's coming."

In fact, the thicket around the fountain shook as if a boar were crashing through, then Jacu appeared. His face was overwrought, although he pretended that finding the two of them was a joke.

"Hey! What are you doing there in the dark? It's time to eat, not to be courting. . . ."

"You're not so hungry; you're thirsty," Zana said sarcastically, lifting the pail, "have a drink, handsome. . . ."

But Jacu threw himself full-length on the ground and drank, panting, from the spring.

During the banquet the doctor laughed, while the priest threw bread crumbs at him and hinted maliciously. He laughed, but from time to time he was distracted, struck by a new idea. After the banquet was over he went off to lie down in the shade among the rocks behind the hut; from there he could see without being seen, and he commanded a view of the area down to the oak in whose shade the shepherd went on shearing. The priest and the others, nearer by, had begun a singing contest, and the women were listening, seated in a row, their hands in their laps.

In the intense silence, the voices, the songs, the laughter were dispelled like the thin white clouds in the blue vastness; and the doctor could hear a horse cropping the grass beyond the rocks, a dog gnawing a bone inside the hut, where Jacu came every so often to empty the sheared wool.

All at once Zana, as the song contest grew more lively, got up and came into the hut. The doctor was smoking; he observed the blue thread that rose from his cigar, and a kind of grin raised his upper lip, showing the gold fillings of his teeth.

Finally Jacu arrived, and Zana's choked voice came like a moan through the cracks in the hut.

"I swear . . . May I be eaten by the hawks . . . if he's even touched my hand. I have my own reasons for smiling at him. . . . It's all for our own good. . . . But this suffering will end . . . end. . . ."

The man, intent perhaps on emptying the wool, was silent. She went on, exasperated, her voice filled with hate: "What about me? Am I ever jealous of your wife? The old crow, the fox. But it's going to end . . . soon. . . ."

Then Jacu laughed; and again there was heard the laughter, the singing, the grazing horse.

But the doctor wanted to enjoy himself a little. He leaped to his feet and began to shout: "Hey! A fox! a fox!"

And the two lovers ran out of the hut, amazed, while below, the group stopped their singing, the women looked all around them, and the dogs started to bark as if a fox had really gone past.

[*Translated by William Fense Weaver*]

Thomas Mann

THOMAS MANN, *one of the greatest novelists of the twentieth century, was born in Lübeck, Germany, in 1875. His family background provided material for his first novel,* Buddenbrooks, *written at the age of twenty-five. The novel is a representative picture of nineteenth century German society and gained its author the Nobel Prize in 1929, but for sheer scope and power,* The Magic Mountain (1924) *and the* Joseph *tetraology* (1933-43), *are even more monumental. Early in the 1930's he recognized and opposed Nazi racism and had to leave his family for temporary residence in Switzerland, becoming an articulate, relentless enemy of fascism in all forms. After several visits to the United States, he settled in Pacific Palisades, and there he wrote* The Holy Sinner *and* Dr. Faustus. *In 1952, when he returned to Germany briefly, he was hailed as a hero. Three years later, while at work on the* Confessions of Felix Krull, *he died in Zurich, where, dissatisfied with the climate of conformity in America, he had taken up residence. "Little Lizzy" is typical of Mann's early interest in pathetic, frustrated, and often freakish persons who lack the ability to cope with life.*

There are marriages which the imagination, even the most practiced literary one, cannot conceive. You must just accept them, as you do in the theater when you see the ancient and doddering married to the beautiful and gay, as the given premises on which the farce is mechanically built up.

Yes, the wife of Jacoby the lawyer was lovely and young, a woman of unusual charm. Some years—shall we say thirty years?

—ago, she had been christened with the names of Anna, Margarete, Rosa, Amalie; but the name she went by was always Amra, composed of the initials of her four real ones; it suited to perfection her somewhat exotic personality. Her soft, heavy hair, which she wore parted on one side and brushed straight back above her ears from the narrow temples, had only the darkness of the glossy chestnut; but her skin displayed the dull, dark sallowness of the south and clothed a form which southern suns must have ripened. Her slow, voluptuous indolent presence suggested the harem; each sensuous, lazy movement of her body strengthened the impression that with her the head was entirely subordinate to the heart. She needed only to have looked at you once, with her artless brown eyes, lifting her brows in the pathetically narrow forehead, horizontally, in a quaint way she had, for you to be certain of that. But she herself was not so simple as not to know it too. Quite simply, she avoided exposing herself, she spoke seldom and little—and what is there to say against a woman who is both beautiful and silent? Yes, the word "simple" is probably the last which should be applied to her. Her glance was artless; but also it had a kind of luxurious cunning—you could see that she was not dull, also that she might be a mischief-maker. In profile her nose was rather too thick; but her full, large mouth was utterly lovely, if also lacking in any expression save sensuality.

This disturbing phenomenon was the wife of Jacoby the lawyer, a man of forty. Whoever looked at him was bound to be amazed at the fact. He was stout, Jacoby the lawyer; but stout is not the word, he was a perfect colossus of a man! His legs, in their columnar clumsiness and the slate-gray trousers he always wore, reminded one of an elephant's. His round, fat-upholstered back was that of a bear; and over the vast round of his belly his funny little gray jacket was held by a single button strained so tight that when it was unbuttoned the jacket came wide open with a pop. Scarcely anything which could be called a neck united this huge torso with the little head atop. The head had narrow watery eyes, a squabby nose, and a wee mouth between cheeks drooping with fullness. The upper lip and the round head were covered with harsh, scanty, light-colored bristles that showed the naked skin, as on an overfed dog. There was no doubt that Jacoby's fatness was not of a healthy kind. His gigantic body, tall as well as stout, was not muscular, but flabby. The blood would sometimes rush to his puffy face, then ebb away leaving it of a yellowish pallor; the mouth would be drawn and sour.

Jacoby's practice was a limited one; but he was well-to-do, partly from his wife's side; and the childless pair lived in a comfortable apartment in the Kaiserstrasse and entertained a good deal. This must have been Frau Amra's taste, for it is unthinkable that the lawyer could have cared for it; he participated with an enthusiasm of a peculiarly painful kind. This fat man's character was the oddest in the world. No human being could have been politer, more accommodating, more complaisant than he. But you unconsciously knew that this over-obligingness was somehow forced, that its true source was an inward insecurity and cowardice—the impression it gave was not very pleasant. A man who despises himself is a very ugly sight; worse still when vanity combines with his cowardice to make him wish to please. This was the case, I should say, with Jacoby: his obsequiousness was almost crawling, it went beyond the bounds of personal decency. He was quite capable of saying to a lady as he escorted her to table: "My dear lady, I am a disgusting creature, but will you do me the honor?" No humor would be mingled with the remark; it was simply cloying, bitter, self-tortured—in a word, disgusting, as he said.

The following once actually happened: the lawyer was taking a walk, and a clumsy porter with a hand-cart ran over his foot. Too late the man stopped his cart and turned round—whereupon Jacoby, quite pale and dazed, his cheeks shaking up and down, took off his hat and stuttered: "I b-beg your pardon." A thing like that is infuriating. But this extraordinary colossus seemed perpetually to suffer from a plague of conscience. When he took a walk with his wife on the Lerchenberg, the Corso of the little city, he would roll his eyes round at Amra, walking with her wonderful elastic gait at his side, and bow so anxiously, diligently, and zealously in all directions that he seemed to be begging pardon of all the lieutenants they met for being in unworthy possession of such a beautiful wife. His mouth had a pathetically ingratiating expression, as though he wanted to disarm their scorn.

I have already hinted that the reason why Amra married Jacoby is unfathomable. As for him, he was in love with her; ardently, as people of his physical make-up seldom are, and with such anxious humility as fitted the rest of his character. Sometimes, late in the evening, he would enter their large sleeping-chamber with its high windows and flowered hangings—softly, so softly that there was no sound, only the slow shaking of floor and furniture. He would come up to Amra's massive bed, where she already lay, kneel down, and with infinite caution take her hand. She would lift her brows in a level line, in the quaint way she had, and look at her husband, abject before her in the dim light, with a look of malice and sensuality combined. With his puffy, trembling hands he would softly stroke back the sleeve and press his tragic fat face into the soft brown flesh of her wrist, where little blue veins stood out. And he would speak to her, in a shaking, half-smothered voice, as a sensible man in everyday life never speaks:

"Amra, my dear Amra! I am not disturbing you? You were not asleep yet? Dear God! I have been thinking all day how beautiful you are and how much I love you. I beg you to listen, for it is so very hard to express what I feel: I love you so much that some-times my heart contracts and I do not know where to turn. I love you beyond my strength. You do not understand that, I know; but you believe it, and you must say, just one single time, that you are a little grateful to me. For, you see, such a love as mine to you is precious, it has its value in this life of ours. And that you will never betray or deceive me, even if you cannot love me, just out of gratitude for this love. I have come to you to beg you, as se-riously, as fervently as I can . . ." here the lawyer's speech would be dissolved in sobs, in low, bitter weeping, as he knelt. Amra would feel moved; she would stroke her husband's bristles and say over and over, in the soothing, contemptuous singsong one uses to a dog who comes to lick one's feet: "Yes, yes, good doggy, good doggy!"

And this behavior of Amra's was certainly not that of a moral woman. For to relieve my mind of the truth which I have so far withheld, she did already deceive her husband; she betrayed him for the embraces of a gentleman named Alfred Läutner, a gifted young musician, who at twenty-seven had made himself a small reputation with amusing little compositions. He was a slim young chap with a provocative face, a flowing blond mane, and a sunny smile in his eyes, of which he was quite aware. He belonged to the present-day race of small artists, who do not demand the utmost of themselves, whose first requirement is to be jolly and happy, who employ their pleasing little talents to heighten their personal charms. It pleases them to play in society the rôle of the naïve genius. Consciously childlike, entirely unmoral and unscrupulous, merry and self-satisfied as they are, and healthy enough to enjoy even their disorders, they are agreeable even in their vanity, so long as that has not been wounded. But woe to these wretched little poseurs when serious misfortune befalls them, with which there is no coquetting, and when they can no longer be pleasant in their own eyes. They will not know how to be wretched decently and in order, they do not know how to attack the problem of suffering. They will be destroyed. All that is a story in itself. But Herr Alfred Läutner wrote pretty things, mostly waltzes and mazurkas. They would have been rather too gay and popular to be considered music as I understand it, if each of them had not contained a passage of some originality, a modulation, a harmonic phrasing, some sort of bold effect that betrayed wit and invention, which was evidently the point of the whole and which made it interesting to genuine musicians. Often these two single measures would have a strange plaintive, melancholy tone which would come out abruptly in the midst of a piece of dance-music and as suddenly be gone.

Amra Jacoby was on fire with guilty passion for this young man, and as for him he had not enough moral fibre to resist her seductions. They met here, they met there, and for some years an immoral relation had subsisted between them, known to the whole town, who laughed at it behind the lawyer's back. But what did he think? Amra was not sensitive enough to betray herself on account of a guilty conscience, so we must take it as certain that, however the lawyer's heart, he could cherish no definite suspicions.

Spring had come, rejoicing all hearts; and Amra conceived the most charming idea.

"Christian," said she—Jacoby's name was Christian—"let us give a party, a beer party to celebrate the new beer—of course quite simple, but let's have a lot of people."

"Certainly," said the lawyer, "but could we not have it a little later?"

To which Amra made no reply, having passed on to the consideration of details.

"It will be so large that we cannot have it here, we must hire a place, some sort of outdoor restaurant where there is plenty of room and fresh air. You see that, of course. The place I am thinking of is Wendelin's big hall at the foot of the Lerchenberg. The hall is independent of the restaurant and brewery, connected by a passage only. We can decorate it for the occasion and set up long tables, drink our bocks, and dance—we must have music and even perhaps some sort of entertainment. There is a little stage, as I happen to know, that makes it very suitable. It will be a very original party and no end to fun."

The lawyer's face had gone a pale yellow as she spoke, and the corners of his mouth went down. He said:

"My dear Amra! How delightful it will be! I can leave it all to you, you are so clever. Make any arrangements you like."

And Amra made her arrangements. She took counsel of various ladies and gentlemen, she went in person to hire the hall, she even formed a committee of people who were invited or who volunteered to co-operate in the entertainment. These were exclusively men, except for the wife of Herr Hildebrandt, an actor at the

Hoftheater, who was herself a singer. Then there was Herr Hilde-brandt, an Assessor Witznagel, a young painter, Alfred Läutner the musician, and some students brought in by Herr Witznagel, who were to do Negro dances.

A week after Amra had made her plan, this committee met in Amra's drawing-room in the Kaiserstrasse—a small, crowded, over-heated room, with a heavy carpet, a sofa with quantities of cush-ions, a fan table, English leather chairs, and a splay-legged ma-hogany table with a velvet cover, upon which rested several large illustrated morocco-bound volumes. There was a fireplace too, with a small fire still burning, and on the marble chimney-top were plates of dainty sandwiches, glasses, and two decanters of sherry. Amra reclined in one corner of the sofa under the fan palm, with her legs crossed. She had the beauty of a warm summer night. A thin blouse of light-colored silk covered her bosom, but her skirt was of heavy dark stuff embroidered with large flowers. Sometimes she put up one hand to brush back the chestnut hair from her narrow forehead. Frau Hildebrandt sat beside her on the sofa; she had red hair and wore riding clothes. Opposite the two all the gentlemen formed a semicircle—among them Jacoby himself, in the lowest chair he could find. He looked unutterably wretched, kept drawing a long breath and swallowing as though struggling against increasing nausea. Herr Alfred Läutner was in tennis clothes—he would not take a chair, but leaned decoratively against the chimney-piece, saying merrily that he could not sit still so long.

Herr Hildebrandt talked sonorously about English songs. He was a most respectable gentleman, in a black suit, with a Roman head and an assured manner—in short a proper actor for a court theater, cultured, knowledgeable, and with enlightened tastes. He liked to hold forth in condemnation of Ibsen, Zola, and Tolstoi, all of whom had the same objectionable aims. But today he was benignly interested in the small affair under discussion.

"Do you know that priceless song 'That's Maria!'?" he asked. "Perhaps it is a little racy—but very effective. And then" so-and-so—he suggested other songs, upon which they came to an agree-ment and Frau Hildebrandt said that she would sing them. The young painter, who had sloping shoulders and a very blond beard, was to give a burlesque conjuring turn. Herr Hildebrandt offered to impersonate various famous characters. In short, everything was developing nicely, the programme was apparently arranged, when Assessor Witznagel, who had command of fluent gesture and a good many duelling scars, suddenly took the word.

"All very well, ladies and gentlemen, it looks like being most amusing. But if I may say so, it still lacks something; it wants some kind of high spot, a climax as it were, something a bit startling, perhaps, to round the thing off. I leave it to you, I have nothing particular in mind, I only think . . ."

"That is true enough!" Alfred Läutner's tenor voice came from the chimney-piece where he leaned. "Witznagel is right. We need a climax. Let us put our heads together!" He settled his red belt and looked engagingly about him.

"Well, if we do not consider the famous characters as the high spot," said Herr Hildebrandt. Everybody agreed with the Assessor. Something piquant was wanted for the principal number. Even Jacoby nodded, and murmured: "Yes, yes, something jolly and striking. . . ." They all reflected.

At the end of a minute's pause, which was broken only by stifled exclamations, an extraordinary thing happened. Amra was sitting reclined among the cushions, gnawing as busily as a mouse at the pointed nail of her little finger. She had a very odd look on her face: a vacant, almost an irresponsible smile, which betrayed a sensuality both tormented and cruel. Her eyes, very bright and wide, turned slowly to the chimney-piece, where for a second they met the musician's. Then suddenly she jerked her whole body to one side as she sat, in the direction of her husband. With both hands in her lap she stared into his face with an avid and clinging gaze, her own growing visibly paler, and said in her rich, slow voice:

"Christian, suppose you come on at the end as a *chanteuse*, in a red satin baby frock, and do a dance."

The effect of these few words was tremendous. The young painter essayed to laugh good-humoredly; Herr Hildebrandt, stony-faced, brushed a crumb from his sleeve; his wife colored up, a rare thing for her; the students coughed and used their handkerchiefs loudly; and Herr Assessor Witznagel simply left the field and got himself a sandwich. The lawyer sat huddled on his little chair, yellow in the face, with a terrified smile. He looked all around the circle, and stammered:

"But, by God . . . I—I—I am not up to—not that I—I beg pardon, but . . ."

Alfred Läutner had lost his insouciant expression; he even seemed to have reddened a little, and he thrust out his neck to peer searchingly into Amra's face. He looked puzzled and upset.

But she, Amra, holding the same persuasive pose, went on with the same impressiveness:

"And you must sing, too, Christian, a song which Herr Läutner shall compose, and he can accompany you on the piano. We could not have a better or more effective climax."

There was a pause, an oppressive pause. Then this extraordinary thing happened, that Herr Läutner, as it were seized upon and carried away by his excitement, took a step forward and his voice fairly trembled with enthusiasm as he said:

"Herr Jacoby, that is a priceless idea, and I am more than ready to compose something. You must have a dance and song, anything else is unthinkable as a wind-up to our affair. You will see, it will be the best thing I have ever written or ever shall write. In a red satin baby frock. Oh, your wife is an artist, only an artist could have hit upon the idea! Do say yes, I beg of you. I will do my part, you will see, it will be an achievement."

Here the circle broke up and the meeting became lively. Out of politeness, or out of malice, the company began to storm the lawyer with entreaties—Frau Hildebrandt went so far as to say, quite loudly, in her Brünnhilde voice:

"Herr Jacoby, after all, you are such a jolly and entertaining man!"

But the lawyer had pulled himself together and spoke, a little yellow, but with a strong effort at resolution:

"But listen to me, ladies and gentlemen—what can I say to

you? It isn't my line, believe me. I have no comic gift, and besides . . . in short, no, it is quite impossible, alas!"

He stuck obstinately to his refusal, and Amra no longer insisted, but sat still with her absent look. Herr Läutner was silent too, staring in deep abstraction at a pattern in the rug. Herr Hildebrandt changed the subject, and presently the committee meeting broke up without coming to a final decision about the "climax."

On the evening of the same day Amra had gone to bed and was lying there with her eyes wide open; her husband came lumbering into the bedroom, drew a chair up beside the bed, dropped into it, and said, in a low, hesitating voice:

"Listen, Amra; to be quite frank, I am feeling very disturbed. I refused them today—I did not mean to be offensive—goodness knows I did not mean that. Or do you seriously feel that—I beg you to tell me."

Amra was silent for a moment, while her brows rose slowly. Then she shrugged her shoulders and said:

"I do not know, my dear friend, how to answer you. You behaved in a way I should not have expected from you. You were unfriendly, you refused to support our enterprise in a way which they flatteringly considered to be indispensable to it. To put it mildly, you disappointed everybody and upset the whole company with your rude lack of compliance. Whereas it was your duty as host—"

The lawyer hung his head and sighed heavily. He said:

"Believe me, Amra, I had no intention to be disobliging. I do not like to offend anybody; if I have behaved badly I am ready to make amends. It is only a joke, after all, an innocent little dressing-up—why not? I will not upset the whole affair, I am ready to . . ."

The following afternoon Amra went out again to "make preparations." She drove to Number 78 Holzstrasse and went up to the second storey, where she had an appointment. And when she lay relaxed by the expression of her love she pressed her lover's head passionately to her breast and whispered:

"Write it for four hands. We will accompany him together while he sings and dances. I will see to the costume myself."

And an extraordinary shiver, a suppressed and spasmodic burst of laughter went through the limbs of both.

For anyone who wants to give a large party out of doors Herr Wendelin's place on the slope of the Lerchenberg is to be recommended. You enter it from the pretty suburban street through a tall trellised gateway and pass into the parklike garden, in the center of which stands a large hall, connected only by a narrow passage with restaurant, kitchen, and brewery. It is a large, brightly painted wooden hall, in an amusing mixture of Chinese and Renaissance styles. It has folding doors which stand open in good weather to admit the woodland air, and it will hold a great many people.

On this evening as the carriages rolled up they were greeted from afar by the gleam of colored lights. The whole gateway, the trees, and the hall itself were set thick with lanterns, while the interior made an entrancing sight. Heavy garlands were draped across the ceiling and studded with paper lanterns. Hosts of electric lights hung among the decorations of the walls, which consisted of pine boughs, flags, and artificial flowers; the whole hall was brilliantly lighted. The stage had foliage plants grouped on either side, and a red curtain with a painted design of a presiding genius hovering in the air. A long row of decorated tables ran almost the whole length of the hall. And at these tables the guests of Attorney Jacoby were doing themselves well on cold roast veal and bock beer. There were certainly more than a hundred and fifty people: officers, lawyers, business men, artists, upper officials, with their wives and daughters. They were quite simply dressed, in black coats and light spring toilettes, for this was a jolly, informal occasion. The gentlemen carried their mugs in person to the big casks against one of the walls; the spacious, festive, brightly lighted room was filled with a heavy sweetish atmosphere of evergreen boughs, flowers, beer, food, and human beings; and there was a clatter and buzz of laughter and talk—the loud, simple talk and the high, good-natured, unrestrained, carefree laughter of the sort of people there assembled.

The attorney sat shapeless and helpless at one end of the table, near the stage. He drank little and now and then addressed a labored remark to his neighbor, Frau Regierungsrat Havermann. He breathed offensively, the corners of his mouth hung down, he stared fixedly with his bulging watery eyes into the lively scene, with a sort of melancholy remoteness, as though there resided in all this noisy merriment something inexpressibly painful and perplexing.

Large fruit tarts were now being handed round for the company to cut from; they drank sweet wine with these, and the time for the speeches arrived. Herr Hildebrandt celebrated the new brew in a speech almost entirely composed of classical quotations, even Greek. Herr Witznagel, with florid gestures and ingenious turns of phrase, toasted the ladies, taking a handful of flowers from the nearest vase and comparing each flower to some feminine charm. Amra Jacoby, who sat opposite him in a pale-yellow silk frock, he called "a lovelier sister of the Maréchal Niel."

Then she nodded meaningfully to her husband, brushing back her hair from her forehead; whereupon the fat man arose and almost ruined the whole atmosphere by stammering a few words with painful effort, smiling a repulsive smile. Some half-hearted bravos rewarded him, then there was an oppressive pause, after which jollity resumed its sway. All smoking, all a little elevated by drink, they rose from table and with their own hands and a great deal of noise removed the tables from the hall to make way for the dancing.

It was after eleven and high spirits reigned supreme. Some of the guests streamed out into the brightly lighted garden to get the fresh air; others stood about the hall in groups, smoking, chatting, drawing beer from the kegs, and drinking it standing. Then a loud trumpet call sounded from the stage, summoning everybody to the entertainment. The band arrived and took its place before the curtains; rows of chairs were put in place and red programmes distributed on them; the gentlemen ranged themselves along the walls. There was an expectant hush.

The band played a noisy overture, and the curtains parted to reveal a row of Negroes horrifying to behold in their barbaric costumes and their blood-red lips, gnashing their teeth and emitting savage yells.

Certainly the entertainment was the crowning success of Amra's party. As it went on, the applause grew more and more enthusiastic. Frau Hildebrandt came on in a powdered wig, pounded with a shepherdess' crook on the floor and sang—in too large a voice— "That's Maria!" A conjuror in a dress coat covered with orders performed the most amazing feats; Herr Hildebrandt impersonated Goethe, Bismarck, and Napoleon in an amazingly lifelike manner; and a newspaper editor, Dr. Wiesensprung, improvised a humorous lecture which had as its theme bock beer and its social significance. And now the suspense reached its height, for it was time for the last, the mysterious number which appeared on the programme framed in a laurel wreath and was entitled: *"Little Lizzy.* Song and Dance. Music by Alfred Läutner."

A movement swept through the hall, and people's eyes met as the band sat down at their instruments and Alfred Läutner came from the doorway where he had been lounging with a cigarette between his pouting lips to take his place beside Amra Jacoby at the piano, which stood in the center of the stage in front of the curtains. Herr Läutner's face was flushed and he turned over his manuscript score nervously; Amra for her part was rather pale. She leaned one arm on the back of her chair and looked loweringly at the audience. The bell rang, the pianist played a few bars of an insignificant accompaniment, the curtains parted, little Lizzy appeared.

The whole audience stiffened with amazement as that tragic and bedizened bulk shambled with a sort of bear-dance into view. It was Jacoby. A wide, shapeless garment of crimson satin, without folds, fell to his feet; it was cut out above to make a repulsive display of the fat neck, stippled with white powder. The sleeves consisted merely of a shoulder puff, but the flabby arms were covered by long lemon-colored gloves; on the head perched a high blond wig with a swaying green feather. And under the wig was a face, a puffy, pasty, unhappy, and desperately mirthful face, with cheeks that shook pathetically up and down and little red-rimmed eyes that strained in anguish towards the floor and saw nothing else at all. The fat man hoisted himself with effort from one leg to the other, while with his hands he either held up his skirts or else weakly raised his index fingers—these two gestures he had and knew no others. In a choked and gasping voice he sang, to the accompaniment of the piano.

The lamentable figure exhaled more than ever a cold breath of anguish. It killed every light-hearted enjoyment and lay like an oppressive weight upon the assembled audience. Horror was in the depths of all these spellbound eyes, gazing at this pair at the piano and at that husband there. The monstrous, unspeakable scandal lasted five long minutes.

Then came a moment which none of those present will forget as long as they live. Let us picture to ourselves what happened in that frightful and frightfully involved little instant of time.

You know of course the absurd little jingle called "Lizzy." And you remember the lines:

> *I can polka until I am dizzy,*
> *I can waltz with the best and beyond,*
> *I'm the popular pet, little Lizzy,*
> *Who makes all the menfolks so fond—*

which form the trivial and unlovely refrain to three longish stanzas. Alfred Läutner had composed a new setting to the verses I have quoted, and it was, as he had said it would be, his masterpiece. He had, that is, brought to its highest pitch his little artifice of introducing into a fairly vulgar and humorous piece of hackwork a sudden phrase of genuine creative art. The melody, in C-sharp major, had been in the first bars rather pretty and perfectly banal. At the beginning of the refrain the rhythm became livelier and dissonances occurred, which by means of the constant accentuation of a B-natural made one expect a transition into F-

sharp major. These dissonances went on developing until the word
"beyond"; and after the "I'm the" a culmination into F-sharp
major should have followed. Instead of which the most surprising
thing happened. That is, through a harsh turn, by means of an
inspiration which was almost a stroke of genius, the key changed
to F-major, and this little interlude which followed, with the use
of both pedals on the long-drawn-out first syllable of the word
"Lizzy," was indescribably, almost gruesomely effective. It was a
complete surprise, an abrupt assault on the nerves, it shivered down
the back, it was a miracle, a revelation, it was like a curtain suddenly torn away to reveal something nude.

And on the F-major chord Attorney Jacoby stopped dancing. He
stood still, he stood as though rooted to the stage with his two
forefingers lifted, one a little lower than the other. The word
"Lizzy" stuck in his throat, he was dumb; almost at the same time
the accompaniment broke sharp off, and the incredible, absurd,
and ghastly figure stood there frozen, with his head thrust forward
like a steer's, staring with inflamed eyes straight before him. He
stared into the brightly lighted, decorated, crowded hall, in which,
like an exhalation from all these people, the scandal hung and
thickened into visibility. He stared at all these upturned faces,
foreshortened and distorted by the lighting, into these hundreds
of pairs of eyes all directed with the same knowing expression
upon himself and the two at the piano. In a frightful stillness, unbroken by the smallest sound, his gaze traveled slowly and un-
easily from the pair to the audience, from the audience to the pair,
while his eyes widened more and more. Then knowledge seemed
to flash across his face, like a sudden rush of blood, making it red
as the frock he wore, only to give way to a waxen yellow pallor—
and the fat man collapsed, making the platform creak beneath his
weight.

For another moment the stillness reigned. Then there came
shrieks, hubbub ensued, a few gentlemen took heart to spring
upon the platform, among them a young doctor—and the curtains
were drawn together.

Amra Jacoby and Alfred Läutner still sat at the piano. They

had turned a little away from each other, and he, with his head bent, seemed to be listening to the echo of his F-major chord, while she, with her birdlike brain, had not yet grasped the situation, but gazed round her with vacant face.

The young doctor came back presently. He was a little Jewish gentleman with a serious face and a small pointed beard. Some people surrounded him at the door with questions—to which he replied with a shrug of the shoulders and the words:

"All over."

[*Translated by H. T. Lowe-Porter*]

Sinclair Lewis

WHAT THAT KIND OF MUSH GETS YOU

SINCLAIR LEWIS *refused the Pulitzer Prize in 1925 for his novel* Arrowsmith, *declaring that he did not believe in prizes; but in 1930 he journeyed to Stockholm to accept the Nobel Prize as the first American to be honored by the Swedish Academy. The son of a doctor, Lewis was born in 1885 in Sauk Center, Minnesota, a town which closely resembled the Gopher Prairie of* Main Street *(1920), the novel which brought him literary prominence. Lewis interrupted his studies at Yale, to join Upton Sinclair's socialist colony, then returned to graduate before setting out on a career of free-lance writing that took him across the United States and through Europe. A keen and satiric observer of his fellow men, in his novels Lewis reported American life as he saw it. His success in portraying the American businessman made popular the word* babbitt, *derived from his novel* Babbitt *(1922). Lewis died in 1951, in Rome.*

Orlo Vay, the Chippewa Avenue Optician, Smart-Art Harlequin Tinted-Tortus Frames Our Specialty, was a public figure, as public as a cemetery. He was resentful that his profession, like that of an undertaker, a professor of art, or a Mormon missionary, was not appreciated for its patience and technical skill, as are the callings of wholesale grocer or mistress or radio-sports-commentator, and he tried to make up for the professional injustice by developing his personal glamor.

He wanted to Belong. He was a speaker. He was hearty and public about the local baseball and hockey teams, about the Kiwanis

Club, about the Mayflower Congregational Church, and about all war drives. At forty-five he was bald, but the nobly glistening egg of his face and forehead, whose arc was broken only by a pair of Vay Li-Hi-Bifocals, was an adornment to all fund-raising rallies.

He urged his wife, Virga, to co-operate in his spiritual efforts, but she was a small, scared, romantic woman, ten years his junior; an admirer of passion in Technicolor, a clipper-out of newspaper lyrics about love and autumn smoke upon the hills. He vainly explained to her, "In these modern days, a woman can't fritter away her time daydreaming. She has to push her own weight, and not hide it under a bushel."

Her solace was in her lover, Dr. Allan Cedar, the dentist. Together, Virga and Allan would have been a most gentle pair, small, clinging, and credulous. But they could never be openly together. They were afraid of Mr. Vay and of Allan's fat and vicious wife, Bertha, and they met at soda counters in outlying drug stores and lovingly drank black-and-whites together or Jumbo Malteds and, giggling, ate ferocious banana splits; or, till wartime gasoline-rationing prevented, they sped out in Allan's coupé by twilight, and made shy, eager love in mossy pastures or, by the weak dashlight of the car, read aloud surprisingly good recent poets: Wallace Stevens, Sandburg, Robert Frost, Jeffers, T. S. Eliot, Lindsay.

Allan was one of the best actors in the Masquers, and though Virga could not act, she made costumes and hung about at rehearsals, and thus they were able to meet, and to stir the suspicions of Bertha Cedar.

Mrs. Cedar was a rare type of the vicious woman; she really hated her husband, though she did not so much scold him as mock him for his effeminate love of acting, for his verses, for his cherubic mustache, and even for his skill with golden bridge-work. She jeered, in the soap-reeking presence of her seven sisters and sisters-in-law, all chewing gum and adjusting their plates, that as a lover "Ally" had no staying-powers. That's what *she* thought.

She said to her mother, "Ally is a bum dentist; he hasn't got a single rich patient," and when they were at an evening party, she communicated to the festal guests, "Ally can't even pick out a necktie without asking my help," and on everything her husband said she commented, "Oh, don't be silly!"

She demanded, and received, large sympathy from all the females she knew, and as he was fond of golf and backgammon, she refused to learn either of them.

Whenever she had irritated him into jumpiness, she said judiciously, "You seem to be in a very nervous state." She picked at him about his crossword puzzles, about his stamp-collection, until he screamed, invariably, "Oh, let me *alone!*" and then she was able to say smugly, "I dont' know what's the matter with you, so touchy about every little thing. You better go to a mind-doctor and have your head examined."

Then Bertha quite unexpectedly inherited seven thousand dollars and a house in San Jose, California, from a horrible aunt. She did not suggest to her husband but told him that they would move out to that paradise for chilled Minnesotans, and he would practice there.

It occurred to Allan to murder her, but not to refuse to go along. Many American males confuse their wives and the policeman on the beat.

But he knew that it would be death for him to leave Virga Vay, and that afternoon, when Virga slipped into his office at three o'clock in response to his code telephone call of "This is the Superba Market and we're sending you three bunches of asparagus," she begged, "Couldn't we elope some place together? Maybe we could get a little farm."

"She'd find us. She has a cousin who's a private detective in Duluth."

"Yes, I guess she would. Can't we *ever* be together always?"

"There is one way—if you wouldn't be afraid."

He explained the way.

"No. I wouldn't be afraid, if you stayed right with me," she said.

Dr. Allan Cedar was an excellent amateur machinist. On a Sunday afternoon when Bertha was visiting her mother, he cut a hole through the steel bottom of the luggage compartment of his small dark-gray coupé. This compartment opened into the body of the car. That same day he stole the hose of their vacuum-cleaner and concealed it up on the rafters of their galvanized-iron garage.

On Tuesday—this was in February—he bought a blue ready-made suit at Goldenkron Brothers', on Ignatius Street. He was easy to fit, and no alterations were needed. They wanted to deliver the suit that afternoon, but he insisted, "No, hold it here for me and I'll come in and put it on tomorrow morning. I want to surprise somebody."

"Your Missus will love it, Doc," said Monty Goldenkron.

"I hope she will—when she sees it!"

He also bought three white-linen shirts and a red bow-tie, and paid cash for the lot.

"Your credit is good here, Doc—none better," protested Monty.

Allan puzzled him by the triumphant way in which he answered, "I want to keep it good, just now!"

From Goldenkrons' he walked perkily to the Emporium, to the Golden Rule drug store, to the Co-operative Dairy, paying his bills in full at each. On his way he saw a distinguished fellow-townsman, Judge Timberlane, and his pretty wife. Allan had never said ten words to either of them, but he thought affectionately, "There's a couple who are intelligent enough and warm-hearted enough to know what love is worth."

That evening he said blandly to his wife, "Strangest thing happened today. The University school of dentistry telephoned me."

"Long distance?"

"Surely."

"Well!" Her tone was less of disbelief than of disgust.

"They're having a special brush-up session for dentists and they want me to come down to Minneapolis first thing tomorrow morning to stay for three days and give instruction in bridge-work. And of course you must come along. It's too bad I'll have to work from nine in the morning till midnight—they do rush those special courses so—but you can go to the movies by yourself, or just sit comfortably in the hotel."

"No—thank—*you!*" said Bertha. "I prefer to sit here at home. Why you couldn't have been an M.D. doctor and take out gall-bladders and make some real money! And I'll thank you to be home not later than Sunday morning. You know we have Sunday dinner with Mother."

He knew.

"I hope that long before that I'll be home," he said.

He told her that he would be staying at the Flora Hotel, in Minneapolis. But on Wednesday morning, after putting on the new suit at Goldenkrons', he drove to St. Paul, through light snow-flakes which he thought of as fairies. "But I haven't a bit of real poet in me. Just second-rate and banal," he sighed. He tried to make a poem, and got no farther than:

> *It is snowing*
> *The wind is blowing*
> *But I am happy to be going.*

In St. Paul he went to the small, clean Hotel Orkness, registered as "Mr. A.M. Romeo & wife," asked for a room with a double bed, and explained to the clerk, "My wife is coming by train. She should be here in about seventeen minutes now, I figure it."

He went unenthusiastically to the palsied elevator, up to their room. It was tidy, and on the wall was an Adolph Dehn litho-graphed instead of the fake English-hunting-print that he had dreaded. He kneaded the bed with his fist. He was pleased.

Virga Vay arrived nineteen minutes later, with a bellboy carry-ing her new imitation leather bag.

"So you're here, husband. Not a bad room," she said indif-ferently.

The bellboy knew from her indifference and from her calling the man "husband" that she was not married to him, but unstint-ingly in love. Such paradoxes are so common in his subterranean business that he had forgotten about Virga by the time he reached his bench in the lobby. Six stories above him, Virga and Allan were lost and blind and quivering in their kiss.

Presently she said, "Oh, you have a new suit! Turn around.

Why, it fits beautifully! And such a nice red tie. You do look so young and cute in a bow-tie. Did you get it for me?"

"Of course. And then—I kind of hate to speak of it now, but I want us to get so used to the idea that we can just forget it—I don't want us to look frowsy when they find us. As if we hadn't been happy. And we *will* be—we are!"

"Yes."

"You're still game for it?"

"With you? For anything."

"He was taking off the new suit; she was tenderly lifting from her bag a nightgown which she had made and embroidered this past week.

They had all their meals in the room; they did not leave it till afternoon of the next day. The air became a little close, thick from perfume and cigarette smoke and the bubble baths they took together.

Late the next afternoon they dressed and packed their bags, completely. He laid on the bureau two ten-dollar bills. They left the luggage at the foot of their bed, which she had made up. She took nothing from the room, and he nothing except a paper bag containing a bottle of Bourbon whisky, with the cork loosened, and a pocket anthology of new poetry. At the door she looked back, and said to him, "I shall remember this dear room as long as we live."

"Yes. . . . As long as we live."

He took his dark-gray coupé out of the hotel garage, tipping an amazed attendant one dollar, and they drove to Indian Mounds Park, overlooking the erratic Mississippi. He stopped in the park, at dusk, and said, "Think of the Indians that came along here, and Pike and Lewis Cass!"

"They were brave," she mused.

"Brave, *too!*" They nervously laughed. Indeed, after a moment of solemnity when they had left the hotel, they had been constantly gay, laughing at everything, even when she sneezed and he piped, "No more worry about catching pneumonia!"

He drove into a small street near by and parked the car, distant from any house. Working in the half-darkness, leaving the engine running, he pushed the vacuum-cleaner hose through the hole in the bottom of the luggage compartment, wired it to the exhaust pipe, and hastily got back into the car. The windows were closed. Already the air in the car was sick-sweet with carbon monoxide.

He slipped the whisky bottle out of the paper bag and tenderly urged, "Take a swig of this. Keep your courage up."

"Dearest, I don't need anything to keep it up."

"I do, by golly. I'm not a big he-man like you, Virg!"

They both laughed, and drank from the bottle, and kissed lingeringly.

"I wonder if I could smoke a cigarette. I don't *think* C_2O_2 is explosive," he speculated.

"Oh, sweet, be careful! It *might* explode!"

"Yes, it——" Then he shouted, "Listen at us! As if we cared if we got blown up now!"

"Oh, I am too brainless, Allan! I don't know if you'll be able to stand me much longer."

"As long as we live, my darling, my very dear, oh, my dear love!"

"As long as we live. Together now. Together."

His head aching, his throat sore, he forgot to light the cigarette. He switched on the tiny dashlight, he lifted up the book as though it were a bar of lead, and from Conrad Aiken's "Sea Holly" he began to read to her:

> *It was for this*
> *Barren beauty, barrenness of rock that aches*
> *On the seaward path, seeing the beautiful sea,*
> *Hearing the lark of rock that sings—*

He was too drowsy to read more than just the ending:

> *Stone pain in the stony heart,*
> *The rock loved and labored; and all is lost.*

The book fell to the seat, his head drooped, and his arm groped drowsily about her. She rested contentedly, in vast dreams, her head secure upon his shoulder.

Harsh screaming snatched them back from paradise. The car windows were smashed, someone was dragging them out . . . and Bertha was slapping Virga's face, while Bertha's cousin, the detective, was beating Allan's shoulders with a blackjack, to bring him to. In doing so, he broke Allan's jaw.

Bertha drove him back to Grand Republic and nursed him while he was in bed, jeering to the harpies whom she had invited in, "Ally tried to—you know—with a woman, but he was no good, and he was so ashamed he tried to kill himself."

He kept muttering, "Please go away and don't torture me."

She laughed.

Later, Bertha was able to intercept every one of the letters that Virga sent to him from Des Moines, where she had gone to work in a five-and-ten-cent store after Orlo had virtuously divorced her.

"Love! Ally is learning what that kind of mush gets you," Bertha explained to her attentive women friends.

Ivan Bunin

SUNSTROKE

IVAN BUNIN, *the first Russian writer to win the Nobel Prize
(1931), was born in 1870 to an aristocratic family in Vorornezh. After
attending the University of Moscow briefly, he brought out his first
book, a volume of verse. For this and his realistic accounts of the decay
of the Russian nobility, he was awarded the Pushkin Prize for Literature and elected to the Russian Academy. He fled to western Europe, following the Revolution, and lived mainly in Paris, sometimes
nearly destitute, until his death at the age of eighty-three. His study of
the dying patriarchy among Russian peasants raises him into the front
rank of European novelists, but his present reputation rests on his
short stories, in such collections as* The Gentleman from San Fran-
cisco *and* The Grammar of Love. *In many of his stories he contrasts
the transitoriness of human life with the endurance of beauty and
nature. Somerset Maugham has called "Sunstroke" one of the world's
best stories.*

They had had their dinner, and they left the brilliantly
lighted dining room and went on deck, where they
paused by the rail. She closed her eyes and, palm turned outward,
pressing her hand to her cheek, laughed with unaffected charm.
Everything was charming about this little woman. She said:
"I'm quite intoxicated . . . Or I've gone wholly out of my
mind. Where did you drop down from? But three hours ago I
scarcely suspected your existence. I don't even know where you

came on board. Was it Samara? Well, it doesn't matter, my dear. Really, my head's in a whirl, or is it the boat turning?"

Before them was darkness—and lights. Out of the darkness a strong soft breeze blew in their faces, while the lights glided past them: with Volga friskiness the steam cut a sharp curve, as it approached the small pier.

The lieutenant took her hand, lifting it to his lips. The strong small hand smelt of sunburn. Bliss and anguish caused his heart to grow tremulous at the thought that underneath this light linen dress she was doubtless all strong and tanned after a whole month's lying under the southern sun upon the hot sea sands (she had said she was coming from Anapu). The lieutenant murmured: "Let's get off here. . . ."

"Where?" she asked in astonishment.

"Here, on this pier."

"Why?"

He was silent. Again she laid the back of her hand upon her hot cheek.

"You're mad. . . ."

"Let's get off," he repeated dully. "I implore you. . . ."

"*Akh*, do as you like," she said, turning away.

The moving steamer crashed with a dull thud against the dimly lighted pier, and the pair almost fell upon each other. The end of a cable came flying above their heads, then the ship reeled and the water clamorously seethed, the gangplank rattled. . . . The lieutenant ran for the luggage.

Presently, they passed through the tiny drowsy pier shed and, once out of doors, found themselves ankle-deep in sand; in silence they seated themselves in the dust-covered hackney cab. The ascent of the steep road, soft with dust, punctuated with infrequent lamp posts standing awry, seemed endless. At last they emerged on top, the carriage rattled along a paved street; here was a square, some administrative buildings, a belfry, the warmth and the smells of a summer night in a provincial town. . . . The cabby stopped before a lighted entrance; through the open doors could be seen the steep wooden stairway. An old unshaven servant in a pink shirt and frock coat reluctantly took their bags and went forward on his tired feet. They entered a large but terribly stuffy room still hot from the day's sun, its windows hung with white curtains, its mirror-topped mantelpiece decorated with two unused candles—and no sooner had they entered and the servant closed the door upon them than the lieutenant impetuously flung himself upon her and they both lost themselves in a kiss of such agonizing rapture that the moment was long to be remembered by them: nothing like it had ever been experienced by either one or the other.

At ten o'clock the next morning, a morning hot and sunny and gay with the ringing of church bells, with the humming in the market-place facing the hotel, with the smell of hay and tar and all those complex odors with which every provincial Russian town reeks, she, this nameless little woman, for she refused to reveal her name, jestingly called herself the lovely stranger, left him, resuming her journey. They had slept little, but when she emerged from behind the screen near the bed, within five minutes all washed and dressed, she looked as fresh as a seventeen-year-old girl. Was she embarrassed? Very little. As before, she was simple, gay and—quite rational.

"No, no my dear," she said in response to his suggestion that they pursue the journey together. "No, you must remain here until the next boat. If we go on together, everything will be spoiled. I wouldn't like that. Please believe me, I'm not at all the sort of woman I may have led you to think. All that happened here never happened before and never will again. It's as if I suffered an eclipse . . . Or, to be more precise, it's as if we both experienced something in the nature of a sunstroke."

The lieutenant rather lightly agreed with her. In gay happy spirits he escorted her in a carriage to the pier, which they reached just as the rose-tinted steamer was on the point of departure, and, on deck, in the presence of other passengers, he kissed her, and barely managed to jump on to the already receding gangplank.

With the same lightness of spirit he returned to the hotel. Yet something had changed. Their room without her seemed quite different. It was still full of her—and empty. That was strange! It still smelt of her excellent English eau-de-cologne, her unfinished cup was still on the tray, but she was no longer there. . . . And the lieutenant's heart suddenly felt such tremors of tenderness that he made haste to smoke, and slapping his boot-leg with a crop, he paced up and down the room.

"A strange occurrence!" he said aloud, laughing, yet conscious of tears in his eyes. " 'Please believe me, I'm not at all the sort of woman I may have led you to think. . . .' And now she's gone. . . . An absurd woman!"

The screen was pushed to one side, the bed had not yet been made. And he felt that now he simply hadn't the courage to look upon this bed. He arranged the screen around it, closed the window that he might avoid hearing the market hum and the creaking of cart wheels, lowered the blown-out white curtains, and sat down on the divan. . . . Well, so that was the end to the "chance encounter!" She was gone—and was now far away, doubtless sitting in the glassed-in white salon or on the deck, gazing at the immense sun-glinting river, at the passing barges, the yellow sandbanks, the distant radiance of water and sky, at the whole immeasurable expanse of the Volga. . . . And farewell, for ever, for eternity. . . . For how could they ever meet again? "I can't, after all," he mused, "for one reason or another, visit the town where her husband is, and her three-year-old daughter, and the rest of her family, the place where she leads her everyday life!"—And that town suddenly appeared to him as a most exceptional, a forbidden town, and the thought that she would go on living in it her lonely life, perhaps frequently remembering him, remembering their chance transient encounter, while he would never see her again, this thought stunned and unmanned him. No, this could not be! It was wholly absurd, unnatural, incredible! And he felt such anguish, such futility of existence in the years to come, that he was seized with terror, with despair.

"What the devil!" he thought, rising, and, again pacing up and down the room, he tried to avoid the sight of the bed behind the screen. "What's the matter with me? Who'd have thought it possible that the first time—and there. . . . What is there about her, and what exactly has happened? Really, it is as if there were some sort of sunstroke! But the main thing is, how am I to spend the whole day without her in this God-forsaken place?"

He vividly remembered her as she was, with all of her most intimate traits; he remembered the smell of her sunburn and of her linen dress, of her strong body, the live, simple, gay sound of her voice. . . . The mood of but lately experienced delights of her feminine loveliness, was still singularly strong upon him; nevertheless, the main thing was another altogether new mood—that strange, incomprehensible mood, non-existent while they were still together, a mood which he could not have even imagined yesterday, when he first made this new, merely diverting, as he had thought, acquaintance, and concerning which he could no longer speak to anyone, no, not to anyone! "Yes, the main thing," he went on thinking, "is that you'll never be able to talk about it! And what is one to do, how is one to pass this endless day, with these memories, with this intolerable anguish, in this God-forsaken little town by that same radiant Volga, upon whose waters this rose-tinted steamer has borne her away!"

It was necessary to save himself, to occupy himself with something, to find amusement, to go somewhere. He resolutely put his cap on; strode vigorously, clinking his spurs, down the empty corridors; ran down the steep stairway toward the entrance . . . Well, where should he go? At the entrance was a young cabby in a smart peasant's coat, calmly smoking a tiny cigar, apparently waiting for someone. The lieutenant glanced at him in distraught wonder: how was it possible for anyone to sit so calmly on a coach-box, and smoke, and seem so unconcerned, so indifferent? "Evidently, in this whole town I alone am so terribly unhappy," he thought, turning in the direction of the market place.

The market was dispersing. Unwittingly he trod upon the fresh manure among the wagons, among the cart loads of cucumbers, among the new pots and pans, and the women, who sat on the ground, vied with one another in trying to call his attention to their pots, which they took in their hands and made ring with their fingers, demonstrating their quality, while the peasants dinned in his ears: "Here are first-class cucumbers, Your Honor!" All this was stupid, absurd, and he ran from the place. He entered the church, where chanting was going on; it was loud and cheerful and determined, as if the chanters were conscious of the fulfillment of a duty; then he strode on through the streets, and in the heat of the sun wandered along the paths of a tiny neglected garden on the slope of a hill, overlooking the broad river with its splendor as of glinting steel. The shoulder straps and buttons of his white summer uniform grew so hot that it was impossible to touch them. The inner band of his cap was wet with perspiration, his face flamed. . . .

On returning to the hotel he found delicious relief in the shelter of the large, empty, cool dining room; he removed his cap, sat down at a little table before an open window, through which the heat blew—a breeze for all that—and ordered an iced soup of pot herbs. Everything was good, in everything there was immeasurable happiness, intense joy, even in this sultriness and in these market smells; in the whole unfamiliar little town and in this old provincial hotel it was present, this happiness, and with it all, his heart was simply being rent into shreds. He drank several small glasses of vodka, and made a snack of pickled cucumbers, and he felt that without the least faltering he would choose to die tomorrow, if only by some miracle he could return here and spend but this one day with her—if only to have a chance to tell her and somehow prove to her, persuade her of his harrowing and marvelous love . . . But why prove it to her? Why persuade her? He could not tell why, yet it seemed more necessary than life itself.

"My nerves are playing me pranks," he thought, as he poured himself a fifth glass of vodka.

He consumed an entire small decanter, hoping in intoxication to forget, to bring to an end his agonized exultation. But, no, it only grew more intense.

He pushed away the cold herb soup, asked for black coffee, and began to smoke and resolutely to deliberate upon ways and means of freeing himself from this unexpected, sudden love. But to free himself—he felt this acutely—was impossible. And, suddenly, with a rapid movement, he rose, picked up his cap and crop, and, asking where the post office was, quickly went in the direction indicated, with the phrasing of a telegram already in his head: "Henceforth my life is wholly yours, unto death, to do with what you will." On reaching the thick-walled house, which sheltered the post and telegraph office, he paused in horror: he knew the town where she lived, he knew that she had a husband and a three-year-old daughter, but he knew neither her first name nor her surname! Several times in the course of the evening he had asked her, and each time she laughed and said:

"Why must you know who I am? I am Maria Green, Fairyland Queen. . . . Or simply the lovely stranger. . . . Isn't that enough for you?"

On the corner, near the post office, was a photographic showcase. He looked steadily at a large portrait of a military man with elaborate epaulettes, with bulging eyes and low forehead, with surprisingly magnificent whiskers and expansive chest, all decorated with orders. . . . How absurdly ridiculous, how horribly ordinary it all was, because his heart had been vanquished, he understood it now—by this terrible "sunstroke," this intense love, this intense happiness. He glanced at a bridal couple—a young man in a long frock coat and white necktie, his hair cut in hedge-hog style; on his arm, in bridal veil—but he then diverted his gaze to the portrait of a good-looking, spirited girl in a student's cap perched awry. . . . Then, tormented by a harrowing envy toward all these strangers, *non-suffering* human beings, he began to look fixedly down the street.

"Where can I go? What can I do?" the insoluble, oppressive question persisted in his mind and soul.

The street was deserted. The houses were all alike, white two-storied, middle class, with large gardens, and they gave the appearance of being uninhabited; a thick white dust covered the pavement; all this dazzled; everything was drenched with the hot, flaming, joyous, seemingly aimless sunshine. In the distance the street rose, humped and pressed against the pure, cloudless, grayish horizon, reflecting lilac. There was something southern in this, reminiscent of Sebastopol, Kertch . . . Anapu. The thought of the last was particularly unbearable. And the lieutenant, with lowered head, screwing up his eyes against the light, with fixed gaze on the ground, reeling, stumbling, spur catching on spur, retraced his footsteps.

He returned to the hotel, shattered with fatigue, as if he had performed a long journey in Turkestan or the Sahara. Gathering his last strength, he entered his large, desolate room. The room had already been cleaned, and her last traces removed—only a solitary hairpin, forgotten by her, lay on the tiny table by the bed! He took off his jacket and glanced in the mirror: his face—the ordinary face of an officer, swarthy from sunburn, with whitish sun-bleached mustaches and bluish-white eyes, seeming against the sunburn whiter than they were—now showed a disraught, insane expression, and in his thin white shirt with standing starched collar there was something youthful and infinitely pathetic. He lay down on the bed, on his back, and rested his dust-covered boots on the footboard. The windows were open, the curtains lowered, and from time to time the light breeze filled them, blowing into the room sultriness and the odor of hot roofs and of all that luminous, now quite desolate, mute, unpeopled world of the Volga. He lay with his arms under his head and gazed fixedly into space. His head held the dim picture of the remote south, of the sun, the sea, Anapu, and it was something fabulous—as if the town to which she had gone, the town in which she had doubtless arrived, was like no other town—and with it all there ripened the persistent thought of pungent, hot tears—and at last fell asleep. When he again opened his eyes there was already visible, through the curtains, the darkening reddish evening sun. The breeze had died down, the room was stuffy and dry, as in a wind furnace. . . . And he remembered yesterday and this morning precisely as if they had been ten years ago.

In no great haste he rose, in no great haste he washed himself; then he pulled the curtains aside, rang for the servant, asked for a samovar and his bill, and for a long time he drank tea with lemon.

Then he ordered a cab and had his luggage taken out, and, seating himself in the reddish, burnt-out seat of the carriage, he gave the servant a whole five rubles as a tip.

"It looks, Your Honor, as though I brought you here last night!" said the cabby cheerfully, as he seized the reins.

When they reached the pier, the blue summer night already darkened above the Volga and many varicolored flames were scattered upon the river and flames hung in the mast of the approaching steamer.

"Got you here just in time!" said the cabby ingratiatingly.

The lieutenant also gave him five rubles, then with ticket in hand went to the pier. . . . Even as yesterday there was the soft sound of the hawsers, and the light dizziness from the vacillation under foot; then came the flying end of the cable, the clamor of the seething waters under the wheels of the steamer receding from the impact. . . . And the sight of the much-peopled steamer, ablaze with light, and the smells of its kitchens, seemed to extend a warm welcome.

Another minute, and the steamer was under way, going up the river, in the direction in which it had borne her away that same morning.

Ahead of it, the dark summer sunset was rapidly fading; gloomily, dreamily and iridescently, it was reflected in the river, showing patches glimmering with tremulous ripples in the distance under the sunset, and the flames scattered in the darkness round the steamer went on receding and receding.

The lieutenant sat under cover on deck, conscious of having aged by ten years.

[*Translated by Teka Matheson*]

Luigi Pirandello

WAR

LUIGI PIRANDELLO, *poet, playwright, novelist, and short-story writer, was born in Sicily in 1867. After taking a doctorate at the University of Bonn, he became a professor of literature at a teachers' college in Rome, where he spent most of his early career. He published a volume of poetry in 1889 and soon began to write fiction in the naturalistic mode, bearing the typical Pirandello note of benevolent irony and pity toward men and women who are caught in the web of human life, who suffer without understanding. His first plays were dramatic versions of his early Sicilian stories. By 1918 he was devoting his full energies to the stage: he founded his own theater in Rome and took his own acting companies on tours with his plays throughout Europe. Before long, his symbolical and satirical dramas became internationally famous and aroused controversy because of their alleged obscurity. He was awarded the Nobel Prize in 1934. Subsequently, many of his works, such as* Henry IV *and* As You Desire Me, *were effectively filmed, and quite recently, New York saw a successful revival of* Six Characters in Search of an Author. *Pirandello died in Rome in 1936.* "War" *shows his ability to suggest in a word or phrase as much as others less skillful convey in a page.*

The passengers who had left Rome by the night express had had to stop until dawn at the small station of Fabriano in order to continue their journey by the small old-fashioned local joining the main line with Sulmona.

At dawn, in a stuffy and smoky second-class carriage in which five people had already spent the night, a bulky woman in deep mourning was hoisted in—almost like a shapeless bundle. Behind her—puffing and moaning, followed her husband—a tiny man, thin and weakly, his face death-white, his eyes small and bright and looking shy and uneasy.

Having at last taken a seat he politely thanked the passengers who had helped his wife and who had made room for her; then he turned around to the woman trying to pull down the collar of her coat, and politely inquired:

"Are you all right, dear?"

The wife, instead of answering, pulled up her collar again to her eyes, so as to hide her face.

"Nasty world," muttered the husband with a sad smile.

And he felt it his duty to explain to his traveling companions that the poor woman was to be pitied, for the war was taking away from her her only son, a boy of twenty to whom both had devoted their entire life, even breaking up their home at Sulmona to follow him to Rome, where he had to go as a student, then allowing him to volunteer for war with an assurance, however, that at least for six months he would not be sent to the front and now, all of a sudden, receiving a wire saying that he was due to leave in three days' time and asking them to go and see him off.

The woman under the big coat was twisting and wriggling, at times growling like a wild animal, feeling certain that all those explanations would not have aroused even a shadow of sympathy from those people who—most likely—were in the same plight as herself. One of them, who had been listening with particular attention, said:

"You should thank God that your son is only leaving now for the front. Mine has been sent there the first day of the war. He has already come back twice wounded and been sent back again to the front."

"What about me? I have two sons and three nephews at the front," said another passenger.

"Maybe, but in our case it is our *only* son," ventured the husband.

"What difference can it make? You may spoil your only son with excessive attention, but you cannot love him more than you would all your other children if you had any. Paternal love is not like bread that can be broken into pieces and split amongst the children in equal shares. A father gives *all* his love to each one of his children without discrimination, whether it be one or ten, and if I am suffering now for my two sons, I am not suffering half for each of them but double . . ."

"True . . . true . . ." sighed the embarrassed husband, "but suppose (of course we all hope it will never be your case) a father has two sons at the front and he loses one of them, there is still one left to console him . . . while . . ."

"Yes," answered the other, getting cross, "a son left to console him but also a son left for whom he must survive, while in the case of the father of an only son if the son dies the father can die too and put an end to his distress. Which of the two positions is the worse? Don't you see how my case would be worse than yours?"

"Nonsense," interrupted another traveler, a fat, red-faced man with bloodshot eyes of the palest gray.

He was panting. From his bulging eyes seemed to spurt inner violence of an uncontrolled vitality which his weakened body could hardly contain.

"Nonsense," he repeated, trying to cover his mouth with his hand so as to hide the two missing front teeth. "Nonsense. Do we give life to our children for our own benefit?"

The other travelers stared at him in distress. The one who had had his son at the front since the first day of the war sighed: "You are right. Our children do not belong to us; they belong to the Country. . . ."

"Bosh," retorted the fat traveler. "Do we think of the Country when we give life to our children? Our sons are born because . . . well, because they must be born and when they come to life they take our own life with them. This is the truth. We belong to them but they never belong to us. And when they reach twenty they are exactly what we were at their age. We too had a father and a mother, but there were so many other things as well . . . girls, cigarettes, illusions, new ties . . . and the Country, of course, whose call we would have answered—when we were twenty—even if father and mother had said no. Now at our age, the love of our Country is still great, of course, but stronger than it is the love of our children. Is there any one of us here who wouldn't gladly take his son's place at the front if he could?"

There was a silence all round, everybody nodding as to approve.

"Why the ——" continued the fat man, "shouldn't we consider the feelings of our children when they are twenty? Isn't it natural that at their age they should consider the love for their Country (I am speaking of decent boys, of course) even greater than the love for us? Isn't it natural that it should be so, as after all they must look upon us as upon old boys who cannot move any more and must stay at home? If Country exists, if Country is a natural necessity, like bread, of which each of us must eat in order not to die of hunger, somebody must go to defend it. And our sons go, when they are twenty, and they don't want tears, because if they die, they die inflamed and happy (I am speaking, of course, of decent boys). Now, if one dies young and happy, without having the ugly sides of life, the boredom of it, the pettiness, the bitterness of disillusion . . . what more can we ask for him? Everyone should stop crying; everyone should laugh, as I do . . . or at least thank God—as I do—because my son, before dying, sent me a message saying that he was dying satisfied at having ended his life in the best way he could have wished. That is why, as you see, I do not even wear mourning. . . ."

He shook his light fawn coat so as to show it; his livid lip over his missing teeth was trembling, his eyes were watery and motionless, and soon after he ended with a shrill laugh which might well have been a sob.

"Quite so . . . quite so . . ." agreed the others.

The woman who, bundled in a corner under her coat, had been sitting and listening had— for the last three months—tried to find in the words of her husband and her friends something to console her in her deep sorrow, something that might show her how a mother should resign herself to send her son not even to death but to a probably dangerous life. Yet not a word had she found amongst the many which had been said . . . and her grief had been greater in seeing that nobody—as she thought—could share her feelings.

But now the words of the traveler amazed and almost stunned her. She suddenly realized that it wasn't the others who were wrong and who could not understand her but herself who could not rise up to the same height of those fathers and mothers willing to resign themselves, without crying, not only to the departure of their sons but even to their death.

She lifted her head, she bent over from her corner trying to listen with great attention to the details which the fat man was giving to his companions about the way his son had fallen as hero, for his King and his Country, happy and without regrets. It seemed to her that she had stumbled into a world she had never dreamed of, a world so far unknown to her and she was so pleased to hear everyone joining in congratulating that brave father who could so stoically speak of his child's death.

Then suddenly, just as if she had heard nothing of what had been said and almost as if waking up from a dream, she turned to the old man, asking him:

"Then . . . is your son really dead?"

Everybody stared at her. The old man, too, turned to look at her, fixing his great, bulging, horribly watery light gray eyes, deep in her face. For some little time he tried to answer, but words failed him. He looked and looked at her, almost as if only then— at that silly, incongruous question—he had suddenly realized at least that his son was really dead—gone for ever—for ever. His face contracted, became horribly distorted, then he snatched in haste a handkerchief from his pocket and, to the amazement of everyone, broke into harrowing, heart-rending, uncontrollable sobs.

[*Translated by Micheal Pettinati*]

Roger Martin Du Gard

THE OPERATION

ROGER MARTIN DU GARD *was born in* 1881 *near Paris and educated there as an archivist-paleographer. His deep respect for historical truth and painstaking documentation which he acquired from this training is discernible in* Jean Barois, *his first successful novel, and* Les Thibaults, *the great roman-fleuve that brought the author the Nobel Prize in* 1937. *Conceived originally as a study of one family (a broader* Jean Barois), Les Thibaults *grew over a period of sixteen years into a ten-volume panorama of French life during the period prior to World War I. Martin du Gard's response to the interplay between the physical and the spiritual, his gift for depicting scenes of action, his fascination with intense, almost brutally physical, life are nowhere better concentrated than in the following story from this work. His most important recent publication is the brief but revealing memoir of his master, Andre Gide. He died in* 1958.

When the taxi pulled up near the Tuileries in front of the house in the Rue d'alger where the Chasles lived, Antoine had pieced together from the concierge's flustered explanations, an outline of the accident. The victim was a little girl who used to meet "M. Jules" each evening on his way back. Had she tried to cross the Rue de Rivoli on this occasion, as M. Jules was late in coming home? A delivery tri-car had knocked her down and passed over her body. A crowd had gathered and a newspaper-vender who was present had recognized the child by her plaited hair, and furnished her address. She had been carried unconscious to the flat.

M. Chasle, crouching in a corner of the taxi, shed no tears, but each new detail drew from him a racking sob, half muffled by the hand he pressed against his mouth.

A crowd still lingered around the doorway. They made way for M. Chasle, who had to be helped up the stairs as far as the top landing by his two companions. A door stood open at the end of a corridor, down which M. Chasle made his way on stumbling feet. The concierge stood back to let Antoine pass, and touched him on the arm.

"My wife, who's got a head on her shoulders, ran off to fetch the young doctor who dines at the restaurant next door. I hope she found him there."

Antoine nodded approval and followed M. Chasle. They crossed a sort of anteroom, redolent of musty cupboards, then two low rooms with tiled floors; the light was dim and the atmosphere stifling despite the open windows fronting on a courtyard. In the further room Antoine had to edge around a circular table where a meal for four was laid on a strip of dingy oilcloth. M. Chasle opened a door and, entering a brightly lit room, stumbled forward with a piteous cry:

"Dédette! Dédette!"

"Now, Jules!" a raucous voice protested.

The first thing Antoine noticed was the lamp which a woman in a pink dressing gown was lifting with both hands; her ruddy hair, her throat and forehead were flooded with the lamplight. Then he observed the bed on which the light fell, and shadowy forms bending above it. Dregs of the sunset, filtering through the window, merged in the halo of the lamp, and the room was bathed in a half-light where all things took the semblance of a dream. Antoine helped M. Chasle to a chair and approached the bed. A young man wearing pince-nez, with his hat still on, was bending forward and slitting up with a pair of scissors the bloodstained garments of the little girl. Her face, ringed with matted hair, lay buried in the bolster. An old woman on her knees was helping the doctor.

"Is she alive?" Antoine asked.

The doctor turned, looked at him, and hesitated; then mopped his forehead.

"Yes." His tone lacked assurance.

"I was with M. Chasle when he was sent for," Antoine explained, "and I've brought my first-aid kit. I'm Dr. Thibault," he added in a whisper, "house-physician at the Children's Hospital."

The young doctor arose and was about to make way for Antoine.

"Carry on! Carry on!" Antoine drew back a step. "Pulse?"

"Almost imperceptible," the doctor replied, intent once more on his task.

Antoine raised his eyes toward the red-haired young woman, saw the anxiety in her face, and made a suggestion.

"Wouldn't it be best to telephone for an ambulance and have your child taken at once to my hospital?"

"No!" an imperious voice answered him.

Then Antoine descried an old woman standing at the head of the bed—was it the child's grandmother?—and scanning him intently with eyes limpid as water, a peasant's eyes. Her pointed nose and resolute features were half submerged in a vast sea of fat that heaved in billowy folds upon her neck.

"I know we look like paupers," she continued in a resigned tone, "but, believe me, even folk like us would rather die at home in our own beds. Dédette shan't go to the hospital."

"But why not, Madame?" Antoine protested.

She straightened up her back, thrust out her chin, and sadly but sternly rebuked him.

"We prefer not," was all she said.

Antoine tried to catch the eye of the younger woman, but she was busy brushing off the flies that obstinately settled on her glowing cheeks, and seemed of no opinion. He decided to appeal to M. Chasle. The old fellow had fallen on his knees in front of the chair to which Antoine had led him; his head was buried on his folded arms as though to shut out all sights from his eyes; and, from his ears, all sounds. The old lady, who was keenly watching Antoine's movements, guessed his intention and forestalled him.

"Isn't that so, Jules?"

M. Chasle started.

"Yes, Mother."

She looked at him approvingly and her voice grew mothering. "Don't stay there, Jules. You'd be much better in your room."

A pallid forehead rose into view, eyes tremulous behind their spectacles; then without a protest, the poor old fellow stood up and tip-toed from the room.

Antoine bit his lips. Meanwhile, pending an occasion further to insist, he took off his coat and rolled up his sleeves above the elbows. Then he knelt at the bedside. He seldom took thought without at the same time beginning to take action—such was his incapacity for long deliberation on any issue raised, and such his keenness to be up and doing. The avoidance of mistakes counted less with him than bold decision and prompt activity. Thought, as he used it, was merely the lever that set an act in motion—premature thought it might be.

Aided by the doctor and the old woman's trembling hands, he had soon stripped off the child's clothing; pale, almost gray, her body lay beneath their eyes in its frail nakedness. The impact of the car must have been very violent, for she was covered with bruises, and a black streak crossed her thigh transversely from hip to knee.

"It's the right leg," Antoine's colleague observed. Her right foot was twisted, bent inwards, and the whole leg was spattered with blood and deformed, shorter than the other one.

"Fracture of the femur?" suggested the doctor.

Antoine did not answer. He was thinking. "That's not all," he said to himself; "the shock is too great for that. But what can it be?" He tapped her kneecap, then ran his fingers slowly up her thigh; suddenly there spurted through an almost imperceptible lesion on the inner side of the thigh, some inches above the knee, a jet of blood.

"That's it," he said.

"The femoral artery!" the other exclaimed.

Antoine rose quickly to his feet. The need to make, unaided, a decision gave him a new access of energy and, as ever when others were present, his sense of power intensified. A surgeon? he speculated. No, we'd never get her alive to the hospital. Then who? I? Why not? And anyhow, there's no alternative.

"Will you try a ligature?" asked the doctor, piqued by Antoine's silence.

But Antoine did not heed the question. It must be done, he was thinking, and without a moment's delay; it may be too late already, who knows? He threw a quick glance round him. A ligature. What can be used? Let's see. The red-headed girl hasn't a belt; no loops on the curtains. Something elastic. Ah, I have it! In a twinkling he had thrown off his waistcoat and unfastened his braces. Snapping them with a jerk, he knelt down again, made them a tourniquet, and clamped it tightly around the child's groin.

"Good! Two minutes' breathing-time," he said as he rose. Sweat was pouring down his cheeks. He knew that every eye was fixed on him. "Only an immediate operation," he said decisively, "can save her life. Let's try."

The others moved away at once from the bed—even the woman with the lamp, even the young doctor, whose face had paled.

Antoine clenched his teeth, his eyes narrowed and grew hard, he seemed to peer into himself. Must keep calm, he mused. A table? That round table I saw, coming in.

"Bring the lamp!" he cried to the young woman, then turned to the doctor. "You there—come with me!" He strode quickly into the next room. Good, he said to himself; here's our operating theater. With a quick gesture, he cleared the table, stacked the plates in a pile. "That's for my lamp." Like a general in charge of a campaign, he allotted each thing its place. "Now for our little patient." He went back to the bedroom. The doctor and the young woman hung on his every gesture and followed close behind him. Addressing the doctor, he pointed to the child:

"I'll carry her. She's light as a feather. Hold up her leg, you."

As he slipped his arms under the child's back and carried her to the table, she moaned faintly. He took the lamp from the red-haired woman and, removing the shade, stood it on the pile of plates. As he surveyed the scene, a thought came suddenly and went: "I'm a wonderful fellow!" The lamp gleamed like a brazier, reddening the ambient shadow, where only the young woman's glowing cheeks and the doctor's pince-nez showed up as high-lights; its rays fell harshly on the little body, which twitched spasmodically. The swarming flies seemed worked up to a frenzy by the oncoming storm. Heat and anxiety brought beads of sweat to Antoine's brow. Would she live through it? he wondered, but some dark force he did not analyze buoyed up his faith; never had he felt so sure of himself.

He seized his bag and, taking out a bottle of chloroform and some gauze, handed the former to the doctor.

"Open it somewhere. On the sideboard. Take off the sewing-machine. Get everything out."

As he turned, holding the bottle, he noticed two dim figures in the dark doorway, two old women like statues posted there. One, M. Chasle's mother, had great, staring eyes, an owl's eyes; the other was pressing her breast with her clasped hands.

"Go away!" he commanded. They retreated some steps into the shadows of the bedroom, but he pointed to the other end of the flat. "No. Out of the room. That way." They obeyed, crossed the room, vanished without a word.

"Not you!" he cried angrily to the red-haired woman, who was about to follow them.

She turned on her heel, and, for a moment, he took stock of her. She had a handsome, rather fleshy face, touched with a certain dignity, it seemed, by grief; an air of calm maturity that pleased him. Poor woman! he could not help thinking . . . But I need her!

"You're the child's mother?" he asked.

"No." She shook her head.

"All the better."

As he spoke he had been soaking the gauze and now he swiftly stretched it over the child's nose. "Stand here, and keep this." He handed her the bottle. "When I give the signal, you'll pour some more of it on."

The air grew heavy with the reek of chloroform. The little girl groaned, drew a deep breath or two, grew still.

A last look around. The field was clear; the rest lay with the surgeon's skill. Now that the crucial moment had come, Antoine's anxieties vanished as if by magic. He went to the sideboard where the doctor, holding the bag, was laying on a napkin the last of its contents. "Let's see," he murmured, as though to gain a few seconds' respite. "There's the instrument box; good. The scalpel, the artery forceps. A packet of gauze, cotton-wool, that'll do. Alcohol. Caffeine. Tincture of iodine. And so forth . . . All's ready. Let's begin." And yet again there came to him that sense of buoyancy, of boundless confidence, of vital energies tautened to breaking-point, and crowning all, a proud awareness of being lifted high above his workaday self.

Raising his head, he looked his junior for a moment in the eyes. "Have you the nerve?" his eyes seemed to inquire. "It's going to be a tough job. Now for it."

The young man did not flinch. And now he hung on Antoine's gestures with servile assiduity. Well he knew that in this operation lay their only hope, but never would he have dared to take the risk, alone. With Antoine, however, nothing seemed impossible.

He's not so bad, this young chap, thought Antoine. Lucky for me! Let's see. A basin? No matter—this will do as well. Grasping the bottle of iodine he sluiced his arms up to the elbow with the liquid.

"Your turn!" He passed the bottle to the doctor, who was feverishly polishing the lenses of his pince-nez.

A vivid lightning flash, closely followed by a deafening clap of thunder, lit up the window.

"A bit previous, the applause," Antoine said to himself. "I hadn't even taken up my lancet. The young woman didn't turn a hair. It'll cool things down; good for our nerves. Must be pretty nearly a hundred degrees in this room."

He had laid out a series of compresses round the injured limb, delimiting the operative field. Now he turned toward the young woman.

"A whiff of chloroform. That'll do. Right!"

She obeys orders, he mused, like a soldier under fire. Women! Then, fixing his eyes on the swollen little thigh, he swallowed his saliva and raised his scalpel.

"Here goes!"

With one neat stroke he cut the skin.

"Swab!" he commanded the doctor bending beside him. "What a thin child!" he said to himself. "Well, we'll be there all the sooner. Hello, there's little Dédette starting to snore!" Good! Better be quick about it. Now for the retractors."

"Now you," he said aloud, and the other let fall the blood-stained swabs of cotton-wool and grasping the retractors, held the wound open.

Antoine paused a moment. "Good!" he murmured. "My probe? Here it is. In Hunter's Canal. The classical ligation; all's well. Zip! Another flash! Must have landed pretty near. On the Louvre. Perhaps on the 'gentleman at Saint-Roch.'" He felt quite calm—no more anxiety for the child, none for death's imminence—and cheerfully repeated under his breath: "The ligature of the femoral artery in Hunter's Canal."

Zip! There goes another! Hardly any rain, either. It's stifling. Artery is injured at the site of the fracture; the end of the bone tore it open. Simple as anything. Still she hadn't much blood to spare. He glanced at the little girl's face. Hello! Better hurry up. Simple as anything—but could be fatal, too. A forceps; right! Another; that will do. Zip! These flashes are getting a bore; cheap effect! I've only plaited silk; must make the best of it. Breaking a tube, he pulled out the skein and made a ligature beside each forceps. Splendid! Almost finished now. The collateral circulation will be quite enough, especially at that age. I'm really wonderful! Can I have missed my location? I've all the makings of a surgeon, sure enough; a great surgeon. In the silent interval between two thunder-claps dying into the distance, the sharp metallic click of scissors snipping the loose ends of the silk was audible. Yes; quickness of eye, coolness, energy, dexterity. Suddenly he picked up his ears and his cheeks paled.

"The devil!" he muttered under his breath.

The child had ceased to breathe.

Brushing aside the woman, he tore away the gauze from the unconscious child's face and pressed his ear above her heart. Doctor and young woman waited in suspense, their eyes fixed on Antoine.

"No!" he murmured. "She's breathing still."

He took the child's wrist, but her pulse was so rapid that he did not attempt to count it. "Ouf!" He drew a deep breath, the lines of anxiety deepened on his forehead. The two others felt his gaze pass across their faces, but he did not see them.

He rapped out a brief command.

"You, doctor, remove the forceps, put on a dressing, and then undo the tourniquet. Quickly. You, Madame, get me some note-paper—no, you needn't; I've my notebook." He wiped his hands feverishly with a wad of cotton-wool. "What's the time? Not nine yet. The pharmacist's open. You'll have to hurry."

She stood before him, waiting; her tentative gesture—to wrap the dressing gown more closely around her body—told him of her reluctance at going thus, half-dressed, into the streets, and for the fraction of a second a picture of the opulent form under the garment held his imagination. He scribbled a prescription, signed it. "A two-pint ampoule. As quickly as you can."

"And if—?" she stammered.

"If the pharmacist's shut, ring, and keep on hammering on the door till they open it. Be quick!"

She was gone. He followed her with his eyes to make sure she was running, then addressed the doctor.

"We'll try the saline. Not subcutaneously; that's hopeless now.

Intravenously. Our last hope." He took two small phials from the sideboard. "You've removed the tourniquet? Right. Give her an injection of camphor to begin with, then the caffeine—only half of it for her, poor kid! Only, for God's sake, be quick about it!"

He went back to the child and took her thin wrist between his fingers; now he could feel nothing more than a vague, restless fluttering. "It's got past counting," he said to himself. And suddenly a feeling of impotence, or sheer despair, swept over him.

"God damn it!" he broke out. "To think it went off perfectly—and it was all of no use!"

The child's face became more livid with every second. She was dying. Antoine observed, beside the parted lips, two slender strands of curling hair, lighter than gossamer, that rose and fell; anyhow, she was still breathing.

He watched the doctor giving the injections. Neat with his fingers, he thought, considering his short sight. But we can't save her. Vexation rather than grief possessed him. He had the callousness common to doctors, for whom the sufferings of others count only as so much new experience, or profit, or professional advantage; men to whose fortunes death and pain are frequent ministers.

But then he thought he heard a banging door and ran toward the sound. It was the young woman coming back with quick, lithe steps, trying to conceal her breathlessness. He snatched the parcel from her hands.

"Bring some hot water." He did not even pause to thank her. "Boiled?"

"No. To warm the solution. Be quick!"

He had hardly opened the parcel when she returned, bringing a steaming saucepan.

"Good! Excellent!" he murmured, but did not look toward her.

No time to lose. In a few seconds he had nipped off the tips of the ampoule and slipped on the rubber tubing. A Swiss barometer in carved wood hung on the wall. With one hand he unhooked it, while with the other he hung the ampoule on the nail. Then he took the saucepan of hot water, hesitated for the fraction of a second, and looped the rubber tubing round the bottom of it. That'll heat the saline as it flows through, he said to himself. Smart idea, that! He glanced toward the other doctor to see if he had noticed what he had done. At last, he came back to the child, lifted her inert arm, and sponged it with iodine. Then, with a stroke of his scalpel, he laid bare the vein, slipped his probe beneath it and inserted the needle.

"It's flowing in all right," he cried. "Take her pulse. I'll stay where I am."

The ten minutes that followed seemed an eternity. No one moved or spoke.

Streaming with sweat, breathing rapidly, with knitted brows, Antoine waited, his gaze riveted on the needle. After a while he glanced up at the ampoule.

"How much gone?"

"Nearly a pint."

"The pulse?"

The doctor silently shook his head.

Five more minutes passed, five minutes more of sickening suspense. Antoine looked up again.

"How much left?"

"Just over half a pint."

"And the pulse?"

The doctor hesitated.

"I'm not sure. I almost think . . . it's beginning to come back a little."

"Can you count it?"

A pause.

"No."

If only the pulse came back! sighed Antoine. He would have given ten years of his own life to restore life to this little corpse. Wonder what age she is? Seven? And, if I save her, she'll fall a victim to consumption within the next ten years, living in this hovel. But shall I save her? It's touch and go; her life hangs on a thread. Still—damn it!—I've done all I could. The saline's flowing well. But it's too late. There's nothing more to be done, nothing else to try. We can only wait. . . . That red-haired girl did her bit. A good-looker. She's not the child's mother; who can she be then? Chasle never breathed a word about all these people. Not his daughter, I imagine. Can't make head or tail of it! And that old woman, putting on airs . . . Anyhow, they made themselves scarce, good riddance! Curious how one suddenly gets them in hand. They all knew the sort of man they had to deal with. The strong hand of the masterful man. But it was up to me to bring it off. Shall I now? No, she lost too much blood on the way here. No signs of improvement so far, worse luck! Oh, damn it all!

His gaze fell on the child's pale lips and the two strands of golden hair, rising and falling still. The breathing struck him as a little better. Was he mistaken? Half a minute passed. Her chest seemed to flutter with a faint sigh which slowly died into the air, as though a fragment of her life were passing with it. For a moment Antoine stared at her in perplexity. No, she was breathing still. Nothing to be done but to wait, and keep on waiting.

A minute later she sighed again, more plainly now.

"How much left?"

"The ampoule's almost empty."

"And the pulse? Coming back?"

"Yes."

Antoine drew a deep breath.

"Can you count it?"

The doctor took out his watch, settled his pince-nez, and, after a minute's silence, announced:

"A hundred and forty. A hundred and fifty, perhaps."

"Better than nothing!" The exclamation was involuntary, for Antoine was straining every nerve to withstand the flood of huge relief that surged across his mind. Yet it was not imagination; the improvement was not to be gainsaid. Her breathing was steadier; it was all he could do to stay where he was; he had a childish longing to sing or whistle. *Better than nothing tra-la-la—* he tried to fit the words to the tune that had been haunting him all day. *In my heart tra-la-la. In my heart sleeps* . . . Sleeps— sleeps *what?* Got it. *The pale moonlight.*

In my heart sleep the pale moonlight
Of a lovely summer night . . .

The cloud of doubt lifted, gave place to radiant joy.
"The child's saved," he murmured. "She's *got to be* saved!"

. . . a lovely summer night!

"The ampoule's empty," the doctor announced.
"Capital!"

Just then the child, whom his eyes had never left, gave a shudder. Antoine turned almost gaily to the young woman, who, leaning against the sideboard, had been watching the scene with steady eyes for the past quarter of an hour.

"Well, Madame!" he cried with affected gruffness. "Gone to sleep, have we? And how about the hot-water bottle?" He almost smiled at her amazement. "But my dear lady, nothing could be more obvious. A bottle, piping hot, to warm her little toes."

A flash of joy lit up her eyes as she hastened from the room.

Then Antoine, with redoubled care and gentleness, bent down and drew out the needle, and with the tips of his fingers applied a compress to the tiny wound. He ran his fingers along the arm from which the hand still hung limp.

"Another injection of camphor, old man, just to make sure; and then we'll have played our last card. Shouldn't wonder," he added under his breath, "if we've pulled it off." Once more that sense of power that was half joy elated him.

The woman came back carrying a jar in her arms. She hesitated, then, as he said nothing, came and stood by the child's feet.

"Not like that!" said Antoine, with the same brusque cheerfulness. "You'll burn her. Give it here. Just imagine my having to show you how to wrap up a hot-water bottle!"

Smiling now, he snatched up a rolled napkin that caught his eye and, flinging the ring onto the sideboard, wrapped the jar in it and pressed it to the child's feet. The red-haired woman watched him, taken aback by the boyish smile that made his face seem so much younger.

"Then she's—saved?" she ventured to ask.

He dared not affirm it as yet.

"I'll tell you in an hour's time." His voice was gruff, but she took his meaning and cast on him a bold, admiring look.

For the third time Antoine asked himself what this handsome girl could be doing in the Chasle household. Then he pointed to the door.

"What about the others?"

A smile hovered on her lips.

"They're waiting."

"Hearten them up a bit. Tell them to go to bed. You too, Madame, you'd better take some rest."

"Oh, as far as I'm concerned . . ." she murmured, turning to go.

"Let's get the child back to bed," Antoine suggested to his colleague. "The same way as before. Hold up her leg. Take the bolster away; we'd better keep her head down. The next thing is to rig up some sort of a gadget . . . That napkin, please, and the string from the parcel. Some sort of extension, you see. Slip the string between the rails; handy things these iron bedsteads. Now for a weight. Anything will do. How about this saucepan? No, the flat-iron there will be better. We've all we need here. Yes, hand it over. Tomorrow we'll improve on it. Meanwhile it will do if we stretch the leg a bit, don't you think so?"

The young doctor did not reply. He gazed at Antoine with spellbound awe—the look that Martha may have given the Savior when Lazarus rose from the tomb. His lips worked and he stammered timidly:

"May I . . . shall I arrange your instruments?" The faltered words breathed such a zeal for service and for devotion that Antoine thrilled with the exultation of an acknowledged chief. They were alone. Antoine went up to the younger man and looked him in the eyes.

"You've been splendid, my dear fellow."

The young man gasped. Antoine, who felt even more embarrassed than his colleague, gave him no time to put in a word.

"Now you'd better be off home; it's late. There's no need for two of us here." He hesitated. "We may take it that she's saved, I think. That's my opinion. However, for safety's sake, I'll stay here for the night, if you'll permit me." The doctor made a vague gesture. "If you permit me, I repeat. For I don't forget that she's your patient. Obviously. I only gave a hand, as there was nothing else for it. That's so, eh? But from tomorrow on I leave her in your hands. They're competent hands and I have no anxiety." As he spoke he led the doctor toward the door. "Will you look in again toward noon? I'll come back when I'm done at the hospital and we will decide on the treatment to follow."

"Sir, it's . . . it's been a privilege for me to . . . to . . ."

Never before had Antoine been "sirred" by a colleague, never before been treated with such deference. It went to his head, like generous wine, and unthinkingly he held out both hands toward the young man. But in the nick of time he regained his self-control.

"You've got the wrong impression," he said in a subdued tone. "I'm only a learner, a novice—like you. Like so many others. Like everyone. Groping our way. We do our best—and that's all there is to it."

Antoine had looked forward to the young man's exit with something like impatience. To be alone, perhaps. Yet, when he heard approaching footsteps, the young woman's, his face lit up.

"Look here, don't you intend to go to bed?"

"No, doctor."

He did not press her further.

The little girl moaned, was shaken by a hiccup, expectorated.

"Good girl, Dédette," he said. "That's a good girl." He took her pulse. "A hundred and twenty. Steady improvement." He looked at the woman, unsmiling. "I think I can say now that we're out of the wood."

She did not reply, but he felt she had faith in him. He wanted to talk to her and cast about for an opening.

"You were very plucky," he said. Then—as was his wont when

he felt shy—he went directly to the point. "What are you here, exactly?"

"I? Nothing. I'm not even a friend of theirs. It's only that I live on the fifth floor, just below."

"But who is the child's mother then? I can't make head or tail of it."

"Her mother is dead, I think. She was Aline's sister."

"Aline?"

"The servant."

"The old thing with the shaky hands?"

"Yes."

"So the child's not in any way related to the Chasles?"

"No. Aline's bringing up her little niece here—M. Jules pays, of course."

They spoke in undertones, bending a little toward each other, and Antoine had a nearer view of her lips and cheeks, and the pale beauty of her skin, touched with a curious glamor by fatigue. He felt over-tired and restless, at the mercy of every impulse.

The child stirred in her sleep. As they approached the bed together her eyelids fluttered, then closed again.

"Perhaps the light worries her," the young woman suggested, taking the lamp and placing it further from the bed. Then, returning to the bedside, she wiped the beads of perspiration from the child's forehead. Antoine followed her movements with his eyes and, as she stooped, he felt a sudden thrill; outlined as in a shadow-play under the flimsy dressing-gown, the young woman's body was silhouetted, frankly provocative as if she stood naked before him. He held his breath; a dark fire seemed to sear his eyes, watching through misty shadows the languid rise and fall of her bosom rhythmed to her breath. Antoine's hands grew suddenly cold as ice, contracted as if in a spasm. Never before with such an urgency of passion had he desired another human being.

"Mlle. Rachel," a voice whispered.

She drew herself up.

"It's Aline; she wants to come and see the child."

Smiling, she seemed to plead the servant's cause and, though vexed by the intrusion, he dared not deny her.

"So your name's Rachel," he stammered. "Yes, let her come." He hardly noticed the old woman kneeling beside the bed. He went to an open window; his temples were throbbing. No cooling breeze came from without; far above the housetops the distant glimmer of a star or two spangled the darkness. Now at length he realized his weariness; he had been on his feet for three or four hours on end. He looked round for a seat. Between the windows two small mattresses resting on the tiled floor formed a sort of couch. Here, no doubt, Dédette usually slept; the room was evidently Aline's bedroom. He ran onto the pallet, propping his back against the wall, and again an uncontrollable desire swept over him—to see once again, half veiled beneath the tenuous fabric, Rachel's firm breasts, their rhythmic rise and fall. But she was no longer standing in the light.

"Didn't the child move her leg?" he inquired without rising. As she walked toward the bed, her body lithely swayed beneath the wrap.

"Is she still as pale as she was?"

"A little less."

"Move her head straight, will you? Quite flat and straight." Now she stepped into the zone of light, but only for a moment, as she passed between the lamp and Antoine. The moment sufficed, however, to quicken his desire anew. He had to shut his eye, jam his back against the wall and thus remain, clenching his teeth, struggling to keep his eyelids closed upon their secret vision. The stench of cities in the summer, a mingled reek of horse-dung, smoke, and dusty asphalt stifled the air. Flies pattered on the lampshade, hovered on Antoine's damp cheeks. Now and again thunder rumbled still, above the remoter suburbs.

Little by little, fever, heat, and the very urgency of his emotion sapped his powers of resistance. He was unconscious of the slow tide of lethargy advancing; his muscles relaxed, his shoulders settled down against the wall, he fell asleep. . . .

It was as if a summons, gently insistent, were calling him from sleep and, still on the verge of dreams, he was vaguely aware of the pleasurable feeling. For a long while he hovered in an ecstatic limbo, unable to discover by what channel and at what point on the surface of his body the warm tide of well-being was seeping in. Presently he traced it to his leg and, at the same moment, grew conscious that someone was seated at his side; that the warmth along his thigh emanated from a living body; that this warmth and the body were Rachel's and the sensation was really one of sensual pleasure, enhanced now that he knew its origin. Her body must have slipped toward him as she slept. He had self-control enough to sit quite still . . . Now he was wide-awake. All the feelings of his body were centered in a little space, no wider than a hand's breadth, where, across the thin covering of their garments, thigh touched thigh. He stayed thus, motionless, breathing rapidly yet fully lucid, finding in the mingling of his body's warmth with hers a thrill more potent than the subtlest of caresses.

Suddenly Rachel awoke and stretched her arms; drawing away from him, but without haste, she sat up. He made as if he, too, were just awaking, roused by her movement.

"I dozed off," she confessed with a smile.

"So did I."

"It's almost daylight," she murmured as she raised her arms to settle her hair.

Antoine glanced at his watch; it was just on four.

The child lay all but motionless. Aline's hands were clasped, as if in prayer. Antoine went to the bed and drew aside the blankets.

"Not a drop of blood—that's good."

While his eyes followed Rachel's movements, he took the child's pulse; a hundred and ten.

How warm her leg was! he was thinking.

Rachel was examining her reflection in a strip of looking-glass, tacked with three nails to the wall, and smiling. With her shock of red hair, open collar, strong bare arms, and her bold, free-and-easy, slightly scornful air, she might have stood for a heroine of the Revolution, a Marseillaise on the barricades.

"I'm a fine sight!" She pouted at her reflected self, though well aware that the young bloom of her cheeks lost, even in the acid test of waking, nothing of its charm. This was plain to read on Antoine's face, as moving to her side, he peered into the mirror. She noticed that the young man's gaze fastened not on her eyes, but on her lips.

But then Antoine took stock of his own appearance—sleeves rolled up, arms burnt with iodine, his shirt crumped and stained with blood.

"And to think I was due to dine at Packmell's!" he exclaimed.

A curious smile flickered on Rachel's face.

"Say! So you go to Packmell's sometimes?"

Their eyes were smiling, and Antoine's heart leapt with joy. He knew little of women other than those of easy virtue. Now suddenly Rachel seemed to become less inaccessible to his desire.

"I'll go downstairs to my flat," she said and turned to Aline, who was watching them. "If I can be of any help, don't hesitate to call me."

Then, without bidding Antoine good-bye, she drew the flaps of her dressing-gown together and discreetly made her exit.

No sooner had she gone than he too felt a wish to leave. "A breath of fresh air," he murmured, glancing over the housetops toward the morning sky. "Must go home too, and explain to Jacques. I can return when I've done with the hospital. Washed, presentable. Might have them send for her to help with the dressing. Or shall I look in on my way up? But I don't even know if she's living by herself."

He explained to Aline what to do, should the child wake before his return. Then, just as he was leaving, a scruple held him back; how about M. Chasle?

"His room opens into the hall alongside the stove," the servant explained.

Antoine discovered a cupboard door beside the stove, answering to her description. Opening it, he saw a triangular recess, lit from the far end by a makeshift window let into the party-wall of the staircase. This was the so-called bedroom. M. Chasle lay fully dressed on an iron bedstead, his mouth wide open, placidly snoring.

"Sure enough, the old loon's plugged his ears with cotton-wool!" Antoine exclaimed.

He decided to wait a minute or two, hoping the old fellow would decide to open his eyes. Pious pictures on colored cardboard mounts lined the walls. Books—devotional, too—filled a whatnot, on whose topmost shelf stood a terrestrial globe, flanked by two rows of empty scent-bottles.

"The Chasle case!" I've a mania for seeing "cases" everywhere, Antoined reflected. Nothing complex about him, really; a second-hand face and a fool's life! Whenever I try to see into people, I distort, exaggerate. Bad habit! The servant-girl at Toulouse, for instance. Now why should I think of her? Because her bedroom window opened onto a staircase, too? No; must be the stale smell of toilet-soap. Funny things, associations of ideas! . . . He was conscious of a vivid sense of pleasure in recalling the juvenile experience; the chambermaid with whom, when travelling with his father to attend a congress, he had passed a night in an attic room in the hotel. And, at this very minute, he would have given much to possess the buxom maid as he had known her then between the rough sheets of her bed.

M. Chasle went on snoring. Antoine decided not to wait, and returned to the hall.

No sooner had he begun to descend the stairs than he remembered that Rachel occupied the floor below. Coming round the bend of the stairs, he glanced down toward her door; it was open! No other door was visible, so it must be hers. Why was it open?

No time to hesitate; it would seem odd if he halted on the way down. Soon he was on her landing.

Rachel was in the hall of her flat and, hearing footsteps outside, glanced around. Her hair was tidy, she looked neat and cool. The pink dressing-gown had given place to a white kimono. Above its silken whiteness her red hair glowed like the flame upon an altar candle.

He addressed her first:

"*Au revoir!*"

She came to the door. "Won't you come in, doctor, and have something before going out? I've just made some chocolate."

"No, really, thanks—I'm too filthy to come in. *Au revoir!*"

He held out his hand. A smile hovered on her lips, but she did not imitate his gesture.

"*Au revoir!*" he repeated. Smiling still, she still refrained from taking his proffered hand, to his surprise. "You won't shake hands with me then?"

He saw the smile freeze on her lips, her eyes grow set. Then she held out her hand. But, before Antoine could touch it, she had grasped him firmly and, with a brusque movement, drawn him over the threshold. She slammed the door behind them. They stood in the hall facing each other. She had ceased to smile, but her lips were parted still; he saw the white gleam of her teeth. The perfume of her hair drifted toward him and he remembered a naked breast, the warm contact of her limbs. Deliberately, he brought his face near to Rachel's, his eyes bored into hers, grown large in nearness. She did not flinch; he felt, or seemed to feel, her wavering in his embrace and it was she who raised her lips to his mouth's kiss. Then with an effort she drew back from Antoine and stood with lowered head, smiling again.

"A night like that works you up . . . !" she murmured.

Through an open door at the far end of the passage he had a glimpse of a bed and, all about it, the glimmer of pink silk; under the waxing light the alcove, distant and so near, seemed the great calyx of a flower aglow there in the dawn.

[*Translated by Stuart Gilbert*]

Johannes V. Jensen

JOHANNES V. JENSEN *was born of peasant stock in Forsö, Denmark, in 1873. He went to Copenhagen to study medicine but left without finishing when the wanderlust gripped him. Though some of his best poetry and his early novels were set in foreign lands (two were based upon his visit to the United States in 1897), a three-volume collection of short stories, which includes "Lost Forests," indicates that he returned for inspiration to his own people and his own land. His major work, for which he received the Nobel Prize in 1944, is a six-part epic entitled* The Long Journey, *in which he traces the development of man from his survival as a brute superanthropoid, with a gradually wakening intelligence, down to the discovery of America, when man emerges as a builder, discoverer, and inventor. He died in the city where he had studied and settled in 1950.*

Korra was the name of a man who tilled the soil. When he had saved some money, he went to town to buy a slave.

The dealer showed him several slaves, but Korra was not satisfied.

"I suppose you want me to drag them all out here," the dealer grumbled. It was noon, and the slaves were all asleep.

"I can always go elsewhere," Korra said simply.

"Well, well!" The dealer pulled the chains, and the slaves filed out sleepily. Korra looked at them all, examining each one very carefully.

"Feel this one, he's a fine husky fellow," said the dealer, and pushed one of the slaves forward. "What do you think of him? Hasn't he a powerful chest? Strike it and see. And look here at his wrists; the tendons are like the strings of a violin. Open your mouth!"

The dealer thrust a finger in the slave's mouth and turned him toward the light. "Now you'll see some teeth," he boasted. He drew the back of a knife across the slave's teeth. "Look! Those teeth are like steel. They can bite a nail in two."

Korra bethought himself yet awhile. He ran his hand over the slave appraisingly, pressing the smooth muscles with the tips of his fingers to see if they were firm. Finally he made up his mind to buy him, paid the price with a scowl, had the slave unmanacled, and took him home.

Before many days had passed, the slave fell sick and began to pine away. Now that he was no longer in the market, but had settled down permanently, he began to long for the forests whence he had come. It was an excellent sign; Korra knew the symptoms. One day he sat down beside the slave, who was lying flat on his back with no interest in life, and began to talk thoughtfully to him.

"You shall get back to your forests, never fear. That I promise you, and you can rely on my promises. You are still young, you know. . . . If you will till my fields for me, willingly and industriously, for five years, I will give you your freedom, even though I have paid for you. Five years. Is it a bargain?"

And the slave worked. He took hold like a demon. It was a joy for Korra to sit in his doorway and watch those muscles knot and quiver under the brown skin, and Korra did this for many hours a day, for there was nothing he would rather do. He began to realize that the body is a beautiful thing and a delight to the eye.

Five years, the slave figured—as many solstices as he had fingers. The sun had to turn ten times. Every evening he watched the sun go down, and he kept track of the number of times with markers of stones and knolls. When the sun had turned the first time, he counted on the thumb of his right hand. After the passage of another solstice—and it seemed an eternity—the index finger was free. These two fingers he loved above the others which still served to mark his bondage.

Thus telling the days and marking the passage of time became the religion of the slave, his inner wealth, his spiritual treasure, which none could take from him or dispute with him.

As the time passed, his calculations expanded, became broader and deeper. The years drove by as great boundless abstractions which he could not grasp; but with every new sunset glow the slave recreated his hope and reconsecrated his faith. Time, which was evanescent in the present, appeared interminable, once it was in the past; and the future seemed infinitely distant.

In such wise the slave's spirit was deepened. As his longing brought infinity into time, so his world became infinite, and his thoughts boundless. Every evening the slave stared thoughtfully into the distant west, and each sunset brought more and more depth into his soul.

When, finally, the five years had ebbed away—it is so easy to say the words—the slave came to his master and asked for his freedom. He wanted to go to his home in the forests.

"You have been a faithful worker," Korra admitted meditatively. "Tell me, where is your home? Is it in the west? I have often watched you staring in that direction."

Yes, his home was in the west.

"It is far away then," said Korra.—The slave nodded—far away. —"And you have no money, have you?"

The slave was silent, dismayed. No, that was right, he had no money.

"Look you, you can get nowhere without money. If you work for me for three more years—no, let it be two—I will give you enough money for your travels."

The slave bowed his head, and went into harness again. He worked well, but no longer did he keep track of the passing days as formerly. On the contrary, he gave way to day-dreaming, and Korra heard him wail and babble in his sleep. After a time he fell sick again.

Then Korra sat down beside him and talked to him long and earnestly. His speech sounded prudent, full of wisdom, as if grounded in honest experience.

"I am an old man," he said. "In my youth, I, too, longed for the west; the great forests beckoned me. But I never had money enough for the journey. I shall never go there now—never until my spirit goes there when I die. You are young and able, and you work hard, but are you any stronger or abler than I was in my youth? Think about all this, and hearken to the advice of an old man. And see to it that you get well again."

But the slave mended slowly, and when he took hold again, it was not with the old enthusiasm. He gave way easily now, his ambition was gone, and he liked to lie down and sleep between jobs. Then one day Korra whipped him. It did him good, and he wept.

So the two years slipped by.

Then Korra really gave the slave his freedom. He went forth into the west; but months later he came back in a miserable plight. He had not been able to find his forests.

"Do you see?" said Korra. "Didn't I warn you? But no one shall say that I am not good to you. Try again, and this time go eastward. It might be that your forests lie in that direction."

Once more the slave set forth, this time with his face toward the rising sun, and finally, after long wanderings, he came to his own forests. *But he knew them not.* Worn out and defeated, he turned his face to the west, came back to his master, and told him that though he had found woods, great woods and small, they were not his own forests.

"Hmm!" Korra coughed.

"Stay with me," he then said warmly. "While I am alive you shall never lack for a home on this earth. And when I have been gathered to my fathers, my son will see that you are taken care of." So the slave stayed.

Korra aged, but his slave was still in his prime. Korra fed him well that he might live long, kept him clean that he might be in good health, and at reasonable intervals whipped him so that he should be meek and respectful. Nor did he stint with rest; every

Sunday the slave was free to sit on top of a knoll and stare out into the west.

Korra's farm yielded in abundance. He purchased woods and cleared them and put them under the plow that his slave might have work, and the slave felled trees with a will. Korra was wealthy now, and one day he brought home a female slave.

The years passed, and in Korra's house there grew up six stalwart slave boys. Like their father, they worked diligently. Only when one is working does the time pass, their father told them. And when the time has passed, weary we are borne into the everlasting forests. Every rest day he took his sons with him up on the knoll where they could watch the setting sun, and he taught them longing.

Korra was old and decrepit. He had, indeed, always been old, but now there was nothing of him left but age. His son had never been strong, but they had nothing to fear from any one, for each of the slaves could fell a man with one blow of a club. They were splendid fellows; the flesh was tight on their iron muscles, and their teeth were like a tiger's. But the times were safe enough. The slaves swung their axes and felled trees.

[Translated by Henry Commager]

Herman Hesse

WITHIN AND WITHOUT

HERMAN HESSE, *the latest literary idol of the "beat generation,"*
was born in Swabia in 1877. After an irregular career as a student,
book-seller, and mechanic, he became famous through two successive
novels: Peter Camenzind (1904) *and* Unter Rad (1905). *In 1911,*
he travelled to India (Siddhartha, 1923), *and upon his return, moved*
to Switzerland. Like his countryman Thomas Mann, Hesse had a total
disregard for political reality in the years preceding World War I; the
heroes of his novels were usually youthful, sensitive outsiders who
clashed with the rude forces of bourgeois society. His world was shat-
tered by the collapse of intellectual values during and after the war.
Demian (1919) *reflects the problems of defeated Germany, and be-*
came almost a Bible for young Germans. Steppenwolf (1927) *is an*
indictment of the chaotic post-war period in which the opposing tend-
encies of man are combined in the protagonist Harry Haller. This
dualism of sense and spirit is the subject of Death and the Lover, *but*
in his last great novel, Magister Ludi (Das Glasperlenspiel, 1943), *the*
conflict is resolved in favor of the spirit. Hesse's verses and his small
but erudite body of essays were not overlooked when he was awarded
the Nobel Prize for 1947. Until recently, his work met with little re-
sponse in America, though both Thomas Mann and André Gide, for
reasons apparent in the following selection, long ago acclaimed him as
one of the truly great writers of our age.

There was once a man by the name of Frederick; he
devoted himself to intellectual pursuits and had a wide
range of knowledge. But not all knowledge was the same to him,

nor was any thought as good as any other: he loved a certain type of thinking, and disdained and abominated the others. What he loved and revered was logic—that so admirable method—and, in general, what he called "science."

"Twice two is four," he used to say. "This I believe; and man must do his thinking on the basis of this truth."

He was not unaware, to be sure, that there were other sorts of thinking and knowledge; but they were not "science," and he held a low opinion of them. Although a freethinker, he was not intolerant of religion. Religion was founded on a tacit agreement among scientists. For several centuries their science had embraced nearly everything that existed on earth and was worth knowing, with the exception of one single province: the human soul. It had become a sort of custom, as time went on, to leave this to religion, and to tolerate its speculations on the soul, though without taking them seriously. Thus Frederick too was tolerant toward religion; but everything he recognized as superstition was profoundly odious and repugnant to him. Alien, uncultured, and retarded peoples might occupy themselves with it; in remote antiquity there might have been mystical or magical thinking; but since the birth of science and logic there was no longer any sense in making use of these outmoded and dubious tools.

So he said and so he thought; and when traces of superstition came to his attention he became angry and felt as if he had been touched by something hostile.

It angered him most of all, however, if he found such traces among his own sort, among educated men who were conversant with the principles of scientific thinking. And nothing was more painful and intolerable to him than that scandalous notion which lately he had sometimes heard expressed and discussed even by men of great culture—that absurd idea that "scientific thinking" was possibly not a supreme, timeless, eternal, foreordained, and unassailable mode of thought, but merely one of many, a transient way of thinking, not impervious to change and downfall. This irreverent, destructive, poisonous notion was abroad—even Frederick could not deny it; it had cropped up here and there as a result of the distress throughout the world brought about by war, revolution, and hunger, like a warning, like a white hand's ghostly writing on a white wall.

The more Frederick suffered from the fact that this idea existed and could so deeply distress him, the more passionately he assailed it and those whom he suspected of secretly believing in it. So far only a very few from among the truly educated had openly and frankly professed their belief in this new doctrine, a doctrine that seemed destined, should it gain in circulation and power, to destroy all spiritual values on earth and call forth chaos. Well, matters had not reached that point yet, and the scattered individuals who openly embraced the idea were still so few in number that they could be considered oddities and crotchety, peculiar fellows. But a drop of the poison, an emanation of that idea, could be perceived first on this side, then on that. Among the people and the half-educated no end of new doctrines could be found anyway, esoteric doctrines, sects, and discipleships; the world was full of them; everywhere one could scent out superstition, mysticism, spiritualistic cults, and other mysterious forces, which it was really necessary to combat, but to which science, as if from a private feeling of weakness, had for the present given free rein.

One day Frederick went to the house of one of his friends, with whom he had often studied. It so happened that he had not seen this friend for some time. While he was climbing the stairs of the house he tried to recall when and where it was that he had last been in his friend's company; but much as he could pride himself on his good memory for other things he could not remember. Because of this he fell imperceptibly into a certain vexation and ill humor, from which, as he stood before his friend's door, he was obliged forcibly to free himself.

Hardly had he greeted Erwin, his friend, when he noticed on his genial countenance a certain, as it were forbearing, smile, which it seemed to him he had never seen there before. And hardly had he seen this smile, which despite its friendliness he at once felt to be somehow mocking or hostile, when he immediately remembered what he had just been searching his memory for in vain—his last previous meeting with Erwin. He remembered that they had parted then without having quarreled, to be sure, but yet with a sense of inner discord and dissatisfaction, because Erwin, as it had seemed to him, had given far too little support to his attacks at that time on the realm of superstition.

It was strange. How could he have forgotten that entirely? And now he also knew that this was his only reason for not having sought out his friend for so long, merely this dissatisfaction, and that he had known this all the time, although he had invented for himself a host of other excuses for his repeated postponement of this visit.

Now they confronted one another; and it seemed to Frederick as if the little rift of that day had meantime tremendously widened. He felt that in this moment something was lacking between him and Erwin that had always been there before, an aura of solidarity, of spontaneous understanding—indeed, even of affection. Instead of these there was a vacuum. They greeted each other; spoke of the weather, their acquaintances, their health; and —God knows why!—with every word Frederick had the disquieting sensation that he was not quite understanding his friend, that his friend did not really know him, that his words were missing their mark, that they could find no common ground for a real conversation. Moreover Erwin still had that friendly smile on his face, which Frederick was beginning almost to hate.

During a pause in the laborious conversation Frederick looked about the studio he knew so well and saw, pinned loosely on the wall, a sheet of paper. This sight moved him strangely and awakened ancient memories; for he recalled that, long ago in their student years, this had been a habit of Erwin's, a way he sometimes chose of keeping a thinker's saying or a poet's verse fresh in his mind. He stood up and went to the wall to read the paper.

There, in Erwin's beautiful script, he read the words: "Nothing is without, nothing is within; for what is without is within."

Blanching, he stood motionless for a moment. There it was! There he stood face to face with what he feared! At another time he would have let this leaf of paper pass, would have tolerated it charitably as a whim, as a harmless foible to which anyone was entitled, perhaps as a trifling sentimentality calling for indulgence. But now it was different. He felt that these words had not been set down for the sake of a fleeting poetic mood; it was not a vagary that Erwin had returned after so many years to a practice of his youth. What stood written here, as an avowal of his friend's concern at the moment, was mysticism! Erwin was unfaithful!

Slowly he turned to face him, whose smile was again radiant.

"Explain this to me!" he demanded.

Erwin nodded, brimming with friendliness.

"Haven't you ever read this saying?"

"Certainly!" Frederick cried. "Of course I know it. It's mysticism, it's Gnosticism. It may be poetic, but—well, anyway, explain the saying to me, and why's it's hanging on your wall!"

"Gladly," Erwin said. "The saying is a first introduction to an epistemology that I've been going into lately, and which has already brought me much happiness."

Frederick restrained his temper. He asked, "A new epistemology? Is there such a thing? And what is it called?"

"Oh," Erwin answered, "it's only new to me. It's already very old and venerable. It's called magic."

The word had been uttered. Profoundly astonished and startled by so candid a confession, Frederick, with a shudder, felt that he was confronted eye to eye with the arch-enemy, in the person of his friend. He did not know whether he was nearer rage or tears; the bitter feeling of irreparable loss possessed him. For a long time he remained silent.

Then, with a pretended decision in his voice, he began, "So now you want to become a magician?"

"Yes," Erwin replied unhesitatingly.

"A sort of sorcerer's apprentice, eh?"

"Certainly."

A clock could be heard ticking in the adjoining room, it was so quiet.

Then Frederick said, "This means, you know, that you are abandoning all fellowship with serious science, and hence all fellowship with me."

"I hope that is not so," Erwin answered. "But if that's the way it has to be, what else can I do?"

"What else can you do?" Frederick burst out. "Why, break, break once and for all with this childishness, this wretched and contemptible belief in magic! That's what else you can do, if you want to keep my respect."

Erwin smiled a little, although he too no longer seemed cheerful.

"You speak as if," he said, so gently that through his quiet words Frederick's angry voice still seemed to be echoing about the room, "you speak as if that lay within my will, as if I had a choice, Frederick. That is not the case. I have no choice. It was not I that chose magic: magic chose me."

Frederick sighed deeply. "Then goodby," he said wearily, and stood up, without offering to shake hands.

"Not like that!" Erwin cried out. "No, you must not go from me like that. Pretend that one of us is lying on his deathbed—and that is so!—and that we must say farewell."

"But which of us, Erwin, is dying?"

"Today it is probably I, my friend. Whoever wishes to be born anew must be prepared to die."

Once more Frederick went up to the sheet of paper and read the saying about within and without.

"Very well," he said finally. "You are right, it won't do any good to part in anger. I'll do what you wish; I'll pretend that one of us is dying. Before I go I want to make a last request of you."

"I'm glad," Erwin said. "Tell me, what kindness can I show you on our leavetaking?"

"I repeat my first question, and this is also my request: explain this saying to me, as well as you can."

Erwin reflected a moment and then spoke:

"Nothing is without, nothing is within. You know the religious meaning of this: God is everywhere. He is in the spirit, and

also in nature. All is divine, because God is all. Formerly this was
called pantheism. Then the philosophic meaning: we are used to
divorcing the within from the without in our thinking, but this is
not necessary. Our spirit is capable of withdrawing behind the
limits we have set for it, into the beyond. Beyond the pair of
antitheses of which our world consists a new and different knowledge begins. . . . But, my dear friend, I must confess to you—
since my thinking has changed there are no longer any un-
ambiguous words and sayings for me: every word has tens and
hundreds of meanings. And here what you fear begins—magic."

Frederick wrinkled his brow and was about to interrupt, but
Erwin looked at him disarmingly and continued, speaking more
distinctly, "Let me give you an example. Take something of mine
along with you, any object, and examine it a little from time to
time. Soon the principle of the within and the without will reveal
one of its many means to you."

He glanced about the room, took a small clay figurine from a
wall shelf, and gave it to Frederick, saying:

*"Take this with you as my parting gift. When this thing that I
am now placing in your hands ceases to be outside you and is
within you, come to me again! But if it remains outside you, the
way it is now, forever, then this parting of yours from me shall
also be forever!"*

Frederick wanted to say a great deal more; but Erwin took his
hand, pressed it, and bade him farewell with an expression that
permitted no further conversation.

Frederick left; descended the stairs (how prodigiously long ago
he had climbed them!); went through the streets to his home, the
little earthen figure in his hand, perplexed and sick of heart. In
front of his house he stopped, shook the fist fiercely for a moment
in which he was clutching the figurine, and felt a great urge to
smash the ridiculous thing to the ground. He did not do so; he
bit his lip and entered the house. Never before had he been so
agitated, so tormented by conflicting emotions.

He looked for a place for his friend's gift, and put the figure on
top of a bookcase. For the time being it stayed there.

Occasionally, as the days went by, he looked at it, brooding on it and on its origins, and pondering the meaning that this foolish thing was to have for him. It was a small figure of a man or a god or an idol, with two faces, like the Roman god Janus, modeled rather crudely of clay and covered with a burnt and somewhat cracked glaze. The little image looked coarse and insignificant; certainly it was not Roman or Greek workmanship; more likely it was the work of some backward, primitive race in Africa or the South Seas. The two faces, which were exactly alike, bore an apathetic, indolent faintly grinning smile—it was downright ugly the way the little gnome squandered his stupid smile.

Frederick could not get used to the figure. It was totally unpleasant and offensive to him, it got in his way, it disturbed him. The very next day he took it down and put it on the stove, and a few days later moved it to a cupboard. Again and again it got in the path of his vision, as if it were forcing itself upon him; it laughed at him coldly and dull-wittedly, put on airs, demanded attention. After a few weeks he put it in the anteroom, between the photographs of Italy and the trivial little souvenirs which no one ever looked at. Now at least he saw the idol only when he was entering or leaving, and then he passed it quickly, without examining it more closely. But here too the thing still bothered him, though he did not admit this to himself.

With this shard, this two-faced monstrosity, vexation and torment had entered his life.

One day, months later, he returned from a short trip—he undertook such excursions now from time to time, as if something were driving him restlessly about; he entered his house, went through the anteroom, was greeted by the maid, and read the letters waiting for him. But he was ill at ease, as if he had forgotten something important; no book tempted him, no chair was comfortable. He began to rack his mind—what was the cause of this? Had he neglected something important? eaten something unsettling? In reflecting it occurred to him that this disturbing feeling had come over him as he had entered the apartment. He returned to the anteroom and involuntarily his first glance sought the clay figure.

A strange fright went through him when he did not see the idol. It had disappeared. It was missing. Had it walked away on its little crockery legs? Flown away? By magic?

Frederick pulled himself together, and smiled at his nervousness. Then he began quietly to search the whole room. When he found nothing he called the maid. She came, was embarrassed, and admitted at once that she had dropped the thing while cleaning up.

"Where is it?"

It was not there any more. It had seemed so solid, that little thing; she had often had it in her hands; and yet it had shattered to a hundred little pieces and splinters, and could not be fixed. She had taken the fragments to a glazier, who had simply laughed at her; and then she had thrown them away.

Frederick dismissed the maid. He smiled. That was perfectly all right with him. He did not feel bad about the idol, God knows. The abomination was gone; now he would have peace. If only he had knocked the thing to pieces that very first day! What he had suffered in all this time! How sluggishly, strangely, craftily, evilly, satanically that idol had smiled at him! Well, now that it was gone he could admit it to himself: he had feared it, truly and sincerely feared it, this earthen god. Was it not the emblem and symbol of everything that was repugnant and intolerable to him, everything that he had recognized all along as pernicious, inimical, and worthy of suppression—an emblem of all superstitions, all darkness, all coercion of conscience and spirit? Did it not represent that ghastly power that one sometimes felt raging in the bowels of the earth, that distant earthquake, that approaching extinction of culture, that looming chaos? Had not this contemptible figure robbed him of his best friend—nay, not merely robbed, but made of the friend an enemy? Well, now the thing was gone. Vanished. Smashed to pieces. Done for. It was good so; it was much better than if he had destroyed it himself.

So he thought, or said. And he went about his affairs as before.

But it was like a curse. Now, just when he had got more or less used to that ridiculous figure, just when the sight of it in its usual place on the anteroom table had gradually become a bit familiar and unimportant to him, now its absence began to torment him! Yes, he missed it every time he went through that room; all he could see there was the empty spot where it had formerly stood, and emptiness emanated from the spot and filled the room with strangeness.

Bad days and worse nights began for Frederick. He could no longer go through the anteroom without thinking of the idol with the two faces, missing it, and feeling that his thoughts were tethered to it. This became an agonizing compulsion for him. And it was not by any means simply on the occasions when he went through that room that he was gripped by this compulsion—ah, no. Just as emptiness and desolation radiated from the now empty spot on the anteroom table, so this compulsive idea radiated within him, gradually crowded all else aside, rankling and filling him with emptiness and strangeness.

Again and again he pictured the figure with utmost distinctness, just to make it clear to himself how preposterous it was to grieve its loss. He could see it in all its stupid ugliness and barbarity, with its vacuous yet crafty smile, with its two faces—indeed, as if under duress, full of hatred and with his mouth drawn awry, he found himself attempting to reproduce that smile. The question pestered him whether the two faces were really exactly alike. Had not one of them, perhaps only because of a little roughness or a crack in the glaze, had a somewhat different expression? Something quizzical? Something sphinxlike? And how peculiar the color of that glaze had been! Green, and blue, and gray, but also red, were in it—a glaze that he now kept finding often in other objects, in a window's reflection of the sun or in the mirrorings of a wet pavement.

He brooded a great deal on this glaze, at night too. It also struck him what a strange, foreign, ill-sounding, unfamiliar, almost malignant word "glaze" was. He analyzed the word, and once he even reversed the order of its letters. Then it read "ezalg." Now where the devil did this word get its sound from? He knew this word "ezalg," certainly he knew it; moreover, it was an unfriendly and bad word, a word with ugly and disturbing connotations. For a long while he tormented himself with this question. Finally he hit upon it: "ezalg" reminded him of a book that he had bought and read many years ago on a trip, and that had dismayed, plagued, and yet secretly fascinated him; it had been entitled *Princess Ezalka*. It was like a curse: everything connected with the figurine—the glaze, the blue, the green, the smile—signified hostility, tormenting and poisoning him. And how very peculiarly *he*, Erwin, his erstwhile friend, had smiled as he had given the idol into his hand! How very peculiarly, how very significantly, how very hostily.

Frederick resisted manfully—and on many days not without success—the compulsive trend of his thoughts. He sensed the danger clearly: he did not want to go insane! No, it were better to die. Reason was necessary, life was not. And it occurred to him that perhaps *this* was magic, that Erwin, with the aid of that figure, had in some way enchanted him, and that he should fall as a sacrifice, as the defender of reason and science against these dismal powers. But if this were so, if he could even conceive of that as possible, then there *was* such a thing as magic, then there *was* sorcery. No, it were better to die!

A doctor recommended walks and baths; and sometimes, in search of amusement, he spent an evening at an inn. But it helped very little. He cursed Erwin; he cursed himself.

One night, as he often did now, he retired early and lay restlessly awake in bed, unable to sleep. He felt unwell and uneasy. He wanted to meditate; he wanted to find solace, wanted to speak sentences of some sort to himself, good sentences, comforting, reassuring ones, something with the straightforward serenity and lucidity of the sentence, "Twice two is four." Nothing came to mind; but, in a state almost of lightheadedness, he mumbled sounds and syllables to himself. Gradually words formed on his lips, and several times, without being sensible of its meaning, he said the same short sentence to himself, which had somehow taken form in him. He muttered it to himself, as if it might stupefy him, as if he might grope his way along it, as along a parapet, to the sleep that eluded him on the narrow, narrow path that skirted the abyss.

But suddenly, when he spoke somewhat louder, the words he was mumbling penetrated his consciousness. He knew them: they were, "Yes, now you are within me!" And instantly he knew. He knew what they meant—that they referred to the clay idol and that now, in this gray night hour, he had accurately and exactly fulfilled the prophecy Erwin had made on that unearthly day, that now the figure, which he had held contemptuously in his fingers then, was no longer outside him but within him! "For what is without is within."

Bounding up in a leap, he felt as if transfused with ice and fire. The world reeled about him, the planets stared at him insanely. He threw on some clothes, put on the light, left his house and ran in the middle of the night to Erwin's. There he saw a light burning in the studio window he knew so well; the door to the house was unlocked: everything seemed to be awaiting him. He rushed up the stairs. He walked unsteadily into Erwin's study, supported himself with trembling hands on the table. Erwin sat by the lamp, in its gentle light, contemplative, smiling.

Graciously Erwin arose. "You have come. That is good."

"Have you been expecting me?" Frederick whispered.

"I have been expecting you, as you know, from the moment you left here, taking my little gift with you. Has what I said then happened?"

"It has happened," Frederick said. "The idol is within me. I can't bear it any longer."

"Can I help you?" Erwin asked.

"I don't know. Do as you will. Tell me more of your magic! Tell me how the idol can get out of me again."

Erwin placed his hand on his friend's shoulder. He led him to an armchair and pressed him down in it. Then he spoke cordially to Frederick, smiling in an almost brotherly tone of voice:

"The idol will come out of you again. Have trust in me. Have trust in yourself. You have learned to believe in it. Now learn to love it! It is within you, but it is still dead, it is still a phantom to you. Awaken it, speak to it, question it! For it is you yourself! Do not hate it any longer, do not fear it, do not torment it—how you have tormented this poor idol, who was yet you yourself! How you have tormented yourself!"

"Is this the way to magic?" Frederick asked. He sat deep in the chair, as if he had grown older, and his voice was low.

"This is the way," Erwin replied, "and perhaps you have already taken the most difficult step. You have found by experience: the without can become the within. You have been beyond the pair of antitheses. It seemed hell to you; learn, my friend, it is heaven! For it is heaven that awaits you. Behold, this is magic: to interchange the without and the within, not by compulsion, not in anguish, as you have done it, but freely, voluntarily. Summon up the past, summon up the future: both are in you! Until today you have been the slave of the within. Learn to be its master. That is magic."

[*Translated by T. K. Brown, III*]

William Faulkner

WILLIAM FAULKNER, *was born in 1897 in New Albany, Missis-sippi, and grew up in Oxford in Lafayette County, which in his fiction became Jefferson City and Yoknapatawpha County. He started out to be a poet (A Green Bough), but soon turned to fiction and discovered in the disturbed Southern society he depicted a reflection of the problems of the modern world. He captures in his novels and short stories like "That Evening Sun" the anguish of the human spirit caught in a world of conflicting values. During World War I, Faulkner served in the Canadian Air Force and before publishing his first novel in 1926, took a trip to France and later worked for a New Orleans newspaper. The Sound and the Fury, his fourth novel, brought him critical acclaim, and Sanctuary, two years later in 1931, national prominence. He was awarded the Nobel Prize in 1950.*

Monday is no different from any other weekday in Jefferson now. The streets are paved now, and the telephone and electric companies are cutting down more and more of the shade trees—the water oaks, the maples and locusts and elms—to make room for iron poles bearing clusters of bloated and ghostly and bloodless grapes, and we have a city laundry which makes the rounds on Monday morning, gathering the bundles of clothes into bright-colored, specially made motorcars: the soiled wearing of a whole week now flees apparitionlike behind alert and irritable electric horns, with a long diminishing noise of rubber and as-

phalt like tearing silk, and even the Negro women who still take
in white people's washing after the old custom, fetch and deliver
it in automobiles.

But fifteen years ago, on Monday morning the quiet, dusty,
shady streets would be full of Negro women with, balanced on
their steady, turbaned heads, bundles of clothes tied up in sheets,
almost as large as cotton bales, carried so without touch of hand
between the kitchen door of the white house and the blackened
washpot beside a cabin door in Negro Hollow.

Nancy would set her bundle on the top of her head, then upon
the bundle in turn she would set the black straw sailor hat which
she wore winter and summer. She was tall, with a high, sad face
sunken a little where her teeth were missing. Sometimes we would
go a part of the way down the lane and across the pasture with
her, to watch the balanced bundle and the hat that never bobbed
nor wavered, even when she walked down into the ditch and up
the other side and stooped through the fence. She would go down
on her hands and knees and crawl through the gap, her head
rigid, uptilted, the bundle steady as a rock or a balloon, and rise to
her feet again and go on.

Sometimes the husbands of the washing women would fetch
and deliver the clothes, but Jesus never did that for Nancy, even
before Father told him to stay away from our house, even when
Dilsey was sick and Nancy would come to cook for us.

And then about half the time we'd have to go down the lane to
Nancy's cabin and tell her to come on and cook breakfast. We
would stop at the ditch, because Father told us to not have anything to do with Jesus—he was a short black man, with a razor scar
down his face—and we would throw rocks at Nancy's house until
she came to the door, leaning her head around it without any
clothes on.

"What yawl mean, chunking my house?" Nancy said. "What
you little devils mean?"

"Father says for you to come on and get breakfast," Caddy said.
"Father says it's over a half an hour now, and you've got to come
this minute."

"I ain't studying no breakfast," Nancy said. "I going to get my sleep out."

"I bet you're drunk," Jason said. "Father says you're drunk. Are you drunk, Nancy?"

"Who says I is?" Nancy said. "I got to get my sleep out. I ain't studying no breakfast."

So after a while we quit chunking the cabin and went back home. When she finally came, it was too late for me to go to school. So we thought it was whiskey until that day they arrested her again and they were taking her to jail and they passed Mr. Stovall. He was the cashier in the bank and a deacon in the Baptist church, and Nancy began to say:

"When you going to pay me, white man? When you going to pay me, white man? It's been three times now since you paid me a cent—" Mr. Stovall knocked her down, but she kept on saying, "When you going to pay me, white man? It's been three times now since—" until Mr. Stovall kicked her in the mouth with his heel and the marshal caught Mr. Stovall back, and Nancy lying in the street, laughing. She turned her head and spat out some blood and teeth and said, "It's been three times now since he paid me a cent."

That was how she lost her teeth, and all that day they told about Nancy and Mr. Stovall, and all that night the ones that passed the jail could hear Nancy singing and yelling. They could see her hands holding to the window bars, and a lot of them stopped along the fence, listening to her and the jailer trying to make her stop. She didn't shut up until almost daylight, when the jailer began to hear a bumping and scraping upstairs and he went up there and found Nancy hanging from the window bar. He said that it was cocaine and not whiskey, because no nigger would try to commit suicide unless he was full of cocaine, because a nigger full of cocaine wasn't a nigger any longer.

The jailer cut her down and revived her; then he beat her, whipped her. She had hung herself with her dress. She had fixed it all right, but when they arrested her she didn't have on anything except a dress and so she didn't have anything to tie her hands with, and she couldn't make her hands let go of the window ledge. So the jailer heard the noise and ran up there and found Nancy hanging from the window, stark naked, her belly already swelling out a little, like a little balloon.

When Dilsey was sick in her cabin and Nancy was cooking for us, we could see her apron swelling out; that was before Father told Jesus to stay away from the house. Jesus was in the kitchen, sitting behind the stove, with his razor scar on his black face like a piece of dirty string. He said it was a watermelon that Nancy had under her dress.

"It never come off of your vine, though," Nancy said.

"Off of what vine?" Caddy said.

"I can cut down the vine it did come off of," Jesus said.

"What makes you want to talk like that before these chillen?" Nancy said. "Whyn't you go on to work? You done et. You want Mr. Jason to catch you hanging around his kitchen, talking that way before these chillen?"

"Talking what way?" Caddy said. "What vine?"

"I can't hang around white man's kitchen," Jesus said. "But white man can hang around mine. White man can come in my house, but I can't stop him. When white man want to come in my house, I ain't got no house. I can't stop him, but he can't kick me outen it. He can't do that."

Dilsey was still sick in her cabin. Father told Jesus to stay off our place. Dilsey was still sick. It was a long time. We were in the library after supper.

"Isn't Nancy through in the kitchen yet?" Mother said. "It seems to me that she has had plenty of time to have finished the dishes."

"Let Quentin go and see," Father said. "Go and see if Nancy is through, Quentin. Tell her she can go on home."

I went to the kitchen. Nancy was through. The dishes were put away and the fire was out. Nancy was sitting in a chair, close to the cold stove. She looked at me.

"Mother wants to know if you are through," I said.

"Yes," Nancy said. She looked at me. "I done finished." She looked at me.

"What is it?" I said. "What is it?"

"I ain't nothing but a nigger," Nancy said. "It ain't none of it my fault."

She looked at me, sitting in the chair before the cold stove, the sailor hat on her head. I went back to the library. It was the cold stove and all, when you think of a kitchen being warm and busy and cheerful. And with a cold stove and the dishes all put away, and nobody wanting to eat at that hour.

"Is she through?" Mother said.

"Yessum," I said.

"What is she doing?" Mother said.

"She's not doing anything. She's through."

"I'll go and see," Father said.

"Maybe she's waiting for Jesus to come and take her home," Caddy said.

"Jesus is gone," I said. Nancy told us how one morning she woke up and Jesus was gone.

"He quit me," Nancy said. "Done gone to Memphis, I reckon. Dodging them city po-lice for a while, I reckon."

"And a good riddance," Father said. "I hope he stays there."

"Nancy's scaired of the dark," Jason said.

"So are you," Caddy said.

"I'm not," Jason said.

"Scairy cat," Caddy said.

"I'm not," Jason said.

"You, Candace!" Mother said. Father came back.

"I am going to walk down the lane with Nancy," he said. "She says that Jesus is back."

"Has she seen him?" Mother said.

"No. Some Negro sent her word that he was back in town. I won't be long."

"You'll leave me alone, to take Nancy home?" Mother said. "Is her safety more precious to you than mine?"

"I won't be long," Father said.

"You'll leave these children unprotected, with that Negro about?"

"I'm going too," Caddy said. "Let me go, Father."

"What would he do with them, if he were unfortunate enough to have them?" Father said.

"I want to go, too," Jason said.

"Jason!" Mother said. She was speaking to Father. You could tell that by the way she said the name. Like she believed that all day Father had been trying to think of doing the thing she wouldn't like the most, and that she knew all the time that after a while he would think of it. I stayed quiet, because Father and I both knew that Mother would want him to make me stay with her if she just thought of it in time. So Father didn't look at me. I was the oldest. I was nine and Caddy was seven and Jason was five.

"Nonsense," Father said. "We won't be long."

Nancy had her hat on. We came to the lane. "Jesus always been good to me," Nancy said. "Whenever he had two dollars, one of them was mine." We walked in the lane. "If I can just get through the lane," Nancy said, "I be all right then."

The lane was always dark. "This is where Jason got scaired on Hallowe'en," Caddy said.

"I didn't," Jason said.

"Can't Aunt Rachel do anything with him?" Father said. Aunt Rachel was old. She lived in a cabin beyond Nancy's by herself. She had white hair and she smoked a pipe in the door, all day long; she didn't work any more. They said she was Jesus' mother. Sometimes she said she was and sometimes she said she wasn't any kin to Jesus.

"Yes you did," Caddy said. "You were scairder than Frony. You were scairder than T.P. even. Scairder than niggers."

"Can't nobody do nothing with him," Nancy said. "He say I done woke up the devil in him and ain't but one thing going to lay it down again."

"Well, he's gone now," Father said. "There's nothing for you to be afraid of now. And if you'd just let white men alone."

"Let what white men alone?" Caddy said. "How let them alone?"

"He ain't gone nowhere," Nancy said. "I can feel him. I can feel him now, in this lane. He hearing us talk, every word, hid somewhere, waiting. I ain't seen him, and I ain't going to see him again but once more, with that razor in his mouth. That razor on that string down his back, inside his shirt. And then I ain't going to be even surprised."

"I wasn't scaired," Jason said.

"If you'd behave yourself, you'd have kept out of this," Father said. "But it's all right now. He's probably in Saint Louis now. Probably got another wife by now and forgot all about you."

"If he has, I better not find out about it," Nancy said. "I'd stand there right over them, and every time he wropped her, I'd cut that arm off. I'd cut his head off and I'd slit her belly and I'd shove—"

"Hush," Father said.

"Slit whose belly, Nancy?" Caddy said.

"I wasn't scaired," Jason said. "I'd walk right down this lane by myself."

"Yah," Caddy said. "You wouldn't dare to put your foot down in it if we were not here too."

II

Dilsey was still sick, so we took Nancy home every night until Mother said, "How much longer is this going on? I to be left alone in this big house while you take home a frightened Negro?"

We fixed a pallet in the kitchen for Nancy. One night we waked up, hearing the sound. It was not singing and it was not crying, coming up the dark stairs. There was a light in Mother's room and we heard Father going down the hall, down the back stairs, and Caddy and I went into the hall. The floor was cold. Our toes curled away from it while we listened to the sound. It was like singing and it wasn't like singing, like the sound that Negroes make.

Then it stopped and we heard Father going down the back stairs, and we went to the head of the stairs. Then the sound began again, in the stairway, not loud, and we could see Nancy's eyes halfway up the stairs, against the wall. They looked like cat's eyes do, like a big cat against the wall, watching us. When we came down the steps to where she was, she quit making the sound again, and we stood there until Father came back up from the kitchen, with his pistol in his hand. He went back down with Nancy and they came back with Nancy's pallet.

We spread the pallet in our room. After the light in Mother's room went off, we could see Nancy's eyes again. "Nancy," Caddy whispered, "are you asleep, Nancy?"

Nancy whispered something. It was oh or no, I don't know which. Like nobody had made it, like it came from nowhere and went nowhere, until it was like Nancy was not there at all; that I had looked so hard at her eyes on the stairs that they had got printed on my eyeballs, like the sun does when you have closed your eyes and there is no sun. "Jesus," Nancy whispered. "Jesus."

"Was it Jesus?" Caddy said. "Did he try to come into the kitchen?"

"Jesus," Nancy said. Like this: Jeeeeeeeeeeeeeeeeesus, until the sound went out, like a match or a candle does.

"It's the other Jesus she means," I said.

"Can you see us, Nancy?" Caddy whispered. "Can you see our eyes too?"

"I ain't nothing but a nigger," Nancy said. "God knows. God knows."

"What did you see down there in the kitchen?" Caddy whispered. "What tried to get in?"

"God knows," Nancy said. We could see her eyes. "God knows."

Dilsey got well. She cooked dinner. "You'd better stay in bed a day or two longer," Father said.

"What for?" Dilsey said. "If I had been a day later, this place would be to rack and ruin. Get on out of here now, and let me get my kitchen straight again."

Dilsey cooked supper too. And that night, just before dark, Nancy came into the kitchen.

"How do you know he's back?" Dilsey said. "You ain't seen him."

"Jesus is a nigger," Jason said.

"I can feel him," Nancy said. "I can feel him laying yonder in the ditch."

"Tonight?" Dilsey said. "Is he there tonight?"

"Dilsey's a nigger too," Jason said.

"You try to eat something," Dilsey said.

"I don't want nothing," Nancy said.

"I ain't a nigger," Jason said.

"Drink some coffee," Dilsey said. She poured a cup of coffee for Nancy. "Do you know he's out there tonight? How come you know it's tonight?"

"I know," Nancy said. "He's there, waiting. I know. I done lived with him too long. I know what he is fixing to do fore he know it himself."

"Drink some coffee," Dilsey said. Nancy held the cup to her mouth and blew into the cup. Her mouth pursed out like a spreading adder's, like a rubber mouth, like she had blown all the color out of her lips with blowing the coffee.

"I ain't a nigger," Jason said. "Are you a nigger, Nancy?"

"I hellborn, child," Nancy said. "I won't be nothing soon. I going back where I come from soon."

III

She began to drink the coffee. While she was drinking, holding the cup in both hands, she began to make the sound again. She made the sound into the cup and the coffee sploshed out onto her hands and her dress. Her eyes looked at us and she sat there, her elbows on her knees, holding the cup in both hands, looking at us across the wet cup, making the sound.

"Look at Nancy," Jason said. "Nancy can't cook for us now. Dilsey's got well now."

"You hush up," Dilsey said. Nancy held the cup in both hands, looking at us, making the sound, like there were two of them: one looking at us and the other making the sound. "Whyn't you let Mr. Jason telefoam the marshal?" Dilsey said. Nancy stopped then, holding the cup in her long brown hands. She tried to drink some coffee again, but it sploshed out of the cup, onto her hands and her dress, and she put the cup down. Jason watched her.

"I can't swallow it," Nancy said. "I swallows but it won't go down me."

"You go down to the cabin," Dilsey said. "Frony will fix you a pallet and I'll be there soon."

"Won't no nigger stop him," Nancy said.

"I ain't a nigger," Jason said. "Am I, Dilsey?"

"I reckon not," Dilsey said. She looked at Nancy. "I don't reckon so. What you going to do, then?"

Nancy looked at us. Her eyes went fast, like she was afraid there wasn't time to look, without hardly moving at all. She looked at us, at all three of us at one time. "You member that night I stayed in yawls' room?" she said. She told about how we waked up early the next morning, and played. We had to play quiet, on her pallet, until Father woke up and it was time to get breakfast. "Go and ask your maw to let me stay here tonight," Nancy said. "I won't need no pallet. We can play some more."

Caddy asked Mother. Jason went too. "I can't have Negroes sleeping in the bedrooms," Mother said. Jason cried. He cried until Mother said he couldn't have any dessert for three days if he didn't stop. Then Jason said he would stop if Dilsey would make a chocolate cake. Father was there.

"Why don't you do something about it?" Mother said. "What do we have officers for?"

"Why is Nancy afraid of Jesus?" Caddy said. "Are you afraid of Father, Mother?"

"What could the officers do?" Father said. "If Nancy hasn't seen him, how could the officers find him?"

"Then why is she afraid?" Mother said.

"She says he is there. She says she knows he is there tonight."

"Yet we pay taxes," Mother said. "I must wait here alone in this big house while you take a Negro woman home."

"You know that I am not lying outside with a razor," Father said.

"I'll stop if Dilsey will make a chocolate cake," Jason said. Mother told us to go out and Father said he didn't know if Jason would get a chocolate cake or not, but he knew what Jason was going to get in about a minute. We went back to the kitchen and told Nancy.

"Father said for you to go home and lock the door, and you'll be all right," Caddy said. "All right from what, Nancy? Is Jesus mad at you?" Nancy was holding the coffee cup in her hands again, her elbows on her knees and her hands holding the cup between her knees. She was looking into the cup. "What have you done that made Jesus mad?" Caddy said. Nancy let the cup go. It didn't break on the floor, but the coffee spilled out, and Nancy sat there with her hands still making the shape of the cup. She began to make the sound again, not loud. Not singing and not unsinging. We watched her.

"Here," Dilsey said. "You quit that, now. You get aholt of yourself. You wait here. I going to get Versh to walk home with you." Dilsey went out.

We looked at Nancy. Her shoulders kept shaking, but she quit making the sound. We stood and watched her.

"What's Jesus going to do to you?" Caddy said. "He went away."

Nancy looked at us. "We had fun that night I stayed in yawls' room, didn't we?"

"I didn't," Jason said. "I didn't have any fun."

"You were asleep in Mother's room," Caddy said. "You were not there."

"Let's go down to my house and have some mor
said.

"Mother won't let us," I said. "It's too late now."

"Don't bother her," Nancy said. "We can tell her in the mo
ing. She won't mind."

"She wouldn't let us," I said.

"Don't ask her now," Nancy said. "Don't bother her now."

"She didn't say we couldn't go," Caddy said.

"We didn't ask," I said.

"If you go, I'll tell," Jason said.

"We'll have fun," Nancy said. "They won't mind, just to my
house. I been working for yawl a long time. They won't mind."

"I'm not afraid to go," Caddy said. "Jason is the one that's
afraid. He'll tell."

"I'm not," Jason said.

"Yes, you are," Caddy said. "You'll tell."

"I won't tell," Jason said. "I'm not afraid."

"Jason ain't afraid to go with me," Nancy said. "Is you, Jason?"

"Jason is going to tell," Caddy said. The lane was dark. We
passed the pasture gate. "I bet if something was to jump out from
behind that gate, Jason would holler."

"I wouldn't," Jason said. We walked down the lane. Nancy
was talking loud.

"What are you talking so loud for, Nancy?" Caddy said.

"Who; me?" Nancy said. "Listen at Quentin and Caddy and
Jason saying I'm talking loud."

"You talk like there was five of us here," Caddy said. "You talk
like Father was here too."

"Who; me talking loud, Mr. Jason?" Nancy said.

"Nancy called Jason 'Mister,' " Caddy said.

"Listen how Caddy and Quentin and Jason talk," Nancy said.

"We're not talking loud," Caddy said. "You're the one that's
talking like Father—"

"Hush," Nancy said; "hush, Mr. Jason."

"Nancy called Jason 'Mister' aguh—"

"Hush," Nancy said. She was talking loud when we crossed the ditch and stooped through the fence where she used to stoop through with the clothes on her head. Then we came to her house. We were going fast then. She opened the door. The smell of the house was like the lamp and the smell of Nancy was like the wick, like they were waiting for one another to begin to smell. She lit the lamp and closed the door and put the bar up. Then she quit talking loud, looking at us.

"What're we going to do?" Caddy said.

"What do yawl want to do?" Nancy said.

"You said we would have some fun," Caddy said.

There was something about Nancy's house; something you could smell besides Nancy and the house. Jason smelled it, even. "I don't want to stay here," he said. "I want to go home."

"Go home, then," Caddy said.

"I don't want to go by myself," Jason said.

"We're going to have some fun," Nancy said.

"How?" Caddy said.

Nancy stood by the door. She was looking at us, only it was like she had emptied her eyes, like she had quit using them. "What do you want to do?" she said.

"Tell us a story," Caddy said. "Can you tell a story?"

"Yes," Nancy said.

"Tell it," Caddy said. We looked at Nancy. "You don't know any stories."

"Yes," Nancy said. "Yes I do."

She came and sat in a chair before the hearth. There was a little fire there. Nancy built it up, when it was already hot inside. She built a good blaze. She told a story. She talked like her eyes looked, like her eyes watching us and her voice talking to us did not belong to her. Like she was living somewhere else, waiting somewhere else. She was outside the cabin. Her voice was inside and the shape of her, that Nancy could stoop under a barbed wire fence with a bundle of clothes balanced on her head as though without weight, like a balloon, was there. But that was all. "And so this here queen come walking up to the ditch, where that bad man was hiding. She was walking up to the ditch, and she say, 'If I can just get past this here ditch,' was what she say . . ."

"What ditch?" Caddy said. "A ditch like that one out there? Why did a queen want to go into a ditch?"

"To get to her house," Nancy said. She looked at us. "She had to cross the ditch to get into her house quick and bar the door."

"Why did she want to go home and bar the door?" Caddy said.

IV

Nancy looked at us. She quit talking. She looked at us. Jason's legs stuck straight out of his pants where he sat on Nancy's lap. "I don't think that's a good story," he said. "I want to go home."

"Maybe we had better," Caddy said. She got up from the floor. "I bet they are looking for us right now." She went toward the door.

"No," Nancy said. "Don't open it." She got up quick and passed Caddy. She didn't touch the door, the wooden bar.

"Why not?" Caddy said.

"Come back to the lamp," Nancy said. "We'll have fun. You don't have to go."

"We ought to go," Caddy said. "Unless we have a lot of fun." She and Nancy came back to the fire, the lamp.

"I want to go home," Jason said. "I'm going to tell."

"I know another story," Nancy said. She stood close to the lamp. She looked at Caddy, like when your eyes look up at a stick balanced on your nose. She had to look down to see Caddy, but her eyes looked like that, like when you are balancing a stick.

"I won't listen to it," Jason said. "I'll bang on the floor."

"It's a good one," Nancy said. "It's better than the other one."

"What's it about?" Caddy said. Nancy was standing by the lamp. Her hand was on the lamp, against the light, long and brown.

"Your hand is on that hot globe," Caddy said. "Don't it feel hot to your hand?"

Nancy looked at her hand on the lamp chimney. She took her hand away, slow. She stood there, looking at Caddy, wringing her long hand as though it were tied to her wrist with a string.

"Let's do something else," Caddy said.

"I want to go home," Jason said.

"I got some popcorn," Nancy said. She looked at Caddy and then at Jason and then at me and then at Caddy again. "I got some popcorn."

"I don't like popcorn," Jason said. "I'd rather have candy."

Nancy looked at Jason. "You can hold the popper." She was still wringing her hand; it was long and limp and brown.

"All right," Jason said. "I'll stay a while if I can do that. Caddy can't hold it. I'll want to go home again if Caddy holds the popper."

Nancy built up the fire. "Look at Nancy putting her hands in the fire," Caddy said. "What's the matter with you, Nancy?"

"I got popcorn," Nancy said. "I got some." She took the popper from under the bed. It was broken. Jason began to cry.

"Now we can't have any popcorn," he said.

"We ought to go home anyway," Caddy said. "Come on," Quentin."

"Wait," Nancy said; "wait. I can fix it. Don't you want to help me fix it?"

"I don't think I want any," Caddy said. "It's too late now."

"You help me, Jason," Nancy said. "Don't you want to help me?"

"No," Jason said. "I want to go home."

"Hush," Nancy said; "hush. Watch. Watch me. I can fix it so Jason can hold it and pop the corn." She got a piece of wire and fixed the popper.

"It won't hold good," Caddy said.

"Yes it will," Nancy said. "Yawl watch. Yawl help me shell some corn."

The popcorn was under the bed too. We shelled it into the popper and Nancy helped Jason hold the popper over the fire.

"It's not popping," Jason said. "I want to go home."

"You wait," Nancy said. "It'll begin to pop. We'll have fun then."

She was sitting close to the fire. The lamp was turned up so high it was beginning to smoke. "Why don't you turn it down some?" I said.

"It's all right," Nancy said. "I'll clean it. Yawl wait. The popcorn will start in a minute."

"I don't believe it's going to start," Caddy said. "We ought to start home, anyway. They'll be worried."

"No," Nancy said. "It's going to pop. Dilsey will tell um yawl with me. I been working for yawl long time. They won't mind if yawl at my house. You wait, now. It'll start popping any minute now."

Then Jason got some smoke in his eyes and he began to cry. He dropped the popper into the fire. Nancy got a wet rag and wiped Jason's face, but he didn't stop crying.

"Hush," she said. "Hush." But he didn't hush. Caddy took the popper out of the fire.

"It's burned up," she said. "You'll have to get some more popcorn, Nancy."

"Did you put all of it in?" Nancy said.

"Yes," Caddy said. Nancy looked at Caddy. Then she took the popper and opened it and poured the cinders into her apron and began to sort the grains, her hands long and brown, and we watched her.

"Haven't you got any more?" Caddy said.

"Yes," Nancy said; "yes. Look. This here ain't burnt. All we need to do is—"

"I want to go home," Jason said. "I'm going to tell."

"Hush," Caddy said. We all listened. Nancy's head was already turned toward the barred door, her eyes filled with red lamplight. "Somebody is coming," Caddy said.

Then Nancy began to make that sound again, not loud, sitting there above the fire, her long hands dangling between her knees; all of a sudden water began to come out on her face in big drops, running down her face, carrying in each one a little turning ball of firelight like a spark until it dropped off her chin. "She's not crying," I said.

"I ain't crying," Nancy said. Her eyes were closed. "I ain't crying. Who is it?"

"I don't know," Caddy said. She went to the door and looked out. "We've got to go now," she said. "Here comes Father."

"I'm going to tell," Jason said. "Yawl made me come."

The water still ran down Nancy's face. She turned in her chair. "Listen. Tell him. Tell him we going to have fun. Tell him I take good care of yawl until in the morning. Tell him to let me come home with yawl and sleep on the floor. Tell him I won't need no pallet. We'll have fun. You member last time how we had so much fun?"

"I didn't have fun," Jason said. "You hurt me. You put smoke in my eyes. I'm going to tell."

v

Father came in. He looked at us. Nancy did not get up.

"Tell him," she said.

"Caddy made us come down here," Jason said. "I didn't want to."

Father came to the fire. Nancy looked up at him. "Can't you go to Aunt Rachel's and stay?" he said. Nancy looked up at Father, her hands between her knees. "He's not here," Father said. "I would have seen him. There's not a soul in sight."

"He in the ditch," Nancy said. "He waiting in the ditch yonder."

"Nonsense," Father said. He looked at Nancy. "Do you know he's there?"

"I got the sign," Nancy said.

"What sign?"

"I got it. It was on the table when I come in. It was a hog-bone, with blood meat still on it, laying by the lamp. He's out there. When yawl walk out that door, I gone."

"Gone where, Nancy?" Caddy said.

"I'm not a tattletale," Jason said.

"Nonsense," Father said.

"He out there," Nancy said. "He looking through that window this minute, waiting for yawl to go. Then I gone."

"Nonsense," Father said. "Lock up your house and we'll take you on to Aunt Rachel's."

" 'Twon't do no good," Nancy said. She didn't look at Father now, but he looked down at her, at her long, limp, moving hands. "Putting it off won't do no good."

"Then what do you want to do?" Father said.

"I don't know," Nancy said. "I can't do nothing. Just put it off. And that don't do no good. I reckon it belong to me. I reckon what I going to get ain't no more than mine."

"Get what?" Caddy said. "What's yours?"

"Nothing," Father said. "You all must get to bed."

"Caddy made me come," Jason said.

"Go on to Aunt Rachel's," Father said.

"It won't do no good," Nancy said. She sat before the fire, her elbows on her knees, her long hands between her knees. "When even your own kitchen wouldn't do no good. When even if I was sleeping on the floor in the room with your chillen, and the next morning there I am, and blood—"

"Hush," Father said. "Lock the door and put out the lamp and go to bed."

"I scaired of the dark," Nancy said. "I scaired for it to happen in the dark."

"You mean you're going to sit right here with the lamp lighted?" Father said. Then Nancy began to make the sound again, sitting before the fire, her long hands between her knees. "Ah, damnation," Father said. "Come along, chillen. It's past bed-time."

"When yawl go home, I gone," Nancy said. She talked quieter

now, and her face looked quiet, like her hands. "Anyway, I got my coffin money saved up with Mr. Lovelady." Mr. Lovelady was a short, dirty man who collected the Negro insurance, coming around to the cabins or the kitchens every Saturday morning, to collect fifteen cents. He and his wife lived at the hotel. One morning his wife committed suicide. They had a child, a little girl. He and the child went away. After a week or two he came back alone. We would see him going along the lanes and the back streets on Saturday mornings.

"Nonsense," Father said. "You'll be the first thing I'll see in the kitchen tomorrow morning."

"You'll see what you'll see, I reckon," Nancy said. "But it will take the Lord to say what that will be."

VI

We left her sitting before the fire.

"Come and put the bar up," Father said. But she didn't move. She didn't look at us again, sitting quietly there between the lamp and the fire. From some distance down the lane we could look back and see her through the open door.

"What, Father?" Caddy said. "What's going to happen?"

"Nothing," Father said. Jason was on Father's back, so Jason was the tallest of all of us. We went down into the ditch. I looked at it, quiet. I couldn't see much where the moonlight and the shadows tangled.

"If Jesus *is* hid here, he can see us, can't he?" Caddy said.

"He's not there," Father said. "He went away a long time ago."

"You made me come," Jason said, high; against the sky it looked like Father had two heads, a little one and a big one. "I didn't want to."

We went up out of the ditch. We could still see Nancy's house and the open door, but we couldn't see Nancy now, sitting before the fire with the door open, because she was tired. "I just done got tired," she said. "I just a nigger. It ain't no fault of mine."

But we could hear her, because she began just after we came up out of the ditch, the sound that was not singing and not unsinging. "Who will do our washing now, Father?" I said.

"I'm not a nigger," Jason said, high and close above Father's head.

"You're worse," Caddy said, "you are a tattletale. If something was to jump out, you'd be scairder than a nigger."

"I wouldn't," Jason said.

"You'd cry," Caddy said.

"Caddy," Father said.

"I wouldn't!" Jason said.

"Scairy cat," Caddy said.

"Candace!" Father said.

Par Lagerkvist

THE LIFT THAT WENT DOWN INTO HELL

PAR LAGERKVIST, *novelist, dramatist, and poet, is the most impressive figure in the Swedish literary revival touched off by Verner von Heidenstam. He was born in 1891 in the town of Växjö. While attending Upsala University he published several poems and in 1912 a novel,* People. *He left the University and went to France, where he came under the influence of the Cubists and Fauvists. The effect of these influences is evident in* The Eternal Smile, *a collection of short stories which includes the following piece. As a poet he created a trend in Swedish poetry which approximated that of T. S. Eliot in English, but it is as a novelist that he is most impressive. His novel* Barabbas, *a profoundly moral work concerned with the problem of good and evil—like most of the work of this man who described himself as a "religious atheist"—was translated into English the year he won the Nobel Prize, 1951. The* Dwarf *treats of human bestiality with an irony reminiscent of Swift, and more recently,* The Sybil *brought him the highest praise. In Sweden, he is also regarded as a remarkably fine dramatist.*

Mr. Smith, a prosperous businessman, opened the elegant hotel lift and amorously handed in a gracile creature smelling of furs and powder. They nestled together on the soft seat and the lift started downward. The little lady extended her half-open mouth, which was moist with wine, and they kissed. They had dined up on the terrace, under the stars; now they were going out to amuse themselves.

"Darling, how divine it was up there," she whispered. "So poetic sitting there with you, like being up among the stars. That's when you really know what love is. You do love me, don't you?"

Mr. Smith answered with a kiss that lasted still longer; the lift went down.

"A good thing you came, my darling," he said; "otherwise I'd have been in an awful state."

"Yes, but you can just imagine how insufferable he was. The second I started getting ready he asked where I was going. 'I'll go where I please,' I said. 'I'm no prisoner.' Then he deliberately sat and stared at me the whole time I was changing, putting on my new beige—do you think it's becoming? What do you think looks best, by the way, perhaps pink after all?"

"Everything becomes you, darling," the man said, "but I've never seen you so lovely as this evening."

She opened her fur coat with a gratified smile, they kissed for a long time, the lift went down.

"Then when I was ready to go he took my hand and squeezed it so that it still hurts, and didn't say a word. He's so brutal, you've no idea! 'Well, good-bye,' I said. But not a word from him. He's so unreasonable, so frightfully, I can't stand it."

"Poor little thing," said Mr. Smith.

"As though I can't go out for a bit and enjoy myself. But then he's so deadly serious, you've no idea. He can't take anything simply and naturally. It's as though it were a matter of life and death the whole time."

"Poor pet, what you must have gone through."

"Oh, I've suffered terribly. Terribly. No one has suffered as I have. Not until I met you did I know what love is."

"Sweetheart," Smith said, hugging her; the lift went down.

"Fancy," she said, when she had got her breath after the embrace, "sitting with you up there gazing at the stars and dreaming—oh, I'll never forget it. You see, the thing is—Arvid is impossible, he's so everlastingly solemn, he hasn't a scrap of poetry in him, he has no feeling for it."

"Darling, it's intolerable."

"Yes, isn't it—intolerable. But," she went on, giving him her hand with a smile, "let's not sit thinking of all that. We're out to enjoy ourselves. You do really love me?"

"Do I!" he said, bending her back so that she gasped; the lift went down. Leaning over her he fondled her; she blushed.

"Let us make love tonight—as never before. Hm?" he whispered.

She pressed him to her and closed her eyes; the lift went down. Down and down it went.

At last Smith got to his feet, his face flushed.

"But what's the matter with the lift?" he exclaimed. "Why doesn't it stop? We've been sitting here for ever so long talking, haven't we?"

"Yes, darling, I suppose we have, time goes so quickly."

"Good Heavens, we've been sitting here for ages! What's the idea?"

He glanced out through the grill. Nothing but pitch darkness. And the lift went on and on at a good, even pace, deeper and deeper down.

"Heavens alive, what's the idea? It's like dropping down into an empty pit. And we've been doing this for God knows how long."

They tried to peep down into the abyss. It was pitch dark. They just sank and sank down into it.

"This is all going to hell," Smith said.

"Oh dear," the woman wailed, clinging to his arm, "I'm so nervous. You'll have to pull the emergency brake."

Smith pulled for all he was worth. It was no good. The lift merely plunged down and down interminably.

"It's frightful," she cried. "What are we going to do!"

"Yes, what the devil is one to do?" Smith said. "This is crazy."

The little lady was in despair and burst into tears.

"There, there, my sweet, don't cry, we must be sensible. There's nothing we can do. There now, sit down. That's right, now we'll sit here quietly both of us, close together, and see what happens. It must stop some time or there'll be the devil to pay."

They sat and waited.

"Just think of something like this happening," the woman said. "And we were going out to have fun."

"Yes, it's the very devil," Smith said.

"You do love me, don't you?"

"Darling," Smith said, putting his arms around her; the lift went down.

At last it stopped abruptly. There was such a bright light all around that it hurt the eyes. They were in hell. The Devil slid the grill aside politely.

"Good evening," he said with a deep bow. He was stylishly dressed in tails that hung on the hairy top vertebra as on a rusty nail.

Smith and the woman tottered out in a daze. "Where in God's name are we?" they exclaimed, terrified by the weird apparition. The Devil, a shade embarrassed, enlightened them.

"But it's not as bad as it sounds," he hastened to add. "I hope you will have quite a pleasant time. I gather it's just for the night?"

"Yes, yes!" Smith assented eagerly, "it's just for the night. We're not going to stay, oh no!"

The little lady clung tremblingly to his arm. The light was so corrosive and yellowy green that they could hardly see, and there was a hot smell, they thought. When they had grown a little more used to it they discovered they were standing as it were in a square, around which houses with glowing doorways towered up in the darkness; the curtains were drawn but they could see through the chinks that something was burning inside.

"You are the two who love each other?" the Devil inquired.

"Yes, madly," the lady answered, giving him a look with her lovely eyes.

"Then this is the way," he said, and asked them to follow please. They slunk into a murky side street leading out of the square. An old cracked lantern was hanging outside a filthy, grease-stained doorway.

"Here it is." He opened the door and retired discreetly.

They went in. A new devil, fat, fawning, with large breasts and purple powder caked on the mustache around her mouth, received them. She smiled wheezily, a good-natured, knowing look in her beady eyes; around the horns in her forehead she had twined tufts of hair and fastened them with small blue silk ribbons.

"Oh, is it Mr. Smith and the little lady?" she said. "It's in number eight then." And she gave them a large key.

They climbed the dim, greasy staircase. The stairs were slippery with fat; it was two flights up. Smith found number eight and went in. It was a fairly large, musty room. In the middle was a table with a grubby cloth; by the wall a bed with smoothed-down sheets. They thought it all very nice. They took off their coats and kissed for a long time.

A man came in unobtrusively from another door. He was dressed like a waiter but his dinner jacket was well cut and his shirtfront so clean that it gleamed ghostlike in the semi-darkness. He walked silently, his feet making no sound, and his movements were mechanical, unconscious almost. His features were stern, the eyes looking fixedly straight ahead. He was deathly pale; in one temple he had a bullet wound. He got the room ready, wiped the dressing table, brought in a chamberpot and a slop pail.

They didn't take much notice of him, but as he was about to go Smith said, "I think we'll have some wine. Bring us half a bottle of Madeira." The man bowed and disappeared.

Smith started getting undressed. The woman hesitated.

"He's coming back," she said.

"Pshaw, in a place like this you needn't mind. Just take your things off." She got out of her dress, pulled up her panties coquettishly and sat on his knee. It was lovely.

"Just think," she whispered, "sitting here together, you and I, alone, in such a queer, romantic place. So poetic, I'll never forget it." "Sweetheart," he said. They kissed for a long time.

The man came in again, soundlessly. Softly, mechanically, he put down the glasses, poured out the wine. The light from the table lamp fell on his face. There was nothing special about him except that he was deathly pale and had a bullet wound in his temple.

The woman leaped up with a scream.

"Oh my God! Arvid! Is it you? Is it you? Oh God in Heaven, he's dead! He's shot himself!"

The man stood motionless, just staring in front of him. His face showed no suffering; it was merely stern, very grave.

"But Arvid, what have you done, what have you done! How could you! My dear, if I'd suspected anything like that, you know I'd have stayed at home. But you never tell me anything. You never said anything about it, not a word! How was I to know when you never told me! Oh my God . . ."

Her whole body was shaking. The man looked at her as at a stranger; his gaze was icy and gray, just went straight through everything. The sallow face gleamed, no blood came from the wound, there was just a hole there.

"Oh, it's ghastly, ghastly!" she cried. "I won't stay here! Let's go at once. I can't stand it."

She grabbed her dress, hat and fur coat and rushed out, followed by Smith. They slipped going down the stairs, she sat down, got spittle and cigarette ash on her behind. Downstairs the woman with the mustache was standing, smiling good-naturedly and knowingly and nodding her horns.

Out in the street they calmed down a little. The woman put on her clothes, straightened herself, powdered her nose. Smith put his arm protectingly round her waist, kissed away the tears that were on the point of falling—he was so good. They walked up into the square.

The head devil was walking about there, they ran into him again. "You *have* been quick," he said. "I hope you've been comfortable."

"Oh, it was dreadful," the lady said.

"No, don't say that, you can't think that. You should have been here in the old days, it was different then. Hell is nothing to complain of now. We do all we can not to make it too obvious, on the contrary to make it enjoyable."

"Yes," Mr. Smith said, "I must say it's a little more humane anyway, that's true."

"Oh," the Devil said, "we've had everything modernized, completely rearranged, as it should be."

"Yes, of course, you must keep up with the times."

"Yes, it's only the soul that suffers nowadays."

"Thank God for that," said the lady.

The Devil conducted them politely to the lift. "Good evening," he said with a deep bow, "welcome back." He shut the grill after them, the lift went up.

"Thank God that's over," they both said, relieved, and nestled up to one another on the seat.

"I should never have got through it without you," she whispered. He drew her to him, they kissed for a long time. "Fancy," she said, when she had got her breath after the embrace, "his doing such a thing! But he's always had such queer notions. He's never been able to take things simply and naturally, as they are. It's as though it were a matter of life and death the whole time."

"It's absurd," Smith said.

"He might have *told* me! Then I'd have stayed. We could have gone out another evening instead."

"Yes, of course," Smith said, "of course we could."

"But, darling, let's not sit thinking of that," she whispered, putting her arms around his neck. "It's over now."

"Yes, little darling, it's over now." He clasped her in his arms; the lift went up.

[*Translated by Alan Blair*]

François Mauriac

A MAN OF LETTERS

FRANÇOIS MAURIAC *was born in 1885 in Bordeaux, the scene of much of his fiction. Deeply influenced by the strict religious teachings of his early years, Mauriac has become one of the leading Catholic novelists of the twentieth century. He remained in Bordeaux at the University until he was twenty and then went to Paris to the École de Chartres, which he left when he began to publish poetry and criticism in avant-garde magazines. After completing two books of poems, he founded a magazine to publish Catholic writing. During World War I, he served in the hospital corps in Salonika until he was sent home suffering from malaria. After* The Kiss of the Leper (1922) *his reputation grew rapidly with the publication of* Genetrix (1924), The Desert of Love (1929), The Viper's Tangle (1933), The Weakling (1951) *and* The Enemy (1955). *In 1933, he was elected to the French Academy and in 1952, awarded the Nobel Prize. His play* Asmodée *was produced successfully off-Broadway in 1958. The principal themes of his works are based on the constant struggle between human love and divine love, between sin and divine grace. The following story, first published in 1929 as part of* Trois Récits, *though it does not share this dominant note, is characteristic of Mauriac's bitter vision.*

What could I do for the whimsical child? Her father, a cloth manufacturer of Elboeuf, did not wish her to marry Jerome, who was a playwright in Paris. She followed Jerome and did not marry him. "Nothing in the world," declared the ninny, "must be allowed to stand in the way of our marvelous love." She took every care not to have a child. A child would have prevented her from serving her master alone. But although she found herself honored everywhere as a wife above all wives, as the lady of ladies, and as the spouse of a playwright of distinction, at the end of fifteen years, in accordance with a right she herself had acknowledged, and without being able to hinder him with aught but her tears, Jerome began to drift away from her.

The mere sight of the drawing room where I was waiting for Gabrielle was enough to open my eyes to the folly of the couple who for years had been lacerating each other there. The shabby pieces of furniture, "modern style," were the useless remnant, the forlorn outline, of a passion that had proved too ambitious. The meanest of the chairs testified by its outlandish design to the bungling efforts which had there been made to achieve bliss. In the gloomy light of that afternoon this wreckage of a foundered life drifted before my eyes. I tried not to inhale too much of that musty smell which is wont to hang about a room where a man has once smoked a great deal and now no one smoked.

Some books lay on a small table, but none had been opened for months. How on earth did this woman spend her evenings? No sort of reading could release her from herself; nothing her imagination prompted could prevail against what was torturing her. What creature of a poet's fancy could succeed, even for one minute, in distracting her from the man who had deserted and betrayed her? I pictured her wandering from room to room, wringing her hands in the silence, choked, suffocated by the diatribes, invectives and appeals she was no longer able to shout at anyone's face.

But, confronted by me, the flood gates would at last be opened. The only comfort I could offer her would be to give her a listener. I should be literally all ears. It is odd that no mythology has ever represented the Deity in the form of a gigantic ear— something that makes no reply but perhaps listens. I should be that deity to Gabrielle.

For years Jerome had tortured her. But every evening she had had the relief of calling him to account—what Jerome called "making a scene." Now Gabrielle knew that to be a martyr was nothing so long as one's torturer was at hand day and night and could be shamed for his barbarity. A loving woman, inured to this daily exchange of insults, considers, when no longer able to engage in the sport, that her life was embellished by it. How full of voluptuous pleasure her suffering before his desertion now appeared to her! To yell alone in a sepulchre is beyond the power of any woman.

But for once at least she was going to be able to pour out her woes to someone. Nevertheless, I should have to pretend to give her advice. What should I say to her?—Anything! All I need do would be to pick up the stones she would fling at Jerome, and, when she stopped to take breath, contrive to say something that would start her off again. No doubt, in keeping with my custom at such interviews, I should pretend to change the subject, if only for the pleasure of seeing the young woman seize upon anything. I said that would help her to return to her anguish. Even if I talked to her about an Emperor of China, she would expatiate on Jerome's slanting eyes and yellow complexion, or perhaps also on his skill and inventing unending tortures which destroy everything in their victim, except the capacity for suffering.

It was tiresome that decency would hardly allow me to hold my tongue, or interrupt her merely by a polite "I am listening" or "I am following every word." It seemed probable that my very first words, spoken from the heart and too hard on the faithless man, would provoke her to urge what she could in favor of her idol. And yet, the moment I appeared even half-convinced she would burst out again with insults against the deserter. For if, from her point of view, the only excuse she could discover for her love was that it was inspired by a superman, conversely it followed that the despair his desertion had caused her—that everbleeding wound —made it impossible for her to look on him as anything less than a murderer. Above all, I should have to avoid in such a context trying to reconcile all the aspects of the case by remarking that this man of genius was a delightful murderer! For then I should behold the fury, baffled by the conflict of ideas, turn from one to the other, hesitate, lose her bearings, and collapse in a torrent of tears and wailings. After having wandered all that time about the Palace of Pyrrhus, Hermione still did not know that Love and Hate were two aspects of the one and only god that obsessed her.

I would not hesitate to make the silliest remark. "Try to love someone else," I should doubtless suggest to her; "offer the empty niche to a stranger!" But there was no empty niche. Her life was full, crammed to the brim by an absence. There was no possible access to Gabrielle, except with reference to the absentee. One must either talk about him or hear him talked about. She could not even turn away certain friends of Jerome who, according to the young woman, had betrayed her and whom she hated as her love's accomplices. They were a part of her distress; they belonged to that absence which preoccupied her wholly.

I would have been prepared to see Gabrielle conquered by another man. But the cruelty of certain desertions is that they leave their victim quite useless to any except her torturer. Gabrielle did not know that Jerome's worst crime had been that he had fashioned and refashioned her out of all recognition; that he had, as it were, deformed her and in such wise as to prevent her from ever again fitting any other destiny than his. Just as he furnished his home with those crazy chairs and those exotic couches of unique design, so Jerome wished to possess a mistress different from all others, a companion for his own use. Wishing to refashion her after his own style, he had first been obliged to dismember her. But all he had been able to do was to destroy her. Then, incapable of restoring her, he had turned away from the mutilated and broken creature. Who would ever dare to recover the scattered fragments of that soul, that confused heap of clay all pawed over and thumb-marked?

Above all, I had to beware of such comforting phrases as "Time will heal the wound. One day you will have forgotten him." If it were true that help could reach her from him alone, I must take care not to exasperate her by picturing her life as deprived of what actually composed it. In order to master sleeplessness, the prerequisite is to put all thoughts of sleep out of our minds. And to those who have nothing left on this earth except to forget, we should never speak of forgetting.

With this companion of a dramatist, however, whose mind was adapted to the weaving of literary themes, I feared lest it might be difficult to avoid the question whether Jerome would not have been better dead than a traitor. I already seemed to hear her saying: "His death would not have been so cruel a blow to me as his infidelity," followed by the sublime comment: "In any case, he would have been lost, and I should not have been forced to despise him." Truth to tell, in that case she would not have despised him, she would simply have forgotten him. But with Jerome living, not a minute passed that might not bring back the fugitive, whilst each minute gave the derelict woman fresh cause for disappointment and increased hatred. Yet, over and above it all, the hope remained that the very next second the lift would stop at her landing and she would recognize the short, sharp ring of her bell. It was impossible to cure her. She could have been cured had Jerome died. For death alone closes every avenue of hope, leaving the survivor only the refuge of oblivion (Shades of Proust!).

Everything was in its usual place. Jerome would find the house just as he had left it. I had heard that Gabrielle refused even to get a new frock, and insisted on wearing only what Jerome had once chosen for her. The reverse would have been wiser. She should have tried to become herself again—the young woman she had been before he had reduced her to shreds. Then he might have recognized her. But if she remained in his eyes what she then was—his handiwork which he had tinkered at without respite and turned his back on, unfinished—she forfeited all hope of conquering him again. Could she possibly be unaware of the fact that we authors never open a book that is one of our failures?

II

This visit was the excuse for a strange duologue. But I must first confess a mistake I made. Gabrielle would never have induced me to come to her simply for the pleasure of talking in someone's presence. Though she doubtless did gratify her wish to pour out her heart, she was hoping for much more than mere attention from me. She wished to be helped to discover Jerome's reasons for deserting her. "I don't understand. I should like to understand," she said again and again, as if all her pain would vanish the moment she was completely apprised of the motives of Jerome's behavior. And, had it been possible, this knowledge would in fact, have healed her wound. It is God's omniscience that helps Him to endure the sorrows of the world.

"He is marrying my rival . . . a woman older than myself and the mother of two children who are always ill."

Just as I was blurting out: "If he loves her——" Gabrielle stopped me.

"She gets on his nerves even more than I did. I know all that goes on there from his friends, the X's, who on the pretense of comforting me sometimes come here to rub salt into my wounds. Jerome cannot see the most casual acquaintance in the study but what she showers reproaches on him. And when I remember the care I used to take of his health, it makes me smile to think that she insists on sharing his bed, and that every night she satisfies herself that he has not spent his strength elsewhere.

"I saw to it that his life here was all peace and quiet. I kept in the background. Whether he came home or stayed out, I never let him see my anguish. After escapades lasting whole weeks he would come back to find his place laid at table and no trace of anything in my face except what suffering had, unknown to me, engraved there. Would you believe it?—I had reached the point of never 'making a scene,' except when I felt that secretly he wished for one, either because he did not know what attitude to adopt and a scene seemed to him the most natural way out, or because he hoped that insults and shouts would relax his nerves. I had reached the stage when, no matter how many letters the postman brought, I knew I must not open even a newspaper wrapper in his presence. I knew that he could not stand being spoken to while shaving, that he hated anyone going past the water-closet door when he was inside, and when he was sitting by the fire objected to anyone taking the easy chair opposite him.

"Sometimes I made mistakes. When he came back at night, for instance, I would pretend to be sleeping, although all the time he wished I had been awake to ask him questions. Or it was the other way about. He would find me reading in bed; for, the moment I heard the lift stop at our floor, I would, for appearance sake and after a night of sleepless torment, sometimes pick up a book and pretend to be perfectly serene. Whereupon he would reproach me for ostentatiously keeping awake in his absence so as to compel him to stay at home in future.

"Oh, God knows, I have sacrificed enough to save our relationship. All I cared about was that he should feel free. Had he left me to live alone I might perhaps have understood him. Despite all my skill in not making myself a burden to him, it may be, as I have often heard him declare, that domestic life is slow poison to a man of letters, and that he is right to treat as an enemy everyone who in his presence utters a word, crumples a newspaper, shuts a door, or even breathes. The faithful heart that beats beside an artist fidgets him by its very beat.

"Yes, I could have understood Jerome's leaving me to be alone, and who knows if I myself might not then have found resignation in rest? For one gets very tired living by the side of these badly wounded creatures, pierced with arrows from all sides, from God and the most sublime abstractions as well as from an embittered fellow-writer or a hostile critic. But, no, no! How could I ever have said that?— Nothing could ever console me for having lost him. . . . But at least I should have understood. . . ."

(Thus, at every turn in the conversation, this word "understood" was on the young woman's lips.)

"Well, it turns out that he left me for the worst possible prison

of all—a third-rate flat in the suburbs, woman worn out and embittered, and with delicate children whom he speaks of with disgust. . . ."

"Probably he is a man as incapable of solitude as of fidelity
. . . he'll desert her. . . ."

"No, impossible, for he is marrying her and is ready to recognize
her children as his own. . . ."

"He may perhaps," I suggested, hesitating to state a possibility
which I feared affected Gabrielle, "be wishing to safeguard himself. . . ." But she guessed what was in my mind.

"You mean, to protect himself against me, set an insuperable
barrier between us? You think I am repugnant to him? Well, listen! I promised him not to breathe a word about it; but I must
tell you. Jerome often comes back here. . . . Yes, he kept a key
of this flat and often of an evening, ever since our separation, I
have heard the familiar grating of his key in the lock. And that is
why nothing on earth would make me leave the house at that
hour. He humbly takes a chair, looks at me, listens, but does not
attempt to defend himself. Why, I have seen him cry in the very
chair you are now sitting in. The last time he came he took my
hand and said: 'You alone Gabrielle,' and pressed my hand
against his brow and eyes. But I was stupid enough to whisper in
his ear: 'Stay here!' Then he got up, the door on the landing
closed, and I heard him go downstairs four steps at a time."

"And you have no idea . . . ?"

"None whatever! At first I thought he felt the need of watching
me suffer . . . yes, for his next play. With men of letters this is
the first thing that should occur to one. Well, in my present state
I could be of use to him. I am what he calls a first-class experi-
mental guinea pig. But that isn't it! I know his eyes. I know his
whole manner when he is after copy and has seized what he
wants, his look of a dog hypnotized by a hare sitting stock still.
Now I swear that on that occasion he was not the man of letters.
He was just an ordinary man whom I saw bleeding in the very
chair you are sitting in."

"Has that woman perhaps some hold over him . . . she may have him in her power?"

This suggestion, made quite airily and only to avoid saying nothing at all, seemed to stir Gabrielle profoundly.

"Yes, I thought of that too, though I like to believe he is not the sort to submit to blackmail. It disturbs me to think you have had the same idea. We know nothing of the most secret side of his life. Yes . . . the more I think of it . . . you may be right."

She rose. A plain, old-fashioned frock hung loosely about her emaciated form.

"Those escapades of his . . . Where used he to go? I can't imagine what he did when out of my sight. He came back improved, almost always more ethereal. That was what prevented me from feeling anxious, when all the time I should have interpreted it as satiety. What does a man do when he goes out alone? Where does he go? To what unknown beast does he secretly take its victuals? Have you known the agony of possessing by right, in the creature you love, only one floor, so to speak—to hear something breathing and moving about above and below, and yet to feel certain all the while that you cannot communicate with what is so near and yet so inaccessible? In such circumstances—yes, one must be brave enough to imagine and to fear everything. I implore you to go and see him."

I retorted that Jerome was not a friend of mine, hardly an acquaintance.

"But he admires you. . . . Yes! He venerates you. Perhaps he will make a clean breast of it. Don't wait until tomorrow. The marriage may take place any moment now."

I wished to comfort Gabrielle and assured her that Jerome was behaving exactly as all we men of letters behaved—tramping the streets in pursuit of a character.

"Those journeys about Paris," I added, "that flight from daily routine, that dread of finding ourselves in a setting too well defined, confronting people too well known—that is the experience of all creators. . . . I'll see Jerome, since you wish me to do so. But we are probably wide of the mark. If there were a skeleton in his cupboard we should know about it. In Paris everything is common knowledge, especially in the small world of letters and the theater. . . . Had his rivals been able to sling mud at him . . . But I never heard anything said about him."

"Everything is common knowledge, you say?" Gabrielle interrupted. "That was not Jerome's opinion. He always said that no one knows us and that we know nothing of other people. Nobody takes any notice of us; others are amused at our antics, but get no further than the surface. For at bottom no one is interested in anyone else. Each of us thinks only of self. 'We imagine we are the cynosure of all eyes,' Jerome used to say, 'until we discover that in a work in which we have stripped ourselves naked people do not ever perceive our nakedness! . . .' 'As I grow older,' he used to add, 'I discard one after the other of my masks; but when, having discarded the last, the world sees my unknown features, I doubt whether a single cry of terror will be raised!' "

"He said 'a cry of terror'?"

"I remember his very words. 'Some people,' I also remember his saying, 'are blind owing to indifference—as to the rest, those who love me as you do, Gabrielle, I have long ceased to exist in their minds, except as their love insists on depicting me.' On one occasion he added: 'I alone am afraid of myself!' "

"He's a dramatist, is your Jerome. He dramatizes everything. Do you suppose that people have not long ago found us out? Literature is full of lepers who stand by the roadside and cry, 'Look at my fine sores!' and they bare their skin. But the passers-by do not stop. 'What do you hope to teach us?' they say. 'All that interests us in you were the wiles you employed to express yourself in your works, without revealing yourself completely. The value of your art consisted only in the illusions it suggested. Now that we have seen your sores all you need do is to hold your tongue.' "

I wished by these subtleties to distract Gabrielle from the anxiety her confidences had roused in me. I added that Jerome, an author appreciated by a small group, was nevertheless extremely concerned about his career, that he betrayed a taste for decorations, for academic honors, and that he was not a man to jeopardize his worldly success. . . .

"It is just because he hankers after official honors that this woman has perhaps the chance of blackmailing him."

"Why not accept the simplest explanation? There is no doubt some sensual affinity between them."

These were tactless words which annoyed her. She shook her head.

"And I know," she repeated, "that he does not love her. But she has a hold over him. She does not let him go out. Her power over him is so great she does not allow him to drink. He has stopped drinking."

"Used to drink? Well, then, Gabrielle, that may be the whole secret of his escapades."

"Oh, but he never came home drunk, you know. A stranger would have noticed nothing. I knew instantly that he didn't know what he was saying. He said much more than he intended and, on cocktail night, he who in his cruelest moods was always concerned about form, soon got to high words. He was like a workman who had taken his week's pay and was bringing home only half of it. At other times, on the contrary, he was all tender kindness, gently commiserating, fondled me like a brother, and wished to unburden himself. . . . Alas! when he reverted to these affectionate ways, I accepted them coldly, either because I knew from bitter experience that the very next day he would make me pay dearly for them, or else owing to a vague feeling that I was enjoying them by pure chance, because I happened to be there. But in search of what other impossible creature had this storm cloud scoured the heavens all night in order, for want of a better object, to burst over me, smothering me with a sweetness I had not inspired? Or at other times, still steeped in happiness, he would offer me his lips—too feverishly hot. You know how in August we say, 'That storm did not come our way, but all the same it has cooled the air. It must have poured somewhere?' In the same way I guessed that Jerome had come from a love-tryst.

"For fifteen years now I have lived near this black, impenetrable pool. Ripples wrinkled its surface, bubbles told of commotions on its bed, the causes of which remained unknown. What monsters swam and devoured each other in its depths?"

I watched Gabrielle in her anguish. Not kindliness, but my capacity for putting myself in other people's places, always unfitted me for the calling of hangman. A whole lifetime of falsehoods did not seem too much to spare her one of those tears. How could Jerome live on, knowing what Gabrielle was enduring on his account? For two pins I would have taken her on my lap, inflamed and wet with weeping though she was. With all due respect, I would have clasped that frame, emaciated with suffering, as if it had been a child's. For there are no two ways of "doing good" to young women, and there is only one form of comfort that really meets their case—that which needs no spoken word, no unseemly gesture either, and which breaks the silence only by sighs.

III

I did not dare to get near the weeping creature, and twilight fell without Gabrielle's thinking of lighting up. She had preserved the tastes of the period of her first love, when the poets she then preferred wrote verses about unlit rooms and compared the dark to an enviable death. Meanwhile, I, who had always had a horror of semi-darkness, began to grope about for the electric switch. Then, at that very moment, a key turned in the lock of the front door. Gabrielle sprang to her feet. I did not follow her to the hall. There was whispering and she reappeared with Jerome. He held out a hand to me.

"I am pleased to see you . . . to see you? That sounds dreadfully formal."

A crude light poured down from the hanging lamp. We seemed to be ashamed of our faces, for we all three looked away. It was as if each of us was waiting for the expressions we had not dreamt of dissimulating in the darkness to vanish from our features. But there may still have been too much desire in my look, too much pain in Gabrielle's, and in Jerome's an air too strange (for in his case it was almost permissible to speak of "repulsive good looks"), for us to dare to scrutinize each other's faces before the end of the interview.

At first I wished to leave them together; but with a vehemence which Gabrielle doubtless recognized as the effect of the alcohol, Jerome urged me to stay. I, for my part, had already caught in his breath that foetid smell of acetylene with which the drinkers of cocktails offend one. I understood why Gabrielle had added her entreaties to his when she whispered in my ear: "You will leave together."

She was hoping that the talk I was to have with Jerome would take place that very night. Feeling some curiosity about what they wished to say to each other, I therefore stayed with them. Jerome spoke to me first and thanked me for helping Gabrielle "to weather the nasty passage."

"People always do what they like best. You, Gabrielle, you like to smart. You hate not being in pain."

She shrugged a shoulder and muttered "Idiot!"

"Naturally I want to suffer at your hands," she added suddenly, "simply because I cannot imagine any other bond than pain between us. I don't know what joy in love is like."

"Do you suppose I know that any better than you?"

Furtively I watched Jerome's handsome, worn features as he questioned Gabrielle; then I turned away with confused feelings of shame. He was staring into space.

"Besides, does happiness ever exist in love? Yes—yes, it exists in a world we know nothing about. I believe in lovers whose love is complete, just as I believe in angels. Somewhere people are singing to the harp and there are beatings of wings . . . But where . . . where?"

"He has been drinking," Gabrielle said to me, hardly moving her lips. Then she got up, went over to Jerome and sat beside him.

"Are you happier than when you were last here?"

"I'll answer you as Lucifer answered Eloa when she wished to

know whether he was not pleased at least—'Sadder than ever!'
Well, yes! sadder than ever . . . you want to know why? I would
take too long to tell. I would not like to make your dinner late.
. . . But I can't possibly go home at once; for when I have been
at work in a bar I can never hide the fact from Berthe. If I don't
get back in time for dinner I certainly run the risk of a row . . .
but not such a tremendous row as if she discovers that I have been
trying to keep my spirits up a bit . . . If you must know everything, little Pierre is just getting over whooping-cough. But Raymond is coughing; he's sure to get it. We did all we could to iso-
late Pierre; but it was no good. So we face a few weeks more of
nights disturbed every half-hour by coughing fits. Yes, we had
the kid in our bedroom throughout his illness, else the servant
wouldn't have stood it. . . ."

"They ought to have a change of air. . . ."

"You actually know that, Gabrielle—that children who have
had whooping-cough must have a change of air? That's splendid!
I have never heard you make a more sensible remark."

"Why shouldn't I know it?"

"Because you've never had any children. You did not want
any."

"Your fault!"

"Now if you wanted any, you couldn't . . . You have not been
sterilized? No? It's nothing to cry about. You are . . . you are
outside the stream of life . . . one of d'Annunzio's heroines, a
sublime creature, a muse, a muse contemplating the picture of a
landscape. If my next play is a success, I'll increase your allow-
ance. You'll go to live at the Ritz. Yes, you will! This flat is
making you vegetate. You must live at the Ritz, and your only
possessions will be your trunks and suitcases. You'll hang a few
photographs on the walls—Michelangelo, Vermeer, a Greco; all in
the best taste."

He had risen to his feet and was striding to and fro, his hands
deep in his trouser pockets, his cheek bones and nose rather blue.
(He was one of those fox-like men who always seem to have blood
on their jaws.)

"Yes, well, the kids are going to the country, to their grand-mother near Bordeaux. Berthe, you know, hails from good peas-ant stock, she does. They own quite a decent house in a small vil-lage called Bommes. They make wine quite as good as that of *La Tour Blanche*. It's the same soil, only the railway separates the two properties. The River Ciron flows at the foot of the hill. There are heaps of gudgeon, and at sundown the girls of the vil-lage watch the boys bathing."

"But you won't be able to work, Jerome."

"There, do you hear that?" He was still striding to and fro and growing more and more excited as he spoke. "It's here, in this dusty, impossible flat, by the side of a woman of leisure, always lying in wait for my every thought, gesture, and remark—it's here that I ought to have given up all idea of creative work."

"You were free . . . I left you quite free."

"Exactly! But we create only under constraint. You always be-lieved that a work of art is born of a work of art, that travel, mu-seums, and concerts inspire the artist. You poisoned me in an at-mosphere of what you call 'beauty.' It's at the bedside of a sick child that the artist sips his nectar—yes, in a room where a child lies coughing and where at the same time he clasps to his side a body exhausted by fertility, a body like a patch of ploughed soil. You needn't pull such a face, my child!"

Gabrielle, whose face had lost all trace of tenderness, watched him as he walked to and fro, and tried to get a word in edgewise.

"I know you too well," she cried, "to believe that rubbish. But surely you remember! A dog barking in the street was enough to stop your work. You had a morbid longing for silence. Fancy you with sick kids in your room! You on a farm in the country! Go and tell that to the horse marines, not to me!"

Jerome shrugged his shoulders, pulled a face and appealed to me.

"She can't possibly understand! Ha! She hails from the good old days of companions to men of letters, 'associates' who be-lieved that the poet must be provided with 'loneliness fraught with kisses.' How often for my benefit has she not quoted this line from that wretched old Prudhomme! Oh, that frightful silence all about me, broken only by the faint, spiteful hum of a mosquito whose interruption is like a sting! Smack! I got a kiss; a mosquito I couldn't crush. I dread a kiss as much as a mosquito. She had a way of hovering about me on the tips of her creaking shoes. It made me feel as if the whole planet were grating on its axis. And the time she took to open and fold up a newspaper! Those doors closed with so much care that my heart missed a beat! Now no one asks whether I like what I eat. I eat what suits the children. I forego bananas because they have to be kept for them."

It soothed him to talk. Gradually his voice dropped to a lower key, and in a moment he was over the old ground again, apologizing for having generalized too much. According to him, the same regimen did not suit every artist, not even the whole life of the same artist. The conditions of our lives should change as we evolve.

Gabrielle had resumed her seat and was now surveying him with eyes devoid of anger but also free from kindliness—inquisitive, questioning eyes. Leaning forward, her elbows on her knees, she shook her head, as if incessantly contradicting him. Without trying to interrupt Jerome, she repeated to herself half-audibly: "No, that isn't it. . . . That is of no importance. . . . It's all beating about the bush. . . . There's something else. . . ." She was, in fact, so bereft of anger that when, after a brief silence, Jerome rose and looked for his hat, she asked him in astonished tones: "Are you going already?"

He replied that he had already stayed too long, that he ought never to have come, that she richly deserved henceforward to live in peace. We followed him into the hall.

"Do not leave him," Gabrielle said to me. "Try to find out. . . . You'll come back tomorrow. I shall expect you at the same time."

She did not hear my answer, did not even think of asking me if I were free. Her whole life turned about Jerome and she would have been hard put to it to imagine that I could belong to a different constellation.

It was Jerome who begged me to accompany him. We walked
along the Avenue Victor-Hugo toward the Etoile. His hat, pulled
over his eyes, concealed his worn features. He walked briskly and
I found it hard to keep up with him. Not one of the passers-by
failed to arrest his attention for a few seconds at least. He told me
he liked having all these samples of humanity under his eyes for a
brief space on the pavement.

"How dare we live with creatures of our own invention, when
all this living flesh and blood flows down the street like a flood?
Do you enjoy writing? I hate the necessity which rivets me to my
table. I feel life within me. Willy-nilly it must out and I have to
remain seated before a sheet of paper—I have to disgorge. What a
fate! I am like that gravid bitch I once saw at the beginning of a
shoot. She crawled about the stubble, searching for a scent and
meanwhile began dropping her young. Such was her passion for
hunting that giving birth to a puppy did not interrupt her quest
and she continued to drag herself along on the track of a hare. I,
too, would gladly spend all my time on the streets. Whether the
roar of the traffic and the crowds is at its height, or at four in the
morning, when Paris is like the end of Time, and absolute silence
prevails, there's not a moment of the day or night but what they
enchant me. But creatures within me come to life; a duologue
starts in my mind, which gets lost for ever unless I hurry home.
. . . For, after all, this is all that counts. It would be delightful to
live now; but with us creators it is a matter of living for ever.

"You heard that poor child boasting that she had always left me
free? The ninny cannot see that that is why I ran away from her. I
expect a woman to hold me to her and if she alone cannot contrive to do so let her summon children to her aid—strings of children and a whole chain of relatives, if only collaterals. Protected
by a huge family circumvallation, cemented with worries, tempta-
tions and regrets, I work!"

He quickened his pace, slowed down again, jostled me in order the better to convince me, started the passers-by out of countenance, even turned around at times to keep one of them in view, and then would say: "The impression of that face is still quite fresh in my mind. In a couple of hours all trace of it will have vanished."

I reproached him for comparing real life in the most arbitrary manner with the fictitious life of the creatures of his fancy. I assured him that quite unconsciously he drew the substance of his works from reality. He protested and I made an effort not to sustain with my objections an argument that was diverting us from the purpose of my secret quest. I refrained from contradicting him, and slyly induced him to tell me more about the Paris streets. Although he was a writer, could he not find room in his life for distraction, adventure—could he not live, in fact?

"Thou hast said! Live!" cried Jerome, grasping my arm. "When Gabrielle was leaving me perfectly free to 'live,' I indulged certain fancies of various kinds. But, no matter what they were, I always felt I was descending a slope which grew steeper at every step. I never once returned to my starting point. I had to remain half-way down the hill, bereft of something, impoverished."

(These were a drunkard's ravings, and I felt all their vagueness. But I took care not to give them weight by commenting on them.)

"We creators," he added, "belong to a minority who are awake. That is why we are afraid of ourselves. You say you are not afraid of yourself? Believe me! The majority of men are asleep. All those restless Anglo-Saxons, all those criers at the Bourse, in Parliament —they are asleep, old boy! The dope of business is as good as the dope of politics. It is terrible to be for ever awake, incapable of sleep, attentive and lucid by profession. Not one of my abysses escapes me. And that woman Gabrielle left me free to fling myself into them! At bottom every artist at some moment in his life is seized with panic and tries to protect himself. The clear knowledge of ourselves plays into the hands of Catholicism. If many hesitate and cannot decide, almost all hover around it. Oh, ye poets—fair game for God!

"You who are unmarried," he said, tightening his hold on my arm, "who do not read *L'Information Financière* and who hate cards, what are you doing tonight? I dare you to tell me!"

"And what about you?"

"I?—I shall go home, exhausted. I shall have prepared a little story so that Berthe may not scold too much. I shall hear how often Raymond has coughed and whether he can take any nourishment yet. With the eyes of a dog I shall scan Berthe's worn features, terrified lest I increase her irritation. She'll give me all kinds of things to do. 'You who are not doing anything,' or perhaps, 'Here, make yourself useful.' . . ."

"But if you had not got this refuge (you call it a refuge!), I don't see what risks—"

"My poor fellow! I remember the days of my freedom. Every evening opened before me a path shrouded in mystery. The city became a jungle where, as I penetrated its tangled skein, anything might charge down on me. My heart was tense with delicious apprehension; my body fresh from my ablutions—ready for any kind of acquiescence. And now I'm no longer a youngster. . . ."

"Supposing you had not to return home to your lady friend tonight, what would you do . . . ?"

He hesitated for a moment, then his expression brightened.

"First of all, I would have the most marvellous dinner. I would warm myself through with a bottle of Bordeaux (a Gruad-Larose of a specially good year). The bottle emptied, I would sink into that simplified vision of heaven and earth, the ecstasy of which the restaurants of the *Rue Royale* have often afforded me. I would mark off the map of my life by sticking little flags about it—one on the *Comédie Française*, for instance, where I would have a play accepted; another on the *Institut*, where I myself will perhaps be accepted one of these days, and yet another on that *apartement* on the Left Bank whence every morning a young girl writes to me, making appointments with me in suburban inns. If an orchestra played during my lonely dinner, my dreams would certainly take on a graver hue; I would turn inwards on myself in the city of sepulchres and count my dead—women as well as men. I would discover certain faces and recover intact a buried treasure of love. How often, when surrounded by people, sitting at table under a fierce light, have I not felt astonished at finding myself to be that respectable-looking person with a blank expression whom I saw in a mirror opposite me! It might be at the very moment when I had exhumed from my soul the body of a friend buried there these five and twenty years. And I would have to lift my eyes to the ceiling in order to arrest the sudden surge for all my child-hood's burning tears. At the close of such evenings Gabrielle al-ways appeared before me—so beautiful, so lacerated! I cannot tell you how much I loved her then! In my imagination I devised means of giving her joy at last. 'From tomorrow,' I said to myself, 'Gabrielle will shed no more tears.'"

"And then, Jerome, what else did you do?"

"Full speed to the streets! . . . But even in summer I usually freeze on rising from the table. There were, of course, always the promenades. The promenades—sheltered thoroughfares, warm and thronged with passers-by selected from all those who divert me on my daily round; all whose business is the chase. As a child I carried no gun in the fields, but I loved to see the dogs take up the scent. And there, too, I would watch my fellows, the majority of whom are both hunters and quarry at the same time."

We had reached the Opera. The crowd was eddying about the steps leading to the Underground.

"Through this sewer," said my companion, seizing my hand, "I shall get back to that third-rate flat, the room that has not been aired because of the kid, his coughing fits and vomitings—the joy of a worthy life, meritorious and pure."

"Weren't you enjoying a life just as pure with Gabrielle, and without all the bother of a family?"

"She loved me, and the love a woman bears one is not a wall behind which one can shelter. It is an obstacle to be overcome. It also makes the air too heavy, like a storm which is the more op-pressive for never bursting. Besides, in order to create, we need a semblance of solitude. Berthe, preoccupied with her children, often forgets me. With Gabrielle, I was all her life. Try as she might to keep in the background when we were together, I could hear her thinking about me. I did not write a single line of verse during our fifteen years together. You know bees veil the walls of transparent hives. No honey is ever made under the eyes of a stranger, even if he be full of passion—above all, when he is full of passion, that is to say, attention. What we should aim at in our homes is to reach that habitual kindliness which would consist in not even seeing each other any more. Would you believe that one evening at Berthe's between a child's bed and a table soiled with medicines, I became a poet once again?"

"And yet you go back to Gabrielle?"

"She compels me to go back. She insists on my going back. Those who love us are not devoid of power over us. For fifteen years Gabrielle has worked at me. She is determined to make me what her love would have me be. And now that we are separated whole sections of her interrupted work survive in me. She still reigns over those elements in my being which are the outcome of her resolute efforts. Whole regions remain under her influence and stir in response to her appeal. How difficult it is to separate! For fifteen years I have applied my strength to the task and within me there are still fibers which continue to resist. Of all the lovers who have parted, I feel sure only a few keep asunder. One has only to think of the vast crowd who, after the most strenuous efforts and most terrible shocks, fall back into each other's arms more firmly riveted than ever one to another, and resigned to cohabitation unto death."

For the last few minutes—since, that is to say, he had been speaking of Gabrielle—Jerome had resorted only to literary jargon, devoid of all sincerity. He pulled out his watch and absentmindedly gave me his hand. He said he was glad to have seen me; begged me not to neglect Gabrielle, and just as I was affecting tender solicitude for her—"She is so charming"—he replied without looking at me: "I give her to you," and disappeared down the steps of the Underground.

Should I go to Gabrielle to tell her all I had heard? Already I had but the vaguest memory of it. Should I be able to extract from all that chatter its infinitesimal portion of truth? Insoluble problems had never detained me long. I had nothing more to expect from Gabrielle, who had made a great mistake in hoping to get anything whatsoever from me. I resolved never to see her again. But, then, what was I to do with my evening?

V

For a moment or two I left a letter from Gabrielle unopened on my table. I was certain that it contained only frantic reproaches for my neglect. After all the years that lovers had involved me in their quarrels, I ought to have remembered that not to comply with their wishes was often the best way of helping them. But, truth to tell, Gabrielle, in twelve pages, expressed her gratitude to me. She told me that very shortly after our last meeting Jerome had seen Berthe and her coughing children off to Bordeaux by train and that, promising to join them soon, he had from that moment resolved never to see them again, and Gabrielle gave me the credit of having brought this about.

"One essential thing," she added, "still remains to be done. Jerome often comes to see me in the late afternoon, but I see no hope of his wishing to resume our life together. I beg you not to leave such admirable work unfinished. Consummate our bliss! Jerome, moreover, hopes you will come to see us. I promised that you would come to meet him here tomorrow about eight o'clock, and that you would take him to a cabaret to dinner. As you know, it is one of his greatest pleasures."

I took care not to present myself at Gabrielle's before eight o'clock. I was loath to deprive her of a single minute alone with Jerome. But here again I soon perceived that I had erred in being too tactful. "Oh, here you are at last!" cried Jerome the moment he saw me. Then, hardly allowing me to say a word to Gabrielle, who was blowing her nose in the background and powdering her face still burning with tears, he was so anxious to flee from his victim that he went off without turning round and only on the stairs asked in high spirits: "Where are we dining?"

"What have you done to her now?"

He protested his innocence. According to him, Gabrielle was a walking sore. It was impossible to say a word that did not wound her—aye, sometimes even before he opened his lips!

"The demands of mistresses of that kind are unlimited. Give them little or all, they suffer and cry. One would have to give up all work, every ambition, all pleasure and, generally speaking, everything they cannot share equally with one. Everything that takes place out of their sight, or away from them, or merely beside them, is a crime and a betrayal. It's impossible to get out of it. . . . But it's not interesting! Let's talk of something interesting."

What he thought interesting was one of his plays, refused everywhere and just published in book form. I was imprudent enough to pretend that I had read it, when all the time it would have been so easy to say with an air of deliberate eagerness, as was my wont in such circumstances, that I had laid it aside to read on my holiday. Truth to tell, I am well able to discuss with an author a work of which I know no more than the title. But in Jerome I had a doughty adversary and he plied me with searching questions.

"Come! Acknowledge frankly that you didn't like my third act. You agree with those who think that Rudolph ought to have. . . ."

I faced the music and succeeded in sustaining my pose until the dessert. In order to alter the course of the discussion I asked him what sort of Press he had had and he was dumbfounded when he heard that I had not read "the marvellous Souday," or "the excellent Chaumeix." He had an astonishing gift for discovering in a flash any mention of himself in a newspaper, even if it were only in a footnote on the third page. Jerome was persuaded that his "Press" was the subject of passionate interest to all other writers and to humanity at large. (It is strange to reflect how the same page of the *Figaro*, read by a literary man and by a sportsman, can give two such different views of the world.)

Only with the liqueurs was I able to get an opportunity of discussing our last meeting and of expressing my surprise that Gabrielle should have given me all the credit for the decision he had come to about Berthe. He assured me that I had, in fact, helped in the matter, or at least expedited the result.

"That night, when I was expatiating before you on the delights of a pure and meritorious life, and telling you of the inspiration a man can derive from a badly ventilated room where a child is coughing, I felt, even while speaking, that it was all moonshine and an experience I had finished and done with. And that theory with which I was entertaining you was, if I may say so, all that remained of it. Hardly had I shaken your hand and was sitting in the Underground when I found myself secretly intoning a hymn of deliverance."

When I asked him whether he had ever felt anything for Berthe, he declared that he adored her.

"I am beginning to know myself, my dear fellow," he added. "My love affairs always follow the same graph—an inordinate power of desire and suffering. Then, whether gratified or not, my desire remains stationary until it begins to ebb. But after love has gone, I still stand by. A sure instinct compels me to remain yet a while longer. It is the period of lucidity. My eyes begin to awaken to new and strange beings, to regions I should never have approached had the tempest of a frantic love affair not cast me on their shores. An overpowering interest still seems to bind me to the creature who no longer interests my heart. Although I may be put off and disappointed, in the end I am never robbed. Satiated, gorged, I pillage with a sort of cold rage the wreckage of my foundered passion. You see, the business of an observer is that of a dupe; it takes us no deeper than the surface of our fellow-creatures. Never can one reach the core of a human being except by love—yes, borne thither by love. And when love has gone, it leaves us at the core.

"I terrify you? But you are a writer, aren't you? Admit, then, that you can turn everything to some use. Besides, I do not even spare myself. . . . We always cash in best on ourselves."

I retorted that when once the conflagration of love was extinguished he could work only on the cinders of it in himself.

"At the height of my passion," Jerome replied, averting his eyes to make the daring admission," and burn as I may, do you suppose that I fail to make notes? My old method is contained in the old waltz *When Love Dies*, which used to be played in our youth. . . . When our love dies and our partner is not yet aware of the fact and relies on our blind affection. . . . nothing warns her of our sudden lucidity. All our maneuvers, lies and ruses—everything stands revealed under the cold glare that pours down upon a dead passion."

"And so now you will turn Berthe to some use?"

"Not a bit of it! I shall bury that spoil as a dog buries a bone. I shall recover it some day, but so completely merged into my other human documents that I shan't even recognize it."

From the time I asked for the bill till I tipped the cloakroom attendant, Jerome seemed lost in the clouds and recovered consciousness only when we were in the street. I told him that all his theories did not prevent him from always going back to Gabrielle, and he did not deny it.

"Our fellow-creatures drift through us, but we need a solid river bed. Without that fixed area of affection and suffering, to which we always find ourselves restored—without a Gabrielle—we too would find ourselves carried away. We need this regulating force, this rallying point—"

"Why not have the courage to say we need this refuge, this consolation, Jerome?"

"I admit without shame. There must be someone on earth who knows pretty well what I am and who loves me notwithstanding. There must be someone who accepts all the known and unknown of me."

"Gabrielle is the only one who has ever come to your side, the only one who has traversed the almost infinite distance that separates you from your fellows. You say you turn them to some use? But all your works amount to nothing more than your despair at never being able to reach them. No one has been less hardened by life than you have. You have never really lived. Because now you are mature and are ashamed of your childish features, you disguise them. Gabrielle alone finds in you, over and above your poses and feigned ferocity, a permanent core of purity, candor and weakness. . . ."

I thought Jerome was protesting; but he was doing nothing of the sort. He was muttering to himself a line I recognized: "How deeply I shall love you, you whom for one moment I have pressed to my side!" . . . And suddenly he burst out laughing.

"You should make a note of what you have just said," he observed. "It will make a fine, stirring conclusion to my obituary notice. For I am older than you!"

"Confess that I've hit the nail on the head!"

"How should I know whether you have or not? What does 'coming to the side of a fellow creature' mean? Voluptuousness is nothing but a dismal and stubborn ferocity that yields nothing. Possession is never achieved, never anything more than an over-powering presence. It is the wretched fate of us shamefast creatures, who cannot after all deliver ourselves of the living beings within us except in solitude, never to be able to remain alone in a room. To no form of parturition are silence and isolation more essential than to ours. And that is why I tormented that woman at my side. But, the moment she moves away from me, I reach out for her and call her name. Truth to tell, all the best-trained mistress strives after is victory over our art—to divert us from it if only for one short hour . . .

"Why is it," he added, standing on the curb looking for a taxi, "that friendship is not enough for us? A friend would give us his company; but a creature of the same sex, our like in fact, would be indistinguishable from ourselves, and while we were in labor neither his glance nor his voice would disturb us. Why must it always be a woman who makes us fertile? Unless we can discover in ourselves, as many artists do, the necessary eternal feminine . . ."

Jerome raised his hand to stop a taxi, but I did not hear the address he whispered to the driver.

[Translated by Huntley Patterson]

Haldor Laxness

LILY

The Story of Nebuchadnezzarson in Life and in Death

HALDOR LAXNESS, *born in Reykjavík, Iceland in 1902, was destined by his parents for a career in music. But at the age of sixteen, he abandoned his piano studies to write a novel on the new Romantic back-to-nature theme, the first in a belle-lettristic career practised at home and abroad (three years in the United States) and culminated by the attainment of the Nobel Prize in 1956 for Islandsklukken, a historical trilogy which immortalizes the Icelander's traditional stubbornness, pride, and love of learning. In addition to "Lily," three of his novels*—Salka Valka, The Great Weaver of Cashmere, *and* Independent People—*have been translated into English.*

I gave the man this name just so that people would take notice of the story and think to themselves: "Ah, this must be an amusing story!" Otherwise I might have let it suffice to call him N. N., although neither of these names was used at the funeral which was held in connection with his demise. The truth is that I have either forgotten what his name was or have never really known it for certain. But what does that matter? For as you notice there is another name above that one, and this first name is really much more important, as we shall see when we have finished the story.

It is really a very long story. Indeed, it is so tremendously long that when I start thinking about it, I am often shocked at how long it is. . . . And yet it began with one of the shortest melodies I have ever heard. In fact it could hardly be called a melody. It was rather a fragment of a melody, the latter half of a short melody, and the biggest part of it was a single concluding note. And that one note was so long drawn out that from any consideration of reasonable proportion, one could rightly have imagined it to be the end of a great symphony by one of the better known composers. Thus with the higher art in mind I have passed this fragment of melody on to an acquaintance of mine who aspires to become a composer, so that he may use it in a symphony when he has attained sufficient stature and when the world has begun to take an interest in those melodies which have their origin in the respiratory organs of the people of Snæfellsnes.

Now we shall hear the story.

It was when I was a student and lived in a basement in Reykjavík, in a wretched little hole separated only by a thin partition from the furnace room. One winter I noticed that this melody was always being sung, especially late in the evening after the fire had been banked for the night, in a dull hoarse voice like a wavy and woolly line. And on the last note it was as though the singer had forgotten to take a breath, so that finally the note died out and silence came of itself, as if the singer had died like the tone. Time passed, and nothing more was heard from him. But in a little while a kind of mumbling became audible, and this mumbling struggled hard to become musical notes, with long pauses in between, and it was obvious that the melody continued to live in the singer's breast, although the voice was hoarse and cracked and the tones came to grief on the vocal chords. Yet it never happened that the singer did not ultimately find himself again in this short melody with that long note, which, as has been mentioned before, is destined to become a great symphony.

Thus did he sing for me in the stillness, night after night, as the winter passed, and when I began to investigate the source of this evening song, I discovered that it was the man who looked after the furnace. As midnight approached, he went away.

One evening I went into the little nook where the furnace
stood. The embers glowed red in the darkness behind the half-
open furnace door. And in front of the furnace sat Nebuchadnezzar Nebuchadnezzarson, almost invisible in the darkness, and
sang.

"Good-evening," said I.

"Good-evening," came the answer from the darkness in an old,
hoarse voice.

"It's warm here," said I.

"I'm leaving," said he.

"Isn't this your room?" I asked.

"No," said he.

"Oh, isn't it?" said I. "But still I've often heard you singing
here in the evenings."

"I'm leaving," he said apologetically and got up.

"Oh, please don't go on my account. I just dropped in to see
you because I've so often heard you sing."

"I don't sing," said he.

"But I've often heard you," I protested.

"No," said he. "I've never been able to sing."

"I've learned the melody," I said.

But he merely muttered something to himself and tried to slip
out through the door behind me.

"Don't let me disturb you," I said.

"It's bedtime," he said and left.

One time in frost and snow I was shown a piano case behind
some privies down by the shore. There lived Nebuchadnezzar Nebuchadnezzarson. Perhaps the man gets his inclination for music
from living in a piano box, I thought.

A few evenings passed in silence.

But as time went on he forgot me again and began to sing as
before the same fragment of melody with the same long note that
died away. Then I went in to him again.

"Good-evening," said I.

"Good-evening," said he.

"You're singing," said I.

"No," said he.

"Where did you learn this melody?" I asked.

"Melody? That's no melody."

"But you're always singing one tune."

"I don't sing," he said. "I've never been able to sing."

"You hum," I protested.

Then he said: "I used to long to be able to sing at one time. But that's past. I never even think of it now. I just sit here in front of the furnace sometimes when I have finished banking the fire. But now I'm leaving."

"Where are you from?" I asked.

"From the West," he answered.

"Where in the West?"

"From Olafsvik."

"Is that a good place?"

"The sea is rough at Olafsvik as elsewhere," said he.

"Have you relations in the West?"

"They're dead."

"What did you do in the West?"

"What did I do? I did whatever came along, sometimes on sea, sometimes on land. All depending on what came along."

"Why did you come to Reykjavík?"

He was silent for a long time and finally replied: "It's all up with the West long ago. It's all up with the West."

"You were doubtless right in coming to Reykjavík," I said. "In my opinion Reykjavík is a much more agreeable place to live than anywhere else in the country."

He was silent for a long time and sat there on a box in front of the furnace. This time there was a light in the little furnace room, so he looked straight down at the holes in the toes of his boots.

"My first night here I slept in the cemetery," he said.

"Did you really?" I exclaimed, and added in order to cheer him up: "There are many who have had to be content to sleep more than one night in the cemetery."

"Yes," said he.

His cheeks were grimy and he had a gray beard that did not look as if it had been brushed.

"Your shoes are in bad shape," said I.

"That doesn't bother me," said he. "I found them down at Vatnsmyri the year before last. Somebody must have forgotten them in the peat bog."

He stood up and took down his hat, which was hanging on a nail behind the furnace. It was one of those derbies which business men wear when they are new, but which are generally thrown into the ash can when a rent appears between the crown and the brim or when some child has stuck a knife through the top.

"May I see your hat?" I said.

The hole in the top was big enough for a child's fist.

"Your hat's getting pretty old," I said, looking up at the ceiling through the hole. "But it has obviously been a good hat in its day."

I handed him back his hat. He took it and he too looked through the hole.

"It's not everybody that can read the Lord's Prayer through his hat," said he with a grimace. He had only one tooth.

Then the blessed spring came. It is never so tempting to loll out of the window and look at precisely everything that goes on in the street, especially the most trivial things, as in the spring when one is studying for examinations. At such a time one reads into what goes on in the street various learned significances.

On moving day a new family moved into one of the apartments on the middle floor of the house. I had somehow or other become aware of it, but of course it was no concern of mine. It was a man and his wife. They had one daughter, she might have been eight years old. Her name was Lily, and I guessed from her appearance that the couple were out-of-town people, for she had braids, they were blonde braids, and she wore homemade woollen stockings. The little girl played with the other children in the yard outside my window, and her mother was terribly fond of her, for she leaned out of her window on the second floor most of the day directing the girl like a regiment with resolute commands:

"Look out for the car! Look out for the drunk man! Look out for the dog! Lily! Lily! Look out for the police!"

This was at the time when there were still old stone fences built of ordinary field stones between the lots in the town, and on the other side of the street there was one of these fences with a little green field behind it. But this was a rather quiet street, and on the fence sat Nebuchadnezzar Nebuchadnezzarson in the blue spring sunshine watching the children play in the yard. Admiration shone from the grimy face, through the unkempt beard. But as the day passed, the children grew tired and went home for a bite to eat. Lily was left alone in the yard playing hopscotch all by herself, and then Nebuchadnezzar Nebuchadnezzarson called:

"Lily."

But she pretended not to hear and kept on hopping on one foot as if she were extremely interested in winning the game, and then Nebuchadnezzar Nebuchadnezzarson called again:

"Lily, my dear!"

But she still pretended not to hear and only after a little while did she look up at the window to see whether her mother was still there, but her mother had gone out into the kitchen to cook.

"Hasn't little Lily got anything to say to the old fellow Nebuchadnezzar Nebuchadnezzarson today?" he asked, from the fence. And he drew up out of his pocket a little paper bag which he had kept hidden all this time. At this the little girl walked straight across the street, a bit skeptically, with her hands behind her back, and looked down into his paper bag. Then she looked up at the window. There were raisins, if you please, in the bag. She still acted as if she were not surprised at this and had little or no interest in it. But it wound up with their both sitting on the fence munching raisins, she ten to his one. At first she dangled her legs shyly and looked critically at his unkempt beard. Then she went on playing hop-scotch on the street in front of him. Her mother called down from the window and told her to come in to supper, but she came back in a little while because she knew there was still something left in the bag.

Thus the spring passed, and before long Lily was no longer skeptical of Nebuchadnezzar Nebuchadnezzarson, but ran to meet him when she saw him coming, dived into his pocket, and found for herself the bag of raisins. And sometimes in the evening they sat for a long time on the fence, and I felt sure the old man was telling the little girl stories, because she listened so attentively to what he was saying.

"Are they some relation to you, these people?" I asked, meaning the little girl's parents.

"They're from the West," he said.

"Then you know something about them?"

"Yes," said he. "That's her—Lily."

I couldn't quite make the man out. He seemed to me rather strange, but I didn't bother about that. It was no concern of mine. I had other things to think about. And even if I had discovered that these people were not from the West at all, but from the East, I shouldn't have felt like arguing about it with the old fellow.

He was just about twenty, I heard him say, and they had always known each other. She was just a few months younger. He offered to build her a little house on the Snout, with a tiny lawn and a vegetable patch, as was then the custom. At that time he was fishing on shares with the late Gudmundur, skipper of the *Hope*, and was doing well. But he never could sing. Her name was Lily.

"And then what?" asked the little girl.

But I had no time to eavesdrop any longer and thought to myself: "He's just telling her some old story from the West."

In the autumn, I came back from the North, and one day as I was chatting with some friends on the street corner, I noticed a man standing staring at me a short distance away. He waited for me to say goodbye to them, and when I had done so, he overtook me and stretched out his dirty hand: "Nebuchadnezzar Nebuchadnezzarson."

"What's new?" I asked.

"Nothing," he answered.

"Was there something you wanted?"

"No," said he. "I just wanted to see whether you'd recognize me."

"Of course," I said. "And what's more, I still know our melody. How's your little girl friend?"

"They've taken away my old-age pension," he said, "—that thirty crowns."

"Why?"

"That fellow Joseph said I was using it to buy raisins. But you must know a lot about the law."

"Who is that fellow Joseph?"

"He's a relation of mine. He sometimes helps me out with a little fish or something."

"Look here," I said, "you ought to go to the mayor about that." For I didn't have time.

"I don't know," said he. "It doesn't make much difference. I may perhaps be able to get a house this winter."

"A house?"

"Yes, like last year."

"Aren't you going to look after the furnace in the house you had last year any more?"

"No," said he. "It's all up with everything in that house. It's all up with that house."

"How's that?"

"Oh, I dunno," he said.

"Goodbye," said I.

"Goodbye, sir," said he. "And thanks for your kindness."

He lifted his hat.

I did not see him again to take any notice of him until many years later. I was then a medical student. He was carried into the morgue in a sheet, and I recognized him although he had been cleaned up. I had no feeling for him beyond that which one has for dead men who have been outcasts of society, and it was not until after the funeral held in connection with his demise that I noticed the congruity in his life and death. This was a man of whom nobody expected anything. He was found dead in his piano box. Nobody really knew his name or where he came from, much less what had been the aim of his life. Even on this dissection day I could not remember the melody he had sung. One thing was certain: he was carved up with scientific precision, and we scrutinized his insides with more attention than he had ever been looked at from the outside in all his life.

But why should I be telling about this here? It is long since I lost interest in medical science and turned to other subjects. But as so many years have gone by since then, I shall confess that a little fraud was practiced upon him in the name of science. As a matter of fact, his bones were removed and polished. His skeleton is now used for scientific observation—I shall not say where—but the rest of the corpse was discarded. This was a scientific secret and conspiracy, and we put gravel in the coffin. One of the group took charge of that, and we followed him to the grave, a few of us medical students, in order to prevent anybody from taking a peek at the corpse at the last moment. We carried the coffin into the church and out again.

It was indeed a day of appalling irony. It was just two days before Christmas. The funeral was rushed through before it was quite daylight, and what made it extraordinary was the circumstance that the church was draped in black ceremonial crepe, because at noon on this very same day was to be buried one of the most distinguished consuls-general in the city. As has been said, Nebuchadnezzar Nebuchadnezzarson was squeezed in on account of the effrontery of the cemetery officials, who proclaimed that, because of the Christmas celebrations so near at hand, this man would have to be buried today or never. And it was a downright scandal that such a no-account funeral should be held with the church hung in mourning.

A northeaster was blowing and we hustled the coffin in through a shower of hail. Our chief worry was that the bottom might fall out and the gravel spill down on the church floor in the midst of all this solemnity and sorrow. And when we got half-way up the aisle I became so agitated by the creaking of the shoddy coffin that I could not keep my tongue off the silly fool who had been charged with "laying out" the gravel. Besides, the weight of the coffin was well nigh crushing us. We sat down in the front pew as if we were some sort of relations of the deceased, and the pastor hurried in from the vestry looking rather shamefaced, as was to be expected, over this misuse of the mourning draperies (God help us if the Consul's family should get word of it!), and delivered like a shot the brief funeral sermon he had held the week before over an insignificant woman from out of town. Naturally he tripped up time and again when he was supposed to say "our late beloved brother" and it was written in the sermon "our beloved sister." Once he even blurted out that "this late beloved sister of ours was sorely lamented by her surviving husband and children in another part of the country." I was deathly afraid that some-body would notice this nonsense and looked back over my shoulder into the church. But the funeral procession, aside from the undertaker, consisted solely of one old woman, deaf I hoped, who sat far back in the church, and I tried to console myself with the idea that she had come in only to get out of the hail and had otherwise no interest in who was being buried.

But when we had carried the coffin out again and the hearse had begun to crawl away, who should make as if to follow to the cemetery but this old woman with her black Sunday shawl around her wrinkled face and her blue striped apron? So I and two others saw nothing else for it but to trudge along behind to keep an eye on things and if necessary to prevent the old woman from rais-ing a rumpus at the cemetery. For indeed we could not feel easy about this funeral until the grave had been filled in. Finally, how-ever, my two companions wearied of this wandering, and slipped off into the Café Uppsala, and it fell upon me to keep watch on the funeral procession all the way. So we tramped along after the coffin, this old woman and I, with the pastor and the undertaker, both in high silk hats.

After the grave had been filled in and the pastor and the under-taker had gone, the old woman stood there still, looking at the earth in the hail storm. I lingered at the gate of the cemetery, but she did not come, so I turned back to the grave again.

"What are you waiting for anyway, my good woman?" I asked. "Did you know this man?"

She looked at me half in fear, and when she finally tried to answer, her face contorted with pain, her lips trembled, and the corners of her mouth dropped, so that I could see she had lost her teeth. And her old red eyes filled with tears. I have described somewhere before how unpleasant it is to see old people cry.

"Don't cry, my good woman," I said. "He is with God."

"Yes," she said and dried her tears with the corner of her apron.

"You ought to go home before you get a chill," said I, for I did not want the woman to hang around there any longer.

We walked together through the cemetery.

"Who are you?" I asked.

"I come from the West," she said.

"You are not from Olafsvik?"

"Yes."

"Then you knew him of course."

"Yes, we were of the same age. Then I married in the South. I lived for forty years in Keflavik."

"What is your name?"

"My name is Lily."

"Is your husband living?"

"No, he died long ago."

"Have you any children?"

"Oh, I've brought thirteen of them into the world," answered the woman with such a resigned note in her voice that I understood at once that she must have at least sixty grandchildren.

"There are many strange things," I said. "He was always lonely."

She trudged along silently at my side over the grave mounds and I hardly expected that she would answer me further; a new storm was on its way across Skerjafjörd. So I prepared to take leave of her in the gate of the cemetery and took off my hat.

"Goodbye," I said.

She stretched out to me her old, bony hand and looking straight at me, the only partaker in her grief, she said: "I too was always lonely."

And then her face again got out of control and again she raised the corner of her apron to her eyes and turned away.

And here ends the story of Nebuchadnezzar Nebuchadnezzarson, who spent only one night in the cemetery.

[Translated by Axel Eyberg and John Watkins]

Albert Camus

ALBERT CAMUS *has set most of his fiction in Algeria where he was born in 1913, the son of an agricultural worker. His father died in the battle of the Marne and Camus grew up in surroundings scarred by poverty. His intelligence gained him a scholarship to the lycée, and when he entered the University of Algiers, he began his career as a philosopher. One of the foremost thinkers and writers in the broad philosophical group known as Existentialists, Camus has had a profound effect upon modern thought. Equipped with a talent for lucid classical prose, he has expressed his view of life and of modern man in essays, in plays, in novels, and in short stories. His Myth of Sisyphus is not only an expression of his early philosophy, but also a good gloss on what remains his best novel, The Stranger. His post-war novel The Plague first brought him to the attention of Americans, and his most recent works, The Fall and Exile and the Kingdom have aroused international interest in his work. When he received the Nobel Prize in 1957, Camus was in his early forties, one of the youngest writers ever to be so honored.*

The schoolmaster was watching the two men climb toward him. One was on horseback, the other on foot. They had not yet tackled the abrupt rise leading to the schoolhouse built on the hillside. They were toiling onward, making slow progress in the snow, among the stones, on the vast expanse of the high, deserted plateau. From time to time the horse stumbled. Without hearing anything yet, he could see the breath issuing from the horse's nostrils. One of the men, at least, knew the region. They were following the trail although it had disappeared days ago under a layer of dirty white snow. The schoolmaster calculated that it would take them half an hour to get onto the hill. It was cold; he went back into the school to get a sweater.

He crossed the empty, frigid classroom. On the blackboard the four rivers of France, drawn with four different colored chalks, had been flowing toward their estuaries for the past three days. Snow had suddenly fallen in mid-October after eight months of drought without the transition of rain, and the twenty pupils, more or less, who lived in the villages scattered over the plateau had stopped coming. With fair weather they would return. Daru now heated only the single room that was his lodging, adjoining the classroom and giving also onto the plateau to the east. Like the class windows, his window looked to the south too. On that side the school was a few kilometers from the point where the plateau began to slope toward the south. In clear weather could be seen the purple mass of the mountain range where the gap opened onto the desert.

Somewhat warmed, Daru returned to the window from which he had first seen the two men. They were no longer visible. Hence they must have tackled the rise. The sky was not so dark, for the snow had stopped falling during the night. The morning had opened with a dirty light which had scarcely become brighter as the ceiling of clouds lifted. At two in the afternoon it seemed as if the day were merely beginning. But still this was better than those three days when the thick snow was falling amidst unbroken darkness with little gusts of wind that rattled the double door of the classroom. Then Daru had spent long hours in his room, leaving it only to go to the shed and feed the chickens or get some coal. Fortunately the delivery truck from Tadjid, the nearest village to the north, had brought his supplies two days before the blizzard. It would return in forty-eight hours.

Besides, he had enough to resist a siege, for the little room was cluttered with bags of wheat that the administration left as a

stock to distribute to those of his pupils whose families had suffered from the drought. Actually they had all been victims because they were all poor. Every day Daru would distribute a ration
to the children. They had missed it, he knew, during these bad
days. Possibly one of the fathers or big brothers would come this
afternoon and he could supply them with grain. It was just a
matter of carrying them over to the next harvest. Now shiploads of
wheat were arriving from France and the worst was over. But it
would be hard to forget that poverty, that army of ragged ghosts
wandering in the sunlight, the plateaus burned to a cinder month
after month, the earth shriveled up little by little, literally
scorched, every stone bursting into dust under one's foot. The
sheep had died then by thousands and even a few men, here and
there, sometimes without anyone's knowing.

In contrast with such poverty, he who lived almost like a monk
in his remote schoolhouse, nonetheless satisfied with the little he
had and with the rough life, had felt like a lord with his white-
washed walls, his narrow couch, his unpainted shelves, his well,
and his weekly provision of water and food. And suddenly this
snow, without warning, without the foretaste of rain. This is the
way the region was, cruel to live in, even without men—who
didn't help matters either. But Daru had been born here. Everywhere else, he felt exiled.

He stepped out onto the terrace in front of the schoolhouse. The
two men were now halfway up the slope. He recognized the horseman as Balducci, the old gendarme he had known for a long time.
Balducci was holding on the end of a rope an Arab who was
walking behind him with hands bound and head lowered. The
gendarme waved a greeting to which Daru did not reply, lost as he
was in contemplation of the Arab dressed in a faded blue jellaba,
his feet in sandals but covered with socks of heavy raw wool, his
head surmounted by a narrow, short *chèche*. They were approaching. Balducci was holding back his horse in order not to hurt the
Arab, and the group was advancing slowly.

Within earshot, Balducci shouted: "One hour to do the three
kilometers from El Ameur!" Daru did not answer. Short and

square in his thick sweater, he watched them climb. Not once had the Arab raised his head. "Hello," said Daru when they got up onto the terrace. "Come in and warm up." Balducci painfully got down from his horse without letting go the rope. From under his bristling mustache he smiled at the schoolmaster. His little dark eyes, deep-set under a tanned forehead, and his mouth surrounded with wrinkles made him look attentive and studious. Daru took the bridle, led the horse to the shed, and came back to the two men, who were now waiting for him in the school. He led them into his room. "I am going to heat up the classroom," he said. "We'll be more comfortable there." When he entered the room again, Balducci was on the couch. He had undone the rope tying him to the Arab, who had squatted near the stove. His hands still bound, the *chèche* pushed back on his head, he was looking toward the window. At first Daru noticed only his huge lips, fat, smooth, almost Negroid; yet his nose was straight, his eyes were dark and full of fever. The *chèche* revealed an obstinate forehead and, under the weathered skin now rather discolored by the cold, the whole face had a restless and rebellious look that struck Daru when the Arab, turning his face toward him, looked him straight in the eyes. "Go into the other room," said the schoolmaster, "and I'll make you some mint tea." "Thanks," Balducci said. "What a chore! How I long for retirement." And addressing his prisoner in Arabic: "Come on, you." The Arab got up and, slowly, holding his bound wrists in front of him, went into the classroom.

With the tea, Daru brought a chair. But Balducci was already enthroned on the nearest pupil's desk and the Arab had squatted against the teacher's platform facing the stove, which stood between the desk and the window. When he held out the glass of tea to the prisoner, Daru hesitated at the sight of his bound hands. "He might perhaps be untied." "Sure," said Balducci. "That was for the trip." He started to get to his feet. But Daru, setting the glass on the floor, had knelt beside the Arab. Without saying anything, the Arab watched him with his feverish eyes. Once his hands were free, he rubbed his swollen wrists against each other, took the glass of tea, and sucked up the burning liquid in swift little sips.

"Good," said Daru. "And where are you headed?"

Balducci withdrew his mustache from the tea. "Here, son."

"Odd pupils! And you're spending the night?"

"No. I'm going back to El Ameur. And you will deliver this fellow to Tinguit. He is expected at police headquarters."

Balducci was looking at Daru with a friendly little smile.

"What's this story?" asked the schoolmaster. "Are you pulling my leg?"

"No, son. Those are the orders."

"The orders? I'm not . . ." Daru hesitated, not wanting to hurt the old Corsican. "I mean, that's not my job."

"What! What's the meaning of that? In wartime people do all kinds of jobs."

"Then I'll wait for the declaration of war!"

Balducci nodded.

"O.K. But the orders exist and they concern you too. Things are brewing, it appears. There is talk of a forthcoming revolt. We are mobilized, in a way."

Daru still had his obstinate look.

"Listen, son," Balducci said. "I like you and you must understand. There's only a dozen of us at El Ameur to patrol throughout the whole territory of a small department and I must get back in a hurry. I was told to hand this guy over to you and return without delay. He couldn't be kept there. His village was beginning to stir; they wanted to take him back. You must take him to Tinguit tomorrow before the day is over. Twenty kilometers shouldn't faze a husky fellow like you. After that, all will be over. You'll come back to your pupils and your comfortable life."

Behind the wall the horse could be heard snorting and pawing the earth. Daru was looking out the window. Decidedly, the weather was clearing and the light was increasing over the snowy plateau. When all the snow was melted, the sun would take over again and once more would burn the fields of stone. For days,

still, the unchanging sky would shed its dry light on the solitary
expanse where nothing had any connection with man.

"After all," he said, turning around toward Balducci, "what did
he do?" And, before the gendarme had opened his mouth, he
asked: "Does he speak French?"

"No, not a word. We had been looking for him for a month,
but they were hiding him. He killed his cousin."

"Is he against us?"

"I don't think so. But you can never be sure."

"Why did he kill?"

"A family squabble, I think. One owed the other grain, it
seems. It's not at all clear. In short, he killed his cousin with a
billhook. You know, like a sheep, *kreezk!*"

Balducci made the gesture of drawing a blade across his throat
and the Arab, his attention attracted, watched him with a sort of
anxiety. Daru felt a sudden wrath against the man, against all
men with their rotten spite, their tireless hates, their blood lust.

But the kettle was singing on the stove. He served Balducci more
tea, hesitated, then served the Arab again, who, a second time,
drank avidly. His raised arms made the jellaba fall open and the
schoolmaster saw his thin, muscular chest.

"Thanks, kid," Balducci said. "And now, I'm off."

He got up and went toward the Arab, taking a small rope
from his pocket.

"What are you doing?" Daru asked dryly.

Balducci, disconcerted, showed him the rope.

"Don't bother."

The old gendarme hesitated. "It's up to you. Of course, you
are armed?"

"I have my shotgun."

"Where?"

"In the trunk."

"You ought to have it near your bed."

"Why? I have nothing to fear."

"You're crazy, son. If there's an uprising, no one is safe, we're
all in the same boat."

"I'll defend myself. I'll have time to see them coming."

Balducci began to laugh, then suddenly the mustache covered the white teeth.

"You'll have time? O.K. That's just what I was saying. You have always been a little cracked. That's why I like you, my son was like that."

At the same time he took out his revolver and put it on the desk.

"Keep it; I don't need two weapons from here to El Ameur."

The revolver shone against the black paint of the table. When the gendarme turned toward him, the schoolmaster caught the smell of leather and horseflesh.

"Listen, Balducci," Daru said suddenly, "every bit of this disgusts me, and first of all your fellow here. But I won't hand him over. Fight, yes, if I have to. But not that."

The old gendarme stood in front of him and looked at him severely.

"You're being a fool," he said slowly. "I don't like it either. You don't get used to putting a rope on a man even after years of it, and you're even ashamed—yes, ashamed. But you can't let them have their way."

"I won't hand him over," Daru said again.

"It's an order, son, and I repeat it."

"That's right. Repeat to them what I've said to you: I won't hand him over."

Balducci made a visible effort to reflect. He looked at the Arab and at Daru. At last he decided.

"No, I won't tell them anything. If you want to drop us, go ahead; I'll not denounce you. I have an order to deliver the prisoner and I'm doing so. And now you'll just sign this paper for me."

"There's no need. I'll not deny that you left him with me."

"Don't be mean with me. I know you'll tell the truth. You're from hereabouts and you are a man. But you must sign, that's the rule."

Daru opened his drawer, took out a little square bottle of purple ink, the red wooden penholder with the "sergeant-major" pen he used for making models of penmanship, and signed. The gendarme carefully folded the paper and put it into his wallet. Then he moved toward the door.

"I'll see you off," Daru said.

"No," said Balducci. "There's no use being polite. You insulted me."

He looked at the Arab, motionless in the same spot, sniffed peevishly, and turned away toward the door. "Good-by, son," he said. The door shut behind him. Balducci appeared suddenly outside the window and then disappeared. His footsteps were muffled by the snow. The horse stirred on the other side of the wall and several chickens fluttered in fright. A moment later Balducci reappeared outside the window leading the horse by the bridle. He walked toward the little rise without turning around and disappeared from sight with the horse following him. A big stone could be heard bouncing down. Daru walked back toward the prisoner, who, without stirring, never took his eyes off him. "Wait," the schoolmaster said in Arabic and went toward the bedroom. As he was going through the door, he had a second thought, went to the desk, took the revolver, and stuck it in his pocket. Then, without looking back, he went into his room.

For some time he lay on his couch watching the sky gradually close over, listening to the silence. It was this silence that had seemed painful to him during the first days here, after the war. He had requested a post in the little town at the base of the foothills separating the upper plateaus from the desert. There, rocky walls, green and black to the north, pink and lavender to the south, marked the frontier of eternal summer. He had been named to a post farther north, on the plateau itself. In the beginning, the solitude and the silence had been hard for him on these wastelands peopled only by stones. Occasionally, furrows suggested cultivation, but they had been dug to uncover a certain kind of stone good for building. The only plowing here was to harvest rocks. Elsewhere a thin layer of soil accumulated in the hollows would be scraped out to enrich paltry village gardens. This is the way it was: bare rock covered three quarters of the region. Towns sprang up, flourished, then disappeared; men came by, loved one another or fought bitterly, then died. No one in this desert, neither he nor his guest, mattered. And yet, outside this desert neither of them, Daru knew, could have really lived.

When he got up, no noise came from the classroom. He was amazed at the unmixed joy he derived from the mere thought that the Arab might have fled and that he would be alone with no decision to make. But the prisoner was there. He had merely stretched out between the stove and the desk. With eyes open, he was staring at the ceiling. In that position, his thick lips were particularly noticeable, giving him a pouting look. "Come," said Daru. The Arab got up and followed him. In the bedroom, the schoolmaster pointed to a chair near the table under the window. The Arab sat down without taking his eyes off Daru.

"Are you hungry?"

"Yes," the prisoner said.

Daru set the table for two. He took flour and oil, shaped a cake in a frying-pan, and lighted the little stove that functioned on bottled gas. While the cake was cooking, he went out to the shed to get cheese, eggs, dates, and condensed milk. When the cake was done he set it on the window sill to cool, heated some condensed milk diluted with water, and beat up the eggs into an omelette. In one of his motions he knocked against the revolver stuck in his right pocket. He set the bowl down, went into the classroom, and put the revolver in his desk drawer. When he came back to the room, night was falling. He put on the light and served the Arab. "Eat," he said. The Arab took a piece of the cake, lifted it eagerly to his mouth, and stopped short.

"And you?" he asked.

"After you. I'll eat too."

The thick lips opened slightly. The Arab hesitated, then bit into the cake determinedly.

The meal over, the Arab looked at the schoolmaster. "Are you the judge?"

"No, I'm simply keeping you until tomorrow."

"Why do you eat with me?"

"I'm hungry."

The Arab fell silent. Daru got up and went out. He brought back a folding bed from the shed, set it up between the table and the stove, perpendicular to his own bed. From a large suitcase which, upright in a corner, served as a shelf for papers, he took two blankets and arranged them on the camp bed. Then he stopped, felt useless, and sat down on his bed. There was nothing more to do or to get ready. He had to look at this man. He looked at him, therefore, trying to imagine his face bursting with rage. He couldn't do so. He could see nothing but the dark yet shining eyes and the animal mouth.

"Why did you kill him?" he asked in a voice whose hostile tone surprised him.

The Arab looked away.

"He ran away. I ran after him."

He raised his eyes to Daru again and they were full of a sort of woeful interrogation. "Now what will they do to me?"

"Are you afraid?"

He stiffened, turning his eyes away.

"Are you sorry?"

The Arab stared at him openmouthed. Obviously he did not understand. Daru's annoyance was growing. At the same time he felt awkward and self-conscious with his big body wedged between the two beds.

"Lie down there," he said impatiently. "That's your bed."

The Arab didn't move. He called to Daru:

"Tell me!"

The schoolmaster looked at him.

"Is the gendarme coming back tomorrow?"

"I don't know."

"Are you coming with us?"

"I don't know. Why?"

The prisoner got up and stretched out on top of the blankets, his feet toward the window. The light from the electric bulb shone straight into his eyes and he closed them at once.

"Why?" Daru repeated, standing beside the bed.

The Arab opened his eyes under the blinding light and looked at him, trying not to blink.

"Come with us," he said.

In the middle of the night, Daru was still not asleep. He had gone to bed after undressing completely; he generally slept naked. But when he suddenly realized that he had nothing on, he hesitated. He felt vulnerable and the temptation came to him to put his clothes back on. Then he shrugged his shoulders; after all, he wasn't a child and, if need be, he could break his adversary in two. From his bed he could observe him, lying on his back, still motionless with his eyes closed under the harsh light. When Daru turned out the light, the darkness seemed to coagulate all of a sudden. Little by little, the night came back to life in the window where the starless sky was stirring gently. The schoolmaster soon made out the body lying at his feet. The Arab still did not move, but his eyes seemed open. A faint wind was prowling around the schoolhouse. Perhaps it would drive away the clouds and the sun would reappear.

During the night the wind increased. The hens fluttered a little and then were silent. The Arab turned over on his side with his back to Daru, who thought he heard him moan. Then he listened for his guest's breathing, become heavier and more regular. He listened to that breath so close to him and mused without being able to go to sleep. In this room where he had been sleeping alone for a year, this presence bothered him. But it bothered him also by imposing on him a sort of brotherhood he knew well but refused to accept in the present circumstances. Men who share the same rooms, soldiers or prisoners, develop a strange alliance as if, having cast off their armor with their clothing, they fraternized every evening, over and above their differences, in the ancient community of dream and fatigue. But Daru shook himself; he didn't like such musings, and it was essential to sleep.

A little later, however, when the Arab stirred slightly, the schoolmaster was still not asleep. When the prisoner made a second move, he stiffened, on the alert. The Arab was lifting himself slowly on his arms with almost the motion of a sleepwalker. Seated upright in bed, he waited motionless without turning his head toward Daru, as if he were listening attentively. Daru did not stir; it had just occurred to him that the revolver was still in the drawer of his desk. It was better to act at once. Yet he continued to observe the prisoner, who, with the same slithery motion, put his feet on the ground, waited again, then began to stand up slowly. Daru was about to call out to him when the Arab began to walk, in a quite natural but extraordinarily silent way. He was heading toward the door at the end of the room that opened into the shed. He lifted the latch with precaution and went out, pushing the door behind him but without shutting it. Daru had not stirred. "He is running away," he merely thought. "Good riddance!" Yet he listened attentively. The hens were not fluttering; the guest must be on the plateau. A faint sound of water reached him, and he didn't know what it was until the Arab again stood framed in the doorway, closed the door carefully, and came back to bed without a sound. Then Daru turned his back on him and fell asleep. Still later he seemed, from the depths of his sleep, to hear furtive steps around the schoolhouse. "I'm dreaming! I'm dreaming!" he repeated to himself. And he went on sleeping.

When he awoke, the sky was clear; the loose window let in a cold, pure air. The Arab was asleep, hunched up under the blankets now, his mouth open, utterly relaxed. But when Daru shook him, he started dreadfully, staring at Daru with wild eyes as if he had never seen him and such a frightened expression that the schoolmaster stepped back. "Don't be afraid. It's me. You must eat." The Arab nodded his head and said yes. Calm had returned to his face, but his expression was vacant and listless.

The coffee was ready. They drank it seated together on the folding bed as they munched their pieces of the cake. Then Daru led the Arab under the shed and showed him the faucet where he washed. He went back into the room, folded the blankets and the bed, made his own bed and put the room in order. Then he went through the classroom and out onto the terrace. The sun was already rising in the blue sky; a soft, bright light was bathing the deserted plateau. On the ridge the snow was melting in spots. The stones were about to reappear. Crouched on the edge of the plateau, the schoolmaster looked at the deserted expanse. He thought of Balducci. He had hurt him, for he had sent him off in a way as if he didn't want to be associated with him. He could still hear the gendarme's farewell and, without knowing why, he felt strangely empty and vulnerable. At that moment, from the other side of the schoolhouse, the prisoner coughed. Daru listened to him almost despite himself and then, furious, threw a pebble that whistled through the air before sinking into the snow. That man's stupid crime revolted him, but to hand him over was contrary to honor. Merely thinking of it made him smart with humiliation. And he cursed at one and the same time his own people who had sent him this Arab and the Arab too who had dared to kill and not managed to get away. Daru got up, walked in a circle on the terrace, waited motionless, and then went back into the schoolhouse.

The Arab, leaning over the cement floor of the shed, was washing his teeth with two fingers. Daru looked at him and said: "Come." He went back into the room ahead of the prisoner. He slipped a hunting-jacket on over his sweater and put on walking-shoes. Standing, he waited until the Arab had put on his *chèche* and sandals. They went into the classroom and the schoolmaster pointed to the exit, saying: "Go ahead." The fellow didn't budge. "I'm coming," said Daru. The Arab went out. Daru went back into the room and made a package of pieces of rusk, dates, and sugar. In the classroom, before going out, he hesitated a second in front of his desk, then crossed the threshold and locked the door. "That's the way," he said. He started toward the east, followed by the prisoner. But, a short distance from the schoolhouse, he thought he heard a slight sound behind them. He retraced his steps and examined the surroundings of the house; there was no one there. The Arab watched him without seeming to understand. "Come on," said Daru.

They walked for an hour and rested beside a sharp peak of

limestone. The snow was melting faster and faster and the sun was drinking up the puddles at once, rapidly cleaning the plateau, which gradually dried and vibrated like the air itself. When they resumed walking, the ground rang under their feet. From time to time a bird rent the space in front of them with a joyful cry. Daru breathed in deeply the fresh morning light. He felt a sort of rapture before the vast familiar expanse, now almost entirely yellow under its dome of blue sky. They walked an hour more, descending toward the south. They reached a level height made up of crumbly rocks. From there on, the plateau sloped down, eastward, toward a low plain where there were a few spindly trees and, to the south, toward outcroppings of rock that gave the landscape a chaotic look.

Daru surveyed the two directions. There was nothing but the sky on the horizon. Not a man could be seen. He turned toward the Arab, who was looking at him blankly. Daru held out the package to him. "Take it," he said. "There are dates, bread, and sugar. You can hold out for two days. Here are a thousand francs too." The Arab took the package and the money but kept his full hands at chest level as if he didn't know what to do with what was being given him. "Now look," the schoolmaster said as he pointed in the direction of the east, "there's the way to Tinguit. You have a two-hour walk. At Tinguit you'll find the administration and the police. They are expecting you." The Arab looked toward the east, still holding the package and the money against his chest. Daru took his elbow and turned him rather roughly toward the south. At the foot of the height on which they stood could be seen a faint path. "That's the trail across the plateau. In a day's walk from here you'll find pasturelands and the first nomads. They'll take you in and shelter you according to their law." The Arab had now turned toward Daru and a sort of panic was visible in his expression. "Listen," he said. Daru shook his head: "No, be quiet. Now I'm leaving you." He turned his back on him, took two long steps in the direction of the school, looked hesitantly at the motionless Arab, and started off again. For a few minutes he heard nothing but his own step resounding on the cold ground and did not turn his head. A moment later, however, he turned around. The Arab was still there on the edge of the hill, his arms hanging now, and he was looking at the schoolmaster. Daru felt something rise in his throat. But he swore with impatience, waved vaguely, and started off again. He had already gone some distance when he again stopped and looked. There was no longer anyone on the hill.

Daru hesitated. The sun was now rather high in the sky and was beginning to beat down on his head. The schoolmaster retraced his steps, at first somewhat uncertainly, then with decision. When he reached the little hill, he was bathed in sweat. He climbed it as fast as he could and stopped, out of breath, at the top. The rock-fields to the south stood out sharply against the blue sky, but on the plain to the east a steamy heat was already rising. And in that slight haze, Daru, with heavy heart, made out the Arab walking slowly on the road to prison.

A little later, standing before the window of the classroom, the schoolmaster was watching the clear light bathing the whole surface of the plateau, but he hardly saw it. Behind him on the blackboard, among the winding French rivers, sprawled the clumsily chalked-up words he had just read: "You handed over our brother. You will pay for this." Daru looked at the sky, the plateau, and, beyond, the invisible lands stretching all the way to the sea. In this vast landscape he had loved so much, he was alone.

[*Translated by Justin O'Brien*]

Boris Pasternak

BORIS PASTERNAK, *after studying music, law, and philosophy (the latter in Germany, where he lived until the outbreak of the first World War), began his literary career with two volumes of difficult verse detached from socio-political concerns. However when the Soviet poet Mayakovsky called upon his fellow poets to serve the cause, Pasternak worked toward content and communicability. His poems* 1905 *and* Lieutenant Schmidt *are about political figures and affairs; yet even in these poems he uses lyric forms and emphasizes the fate of the individual. Among his most successful works in prose are his autobiography,* Safe Conduct; *a collection of short stories,* Aerial Ways; *his translations of the German poets and Shakespeare, considered by many the best in the Russian language; and* Doctor Zhivago, *the novel which brought him to the admiring attention of an international audience. In 1958, the award of the Nobel Prize and his decision to refuse acceptance of it was a cause célèbre without parallel in literary history. The present story, composed in 1915, is based upon his visit to Italy at about that time.*

They say that when the Greek artist Apelles discovered that his rival Zeuxis was not at home, he drew a line on the wall, so that Zeuxis would be able to guess who it was who had come in his absence. Zeuxis did not remain long in debt to his fellow-artist. He chose a time when Apelles was known to be away from home and left his mark, which became the proverbial sign of art.

I

On one of the September evenings when the sloping tower of Pisa
led a whole army of oblique colors and sidelong shadows against
Pisa, when all Tuscany, irritated by the night wind, smelt like a
frayed laurel held between the fingers, on one of these evenings,
I even remember the date—23rd August—on this evening Emilio
Relinquimini, not finding Heine in the hotel, demanded paper and
light from the obsequiously fawning lackey. And when the lackey
reappeared, bringing beside the objects he had been asked for an
ink-bottle and a pen-holder, a seal and a stick of wax, Relinquimini dismissed him with a gesture of the utmost fastidiousness.
Taking the pin from his tie, he placed it over the candle and
waited until it was white hot, pricked himself in the finger and,
taking one of the innkeeper's cards from a pile of similar cards, he
bent it around the end of his bleeding finger. Then he handed it
nonchalantly to the lackey with the words, "You are to give Herr
Heine this visiting card. Tomorrow I shall visit him at the same
hour."

The leaning tower of Pisa had pushed its way through a chain
of medieval fortifications. The number of people who could see it
from the bridge were increasing every minute. The red glow of
the sky, like a poursuivant, crawled along the square. The streets
were blocked with tiptilted shadows, some of which were still
fighting in the narrow alleyways. The tower of Pisa continued its
march, moving everything down, until at last one insane, gigantic
shadow covered the sun. The day broke into pieces. And meanwhile the lackey, briefly and confusedly informing Heine of his
recent visit, succeeded several minutes before the final setting of
the sun in presenting the impatient guest with a car bearing a
coagulating yellow stain.

"What an original!" But Heine immediately guessed the name
of the visitor, who was the author of the famous poem "*Il sangue.*"
The accident by which Relinquimini arrived in Pisa from Ferrara
on exactly the same day that Heine arrived from Westphalia—

obeying the even more capricious whimsy of a poet on his holidays
—this fortune did not seem strange to him. He remembered the
anonymous person from whom he had received several days before
a negligently written, defiant letter. The claims of the unknown
passed the frontiers of the permissible. Speaking vaguely about
the blood-call of poetry, the unknown demanded of Heine . . .
his Apelles-like *pièce d'indentitié*. Love (wrote the unknown),
this cloud stained with the blood which ever overlays our cloudless
blood . . . you must speak of it in such a way that it will be as
laconic as the signature of Apelles. Remember only that you belong to the aristocracy of spirit and of blood (these things cannot
be separated). This is the only thing about which Zeuxis is
curious.

P.S. I have profited by your stay in Pisa, of which I was so op-
portunely informed by my publisher Conti, to put an end once
and for all to my tortures of conscience. Within three days I shall
come to you and look at the signature of Apelles.

The servant who appeared at the summons of Heine was given
the following communication:

"I am taking the ten o'clock train for Ferrara. Tomorrow evening, the bearer of the card, who is already known to you, will ask
to see me. You will personally hand him this parcel. Please let me
have the bill and call the *facchino*."*

The ghostly weight of the parcel, which was apparently empty,
was nevertheless due to a thin sheaf of papers, obviously selected
from some manuscripts. And this sheaf of papers comprised only a
part of the phrase, without beginning or end: "But Rondolfina
and Enrico have discarded their old names and changed them into
names hitherto unprecedented: he cried wildly, 'Rondolfina,' she
replied 'Enrico'. . ." †

---

* Porter: in Italian in the original.
† This sentence is in verse in the original—*translator's note*.

II

On the paving stones, on the asphalt market-places, on the balconies of Pisa and the embankments of the Arno, the inhabitants lit the scent of a Tuscan night. Out of the burning darkness of the night, the scent lay heavily on the suffocating passage-ways, and under the dust-laden plane pine trees; and its burning, glittering splendor was crowned with scattered sheaves of light from the stars and clusters of thorny mist. These flashes of light overflowed in the bowl of Italian patience: from the heat of their fervor they uttered curses, as though they were prayers, and wiped the humid sweat from their brows before they even glanced at Cassiopeia. Handkerchiefs gleamed in the dark like shaken thermometers. The readings of these cambric thermometers spread perniciously along the streets: they diffused oppressive heat, like snatched-up rumors, like panic fear. And just as the stagnating town disintegrated unconditionally, the streets, the houses, the courtyards, so in the same way the night air was compounded of separate and motionless collisions, ejaculations, bloody quarrels and encounters, whispers of laughter and drooping voices. Those echoes existed in dust-laden and frequent *interweavings;* they stood out in rows, which grew out of the pavement like the trees in the street, suffocating and colorless in the light of the gas-flares. Fantastically and powerfully, the night of Pisa traced a limit to human endurance. Beyond these frontiers chaos began. Such a chaos reigned over the railway station. Here handkerchiefs and curses disappeared from the scene.

People to whom a moment before a simple and natural movement would have seemed a torture, here, clinging to their bags and parcels, bellowed at the ticket office and like madmen stormed over the charred carriages, made siege on the footboards and, covered with soot so that they looked like chimney sweeps, hurled themselves into compartments partitioned by burning brown veneer which appeared to be warped by the heat, by the violent language and the incessant jolting of the passengers. The carriages were burning, the sleepers were burning, even the signals were

burning, while the engines from far and near uttered their lamentations through the steam. Hobbling with flashlights, like a buzz-
ing insect, the heavy breath of the open furnace fell asleep on the
engine driver's cheeks and the leather jacket of the fireman: the
engine driver and the fireman were both burning. The clock dial
was burning, the iron crossbars of the speedometer and minute
hands were burning; the watchmen were burning. All this was
beyond the range of human endurance. All this could be endured.

A seat by the window. A moment later—an entirely deserted
platform formed of massive stone, massive rumbling sounds and
massive exhortation from the guard: *Pronti!*—and the guard runs
alongside in pursuit of his own exhortations. The columns of the
station slip smoothly away. Lights scurry along, intermingling like
knitting needles. Gleams of light from the reflectors catch the
carriage windows, caught up by the draught, proceed through, beyond and across the opposite windows, lie along the line, trailing,
slide on the rails, rise and disappear behind the cart-sheds. Dwarf
streets, misshapen and hybrid corners—the jaws of the viaduct
swallow them with a hollow roar. The blustering of approaching
gardens close to the blind. The restful space of the curling carpet
of vines. Fields.

Heine travels in a happy-go-lucky fashion. He has nothing to
think about, he attempts to doze, he closes his eyes.

"Something will certainly come of it. There is no sense in making guesses about the future, no sense and no possibility of a
solution. The future is always a delightful mystery."

The wild oranges probably in flower. Scented gardens overflowing. From where the breeze temporarily sleeps on the close-
clinging eyelids of the passenger.

This is playing for safety. Something will certainly come of it.
It can't be without reason—Heine yawned—that in all the amor-
ous poems of Relinquimini, there is the unchangeable annotation:
Ferrara.

Rocks, precipices, his neighbors crestfallen in sleep, the stench of the carriage, the tongues of gaslight. The gaslight licks the rustling noises and shadows from the ceiling, it licks itself and ıs out of breath when rocks and precipices are followed by a tunnel: the rumbling mountain creeps down along the roof of the carriage, spreads smoke from the engine, drives it through the windows, clings between racks and pegs. Tunnels and valleys. A road with a single cart-track wails monotonously above the small mountain river which breaks against the rock, and rushed down from some improbable heights, fast invisible in the darkness. And here the waterfalls smoke and churn, and all night their strident rumbling encircles the train.

The signature of Apelles . . . Rondolfina . . . Probably I shall not succeed in a single day. And I have no more time. I must hide without leaving a trace . . . Tomorrow . . . And how he will run to the station when the lackey informs him of my journey!

Ferrara! The blue-black steely dawn. The sweet-smelling mist saturated with coolness. O, how sonorous is a latin morning!

III

"Impossible, the issue of V*oce* is already in page-proof."

"Yes, but I refuse to surrender my discovery to anyone or for any money; meanwhile I can't stay in Ferrara for more than a day."

"You say this notebook was in the carriage under the seat?"

"Certainly, the notebook of Emilio Relinquimini, a notebook possessing a large number of manuscript pages and an immense quantity of unpublished poetry, rough copies, fragments, aphorisms. The entries were made throughout the year, mostly in Ferrara, as far as can be judged from the dates written underneath.

"Where is it? Have you got it?"

"No, I left my things at the station, but the book was in the travelling-bag."

"A thousand pities! We might have been able to send the book to the house. The publishers know Relinquimini's address in Ferrara, but he has already been away for a month."

"What if Relinquimini is not in Ferrara?"

"That's the trouble. I really can't understand how you can hope to succeed by publishing an advertisement on this discovery of yours."

"Just this—with the help of your newspaper it may be possible to arrange a trustworthy liaison between myself and the owner of the book, and Relinquimini may at any moment profit by the courteous services of Voce in the affair."

"Then there is nothing to be done with you. Please sit down and have the kindness to make a declaration."

"I'm so sorry to worry you, but the telephone—will you allow me?"

"Do anything you like."

"Hotel Torquato Tasso? Could you let me know whether you have any rooms free? What floor? Good, reserve number eight for me."

"*Ritrovamento.* The manuscript of a book by Emilio Relinquimini, recently prepared for publication, has been found. The person occupying number eight in the Hotel Tasso will be expecting the owner of the manuscript or his representatives, while staying in the room throughout the day until eleven o'clock at night. Commencing with the following day the publishers of Voce, in common with the directors of the hotel, will periodically and in good time be informed by the above-mentioned person of each change of his address."

Heine was tired by the journey and slept a dead and leaden sleep. The venetian blinds of his room, warm with the breath of morning, were like copper membranes of a mouth-organ burning. A net of light from the small window fell on the floor, taking the shape of a ravelled straw mat. The straw closes its ranks, crowds together, squeezes together. On the street—faint conversations. Someone loses the train of his thoughts, someone else gathers them together again. The straw is already compressed into a single mass and already the straw mat has become a pool of sunlight spilled on the floor. An hour passes. On the street men are talking nonsense; they nod their heads; on the street voices are being lulled to sleep. Heine sleeps. The sunlight pool is let loose: it seems that the inlaid floor is impregnated with it. Once more it is a thinning straw mat of singed and crumpled straw. Heine sleeps. Conversations on the street. Hours pass. They grow lazy, together with the black patches on the straw mat. Conversations in the street. The straw mat fades, is covered with dust, grows dull. Already it is an old string mat inextricably entangled. Already it is impossible to distinguish the threads and the stitches from the knots. Conversations on the street. Heine sleeps.

In another moment Heine will wake up. In another moment Heine will slip out of bed, remember my words. Let him but see the last chapter of his dream to the end. . . .

Desiccated by the heat, the wheel suddenly cracks as far as the nave. The spokes protrude like a cluster of split pegs, the barrow falls to one side with a thump and a crash, bales of newspapers fall out—a crowd, sunshades, shop windows, awnings—they take the newspaper boy away on a handcart and the chemist's shop is nearby.

Look! What did I say? Heine leaps up. "Immediately!" Someone is knocking at the door furiously and impatiently. Heine, half awake, his hair tousled, still in his cups, reaches for his dressing-gown. "Excuse me for a moment!" With an almost metallic rattling his right leg fell heavily on the floor. "Coming at once!" Heine walked to the door.

"Who is there?"

The voice of the lackey.

"Yes, yes. I have the manuscript. Give the signora my apologies. Is she in the drawing-room?"

The voice of the lackey.

"Ask the signora to wait ten minutes. In ten minutes I shall be entirely at her disposal. Do you hear?"

The voice of the lackey.

"Wait a moment."

The voice of the lackey.

"And don't forget to tell mademoiselle that the signor expresses his sincere regret that he is unable to join her this very minute, that he feels deeply sorry, but he will try . . . Do you hear?"

The voice of the lackey.

". . . but in ten minutes he will try to make complete amends for his inexcusable inadvertence . . . and say it very politely, lackey, because I am not from Ferrara."

The voice of the lackey.

"Very good, very good. Lackey, is the lady in the drawing-room?"

"Yes, signor."

"Is she alone?"

"Alone, signor, if it pleases you. On the left, signor, on the left."

"Good morning, what can I do for the signora?"

"*Pardon.* Are you from room number eight?"

"Yes, that is my room."

"I have come for Relinquimini's notebook."

"Allow me to present myself—Heinrich Heine."

"Excuse me, are you related to the . . . ?"

"Not in the least. An accidental coincidence. Even an embarrassing one. I too have the pleasure . . ."

"You write poetry?"

"I have never written anything else."

"I know German well and spend all my leisure reading poetry, but . . ."

"Do you know the poems which are unpublished during the poet's lifetime?"

"Of course. Now I realize who you are."

"Forgive me, but I have an ardent desire to know your name."

"Camilla Ardenze."

"Extraordinarily pleased. Now, Signora Ardense, did you happen to see my advertisement in the *Voce?*"

"Of course. All about the notebook which has been found. Where is it? Give it to me."

"Signora! Signora Camilla, you—perhaps with all your heart—celebrated by the incomparable Relinquimini . . ."

"Don't! We are not on the stage!"

"You are mistaken, signora. We spend our whole lives on the stage and it is only with the greatest difficulty that some of us assume the naturalness which is bequeathed to us, like the character of an actor on the day of our births."

"Signora Camilla, you love your native town, you love Ferrara, but (I must tell you this) it is the first town I have ever come across which definitely repels me—you are beautiful, Signora Camilla—and my heart shudders at the thought that you and this detestable town are both conspiring against me."

"I fail to understand you."

"Don't interrupt me, signora—this town, I was saying, which lulled me to sleep like the poisoner who lulled to sleep his boon-companion when the hour of his fate draws near, doing it in order to awaken a spark of disdain with regard to his fate in the eyes of the unhappy man who has just entered the tavern, and fate betrays the man who has been lulled. Milady, the poisoner turns to the woman who enters—look at the lie-a-bed; it is your beloved; he beguiled the hours of waiting with stories about you; they were like spurs when they pierced my imagination. Did you not gallop here on its back? Why did you whip it so unmercifully with your gossamer whip? It is lathered in sweat—it is in heat!"

"O these stories! But allow yourself to glance at him. Milady, he is lulled by his own stories about you—you see, the separation has the effect of a lullaby on your beloved. However, we can awaken him. It is not necessary: the poisoner answers for the fate of the man who was poisoned. Needless to alarm him. He sleeps so sweetly and perhaps he even sees me in his dreams. Far better to arrange that I should be provided with a glass of punch. It is cold in the street. I am numb. Please rub my hands."

"You are very strange to me, Herr Heine. But continue, please for your high-falutin speech entertains me."

"Excuse me if I have forgotten Relinquimini's notebook. I shall go up to my room . . ."

"Don't trouble, I won't forget about it. Continue, please. What an amusing man. Continue. 'Please rub my hands,' said fate. Isn't that what she was saying?"

"Yes, signora, and many thanks for listening so attentively."

"Well?"

"Well then, this town has treated me exactly as the poisoner treated his boon-companion—and you, beautiful Camilla, are on the side of the town. The town overheard my thoughts of crumbling dawns, as old as robber castles and as solitary, and it lulled me to sleep because it wanted to take advantage of them steathily, and it allowed me to speak to my heart's content about gardens, borne on immense sails from the red evening air into the night, and it hoisted the sails and left me lying in the port-tavern, and I am sure you will refuse to allow it to awaken me, if the crafty rogue should propose such a thing."

"Listen, my dear. Where am I in all this story? I do hope the lackey definitely woke you."

"Ah, so you think the night comes, there may be a storm, one must hurry, since the time is up, don't wake him."

"O signor Heine, what illusions you have! I say yes, yes, Ferrara, ruffle his hair if he is still asleep; I have no time; rouse him roughly; assemble all your crowds; rumble in all the city squares; rumble until he is awake, there is so little time."

"Ah, but the notebook . . ."

"We'll talk about that afterwards."

"O my dear signora, Ferrara has been cheated in its calculations, Ferrara has been duped, the poisoner runs away, I am awakened, I am awake—I am on my knees before you, my love."

Camilla leapt.

"Enough! Enough! All this becomes you—even those commonplaces—yes, precisely these commonplaces! But it can't go on! You are acting like a wandering buffoon! We are almost strangers to one another. Only half an hour ago—it would be funny even to argue about this—and still—and here am I arguing with you. I never felt more stupid in my life. This whole scene is like a Japanese flower which blossoms instantly in the water. No more and no less! But they are paper flowers! Such cheap flowers!"

"I am still listening to you, signora."

"Signor, I might have listened to you all the more willingly.

You are very clever and, it appears, sarcastic. And yet you have no contempt for commonplaces! It is strange but not at all contradictory. Your theatrical pathos!"

"I beg you, signora. Pathos in Greek means passion, but in Italian it is only an empty kiss. And kisses are compulsory—"*

"Again! Spare your pains! Intolerable! You are hiding something from me—explain yourself. And listen, please don't be angry with me, my dear signor Heine. For all that—you do not blame me for my familiarity? You are such an unusual child. No, that is not the right word—you are a poet. Why didn't I think of the word at once? But to discover it, it was indeed sufficient to look at you. An idler chosen by God and spoilt by fate."

"*Evviva!*" Heine leaped on to the window-sill and leaned out with his whole body.

"Careful, signor Heine!" Camilla cried. "Careful, you are frightening me!"

"Don't trouble yourself, my dear signora!"

"Aiee! *Furfanto!* † Catch him!" Lyres flew over the square. "Only stay a moment! You will receive ten times as many if only you rob a dozen gardens in Ferrara. A *soldo* for each hole in your trousers! Quickly! Don't breathe on the flowers when you are carrying them. The countess has a mimosa-like sensitiveness. Hurry, you old fool!"

"Did you hear it, enchantress? That ragamuffin will return in the costume of Cupid. But let us speak seriously. What perspicacity! With a single line—the line of Apelles—I have to express all my being, all that is essential to my existence!"

"I don't understand you. Or is this one more piece of play-acting. What is it you really want?"

"Yes, one more piece of play-acting. But why am I not allowed to stay for a while under the rays of a perfect illumination? Am I at fault because the most dangerous places in life—bridges and crossroads—are illuminated more strongly than any others? How crude is the light! All the rest is submerged in darkness."

* baccozzo.
† rogue: in Italian in the original.—*Translator's note.*

"Imagine a stage with a man illuminated by perturbed flares, as though he were on exhibition—a man enclosed within balustrades, the panorama of the town, precipices and the signal lights on the quays."

"Signora, you would not have listened to one half of what I have to say if we had not encountered one another in such a dangerous place. I am obliged to imagine that it is dangerous, although I have myself no knowledge of its danger: it is necessary to imagine it, because whole seas of flame were exhausted by people in imagining it, and it is not my fault if we are illuminated so clumsily and crudely."

"Good. Have you finished? All that is true. But it is all unheard-of nonsense! I want to confide in you. It is not just my fancy. It is almost a necessity for me. You are not lying. Your eyes don't lie. Yes, what is it I wanted to say? I have forgotten. Wait a moment. Listen, my dear, only an hour ago . . ."

"Wait, these are only words. Hours exist, but eternities exist too. Quite a large number of them and not one has a beginning. At the first opportunity they break away. And this now is a good opportunity. And then away with words! Do you know, signora, when and by whom they are cast down? Away with words! Such revolutions are known to you, signora? Signora, all my fibers rise within me and I must yield to them, as one yields to the crowd. And one more thing. Do you remember what you called me just now?"

"Yes. I am quite prepared to repeat it."

"Quite unnecessary. And you know how to look freshly. And already you are in possession of the line, the unique one, like life itself. Don't lose it, don't throw it away on me, repel it only as much as it will allow you to. And then trace the line farther."

"What did you get, signora? What is the result? Are you in profile? Or half-face? Or in some other way?"

"I understand." Camilla stretched out her hands towards Heine. "And yet—no, I am no longer a young girl. One must have control over oneself. Such magnetism."

"Signora!" Heine exclaimed theatrically at the feet of Camilla.

"Signora!" he exclaimed in a piercing voice, while he hid his face
with his hands. "Have you already drawn the line?

"How terrible!" He sighed in a whisper, tearing his hands away
from his face which had suddenly grown pale . . . looking into
the eyes of the completely disconcerted signora Ardenze, noticing
to his unspeakable surprise that . . .

IV

. . . that she was really beautiful, that she was beautiful to the
extent of being unrecognizable, that the pulse of his own heart
throbbed like the sea under the stern of a boat, surges, rises, pours
close to the approaching knees, rolls over her in lazy layers of
waves, sways her silk dress, stretches the smooth contours of her
shoulders, lifts her chin and—miracle!—gently raises it a little,
higher and higher—the signora is now up to her neck in his heart,
a wave more—and she will choke and be drowned. Heine seized
the drowning woman—a kiss—a kiss which bore them out of the
whirlpool, but he groaned under the pressure of their breaking
hearts, twitched and tore himself upward, forward, devil knows in
what direction: and she offered no resistance at all. On the contrary if you desire her, her body sings, attracted by the kiss, strad-
dled by the kiss, her outstretched body sings; if you desire her, I
will be a boat for such kisses, only carry me, carry me . . . the
words burst apart with a hoarse sound from Camilla's breast. "A
knocking at the door!" "A knock at the door!" and she tears herself
away from his embrace.

Then:

"A thousand devils! Who is it?"

"The signor has locked the drawing-room, God knows why. It
is not the custom here."

"Silence ! I shall do as I please."

"You must be ill, sir."

There followed swearing in Italian, sensual, fanatical swearing,
like prayers. Heine unlocked the door. The lackey in the corridor

had already come to an end of his swearing, and a short distance behind him there was a little ragamuffin whose head was blossoming out into a small forest of liana, oleander flowers, orange-blossoms, lilies . . . "This good-for-nothing . . ." rose, magnolia, carnations.

"This good-for-nothing asked to be allowed to enter the room which has windows overlooking the square, and the only room of the kind is the drawing room."

"Yes, yes, the drawing room," the boy snarled.

"Naturally, the drawing room—" Heine agreed. "I myself told him . . ."

"Because," the lackey continued impatiently, "there could be no question of letting him into the office, the bathroom or still more the reading room. However, owing to the obvious indecency of his costume . . ."

"Ah, yes," Heine exclaimed, as though he had only just at that moment woken up. "Rondolfina, look at this trousers! Who sewed those breeches of yours out of fishing nets, a transparent conglomeration. . . . ?"

"Signor, the thorns of the prickly hedges in Ferrara are sharpened every year by special gardeners."

"Ha! ha! ha!"

". . . In view of the obvious indecency of his costume," the lackey continued impatiently, laying special emphasis on this last expression because he saw the signora approaching: on her eyes there wrestled the shadow of a sudden perplexity with gleams of a wholly unquenchable mirth. "On account of the indecency of his costume, we suggested to the boy, transferring to our person the demand made by the signor, that he should wait for the answer in the street. But this little swindler . . ."

"Yes, yes, he is right," Heine said, bringing the orator to a full stop. "I ordered him to appear personally before the signora."

"This swindler," the angry Calabrian was babbling, "even began to threaten us."

"Precisely how?" Heine asked. "Isn't this terribly characteristic, signora?"

"The little brat referred to you. Signor, he threatened us, he said that the signor merchant would make use of other *albergi* in the course of his travels through Ferrara if, in defiance of his wishes, he wasn't allowed to see the signor."

"Ha! ha! ha! What an amusing person! Don't you agree, signora? You will carry this tropical plantation, wait a moment!" Heine, turning around, waited for Camilla's orders. "To room number eight," Heine continued without receiving any reply from her.

"In your room, for the moment," Camilla repeated, blushing a little.

"All right, signor. But what about the boy . . ."

"As for you, you monkey, what do you think your trousers are worth?"

"Julio is covered with stripes, Julio grows blue with cold, Julio hasn't any other clothes, Julio has neither father nor mother . . ." the ten-year-old ragamuffin whimpered tearfully and sweatily.

"Answer, how much?"

"A hundred *soldi*, signor," the boy exclaimed diffidently and dreamily as though hallucinated.

"Ha! ha! ha!" they all laughed. Heine laughed, Camilla laughed, even the lackey burst out laughing, the lackey particularly when Heine bringing out his pocketbook, produced a ten-lire note and without ceasing to laugh offered it to the little ragamuffin.

As quick as lightning the boy's outstretched hand dived at the outstretched pocketbook.

"Stop!" Heine shouted. "This is, it appears, your first appearance in the field of commerce. In good time . . . Listen, *cameriere*, your laughter at such a time is positively indecent. It stings the young merchant to the quick and don't you think, my dear fellow, it would be better if, in your future negotiations in Ferrara, you never showed yourself again within the inhospitable walls of the 'Torquato'?"

"Oh, no signor, on the contrary. How many days is the signor still staying in Ferrara?"

"In two hours I shall have left."

"Signor Enrico."

"Yes, signora."

"Come out in the street. It is so much better to leave the stupid drawing room."

"Good. *Cameriere*, these flowers—to number eight. Wait a moment, this rose must still blossom; for this evening the gardens of Ferrara will ensue that you have it, signora."

"*Merci*, Enrico. . . . This black carnation is really devoid of all reticence; the gardens of Ferrara, signor, entrust you with the care of this licentious flower."

"Your hand, signora . . . *Cameriere*, take it to number eight. And bring my hat. You'll find it in the room."

The lackey went out.

"You are not doing this, Enrico."

"Camilla, I don't understand."

"You will stay. Oh, don't answer me—you will stay at least for another day in Ferrara . . . Enrico, Enrico, you have sullied your brow with pollen, let me wipe it away."

"Signora Camilla, there is a fluffy caterpillar on your shoes, may I dispose of it? I shall send a telegram to my home in Frankfurt— and those petals on your dress, signora—I shall send telegrams every day until you refuse to let me do it any more."

"Enrico, I can't see any engagement ring on your finger. Have you ever worn one?"

"A long while ago I noticed one on yours. My hat—and thank you!"

v

The perfumed evening filled all the corners of Ferrara and trickled over the labyrinths of her streets like a drop of seawater, pouring into the ears and filling the skull with deafness.

The coffee house was a hubbub of noise. Only a single, fragile side street led to the coffee house. The town, deafened and stunned, encircled it on all sides, holding its breath because the

evening drove into one of the little side streets and precisely into this one where there was the coffee house at the corner.

Camilla was deep in thought. She was waiting for Heine, who had gone into the post-office next door to the coffee house.

Why in the world didn't he want to write the telegram in the coffee house and send it over by messenger? Is it possible that he is not satisfied with an ordinary formal telegram? Was there a strong and really emotional liaison? But on the other hand he would have entirely forgotten about the telegram if she had not reminded him. And who was Rondolfina? She would have to ask about her. But could she? Obviously, these were intimate things. Heavens, I am like a little girl. I can, I must. Today I have obtained the right to know everything; today I shall lose the right to know everything. They spoil you, my dear—those artists. But this one. . . . And Relinquimini . . . ? What a remote person! In spring? Oh, no, earlier—perhaps on New Year's Eve? No, he was never really close to me . . . And now. . . ."

"What are you talking about, Camilla?"

"Why are you so melancholy, Enrico? Don't grieve. I shall let you free. You can write the telegrams by dictating them to the lackey. Send a telegram like that home, it will only be three hours late, there is a train which leaves Ferrara for Venice at night, and Milan too, and the delay won't be more than. . . .

"What are you talking about, Camilla?"

"Why are you so melancholy, Enrico? Tell me something about Rondolfina?"

Heine trembled and sprang from his chair.

"Who told you? He was here? He was here in my absence? Where is he, where is he, Camilla?"

"You turned pale, Enrico. Who are you talking about? I asked you about a woman. Isn't that so? Or perhaps I didn't pronounce it correctly. Perhaps it is Rondolfino. It all depends on the vowel. Sit down. People are looking at us."

"Who told you about her? Did he tell you anything? But how did it come here? We are only here by accident—I mean, no one knows we are here."

"Enrico, there was no one and nothing happened while you were in the telegraph office, I give you my word. But it is becoming curiouser and curiouser every minute. Are there two of them?"

"It's a miracle—incomprehensible to the reason . . . I'm losing my mind. Who told you this name, Camilla? Where did you find it?"

"This night, in my dreams. It's such a common name. And you still haven't told me who Rondolfina is. Miracles do still happen—but let us leave them alone. Who is she, Enrico?"

"O Camilla, Rondolfina is you!"

"What an incorrigible actor you are! No, no! Let me go! Don't touch me!"

Both jumped up. Camilla's was a single movement, an irrevocably impetuous maneuver. Only the little table separated them. Camilla clutched the back of a chair, something rose between her and her decision; something stirred within her, and like a merry-go-round, in a circular wave, it drew the coffee-pot upwards, sideways . . . She was lost . . . Tear it away, tear her necklace. . . .

In the same loathsome merry-go-round the chain of faces broke away, moved away, floated in the air . . . imperials . . . monocles . . . lorgnettes . . . ; then in large and ever-increasing quantities, the conversations at all the tables stumbled against their unhappy table; she still saw it, still leaned against it, it might pass . . . no . . . the discordant orchestra was falling out of tune.

"*Cameriere*, water!"

VI

She was slightly feverish.

"What a tiny room you have . . . Yes, that's right; thank you very much. I shall lie down for a while. It is malaria, but then . . . I have a flat of my own. Don't leave me. It may come at any moment. Enrico!"

"Yes, darling."

"Why are you so silent? No, no, it is not necessary, better as it is. Ah, Enrico, I can't remember whether there was a morning today. Are they all still there?"

"What, Camilla?"

"The flowers."

"We'll have to take them away during the night. What a heavy perfume it is! How much must the perfume weigh?"

"I shall have them taken away. What are you doing, Camilla?"

"I am getting up. By myself, thank you. It's all over now. I can stand on my own legs . . . Yes, they must be taken away. But where can we take them? Wait a moment. I have a flat of my own in the Ariosto square. Surely you can see it from here!"

"It is dark already. A little cooler, perhaps."

"Why are there so few people in the street?"

"Schsch, they can hear every word."

"What are they speaking about?"

"I don't know, Camilla. Students, probably. Boasting, probably, perhaps about the same things we . . ."

"Let me see it. Now they are standing at the corner. Heavens, how he threw the boy over his head! Now it is quiet again. How oddly the light clings to the branches. But there are no streetlamps to be seen. Are we the last?"

"The last what, Camilla?"

"Are there any floors above us?"

"Probably, Camilla."

Camilla leaned out of the window and peered over the cornice at the street below.

"No . . ."—but Heine did not let her finish her speech. "There is nobody there at all," she repeated, as she disengaged herself from his embrace.

"What is the matter?"

"I thought there was a man there, a lamp in the window, and he threw crumpled leaves and shadows into the street through the window. I wanted to turn my face there, to catch it on the cheeks, but there was no one. . . ."

"This is poetry, Camilla."

"Really? I don't know. There it is, near the theater. Where there is a lilac-colored glow."

"What is there, Camilla?"

"You are a queer fellow! Well, my house!"

"I understand, but it is all a kind of nervous paroxysm. I would like it if we had . . ."

"A room has already been ordered for you."

"How terribly thoughtful of you! What time is it? We must go. We must go and have a look at my room. It's very interesting."

They left number eight, smiling and as excited as schoolboys laying siege to Troy in the courtyard.

VII

Long before morning the churchbells were chattering garrulously about the approach of dawn, jerkily making their low and cold bows, leaping backwards and forward on the tumbling beams. Only one of the hotel lamps was burning. It kindled when the telephone bell crackled corrosively, and it was not extinguished afterward. The law saw the porter, still half asleep as he left his pipe on the desk after a short quarrel with the man at the other end of the line; saw him as he lost himself in the depths of the corridor, emerging a short while later from the half darkness of the hotel. "Yes, the signor is leaving in the morning. He will call you in half an hour if it is really urgent. Have the goodness to leave your number. And tell me, please whom he must call?"

The lamp continued to burn while the man from number eight, who had been called to the telephone, had to walk down the corridor, and the first step he made took place somewhere near room number eight. After a short conversation with the porter his features changed—nervous agitation gave place to sudden recklessness and curiosity, and he seized the telephone boldly and, after going through the whole technical ritual, began to speak with the editor of Voce.

"Listen, it's terrible. Who told you I was suffering from sleeplessness?"

"I imagine you came to the telephone by mistake while you were climbing the steeple. What are they ringing the bells for? What is it all about?"

"Yes, I remained a day longer."

"The lackey was right. I did not give them my home address and I have no intention of giving it to them."

"For you? Not at all! I did not think of publishing it—at any rate not today as you seem to have thought."

"You won't need it at all."

"Don't get into a temper, signor editor. I beg you to be cool."

"Relinquimini will not have to make you the mediator."

"Because he has no need of a mediator."

"May I remind you once more of your incalculable worth when you are calm. Relinquimini has never lost a notebook in his life."

"Excuse me. This is your first unequivocal statement. No, a thousand times no!"

"Still talking about that? Good, I shall admit it. Within the limits of yesterday's issue of *Voce*, it is blackmail. But it is not blackmail at all outside these limits."

"It was yesterday. At six o'clock."

"If you could only guess what rose out of the yeast of this invention, you would call it by still harder names and they would be still further from the truth than the one you had the goodness to utter just now."

"Willingly. Today I have no objections to saying it. Heinrich Heine."

"Just so."

"Very pleased to hear it."

"What are you saying?"

"Very willingly. How to manage it? I am sorry I have to leave today. Come to the station and we'll spend a short time together."

"Nine thirty-five. Whatever the time—a chain of surprises. Better not come."

"Come to the hotel. During the day. It will be better. Or to my flat. During the evening. In tails, and don't forget to bring the flowers."

"Yes, yes, signor editor. You are—a prophet."

"Or tomorrow, on the duelling square outside the town."

"I don't know, perhaps it is quite serious."

"Or if you are busy during the next two days, come to the Compo Santo the day after tomorrow."

"You think so?"

"You think so?"

"What a strange conversation at the beginning of the day. Forgive me, I am tired, I must go back to my room."

"I can't hear? Number eight? Oh, yes. Yes—yes number eight. It is a marvelous room, signor editor—a climate entirely of its own, where there has been eternal spring for five hours. Good-bye, signor editor."

Heine mechanically turned down the switch.

"Don't put it out, Enrico!"—a voice came from the darkness of the corridor.

"Camilla!"

[*Translated by Robert Payne*]